FAIR WINDS OF DOUBT

FAIR WINDS

OF

DOUBT

B. R. WADE, JR.

A WADE PUBLISHING NOVEL

Wade Publishing LLC
1782 Trinity Road, Belington, West Virginia 26250
www.wadepublishing.com

Library of Congress Control Number: 2024922903

ISBN 978-1-7375461-6-0 (paperbound)
ISBN 978-1-7375461-7-7 (e-book)
ISBN 978-1-7375461-8-4 (hardcover)

Printed in the United States of America

This is a work of fiction. Space and time have been rearranged to suit
the convenience of the book, and with the exception of references
to historical figures, any resemblance to persons living or dead is
coincidental. Certain long-standing and factual institutions, ships,
buildings, military facilities and equipment, vehicles, and public places
are mentioned, but the characters involved are wholly imaginary
and their interaction with these actual entities is pure fantasy.

The reference to a tattoo for the Marines that fought at the battle
of the Chosin Reservoir in November-December 1950 is fiction.
The men of the 1st Marine Division and 31st Regimental Combat
Team are remembered herein with the ultimate level of respect.

This work does include some of the author's recollections
of serving in the United States Navy while attending
Yeoman A School at NTC Bainbridge and as a yeoman
at the Naval Investigative Service Office Norfolk.

Many things we know as facts today at one time were looked upon as myths or the ramblings of the insane.

This work is dedicated to those people who consider what might be true and keep an open mind even when facing intense ridicule.

ACKNOWLEDGEMENTS

Writing this story was a lot of fun. It gave me the chance to mix several of my personal interests—military, history, and the unknown—with very special memories of people and places. But after that, the hard part starts, and as I've mentioned in the past, I do my best to avoid that stuff! I am indebted to several people who were there for me when I needed them.

John K. expertly answered my questions on private aircraft servicing facilities and procedures.

Martin S. was extremely helpful with West Virginia Black Bear information.

Alice H. again tackled the initial punctuation and grammar editing chores efficiently and quickly. She also did a beta read of the story and shared her thoughts that led to many significant improvements.

Louise S. provided a level of professional editing that massaged rough words into a readable story. Her encouragement and suggestions are a lasting and appreciated gift.

Stewart W. handled the conversion of Word pages into book format and gave them a very professional look. He also took my vague ideas and created a cover that entices the potential readers.

POINT PLEASANT, WEST VIRGINIA
15 DECEMBER 1967

TEN DAYS BEFORE CHRISTMAS, 1967, at around 5 p.m., workers and shoppers in Point Pleasant, WV were driving home. Truck drivers were completing their runs. The aging, aluminum-painted steel structure known locally as the Silver Bridge, which connected West Virginia to Ohio, was filled with traffic. Then the unthinkable happened: the bridge collapsed. Thirty-one vehicles dropped into the icy waters. At final count, the disaster left forty-six dead. Two bodies were never found. The only good news: twenty-one of those who dropped into the river survived.

The investigation showed that several factors caused the collapse, including lax maintenance. But no inspectors could have noticed the small defect, about a tenth of an inch, in one of the eyebars. That was the first piece to give way.

But perhaps the biggest factor was the load: rush-hour traffic was much heavier than the weight the bridge had been designed to handle forty years earlier. The load caused that one defective eyebar to break, and the failure cascaded to other eyebars.

The Silver *Memorial* Bridge replaced the collapsed bridge. This new bridge opened in 1969, restoring easy travel across the Ohio River. But the deaths and injuries permanently scared the locals and fed a local legend.

For over a year prior to the 1967 collapse of the Silver Bridge and the death of forty-six people, there had been sightings of an unusual creature.

Some felt the sightings were premonitions of the bridge collapse. Others attributed supernatural events to the sightings.

It all started when two young couples on a drive in November 1966 reported seeing a ten-foot-tall, man-like creature with huge wings. They claimed the car's headlights made the creature's eyes glow red, and that it followed them for a distance as they drove away.

The first newspaper report, published in the *Point Pleasant Register* on November 16, was titled "Couples See Man-Sized Bird … Creature … Something." Later, someone in the media coined the name that stuck: the Mothman.

Sightings increased after that first published report. A couple of volunteer firefighters reported seeing something, perhaps a huge gray bird with red eyes. Scientists theorized that a sandhill crane, which fit the firefighters' description, may have strayed into the area.

Mothman sightings continued until the Silver Bridge fell in December 1967, then suddenly stopped. Unofficially, there had been over one hundred sightings of the Mothman, including several of him sitting on the doomed bridge. That created, in local lore, a supernatural connection between the Mothman and the bridge disaster. Many believed the Mothman was a harbinger of doom. West Virginia folklore had been born.

2

CAL HATED THE LATE SHIFT. He only pulled it a couple of times per month—too often, as far as he was concerned. At least he had Friday off to recover and wouldn't have to go back to work until Monday morning. He fully expected that his wife of twelve years would have a list of things for him to fix around the house, so his day of rest—or of restful fishing—was already shot. The honey-do list has priority.

Working wasn't really that bad. The Kingsman Mine had enough shift supervisors for a decent rotating late-shift schedule. Calvin Thompkins was happy he'd been promoted out of the actual mine to work in an aboveground office. There he monitored the amount, grade, and size of bituminous coal loaded into the waiting Norfolk and Western Railway coal cars.

Still, the predawn drive home was difficult. His aching eyes kept closing and the yawns kept a'coming, one after another, never ideal on the tight curves of West Virginia roads. He had planned to nap most of the previous afternoon, but the same old argument with Doris Thompkins had killed that idea: she wanted to visit her folks in Michigan for Christmas and Cal wanted to stay home.

Travel during holidays was disgusting, he believed—and had forcefully said so once too often. Moments before slamming the door on his way to work last night, he heard Doris yelling something about going to Michigan by herself. Part of him wished she would.

But the reality was he loved his wife. He had two great children, a decent house, and a good job. He thought maybe he was overreacting. His mother-in-law's Christmas ham was mouth-watering, so it wasn't all that bad.

That threat had been made as often as there were Christmas holidays. She would be over it by now and, like she always did after an argument, would spend an hour more in the kitchen baking homemade cinnamon buns to make amends. And Cal would do his part for domestic tranquility by again giving up a week of his summer fishing vacation to do family things in Michigan over Christmas.

Two things looked strange when Cal reached his driveway as the dim light of predawn started erasing the deep shadows. No lights were on in the house, and Doris's Buick was gone. The sun was rising, albeit slowly, and headlights were still needed as Cal's Ford pickup turned onto the driveway. "Perhaps she actually left for Michigan," he mumbled out loud.

The headlight beams highlighted the garden shed and Cal's fishing boat and trailer. The beams also caused two red reflections to stand out from the darkness between the shed and house. *Guess she parked the Buick there.* Then he wondered why: it was a stupid place to park, but he knew Doris was not exempt from stupid decisions.

With the pickup in its standard place, Cal shut down the engine and swung his legs out of the vehicle. The creaking of the closing truck door reminded him one more time that he needed to oil those hinges. *Dang West Virginia road salt gets into every vehicle joint and starts the rust monsters.* Another thing to add to his to-do list.

He glanced around like he usually did and ambled toward the dark house. A soft sound got his attention. He halted to eliminate the crunch of the driveway gravel under his boots. The sound came again, only closer.

"That you, Doris?" he quietly asked. He saw no need to yell and wake the neighbors.

Getting no response, Cal looked in all directions. Nothing moved. No one was there. He again started toward the house, continuing to glance around. The kitchen door was unlocked, which was strange.

"Doris, I'm home," he said in a normal voice as he entered the dark house. It was time for their two kids to be up demanding breakfast. But his announcement received total silence.

He walked from room to room, turning on and leaving lights burning, and quickly found the house to be empty. No Doris. No children. No note on the kitchen table. Some of her clothes were still in the closet, but her makeup kit, which she never left home without, was gone from the bathroom counter. All he had to show for his search was a world of silence.

"Guess she did go to Michigan," Cal muttered. Remembering her Buick outside, Cal dashed out to check on it. Maybe she and the kids were in the car.

As he rounded the corner of the house, the area where he was sure the Buick was parked was empty. There were no tire marks in the dew-wet grass. But he had seen the taillights when he pulled in, and that didn't seem right. *Where is the car and where is my family?*

He ran through all the logical possibilities. It was too early to take the kids shopping. Maybe she took them over to her sister's place in Ohio last night; time to call Mary and ask. As he turned to head to the phone, again he heard that soft rustling sound. It was not something familiar. He stopped and listened harder. Nothing.

He again started toward the door and was reaching for the knob when the quiet crunch of leaves stopped him. Someone or something was around the side of the house. Cal spun around in time to see a large shape fly over his head. Wings beat against the morning air as the dark shadow passed from sight.

3

AUTUMN IS THE BEST TIME of year for many West Virginians, and the colors were at their peak that afternoon. The vivid shades of green that had colored the trees in spring and summer were replaced with the brown, red, yellow, and orange hues that portended the leaves' literal fall. The first to fall started a carpet of all those colors covering the forest floor. Like the snows that would come in the next few weeks, the carpet of multicolored leaves hid some of the ugly.

Granted, nature lovers would be the first to argue that nothing in nature's woods is ugly. But for many, not every rock, rotting log, or tree stump inspires awe. And for these people, the dying leaf coverage is a welcome change.

Ryan and his best friend Dudley, both juniors at Princeton High, were slowly walking across the crunchy and somewhat slippery forest floor, scoping out a good place to start their deer hunt in a few weeks. The teens were looking for signs that deer frequented the area.

They had been hunting deer and turkey since their fathers gifted them rifles and shotguns for their twelfth birthdays. But hunting season was fast approaching, and they had yet to find their location for this year. The consensus was, any place was better than last year's, with their score of boys–0, deer–2. It had been a bad year. They had seen too few deer, and the two they tried to take down got away unharmed. Not good when the freezer needed to be refilled.

"Hey man, how much longer are we going to walk, man?" Dudley whined. "If we keep going south, man, we're going to be in Bluefield soon. Hell, we might already be in Virginia!"

Ryan gave him a hard look. "Pipe down, motormouth. You'll scare off any deer before we see them. Anyway, since we only have about three hours of light left, guess we need to head to the car."

They decided to shift their path about fifty yards west for the walk back to Highway 460. They tried to ignore the greenbriers as they trudged along.

Greenbriers, which grow into long tough reeds, thorns lining their leafy sides, don't care what season it is: they ram their thorns into anyone who gets close all year long.

It is accepted that plants do not have intelligence that would incite them to attack warm-bodied animals. The most well-known carnivorous plant, the Venus flytrap, will latch onto and devour a tasty bug, but it doesn't hunt them down: it lies in wait.

However, folks who spend time in the West Virginia woods know for a fact—a guaranteed, take-it-to-the-bank fact—that greenbriers see them coming, team up with other nearby vines, and attack with viciousness. Naturally, scientists who never spent time in West Virginia woods are quick to laugh at reports of this attack feature of the vines.

As the boys improvised their new path, they had to fight through a large patch of briers. Dudley fussed. Ryan, laughing at him, took his eyes off the brush long enough to get himself snared by the tough plants. Their long branches seemed to wrap around his legs, driving their thorns through his blue jeans and into his flesh. They locked him in place, inflicting pain. He hadn't planned to fall, but the ground came up to kiss his face quickly.

Ryan grumbled as he tried to escape the grip of the vines and become vertical again. It was now Dudley's turn to laugh, as Ryan put his hands into a pushup position and started to rise. But nature was not ready to let him up yet. His left hand slipped in the leaf compost slime that covered the damp woods floor, and he kissed the ground again. Repositioning, he came face to face with a hand that wasn't his. A rotting hand.

"What the hell?" Ryan yelled as he tried to push away from the hand. He noticed the hand was attached to an arm, and like the old song, the arm bone was connected to the shoulder bone, and so on. The body was covered with leaves and other pieces of forest debris. For once, the green-briers could not slow the boys down as they ran from the area.

4

THE SENTRIES MANNING THE MAIN gates at the Naval Training Center (NTC) were usually looking for an auto's officer sticker, which would require a salute, and for potential recruits trying to desert. There were too many of the former and, thankfully, few of the latter.

Vehicles without a base sticker were stopped on the way in. If the driver's presence was justified, they were provided with a cardboard pass to place on their dashboard and directions to their destination. Commercial vehicles also received a cardboard pass and were entered into the log, along with entry time and destination.

The same vehicles leaving the NTC were rarely stopped for long; they had been inspected on the way in to make sure they had a reason to be on base and were not bringing in a bomb. But on the way out, a quick glance at their signed waybills was all that was needed to gain a wave-by. Naturally, a note in the log documented their departure.

At a few minutes to midnight that Sunday, few vehicles were coming in and even fewer were leaving the base. One twenty-foot-long box truck had been on the base nearly six hours. For most of those hours, the truck remained backed up to a loading dock of the base hospital. Deliveries of hospital supplies were common.

If anyone had been watching, they would have seen the driver slowly rolling hand-truck-loads of average-sized boxes into, and out of, the truck. He didn't seem in a hurry, nor did he act nervous. The driver did stop for a smoke break frequently, but that was normal. He was an average guy doing a boring job.

A chief petty officer monitored the loading. His presence would have added a sense of authority to the scene had anyone taken the time to look. No one had.

The truck had a light beige paint job with lettering solely on the door. That lettering was both small and unmemorable. A few initials in bold black lettering were centered on each door, with a smaller Illinois commercial-carrier license number below. The truck was clean, all lights were functioning, and no dents were visible. In short, it was a boring truck that would not impress anyone seeing it.

Like the truck, the driver's appearance did not leave an impression. He was dressed in dark blue work pants and tan shirt, and the red ball cap on his head sported no logo or lettering. He was clean-shaven, with hair a bit longer than the average military cut. The *thanks* he gave the sentry was so quick that any accent could not be heard.

The exit from the base required the driver to stop the truck and turn in the cardstock dashboard pass. The nondescript driver handed the pass to the sentry through the window of the nondescript truck. Even with the light midnight traffic, those sailors pulling guard duty would not remember the event, the truck, or the driver.

The drive into the south side of Chicago brought the truck to its last stop, in an extremely bad neighborhood. It nosed up to a run-down warehouse that had a single light fixture hanging over a rusty freight door. The few windows were painted over. The only identifiers on the building were a couple of "private property" and "no trespassing" signs that were faded and rusted. The door quickly rolled up when the truck arrived, allowing the truck to drive inside before it slammed shut. Then all was quiet.

The event had been repeated every week for the last month. The times varied and the truck door lettering was changed for each visit. There were several drivers, and none ever made two trips in a row. There were two constants to the base visits: the same chief petty officer was always on duty, and the inventory value remained the same.

And in between these base visits, a different truck arrived from an out-of-town location and was sequestered in the warehouse for a few hours of unloading. Sometime later, it was sent off to a remote parking area until needed, and the cycle continued.

5

THE WEEKEND HAD BEEN A quiet one; at least the phone hadn't been ringing much. There were the normal weekend issues, with a couple of car wrecks on the highway early Sunday morning. A couple of drivers had decided one more drink wouldn't hurt. It would, and now two more people were in the morgue because of DUI incidents. Otherwise, the deputies on duty hadn't needed to call the sheriff to handle unusual issues. They'd had it all under control.

The sheriff strolled in a bit before the official start of the day shift. He looked around, pleased that things seemed calm. Four deputies and two clerical staff members were at their desks, three deputies were on patrol, and three had the day off. No panic was evident. It was a good way to start the day.

The people had elected Godfrey Timmons III as sheriff the previous year. Most folks simply called him GT. While he was new to the badge and new to the age of thirty-one, he was not new to the job. GT had been a deputy for years before he got the big office. His career began when, drafted a year after high school, he spent his two Army years in Vietnam as a military police officer. On top of that, he had received verbal police training all of his life.

He glanced at the mirror on the back of his office door to check that all his parts were in place. A small gut was starting, but at 5'11" he carried his 190 pounds well. He made a mental note to exercise a bit more. His black hair was cut short in a military style: high and tight on the sides and about an inch long on top. GT figured he had more important things to do than keep it combed, and that length never got messed up by his cap. No facial hair hid his tanned, boyish face, though some age lines were starting around his eyes from squinting in the West Virginia sun. He made another mental note to get a new pair of mirrored sunglasses soon; he had no idea where the last pair had gone.

His father, Godfrey Timmons Jr., had been Mercer County Sheriff for the previous thirty-five years and was known to all, in and out of the county, as Junior. His father before him, the first Godfrey Timmons, had been the county sheriff for nearly forty years before dying at the hand of a robber who beat him to the draw. Folks had always called GT's grandfather Sheriff Timmons, with many adding a "sir," either out of fear or respect. His stern, all-business attitude had had that effect on people. No nicknames were allowed. Perhaps his thick handlebar mustache pushed that stern image, like it did for Wyatt Earp.

Sheriff GT settled into his office with the first of many cups of acidic black coffee. He pulled his copy of the shift schedule out of the drawer and glanced at the names of those on duty that day and night. It was a good selection of well-trained people. That helped reduce the day's stress.

GT glanced over the daily notices from his in-basket, missives from surrounding counties. They were not fancy notices, but short blurbs to let others know what was going on across county lines. It was a fact that problems across those lines, drawn only on a map, could quickly become his problems. *Semper Paratus*, the motto of the U.S. Coast Guard, applied to his office: they were always ready. At least they tried to be.

GT leaned back to read what evils others were fighting.

A quick rap on the door casing interrupted his read. "Excuse me, Sheriff. There's a man and a boy out here who refuse to talk to anyone but you," Norma said.

A stout lady with graying hair, Norma Kissing was the official mother figure in the office. She had worked many years for his father and was the glue that held the paperwork process together, as she ran the office. Her look was all business, and none of the deputies dared cross her.

"Thank you, Norma. Can't keep the good folks of Mercer County waiting, now can we. Send them in please," GT announced as he stood.

Out of habit more than necessity, he hiked up his loaded duty belt. The trappings of a sheriff carried a lot of weight, as did the responsibilities.

GT's initial analysis concluded that the older man had forced the younger one, probably his son, to come to the office. The kid's look vacillated between anger and concern, and the older man was nervous. GT said, "Mornin' gents. What's up?"

"Thanks for seeing us, Sheriff. I'm Brock Maynard. My boy Ryan here needs to tell you somethin' bad."

GT sat behind his desk and gestured to the two chairs. The two sat. A couple of moments passed before GT said, "And how long do I need to wait to hear from you, Ryan?"

Ryan looked down at his boots and mumbled something. Mr. Maynard poked him in the arm.

"Son, I don't have time to waste. Now speak up and tell me why you're here," GT barked.

Visibly shaken by GT's change in demeanor, Ryan licked his lips and looked toward the ceiling. He lowered his eyes to make contact with GT's. "Sir, me and Dudley …"

Ryan's father again poked his son's arm and interrupted, "Sheriff, that would be Dudley Callens. He's Ryan's best friend."

GT nodded and pointed to Ryan. "Thanks, Mr. Maynard. Go on, Ryan."

"Well, me and Dudley was scouting new deer huntin' spots yesterday afternoon late, down toward Bluefield. Our choices last year sucked, so we need a new area, ya know. So far nothin' was looking good. Anyway, I tripped because of those dang greenbriers and just about landed on a rotting body."

That got GT's attention. "Then what did you do?"

Ryan snickered. "We got the hell out of there, I tell ya. Dang fast."

GT could understand that reaction. Most folks are not accustomed to seeing a body, outside a casket at the funeral home. He smiled. "And why isn't Dudley here with you?"

Ryan shrugged.

His father said, "Sheriff, if I hadn't overheard Ryan on the phone talking about it to one of his buddies, we wouldn't be here now. No idea about Dudley."

His fingers were steepled, with the index fingers nestled in his philtrum. GT stopped thinking about the body and his guests for a quick moment as he wondered why he knew the name for the indent in his upper lip. "Okay, Ryan, I need you to give your official statement to my lead detective. Make sure you go into more detail than what you just told me, okay? Tell him everything and every little detail. And do you think you can find the place again?"

Seeing Ryan nod quickly, GT picked up his phone and dialed a two-digit number. "Allen, I need you to take a statement."

GT looked at Ryan. "Got Dudley's phone number handy?" Ryan gave it to GT before Allen escorted him and his father to an interview room for their statement.

The call to the Callens' house was a dead end: it rang and rang. But a call to the principal at Princeton High let him know Dudley was in class. GT asked the principal to get Dudley to his office in about twenty minutes. The principal promised he would, and that he'd call Dudley's father to be there as well.

The drive to the high school would only take six minutes, so GT used the other fourteen to check with his team. Standing in the squad room, he rapped on a deck to get their attention. Half a dozen people turned to stare at him.

"People, we've got a couple of teens who yesterday found a body in the woods down toward Bluefield. Allen's getting the statement from one, and I'm going to the high school to talk to the other." GT paused to gather his thoughts and absorb the intense concern on the faces before him. "While I'm gone, dig into our missing persons' files, call the neighboring counties, and check with them. Sorry, until we get their statements and go to the scene, we don't know anything about the body except it exists. The young man here said it was rotting, so it's been there for at least a week. I'll get back to you."

The principal met GT in the parking lot. A slight, balding man, who may have weighed 150 pounds fully clothed and dripping wet, Clarence White had been the principal for the last five years. He was about ten years away from retirement and had hoped this sunset position would be an easy one.

Wringing his hands and blinking rapidly, he blurted, "I have Dudley and his father in my office. What did he do? What is going on? Is there any danger to the other students? Will it be okay with you if I sit in, Sheriff?" His speech speed increased the more he talked.

GT recognized the man's stress. He extended his hand. "Principal White, calm down. There are no issues with the school, so there is no reason for you to be there. I just need to talk with Dudley about something that he saw over the weekend. Show me to your office, please." GT placed his arm around White's shoulder as a stress-calming gesture.

"Perhaps I should help with the interview, Sheriff."

GT gave his most disarming smile. "Sir, it's only a friendly chat. More people tend to make things intense. But I appreciate the offer, and if any-thing—anything at all—involves the school, you will be fully informed. Okay?"

While the principal was not convinced, he showed GT into his office and watched GT close his door. He took a seat in the row of chairs usually filled with students sent to his office for punishment. Seemed right, since he felt he was being punished.

"Mr. Callens, thanks for coming in."

"What the hell is this all about, Sheriff? I've got work to do and the boss ain't happy I took off."

GT nodded. "Mr. Callens, I'll be happy to talk with your employer if you like. But right now, we need to talk about something else. Something serious. Has Dudley mentioned anything about his walk in the woods with Ryan yesterday?"

Dudley was looking down like the floor was the most interesting thing in the universe. Perspiration on his forehead betrayed his condition.

Mr. Callens shook his head. "No, sir." He jerked his head toward Dudley and said, "What did you do, boy?"

Dudley mumbled, "Nothing."

GT decided to push the conversation along. He cleared his throat and said, "Dudley, your buddy Ryan says y'all found a dead body. What do you have to say?"

"Yes, sir, we did," Dudley stammered while still looking down.

"Anything else you want to tell me, Dudley?" GT asked.

"No, sir. We saw it and ran like hell."

GT looked over at Mr. Callens. "I know you need to get back to work, so would it be all right if Dudley comes with me to help find that body?"

It was after four p.m. when GT dropped Dudley and Ryan off at their houses. It had taken a while to find the body. The boys were not great scouts.

The medical examiner finally got the body to the morgue a little af-ter six p.m. He called GT and said, "This is a nasty one, Sheriff. Looks like the man was in the woods for about three weeks. Buck naked and no ID was on him. Most of his fingerprints are gone due to munching critters, but I'll get you what I can. Also gone are most of his internal organs—that part is weird. I'll work late and hopefully have more for you in the morning."

GT thanked him for his work, hung up the phone, and looked at the short list of missing persons his team had put together earlier. Since the guy was dead and the hour was late, tomorrow would be the time to dig further.

6

"**Well, that stinks, Dennis,**" **Sheriff** GT Timmons kinda yelled into the phone. The medical examiner was on the other end of the line. "Come on, you got to have something more." Doctor Dennis Bassett had reported that his autopsy resulted in more questions than answers. No firm cause of death was determined.

Bassett cleared his throat. "Okay, GT, I can tell you for sure that the deceased is male. Caucasian. Age around thirty. Dark brown hair was not recently trimmed. Birds got to his eyes, so no color to give ya. Height is 5'10" and since I don't have all of him, no firm weight, but I would guess he weighed at least 165 when he was whole. Hard to say if he had a beer belly, since all that area is gone, but you could add an extra ten pounds to the possible weight. No jewelry was on him. Scars included a five-inch surgical on his left thigh, a suspected old knife-wound scar on his right chest, and a couple of small ones on his forehead—possibly the results of an auto or motorcycle accident. Like I said yesterday, looks like the body has been in the woods about three weeks."

The sheriff tapped his pen against the mostly empty tablet on his desk. His notes on this case were weak so far. He pushed for more from the medical examiner. "Dennis, so you're telling me there are no gunshot wounds, no blunt force trauma to his head, no crushed hyoid bone, no drug injection marks, nothing? Is there enough of his face left to send photos to the FBI, for them to try to develop at least a drawing of how he looked in life?"

"Perhaps, GT. I'll get some good shots for you. And I'll see what I can do about a decent fingerprint or two. Just remember, it will be a day or two before we get the blood work back."

"Okay. Send the photos over with your report. Soon, I hope."

"Yea, I'll get it to you in a few hours. And one more thing, GT. The way he was eviscerated is the weird part. Intestines, stomach, spleen, liver, kidneys, heart, and the bottom part of his lungs are gone. Totally gone. It looks somewhat surgical, but it also has a wild animal attack feel. Kind of like scooping the seeds out of a cantaloupe, if ya know what I mean. And where the hell are all those parts now? No big pool of blood at the scene, so perhaps the body was dumped."

"I see what ya mean about weird. Just include as much detail as ya can in the report. I appreciate your standard great work, Doc."

GT hung up the phone and picked up the list of names. His team had gathered the data Monday, so it was current. The list included missing persons from ten nearby counties in West Virginia and six in Virginia. Some were within the last week, but many were years old. He was surprised at the number. There were seventy-seven people on the list: fifty-three males and twenty-four females. Ages ranged from nine to seventy-four years.

Filtering out all females, and the males under twenty and over forty, narrowed the number down to twenty-two. The victim being Caucasian dropped that number to eighteen. Hair color and height ruled out another eleven. Still a lot, but at least it was better than fifty-plus.

The list now showed check marks next to the unlucky seven. Of those, only one of the missing was from Mercer County, so only one file was handy: Jacob Tucker, missing since February 1968. GT picked up the phone. "Allen, I need you in here. Thanks."

Allen Chambers dropped into a chair in front of GT's desk. A weight trainer who stood a little over six feet tall, he presented an imposing figure. Detective Chambers had been with the force for fifteen years and was divorced, with a young daughter. He was a couple of years older than GT, but he never resented working for a younger man.

The good news for GT was that Allen was one hell of a detective. He saw things no one else did, and worked wonders pulling information from witnesses. He was GT's right-hand man, and that was fine with him.

He enjoyed working with GT, and felt he would hate the semi-political position of sheriff. His smile was honest as he asked, "What's up, boss?"

In less time than he spent with the doctor, GT shared the latest information and the analysis of the list. With a soft chuckle, he handed the marked list to Allen. "Call those four counties and ask them nicely to make us a copy of those files ASAP. Then see who we have available to go pick them up. I'll be hunkered down over the one case in our files. This case is six years old, so I doubt it is our John Doe, but we who read dusty files and risk paper cuts also serve."

Scanning the list, Allen Chambers said with a shrug, "He could be ours if he ran away six years ago and recently returned to town. Maybe whoever he ran from back then finally caught him."

"Yea, and maybe Santa will bring you a new truck this Christmas." Both men laughed at their standard joke. GT continued, "Nice story, but improbable. Get the remote files, please."

As Allen hurried out the door, GT sipped his now-cold coffee and pondered Jacob Tucker. Since he was the only local on the missing person's list that met the criteria, it was time to pull his file and see if he was a match for the body in the morgue.

GT made a quick mental list of things to do as he strolled to the records cabinet. Considering all the factors, it was probable that the John Doe was from way outside the local counties and Allen was spinning his wheels, but you never know. GT decided that when he got the medical examiner's report, he would write up a report to send to the National Crime Information Center (NCIC).

The nationwide compilation of missing persons and crime information had become a great asset. Perhaps they would find a match for his John Doe in their missing persons files. It might be a stretch, but dotting and crossing every *i* and *t* was part of the job. He went to the file room with a specific mission on his mind.

On the way back to his office, Norma waved him over. "Sir, I know you've got a plate-full right now, but there was one more incident you need to be in the loop on. Another weird one. Here is the report Sergeant Walker took over the phone." She handed GT a couple of sheets of paper neatly stapled in the upper left corner.

"Thanks, Norma. My favorite task: more reading to do." GT took the report and did a quick scan as he walked toward his office. He paused as he placed it on top of the missing persons file, and muttered, "Huh. Weird is right."

GT did a quick turn. "Hey, Norma, please call this gent, Cal Thompkins, and ask if he has a recent photo of the wife and kids. Go ahead and gen' up an official missing persons report on them. Notify NCIC and the FBI."

"Can do, Sheriff."

GT kept on top of the case, but as the days passed, the missing family remained that way.

7

THE RAILROAD YARD WAS BUILT in 1905, as the Virginian Railway came to life to haul West Virginia's natural resources—lumber and coal—from the mountains. The eastern end of the line was in Norfolk, in the Tidewater area of Virginia, where large coal piers were built for the rapid dumping of hundred-ton carloads of coal into ships heading to foreign ports. A large, two-story passenger station in Norfolk handled people and freight, as well as housed company offices. Other large brick buildings provided servicing to the huge locomotives and freight cars.

As times changed and businesses altered their shipment methods to stay relevant, the American railroads cut back service to areas that no longer provided decent profits. The growth of the trucking industry took further business and profits from the railroads. Smaller rail lines survived, to some degree, by merging with others.

In December 1959, the Virginian Railway merged with the larger and older Norfolk and Western Railway (N&W). With the merger, the Virginian Railway basically ceased to exist. The good news was that most of the employees still had a job. And it would take decades for all the reminders of the line, those common-as-dirt coal cars carrying the Virginian name, reporting marks, and logo, to finally be scrapped. But through the efforts of historians, model railroaders, and railfans, the Virginian Railway would last forever.

Locomotive maintenance work had all been transferred to the larger N&W shops in Bluefield, West Virginia, and the even bigger N&W shops in the railway's business center of Roanoke, Virginia. With that work gone, the old Virginian shops focused their efforts on keeping the moneymaking coal cars running.

The expected life of a rail car was around forty years. During that time, the coal cars needed repairs due to improper loading, slamming against other cars during switching, and damage from rust. Naturally, some mechanical parts like brake shoes and bearings needed frequent maintenance from everyday use. With thousands of coal cars on the line, it was common for over a hundred to need work.

Homer Grant started his workday as a car mechanic shift supervisor precisely at eight. He punched the time clock, stowed his lunch box and jacket in his locker, and pulled the stack of work orders to see what repairs he and his team faced that day.

As he sat at his desk in the cramped, cluttered back office, Homer thumbed through the small work order stack. Since the railroad didn't run a night shift on weekends, it was surprising more work wasn't waiting. He stabbed out his Camel cigarette stub in the ashtray that still featured the old Virginian Railway logo, drained his coffee dregs, and walked out to the shop floor.

The shop's servicing tracks each had a pit, with stairs at both ends, that allowed easy access to the cars' bottoms. Drains in the floor kept them from becoming swimming pools. The pits were only four feet wide and five feet deep, running most of the length of the track inside the building. Portable bridges could be placed at the ends of the cars so the mechanics could cross safely and easily.

As Grant left his office, he saw most of the day shift employees standing at the end of the pit at the center of the shop building. They were pointing into the pit, their murmurs getting louder.

"What the hell are you people doing?" Grant yelled as he approached. "We have cars to get out of here."

"Homer, you need to take a look at this." The mechanic pointed to the pit.

The light coming in the large open doors was enough to illuminate the shop floor, but the pits needed more. Portable shop lights were used in the pits, and most workers carried flashlights. Grant pulled his out and shined the light into the pit. He nearly dropped the flashlight when the beam illuminated the dead woman lying on her side. Light reflected off the small quantity of blood pooling in the pit floor, with a thin red stream meandering toward the nearest floor drain.

The woman's face was frozen in a look of fear or shock: it was hard to tell the difference. Her hair, which may have been medium brown, was streaked with a grayish-brown substance. Grant swept the light around, but didn't see a purse—or anything except the naked body.

None of his people recognized the lady, they said. When he moved to the side of the pit, he looked closer and realized that her stomach area had been ripped open, leaving a gaping cavity.

Grant made it to the area immediately outside the door before he vomited his breakfast. Dry heaves followed for the same amount of time it took for one of the mechanics to call the police.

8

Bob Ledder was dead tired. He started the first workday of the week ready for a nap, after flying back from eastern Virginia late Sunday following a busy weekend. Now he was tired. He sipped his coffee as he pondered his life, his job, and a buddy he was concerned about.

In West Virginia, he was a heavy equipment operator on one of the larger Caterpillar bulldozers. Due to his fine touch on the control levers, he was a master of the machine. It didn't matter what material he was pushing, how complicated the job, or how soft the soil: Bob was the man.

His expertise safeguarded his position with Loveland Construction Company, but he also served in a Navy Seabee Reserve unit. The Seabees, a pronunciation of the unit's acronym, CB, for Construction Battalion, were formed in World War II. The Navy needed a unit that could build while fighting the enemy, freeing combat troops from being their guards. John Wayne starred in the 1944 movie about the new unit: *The Fighting Seabees*. While fiction, it did its job as a recruiting tool and a bit of propaganda for the good guys.

Bob had enlisted in 1964, his construction experience guiding him directly to the Seabees. On his first tour in Vietnam, as a Second Class petty officer, he took leadership of the unit after an attack killed three officers. His actions garnered him a couple of medals and a battlefield commission as an ensign.

He left the Navy in 1970 as a lieutenant, after two more tours in Vietnam and a stint instructing at the Naval Construction Training Center Gulfport. After four years in the humidity and heat of 'Nam and Mississippi, Bob was ready to get back to the wonderful four seasons of West Virginia, especially the cool weather of fall.

But after settling into civilian life, Bob realized he missed the comradery of the Navy, so he joined the Reserve Seabee unit that trained in Little Creek, Virginia. Getting to the monthly drills was not a problem: Bob was a pilot with his own plane.

Granted, his little puddle jumper was not as nice as the DC-10s of the airlines, but it was at his command. Between being a frugal saver and damn good at poker while on active duty, Bob had paid cash for his plane. He'd fly to Virginia on Friday morning, drill with his friends on Saturday and Sunday, then fly home Sunday evening. But this weekend had been strange. Normally he attended drills with his buddy and coworker Joe, but he'd been a no-show on Friday.

Joe Decker had been a boatswain's mate in the Navy in the mid-1960s, afterwards falling in love with heavy equipment at a tech school. His position at the subdivision site was running one of the graders in the formation of the roads that would eventually lead to fancy new homes.

Over three beers after work a few years back, Bob convinced Joe that joining his Seabee unit would be fun and give him extra money. And he could ride to Virginia in Bob's plane. It had worked well—until this past Friday. When Joe didn't show at the airport Friday morning. He had been at work on Thursday, but they hadn't spoken. A few calls failed to find Joe. The flights to and from Little Creek had been lonely without Joe's company.

Bob was first on site that Monday morning. As he worked on a second cup of coffee from his thermos, he checked the oil level on his bulldozer, inspected the hydraulic lines for cracks and leaks, and fired up the big diesel engine. As its temperature came up, Bob realized he needed a bladder break. He looked toward the portable toilet a half-mile away, then noticed a ditch near the wooded area twenty yards' distant. The decision was easy.

He'd stepped to the edge of the ditch, unzipped, and started his task when a reflection of sunlight on the other side caught his eye. As he was still the only one on site, Bob decided to take a look.

He finished, zipped up, and climbed down to cross the ditch. It took a couple of minutes to root through the brush under the edge of the tree line, but he finally found the reflection's source: the bottom of an empty beer can at the right angle to catch the morning sun.

Chuckling at his wasted effort, Bob turned toward his big yellow beast. He almost missed the irregularity. The brush and debris were thicker around the trees, but something weird stood out in the dim morning light. As his eyes focused, he realized someone was sitting at the base of a tree.

Bob yelled out a greeting. No response. He pushed his way through the brush to get closer, thinking the fellow was sleeping off a beer drunk. When he got to within a few yards, he recognized Joe under the brush. However, something was bad wrong: Joe was naked. And his gut was ripped open. He was dead for sure.

9

THE BUZZ OF THE ALARM ended a pleasant dream. He and Kelly were holding hands and enjoying a glass of wine while watching the sunset behind the Colosseum. When he was relaxed, most of his dreams were snippets from their 1971 honeymoon in Rome. He was amazed that four years of marriage were already behind him. It was true: time does fly when you're having fun.

Marcus turned off the alarm and rolled over to snuggle with Kelly for a moment or two. Softness and warmth was the payment for his effort. Her breathing changed as she came out of her slumber. She softly kissed his lips. "You know we don't have time to finish what you want to start, don't ya?"

"Oh, yea, I'm well aware of my obligations for the day. Sadly, what I want and what I need … and I mean right now, will have to wait until to-night. Pencil me in as a hot date on your social calendar, please," Marcus whispered as he rubbed her back.

Kelly giggled. "Always thrilled to keep my sailor happy. Get your shower and I'll start the coffee." She rolled away and left the bed.

As the soap and hot water ran off his body, Marcus again considered how lucky he was. He was one of the youngest Commanders in the Navy. His duty station was the Naval Investigative Service (NIS), where he was a special investigator in charge of the Internal Affairs Division. And his luck had him working out of the headquarters office in the Washington Navy Yard, the oldest shore facility in the Navy. The place had history and class, and he loved it.

Usually, Marcus would nonchalantly tell people he worked in an office in the Navy Yard. Boring paper-pushing and paperclip-counting tasks were his forte, he'd say. Because when he had to tell non-Navy people where he worked in more accurate detail, he'd get a blank stare, followed by a variation of the question *you do what for whom*? It was easier to explain to civilians that the Navy has a police department. The Shore Patrol (SP) are the beat cops, and the NIS agents are the detectives. It was his job in Internal Affairs to keep the NIS agents and other personnel honest.

If the civilians were interested, he'd get into more detail about the organization of NIS, which wasn't classified material. Washington D.C. is the Naval Investigative Service (NIS) headquarters, where an admiral is in charge. Under NISHQ are multiple NISOs—Naval Investigative Service Offices—which coordinate work in a geographic area such as the 5th Naval District.

The Navy breaks up the world into districts, with a large Navy base as the headquarters (HQ) for each district. For example, Norfolk, Virginia is the home of the 5th Naval District. It extends from northern Virginia down through much of North Carolina, with multiple Navy and Marine bases. And under each NISO are a number of NISRAs—Naval Investigative Service Resident Agencies—which house the agents who do the investigative work at various locations around the district.

Marcus's Internal Affairs Division, consisting of three other officers, several enlisted personnel, and a few civilians, mostly spent time at the NISRA level, weeding out agents who had gone astray. They also made sure that the agents who had made tough decisions like shooting a bad guy had followed all the rules while doing it. That part of the job did not make them any friends in the agent ranks, but it kept the press and politicians happy when they proved proper procedures were followed. And they usually were.

While running Internal Affairs, another part of his job—one not specified in the job description or organizational chart—was being assigned operations and projects that senior brass believed couldn't be done in the conventional manner. Since he had a track record of success with the unconventional, Marcus would get the call. It was one of those unconventional assignments that brought him, through total fluke, face to face with Kelly.

The most senior brass, who frequently tasked Marcus with unconventional assignments, was Admiral William Gallagher. This admiral occupied the Pentagon desk belonging to the Chief of Naval Operations, or CNO, the highest-ranking military person in the Navy. He was deputy to the Secretary of the Navy and a member of the Joint Chiefs of Staff. The JCS consisted of the senior ranking members of each branch of the military, and together they provided professional military advice to the Secretary of Defense and the President. People respected his opinions. So when the CNO called, everyone answered.

Admiral William Gallagher was the classic example of a Navy admiral: a bit under six feet with a small amount of body fat. A weathered face added to his commanding look, with crow's feet beside each eye and a permanent tan on aged skin that had seen too many hours on the bridge wing of a naval vessel. The four stars on his collar gleamed with power. He could have been the poster boy for the office of the Chief of Naval Operations.

One of Marcus's previous missions for Gallagher had been to find a killer thought to be lurking in NISO Norfolk. He'd gone undercover as a low-rated enlisted man, finding the killer and much more.

Had he not been on an undercover assignment and needing to talk in secret with the commanding officer of the unit he was investigating, he would never have met the captain's niece. Kelly was an adorable Old Dominion University student. Her sand-colored hair was usually in a ponytail, and her beautiful face with the brightest smile never needed makeup. Marcus was knocked off his feet instantly by this beauty.

Nearly as quickly, it became clear this lovely lady felt the same about Marcus. And it was only after she caught him, with "forever after" on her mind, that she mentioned being the daughter of the CNO, his real boss's boss. The CO of the unit he was investigating was married to the CNO's little sister.

Marcus was still not sure what she saw in him. He stood six feet tall, and while somewhat athletic, he had a slender look. His face was not Hollywood quality, and his ears stuck out a bit. He also looked younger than his age.

Kelly, before and after marriage, was every man's dream girl. She looked a lot like Grace Kelly in *High Society*, except her hair was longer and she was much prettier. Standing around five-foot-six, she was the perfect height for Marcus to kiss her on top of her head.

Two weeks after their first meeting, they were engaged. Less than six months later, their Norfolk wedding was the social event of the year for Naval Base Norfolk. And life had gotten better with each passing day.

Hands encircling him from the back returned Marcus to the present. Kelly had joined him in the shower.

"Your coffee is ready, Sailor. After I wash your back, you need to get moving. No one in this house is allowed to be UA!" Raised a Navy brat and now a proper Navy wife, Kelly frequently used military terms, acronyms, and initials. And she would never allow Marcus to be late, thereby generating an unauthorized absence charge.

Marcus turned and washed Kelly's back. "If Admiral Chance could see us now, I think the absence would be authorized."

"Don't go there. There are some things even the admiral can't see. Ever!"

10

SHERIFF GT'S FRUSTRATION GREW UNTIL he was completely pissed. The morning had started off decent, with a steak and eggs breakfast after a great night's sleep, followed by a smooth drive into town. Then he walked into the office. It went downhill quickly from there.

As the radio guys say, the hits just kept on coming. And in GT's case, they were all negative. Earlier phone calls had reported that two more dead bodies, one male and one female, had been found. One was in the woods and one in a locked railroad shop building. Both were eviscerated, like that John Doe that Doc still had on hold in the morgue cooler. Adding to GT's frustration was that all the leads on identifying their John Doe had failed. No one around the area knew him. NCIC had not been helpful. The FBI had generated a possible complete face, but even wide circulation had not born fruit.

The office was quiet. Norma and GT were the only ones there, having sent the officers on duty to the two crime scenes. Allen Chambers was the lead on the body found at the rail yard, and Walker took point at the construction site. They had been gone for a little over an hour, and no updates had been called in.

GT tapped his pencil against his coffee mug in frustration as the known information flashed behind his eyes for yet another review. With the body count growing, he mumbled through a slight smile, "Doc will need to hire a larger staff if this crap continues. And get a bigger cooler." Then the humor passed, and he realized the next election might see him booted out if he didn't stop the killings soon. The way he felt at that moment, a new career might be a good thing. He sighed and mumbled louder than he wanted, "I double hate Mondays."

"I agree," Norma yelled from her desk outside GT's office. "Fresh pot of coffee is ready, Sheriff. It might make your day better."

With a smirk improving his angry face, GT chuckled and grabbed his coffee mug. Since Norma was a staunch Baptist, he didn't vocalize his thought about needing a shot of bourbon in the coffee to make the day better. He rapped a signal of gratitude on Norma's desk as he walked past. "Right you are, Norma, as always. Thanks."

"And there are a couple of donuts left in the break room, also," she said to his departing back. "One or two might sweeten you up, Sheriff!"

"Doubtful, but I'll try."

As the hot coffee splashed into his mug, the aroma stimulated his nose as he hoped the caffeine would stimulate his brain. GT checked and found one chocolate and two glazed donuts in the box. The chocolate silently called his name. Alternating between donut bites and coffee sips, GT thought through the parameters of the John Doe case as he wondered if John D. was the first of what might be a serial killing spree. With the day's bodies, the number with similar details was officially three, but there were a lot of woods around West Virginia perfect for hiding bodies. Maybe their John Doe was not the first.

The stroll to his office, mug in one hand and remains of the donut in the other, was a short distance, but it was long enough to realize something did not sit right. The speculation on John Doe was that a wild animal, probably a black bear, had his innards for lunch. And now there was another body in the woods; well, almost in the woods. *Perfect place for a bear to have dinner* was the logic Allen had offered earlier. Yet the second body found that morning was inside a building in the middle of a rail yard. It was inside a *locked* building that must have been at least a mile from the nearest wooded area. The rail yard was definitely not bear territory.

"Norma, call over to the rail yard office and get Allen on the phone for me, please," GT asked as he passed her desk.

He dropped into his chair as if the weight of the world were on his shoulders, and pulled a county map from his desk drawer. GT started at the center of the rail yard and worked his way outward toward the woods. His guess was right: the closest wooded area was at least two miles from the building that contained the woman's body. A long damn way for a bear to drag a body before he picked the door lock.

The map study came to an abrupt end when the phone rang. "Sheriff."

"What ya need, GT?" Allen asked.

"Any ID on the body?"

"No, sir. Just the basics: female, mid-thirties, Caucasian, dirty-blonde hair, wedding ring. None of the workers here knew her. I shot the standard photos and will get them processed on the way in. Anything else?"

GT exhaled slowly. "Okay. It's possible our first assumption this morning about wild animal attacks may not be totally correct. Think about it, buddy. One body was on the edge of the woods and one was found inside a locked building. Both were not near a bear's normal stomping grounds. Check the place, looking for any points of entry. I can't believe I'm saying this, but if it was a bear doing this, how the hell did he get in? And more importantly, why? Damn, I really did say that out loud."

Allen harrumphed. "So, what are you saying? Do we have a human copying the MO of a bear? Or a bear acting like a human? So, is Yogi, who we all know is 'smarter than the average bear,' our murderer?"

The laugh came naturally to both of them. GT got his under control. "That would make the front page for sure, Allen. Maybe some human moved the bear-killed body. Hell, I don't know. Just find out how the body got inside the shop building, okay?"

"As you wish, Mr. Sheriff, sir," Allen replied with heavy sarcasm before he hung up. He was close enough to GT to know a touch of sarcasm might relieve some of his boss's stress.

GT finished the remains of the donut and washed it down with now semi-cold coffee. He checked his notepad and found the comment from Doc about the John Doe body. He reread the comment several times. "It looks somewhat surgical, but it also has a wild animal attack feel." Like many West Virginians, GT and his friends were avid hunters and had seen what animals can do to other animals. But this was different. Like Doc had said, it was weird.

He needed another opinion: one from a true professional. GT pulled his private phone directory from the desk drawer and flipped through the pages. Dialing the eleven digits got him the secretary of the Department of Natural Resources. Kate with the Texan accent was courteous when she answered the phone, but not much help.

"Sorry, Sheriff, Doctor Wallace is not available. He's out in the woods. May I take a message?"

"Sure. Please have him give me a call soon as he can. I need his expert opinion."

With nothing else to do for a moment, GT pulled the map closer and again checked the distances from the middle of the rail yard to the potential bear territory. Wallace would confirm when he called back, but GT could not see a bear dragging a body that far.

Again, the phone took him away from his map. "Sheriff Timmons."

"Sheriff, the body at the construction site is on the way to the morgue. We have combed the area out one hundred yards from the body and found nothing," George Walker said. "No one here knows anything. I'll be here at the construction site trailer for a bit longer if you need me."

GT was quiet for a moment. "Guess you need to check out the area for another hundred, George."

"Will do, but I'm tellin' you, GT, ain't nothing here. The weird thing is that there are no drag marks. No blood trail. No compacted brush except where the guy who called it in approached. It's like the body was dropped from a chopper."

"Okay, I get it. Check further out and make sure nothing is overlooked. Got an ID on the body?"

The sound of notebook pages flipping came over the line. "He is Joseph no-middle-name Decker, according to his buddy who found him. Not married and no local family. I'll swing by his apartment on the way in to see what I can find."

As the phone settled in the cradle, GT leaned back and closed his eyes. It was not what he needed—another freaking weird case.

A couple of hours later, Allen Chambers returned to the office. He plopped down in the chair in front of GT's desk. "Damn mess of a case, GT. At least the medical examiner has the bodies and is doing his magic. I got all the scene photos processed, and here are the eight-by-tens."

GT quickly sifted through the stack of crime scene photos, then suddenly stopped. One had gotten his attention.

"Don't you recognize this deceased, Allen?"

"No, who is it?"

"Unless my eyes are failing in my old age of thirty-one, that is Doris Thompkins. She is the lady who, with her two children and a Buick, vanished at the end of last month. We need to call in her husband for a positive ID. But what the hell are we going to tell him about her cause of death, and where the hell are the children?"

Allen shook his head. "That's why they pay you the big bucks, Sheriff. I'll call him in and stand behind you while you tell him."

GT extended his right hand, one finger raised, in a gesture with negative connotations. He then picked up the phone to update the FBI.

II

THE LAST YEAR HAD BEEN rough for America. A president had re-signed under a dark cloud. Watergate, heretofore a group of buildings housing a hotel, apartments, and offices along the Potomac River, became a household word due to the scandal. A relatively new vice president, now sworn in as president, faced the challenge of reuniting the country. In his attempts to show that all was copacetic, and the government was running well, he privately asked many members of the government and the military to hold off on their retirements. Continuity was important, he said. So far, it had seemed to work.

It didn't surprise Marcus Colt that several people he admired were asked to postpone their retirements. His father-in-law, the Chief of Naval Operations, was one. He had looked forward to spending more time on the golf course, but for the good of the country, that would have to wait months longer. In turn, the CNO had requested that the head of NIS, Vice Admiral John Chance, hang around for another year or so.

Another was the Secretary of State. Marcus and his team of SEALs had come to his rescue in Vietnam five years ago. Since then, SecState had considered Marcus a family member; it was the least he could do for the man who saved his life. After meeting SecState's daughter Susan while investigating a case in Italy four years ago, Marcus was even deeper entrenched in the family.

Of course, having the private phone numbers of such a powerful man had come in handy on at least one case. Marcus didn't abuse the privilege, but he was glad he had it.

Marcus was draining his second cup of coffee as he contemplated the state of the federal government. It could be worse, he realized, as the presidential resignation and subsequent pardon had reduced the cries for trials and punishments. Hopefully the disgraced president would simply fade away like the old soldiers did. Marcus had heard a recording of General MacArthur's farewell address to Congress in 1951, and MacArthur's use of the line from an old Army ballad—"Old soldiers never die—they just fade away"—had always stayed with him.

He glanced at his watch and knew it was time to get his butt in gear. The Monday morning staff meeting for the Internal Affairs division was about to start. Since he was in charge of IA and the meeting was held in his office, he had to be there.

As happened with most military units, there had been some shakeups in his division over the last year. Military personnel were assigned there for a period of time, then transferred out to other units. The Navy lieutenant he'd been leaning on as his backup had been transferred out last year; LT Jake Doty was now stationed in Norfolk, Virginia, assigned to Fleet Intelligence and promoted to lieutenant commander.

To make matters worse, Captain Henry "Hank" Bates, USMC, an outstanding investigator, was up for transfer at year's end. Marcus's recommendation had resulted in him going to JAG, where he would get more use out of his law degree.

That was the problem with having military personnel in the IA division: they didn't stay long enough. By the time they became proficient, they were up for a transfer. And that was the primary reason Marcus had been pushing his boss, Vice Admiral Chance, to staff the IA division with more civilian agents. It was slowly coming to be.

Marcus was the outlier in that he had been in IA for seven years. The admiral didn't want to mess up a good thing, so with the help of the CNO, he had pulled a few strings to keep Marcus Colt in place. Under normal circumstances, the lack of different duty stations would hinder an officer's career path, but the situation worked out well for Marcus. He loved his job and was satisfied with his career path so far. Retiring after twenty years with the rank of an O-6, a captain, would be fine with him.

The good news for that morning's meeting was the introduction of a new staff member. There would be two Marines sitting in on the meeting. Actually three, Marcus reflected, since the civilian who was his friend, gatekeeper, and office manager was a retired Marine. Once a Marine, always a Marine.

That Marine was first to get to the conference table, as usual. Carl Freeman rarely smiled and his past middle-aged eyes seemed to look deep into your soul. Many found him intimidating, but when Marcus came on board and discovered he was a former Marine master gunnery sergeant, Marcus followed the sacred advice given to all young officers: find a good senior NCO and listen to him. They worked well together and had become friends in and out of the office.

"Good morning, Gunny. All right with the world today?" Marcus asked as he wandered to the table.

Carl gave out one of his rare smiles. "Couldn't be better, Commander. Martin just called, and he is taking Diana to the hospital. Labor has started!"

"That's wonderful, Carl. Guess I need to start calling you Grandpa Gunny. You should get on over there," Marcus said as he shook Carl's hand. Carl, along with his son and daughter-in-law, were frequent dinner guests at the Colt house.

"Maybe after the meeting I'll run over and sit with Martin. Doctors said her labor might be a long one since this is her first."

Marcus nodded his sympathy. "Go when you want, Carl—you shouldn't miss the big event."

"Thanks, boss, but there is some business to attend to first. I've got the traffic ready for you."

Marcus grimaced. "Any major heartburn stuff in there?"

Carl shook his head and passed the small stack of radio traffic and NIRs and ROIs over to Marcus. Most of the Naval Investigative Requests, NIRs, were information on the start of an investigation that might, *might*, need the attention of IA. Usually they did not.

The ROI, or Report of Investigation, was *here's what's happening and why*. Sometimes IA took action if requested in the ROI, or if IA staff considered it prudent.

"No, sir, but there's one NIR from Great Lakes that might cause some later," Carl said.

Marcus pulled that request from Great Lakes and agreed: it was heartburn material. He muttered a profanity as he returned it to the pile. Then he took his place at the head of the table.

The rest of the IA team arrived precisely at 0815 hours. Following Captain Hank Bates in was LT Wendy James. She had been with NIS the entire four years of her naval service. She was slender, but her uniform couldn't hide the fact she was well built; Marcus had overheard a guy in the cafeteria saying she was built like the proverbial brick outhouse.

Her reddish-brown hair was drawn into a small bun at the base of her skull, and her smile was intoxicating. Her hair and pale, freckled skin made people think she was Irish, yet her ancestry was Welsh and French.

More importantly for their work, Wendy had degrees in accounting and business management from Washington and Lee University. She was perfect for following money trails and grasping the nuances of business operations. Born and raised in Richmond, VA, she had a disarmingly soft Virginian accent. And when she had people disarmed, she went for the jugular. She fit in well and had been an excellent partner for Marcus on several troublesome cases.

Donald "Doc" Stevens sat to Marcus's right, with coffees for himself and for Marcus, who nodded appreciation. This civilian in a sport coat was the assistant to the director of Internal Affairs.

Doc met Marcus in 1970 in Vietnam. At that time, Doc was an enlisted hospital corpsman assigned to a SEAL team that helped Marcus with a secret rescue mission. The targets were two kidnapped cabinet members. While saving each other's and the targets' lives, Doc and Marcus became good friends.

But when the rescue was over, they'd recovered in separate hospitals before returning to their duty stations. They were reunited eight months later when Marcus needed the SEALs' help with a special case, in Norfolk, Virginia. After Marcus was seriously injured, Doc was assigned to keep Marcus safe and assist him with his work.

The friendship grew deeper, and Doc realized he had a knack for investigative work. So he finished his college degree, left the Navy, and transitioned from corpsman to full-fledged NIS agent. Admiral Chance, seeing how well Doc and Marcus meshed, assigned him to IA quickly. Doc's wife of three years had also been a Navy corpsman, but after they married she went into nursing and now worked at Walter Reed Medical Center.

Two more civilians strolled in, sharing a joke. Bradley "Brad" Neil, a civilian in a three-piece suit, had once been a yeoman, but Marcus had encouraged him to become an agent when his enlistment ended. Born in Southern California, he had a surfer look with his blonde hair and laid-back attitude. But he had the skills of a street fighter, and his casework was always by the book.

The lady laughing with SA Neil was Margarita "Rita" Howland, senior IA secretary. Middle-aged yet attractive, with a cute Cuban accent, she was essential due to her Spanish fluency and extreme efficiency.

Marcus noted the empty chair between Rita and Doc, then glanced at the clock. He realized that 0816 shouldn't be considered late, but with everyone else in place, the last to arrive had to face the stares of those already there. It would be intimidating were the IA team not family.

The wait was short, and the last to arrive did not face harsh stares but rather a round of applause. The stares would have been less embarrassing for the newest member of the IA team.

"Lieutenant Gardener, I'm glad you could finally make it to your first Monday staff meeting. Welcome aboard, Marine!" Marcus said after his hand movements stopped the applause.

"Sir, sorry to be late, sir, but the admiral delayed me in the coffee mess, sir," he said while standing at near attention behind his chair, a slight blush coloring his cheeks. Second LT Richard Gardener, USMC, was a couple of months out of Officer Candidate School and had recently turned twenty-five. Furthermore, he had finished the mandatory five weeks of NIS agent training that past Friday. The bright shine of his new second lieutenant "butter bar" was blinding.

Marcus put on a solemn face. "Did he give you a late note, Lieutenant?" Hearing that, Gardener's blush became more intense.

Wendy was the first to lose control. Through her laughter, she punched Marcus in the arm. "Rick, he's pulling your leg. Take your seat."

Rick Gardener first came to Marcus's attention in late 1971 when he and Wendy were on a case that landed them in Naples, Italy. At that time, Rick was a Marine corporal assigned to the Consulate. After a criminal mastermind injured both Marcus and Wendy in a failed assassination attempt, Rick had been assigned to be their driver-slash-bodyguard. In the end, he played a part way beyond that of driver.

Proof that it's a small world, Rick's Gunnery Sergeant in Naples, Gunny Railey, was a man who had helped Marcus and Doc in Vietnam the year before. Railey worked under the code name "Rattler" when he was in 'Nam because he struck quickly with deadly force. He too was a great help in the Naples investigation.

Watching him in action on the case, Railey and Marcus realized Rick was both officer and special agent material. They helped him get his college education on the Navy's dime and saw him commissioned as a Marine officer. Marcus was elated that Rick had requested his first duty station at NIS.

Marcus broke into laughter as well. "Rick, you handled your first day hazing, as we have come to expect from a Marine. Now here's the good news and the bad news, which, by the way, is the same news. The people around this table have been hearing about you for several years. Your reputation precedes you. And even knowing all that, we are happy to have you as part of our team." The laughter from the group was warm and welcoming.

"I appreciate the warning, Commander." Rick chuckled as he slid into the chair.

With a tap on the table with his college class ring, Marcus got the attention of the team and started the meeting. "Welcome to Monday morning. Hope you all had a great weekend, people, because this week is starting off rather nasty, and I suspect it will only get worse. It usually does." Marcus's standard opening spiel received the expected chuckles, and then they went over the status of ongoing cases.

With everyone on the same page of knowledge, Marcus brought up some general housekeeping. "Since our oldest active-duty Marine is leaving us soon, it is time for him to start clearing his desk. Doc, I want you and Rita to get with Hank this week and start the transition of his inhouse duties. Split them between Wendy, Brad, and Rick. And Hank, you will need to spend time with Rick—get him up to speed on how things run around here and how best to get some tarnish on that new butter bar before it blinds us. Okay?"

"My pleasure, sir." The others simply nodded in agreement.

Then Marcus gave them a rundown on the one new issue from the Great Lakes NTC. It didn't take long to share all the info they had thus far. And when you don't have much to go on, you go with what ya got.

Marcus held up the Great Lakes NISO NIR. He took a sip of lukewarm coffee. "Any volunteers to head to Illinois?"

Wendy James gave a quick nod. "Sounds like they have a strange accounting issue up there. That falls into my area of expertise, boss, and if you concur, I would like to take Brad with me. He's sharp at seeing hidden things."

Brad gave Wendy a thumbs-up and nod.

"I will never stand in the way of those bucking standard military tradition and volunteering. Besides, you two are perfect for the job. Just try to wrap it up in a couple of days since I'm taking off on Friday for a long weekend, okay? Rita, get the travel stuff underway since soon-to-be grandpa Carl is about to dash off to the hospital." Marcus stood and reached for his coffee cup. "Unless there is anything else?"

The shaking heads told him what he needed to know. As the team drifted out, Marcus pointed toward Rick Gardener and said, "Get a fresh cup and return. I'll be right back after a head call."

Marcus returned from his visit to the head, the Navy term for the men's room, and a stop in the coffee mess to find Rick Gardener standing at attention by the door. He pointed to one of the chairs in front of his desk and sat in the other. Marcus crossed his legs and struck a relaxed pose while Rick maintained the still posture of attention, even while sitting. Marcus suppressed his smile.

"At ease, Rick. Did you get more coffee?"

"No, sir, I'm fine." Rick's face showed no emotion, but his posture did lose some of its starch.

Marcus smiled. "As your division officer, it is my job to make sure you are happy, well trained, et cetera, et cetera. There is probably a 'welcome aboard' speech I should give, but that isn't going to happen. But I will tell you that if you are constantly standing at attention around me, we will have some negative words. Got it?"

"Yes, sir."

"Okay, I know I'm going against years of your training at Parris Island and in OCS, but having you fit in with the team is much more important. There will be times when proper military protocol is expected, and that is usually when our, or any other, admiral is on deck. Until then, our work cannot be slowed down by popping to attention, adding too many 'sirs' to a sentence, and so on. We are more relaxed in IA. Hank will go into more detail, and you can learn a lot by watching and listening to his interaction with others on the team."

"I understand, sir." Rick's body relaxed a bit more.

"I also think you will remember our adventure in Naples and let that be part of your behavior guide." Marcus sipped his coffee and study Rick's face. He saw a sparkle of understanding sneaking through the starchy stoic exterior.

"Have you talked with Rattler lately?" Marcus asked.

"No, s-s-s, Commander. I was so covered up in school, OCS, and agent training that many things were overlooked. I haven't talked with him in way too many months, I'm ashamed to admit."

"Try to find time for that this week. He is now Sergeant Major Railey at Camp Lejeune, and I know he would appreciate a 'congrats' from a freshly minted second lieutenant."

"Will do, boss. That is great news!"

"Ah, ha! You are trainable!" Marcus laughed then became somber. "Seriously, Rick, our jobs here are difficult. You saw some of that in Naples. Easing up on the protocol helps some, as does building a good relationship with the rest of the team. Don't be afraid to socialize with any of us outside the office. And for crying out loud, if you have any problems: work related, military, personal, women, whatever. That door"—Marcus pointed toward his office door—"as well as the one to my house, is always open. Carry my home phone number in your wallet, and don't be afraid to use it, no matter the time. Okay?"

"I won't let you down, and I appreciate the opportunities I've been given. Commander Colt, I know how much you and Gunny Railey have helped, and I promise you will not be disappointed." After a moment's hesitation, Rick added, "Sir."

Marcus couldn't stop his grin as he told Rick to go find Hank and start his official indoctrination on fitting into the uniquely run NIS IA division.

As the door softly closed, Marcus said a silent prayer of thanks for the blessings of such a good team. He then turned his full attention to the pile of paperwork that never seemed to vanish. His goal was to have a clean desk when he went on leave Thursday afternoon.

12

THE PRINCETON BUGLE, **THE LOCAL** weekly newspaper that dated to the late 1930s, had summed up GT's feelings in huge headlines: "Now Three Mystery Deaths; Authorities Baffled." He snorted when he read the name the reporter had used: Crazed Bear Murders. GT let out a deep sigh as he tossed the paper on his desk, then mumbled, "No shit, Sherlock—I am baffled."

Normally the paper was published every Wednesday, but editor-in-chief Jerry Masterman felt the people needed to know the facts sooner, so he moved it up a day. Sadly, there were few facts beyond the mutilated bodies in Doc's cooler. Baffled was an understatement.

The sheriff's wife of seven years was constantly telling him to look on the bright side. Right now, the only positive was that there had been no phone call today announcing another body discovery. *Be thankful for small blessings*, GT thought. The loud ring of his phone caused him to think he had jinxed the blessing.

"Sheriff Timmons speaking," he announced formally after seeing it was an outside line—his private line, in fact. Only a select few had that number.

"Sheriff, this is Kate at DNR. Sorry to be so long getting back to you, but Doctor Wallace was out in the field overnight. He just called in, and I passed your message on to him. Since he's in your area, he said he would drive over rather than call."

"That's good news, Kate. Thanks! Any idea when he'll get here?"

"Probably within the hour, Sheriff. He was checking on a reported sleuth of brown bears in western Monroe County. Since we've never had brown bears here, he speculated they're black bears that have an unusual coloring issue called color phasing. They range from various shades of brown, blonde, gray and even cinnamon. Most color phase black bears are out west, but some have been spotted here. He was able to collect some hair and scat samples, so he is happy."

"The man gets excited about the strangest things, right?"

Kate couldn't hide her chuckle. "So true, GT."

"Thanks again, Kate. Next time I'm in Beckley, I owe you lunch, hun. Take care."

GT couldn't stop the smile that brightened his face for the first time that day. Perhaps Doctor Simpson Wallace would see something he and Doc had missed. As the leading ursinologist in this and all the bordering states, Wallace was usually called "that bear guy" or "bear master" by his friends. He was in high demand for his expertise.

Simpson Wallace was a unique character. He grew up in Princeton, but being at least a dozen years older than GT, they ran in different social circles. They'd met when the doctor gave a lecture at Princeton High School in hopes of getting more students interested in zoology. GT had asked most of the questions after the lecture, and they continued their talk when GT asked him home for dinner. A friendship grew from that brief encounter.

Doctor Wallace had gotten his master's and doctorate degrees in wildlife biology at Utah State. His doctoral dissertation was built upon his master's thesis on bear migration, which included lifestyles, mating habits, and nearly every aspect of bears; it was later published as a collegiate textbook. Academics couldn't understand his choice of the West Virginia Division of Natural Resources over his many offers at places like Yale or Oxford. But that was one of his quirks; he didn't want to teach; he wanted to do. He wanted to get in the woods, tag bears, watch their actions, collect scat, and enjoy all the other wonderful things that happen when you get your hands dirty.

Not only did his vast knowledge and choice of employers make him unique, but so did his appearance. Simpson Wallace had started a full beard in his first year of college, and most who looked at him now believe he had never trimmed it since. Aside from his slightly receding hairline, calling his hair style *bushy* was a gross understatement. Some, upon meeting the doctor, recalled P.T. Barnum's *Wild Men of Borneo* exhibit from the 1880s.

In addition to his hair, Simpson never put much thought into his dress. While he tried to wear a suit and tie in the office, there were days when he came in dressed like he'd been on safari for weeks. Matters of appearance, like dressing for the occasion, were not important to him.

"Sheriff, you need to come out here," Norma softly called into GT's office. "Now, Sheriff!" she said with a bit more urgency.

Standing inside the door was a tall and rather bulky man. His 6'3" frame seemed taller because of the mass of curly black hair that covered his head. And the bulk from his coat visually added more to his 260-ish pounds. Most would consider him a hobo at first, and even second glance. Wild hair and beard, unkempt coat and trousers, and muddy boots encouraged that belief until he spoke. Doctor Simpson Wallace had picked up a British accent during an extended lecture tour at Oxford and other schools around the United Kingdom. At times, he sounded more royal than the royals.

"Bloody good to see you, Godfrey! How's dear Sally and the little ones?" Doctor Wallace was one of only a few who could call GT by his first name without getting "the look." Might have been the accent. It had been a couple of years since they worked together on a bear tagging weekend, but GT saw that his friend had not changed a bit.

"They're doing fine, Simpson. You're looking great, as always. Kate told me you had a good time wallowing in the woods last night."

"Indeed. I have gathered sufficient evidence to catalog this new sleuth. But that can wait; your call takes priority. How might I help the sheriff of Mercer County?"

After a round of introductions, GT and Wallace retired to the conference room. GT brought his coffee, and Wallace brought his standard cup of tea that he had prepared in the break room. Detective Allen Chambers quickly arrived with a stack of case folders. They spent at least an hour going through the files, pointing to various things on the photos and making notes on legal pads. Anyone walking in would immediately feel the frustration.

"Bodies number one and two sort of fit into a bear's standard storage methods and probable territory. Well, 'sort of' is the key phrase; number two leaning against a tree is strange as is the lack of clothing. Bears do not remove clothing when they attack. Shred, yes. Completely strip, no."

Heads nodded in agreement.

Simpson continued, "Godfrey, I concur with your theory that a bear would not drag a human body over a mile. So how body number three got to the rail yard, *and* inside a locked building, is a mystery. Holmes and Watson would love this case. As would a real inspector I know at Scotland Yard."

GT said, "The only possible way to get into that shop building that morning was through a roof skylight. There were several that were not secured, and Allen found matching blood traces on the one directly above the body. Looked like she was dropped or lowered from the roof."

Wallace scoffed. "So you are suggesting a bear carried the body several miles, then took it to the roof? Seriously?"

"No, I'm not suggesting anything. Just throwing out more of the confusing information we have." He flipped through his notepad until he found what he needed to share. "And when Sergeant Walker was working the scene with body number two, he jokingly said it looked like the body was left by helicopter. There were no visible signs that the body had been carried or drug to the scene. And there were no blood or body parts anywhere in the area."

Shaking his head, Wallace announced, "We do officially have one solid fact: there are no flying bears!"

GT tried to keep a straight face and failed. Both he and Allen started with a giggle and quickly broke into uncontrolled laughter. Finally catching his breath, GT said, "You sound so sure about that, Simpson!"

"Indeed, I am," Wallace huffed sternly.

"Okay, I'll give you that. But can you say with certainty that the bodies were gutted by a bear?"

Doctor Wallace again scanned the autopsy photos of all three victims. "While these photos are good, Godfrey, I can *not* see what I need to see. The bodies do have all the hallmarks of a bear attack, yet something seems amiss."

"So a bear could be involved?" Allen asked.

"Perhaps. Maybe. But I insist I need to see the actual bodies. Are they available?"

GT nodded. "How about we head to the morgue in the morning. Come home with me, Simpson. Sally will fix us a good dinner, and you can have our guestroom. And I have an untapped bottle of Jim Beam we can use to numb the frustration. Okay?"

"You had me at Sally's dinner—a delightful expectation. And the bourbon is icing on the cake."

13

ALL THE BOOKS BALANCED. THE inventory lists had been checked and double-checked. Bills of lading were verified. Processed orders researched. Special agents Wendy James and Brad Neil had spent the day and previous evening going over the records several times. And that was after the NISO agents spent over a week digging. The result was the same every time: nothing was amiss.

But Supervisory Special Agent Todd Burke, the man in charge of the Great Lakes NISO, was not convinced. He had requested IA to take over the case when his own agents had hit a brick wall. They were following his hunch to look into the base hospital. In reality, he knew there was no official case, but there was something "not right" about the trucks reportedly coming and going there irregularly.

When Burke took over the office several years ago, he had instituted several new reviews in hopes of keeping on top of things. And the latest review of commercial traffic on the base showed an anomaly: a small box truck came on the base every week or so, only in the evenings. It stayed longer than other delivery vehicles of its size, and its destination was always the hospital. Yet no documentation of deliveries matched the timing of the truck's visits.

"Okay, Todd, the paperwork and physical inventory are fine. Hopefully your digging around hasn't spooked anyone. Your thoughts about that?" Wendy asked.

"We should be clear, Wendy. The General Accounting Office and the Navy's Bureau of Medicine in Alexandria, Virginia provided all the documents we've checked out. And we pulled the gate logs like we have done for years, so nothing is amiss there. No agents have visited the hospital or conducted interviews. I wanted your input first," Todd replied.

Wendy glanced at Brad, who gave a quick nod: he knew where she was going. "It has been over a week since the last strange delivery, so it's time to set up 24/7 surveillance on the place."

"But the deliveries are all in the evenings. Why 24/7?" Todd asked.

Brad added, "We need to see what's happening there round the clock. And when the suspect truck arrives, we'll need to follow it back to its lair."

Todd nodded, then put forth an argument, "Yea, but the problem is manpower. My agents total five, including me. Suggestions?"

Wendy removed her glasses and massaged the bridge of her nose. One of the many things Marcus had taught her was to find ways to ponder a problem without looking like a deer caught in a truck's headlights. Fiddling with her glasses provided the means of delaying a response. It gave her the needed time to think. She replaced the glasses and looked at Todd.

"We have a bigger problem to address first. Since nothing is missing, my guess, and I suspect yours also, is that drugs are being funneled through the center. That means just about anybody on the base could be involved, so we can't use any of the Great Lakes resources like Shore Patrol or Marines to help with the surveillance. Any of them might be involved. Ditto for the local police."

Todd slowly let out a deep breath. "So, it's up to the seven of us? Guess we can do it, but it will be rough if it lasts more than a few days."

"Here's the plan, Todd. Set up a two-person team working an eight-hour shift. Each person will have a vehicle in case there is the opportunity to tail the truck. Get the first two on site immediately. They'll need to find a good nest where they can see and not be seen. Brad will be with the first team. Your five, plus Brad, will be enough to cover the first few days before fatigue sets in."

"Okay. Brad, you need to get with Rodney Carth and go find your location. Radio back when you're set."

Brad left to start the surveillance. Wendy picked up all the paperwork and secured it in her briefcase. She turned to Todd. "While you're setting up the other two teams and briefing them about the situation, I'll be in my room working on getting us more help. And I need to check a couple other things in these logs. I'll see you in the morning."

Wendy drove her assigned vehicle, a battleship-gray 1973 Plymouth Fury, to the Navy Lodge. This was an actual hotel built on base and made available to personnel like her on short assignments, or to families visiting their sailor. It was more private and much nicer than the transient Bachelor Officer's Quarters.

Before picking up the phone, she ran the parameters of the case through her mind. As she did, it was easy to see that the unknowns outweighed the knowns, but she knew her boss had done more with less. Now it was her turn, but she needed help. As Marcus had told her many times, never be afraid to ask for help. She dialed the numbers from memory.

"Naval Investigative Service, Internal Affairs. Carl Freeman speaking. How may I help you, sir?"

"Hi Carl. Wendy calling for Marcus. But first, are you a grandpa yet?"

She could hear Carl's smile through the phone. "Oh, yes ma'am, I am! Marcus Carl Freeman arrived at 0200 hours this morning weighing in at seven pounds and five ounces. Diana's doing fine and Martin is beside himself with joy."

"That's wonderful, Carl! Carrying the names of two great men—his future is rock solid. Pass my congrats on to Diana and Martin and tell them I'm looking forward to my turn at babysitting. Hate to put a damper on this good stuff, but is my grouchy boss around?"

"Yes, ma'am, he is … both grouchy and around. Hold one please."

"Afternoon, Wendy. Coming home soon?" Marcus asked after a couple of clicks came through the line.

Wendy grimaced. "Uh, no, sir. I'm here at the lodge so I could call you in private. Not being too paranoid, but you never know what phones are clean."

Marcus chuckled at their shared code. They had used that line on assignment in Panama a year ago; it was code for needing a break from everyone. To think clearly often requires getting away from the action and everyone involved. "Okay. What's up?"

It took less than five minutes for Wendy to share the status of her investigation. Then she requested a few more people.

"Wendy, I can't fault your logic. I can see where illegal drugs can come into the hospital and get shipped out with various supplies. Or the hospital could be the hub for incoming drugs for distribution to civilians in Chicago. Someone might have a big network in play either way it flows. How many people do you need to do it right?"

"Am I being too greedy asking for six? That would give us enough people to cover two days with eight-hour shifts without duplication, or we could break the shifts into four- or six-hour durations and be less painful. Based on the varied delivery schedule, I hope the surveillance will last only a few days, but there are no guarantees. I know you wanted us back sooner, but I'd like to see this through. It looks to be a lot bigger than an accounting error or two."

Marcus leaned back and looked at the overhead: the Navy's term for ceiling. It helped center his focus. He often referred to this maneuver as seeking advice from the "oracles of the overhead." Whatever it was called, it allowed a moment of concentrated thought. After no more than a few seconds, he said, "Makes sense for you to handle it. Todd's a good agent, but you have more experience with surveillance. I'd recommend using three agents on four-hour staggered shifts, but that's all up to you. I'll get with the admiral and call ya back shortly. What's the number there?"

14

GETTING IN TO SEE VICE Admiral Chance was not as fun as it used to be. The last official gatekeeper, Senior Chief Yeoman Victor O'Keef, had retired the previous year. He and Marcus had constantly traded verbal barbs and jokes, as friends are known to do.

The new gatekeeper was a civilian. She was more than good at her job, but didn't have the same level of friendliness as Vic. Fact is, after his first attempt at warming up to her, Mrs. Schaffer—no, he could not call her "Mary," she said—made sure he knew her office was strictly for Navy business and not discussing how her weekend went. Small talk was out of the question.

But at least Mrs. Schaffer knew that when Commander Colt—no, she would not call him "Marcus" like he asked—came through her door, he damn sure needed to talk with the admiral. She picked up the phone to make sure the admiral was free as soon as she saw his face. She nodded an okay toward Marcus and returned to her typing.

Marcus rapped twice on the admiral's door, heard "Enter," and walked in. The admiral directed him to the sofa off to the side, then sat opposite. "Your first visit this week—things must be slow." His warm smile kept the comment from being derogatory.

"Yes, sir, but like you always say, give it a minute and things will change. And it just did," Marcus replied. Then he briefed the admiral on the Great Lakes situation and Wendy's request for additional people. He wrapped it up with, "She asked for six, but I would prefer to send her at least eight agents."

The admiral nodded in agreement. "Logical. Pull two from downstairs and call around. I suspect Charleston, Norfolk, and Philadelphia NISOs can lend a hand or two. If I recall correctly, all three places owe you a favor or two."

Marcus stood. "Thank you, sir. I'll make a few phone calls."

The admiral motioned him back down on the sofa. "I'm sorry I can't be with you on Saturday, Marcus. So is the CNO. The president called for a full security briefing at Camp David. Is there anything else I can do? Sure you have enough time off scheduled?"

"I understand, sir. And everything is under control. But I appreciate your concern. I'll give you a full report next Wednesday morning," Marcus said with a shrug and a partial grin.

"Well, drive safely. Call if you need me."

Calls were next on the list as Marcus carried yet another cup of the special blend coffee to his office; cardamom and cinnamon gave a nice touch to the brew. The calls went well. Ten agents would be arriving at Great Lakes by noon tomorrow. His uncle-in-law, Captain Humphrey Miller, was the commanding officer of NISO Norfolk, and he volunteered three of their agents to help. Charleston and Philly kicked in two each. And the two volunteer agents downstairs asked if a third agent, a new guy who needed the experience, could participate.

Marcus called the lodge at Great Lakes. "Wendy, a few agents will be there by noon tomorrow."

"I appreciate it, Marcus. Will the names of the six be sent as a ROI overnight?"

He chuckled. "Nope. But the roster of all ten will."

"Ten? You gotta be kidding me. That's outstanding! How did that happen?"

Marcus shared the talk with the admiral and the results of calling in a few favors from the various NISOs. It was nice when things went the right way.

"Any words of wisdom to share, boss?"

Marcus chuckled. "Make sure you have someone watching your back at all times, Wendy. Otherwise, you know what has to be done. Call if you need me." He gave her the number where he could be reached while on leave.

"I'll be glad when we know what those trucks are carrying and why they are staying so long on the base. I might be chasing those elusive wild geese."

"Your gut is getting to be as sharp as mine, so if you think something is evil, it probably is."

They chatted for a few more minutes about the case and Carl's grandson. Wendy hoped to return to the office in time for the Monday meeting.

"Wendy, do whatever needs to be done. Doc, Hank, and Rick will be here while I'm on leave. And I'll be back at work next Wednesday."

"Will do. Sorry I can't be with you this weekend. You and Kelly stay safe on your drive, Marcus. We need you."

"I'll do my best."

15

DOCTOR DENNIS BASSETT HAD BEEN the Mercer County medical examiner for over fifteen years. He was damn good at his job and loved doing it. Short and slightly built, Dennis did not cut an imposing figure as he pushed his black-framed glasses back up his nose. Yet this small man, a few years short of age fifty, was rarely given any grief.

Dennis ran his morgue like a boot camp drill instructor. Everything had a place, and it had better be there when not in use. Procedures existed for a reason and they were followed. Autopsies were completed, reports and photos were filed, and bodies were released to the next of kin as quickly as possible. He treated his people with respect, but woe betide ones who didn't follow procedures.

Upsetting his "tight ship" right now were the eviscerated bodies stored in three of his eighteen refrigerated lockers. They were on hold due to the circumstances of their demise. Well, that and the fact that one was still a "John Doe" and another didn't have family. Bassett had added his own padlocks to the three doors to keep the inquisitive away. The Crazed Bear comment in the paper had excited curiosity.

GT had called late yesterday and told Dennis he was bringing by a bear expert to look at the three bodies at eight in the morning. Dennis had arrived a bit earlier than usual, allowing time to copy the three autopsy files. The expert would probably want his own copies for research or note taking. Dennis tried to anticipate the needs of his visitors.

GT led the group into the morgue a few minutes earlier than expected. Detective Allen Chambers and Doctor Simpson Wallace followed closely behind. Dennis nearly came to attention when he recognized the renowned Doctor Wallace. GT handled the introductions.

Dennis looked up at Simpson Wallace. "A great honor to meet you, Doctor. Your book on bear migration was excellent."

Simpson smiled down at Dennis. "Thank you, sir. And I must say that your autopsy reports were well done, Doctor Bassett."

GT was getting frustrated. "Okay, doctors, enough of the mutual admiration society blather. Let's get on a first name basis and do what we came to do. Okay?"

Dennis asked, "Right. Where to start? Shall we go in date order?"

"If you don't mind, Dennis, I would prefer to see all three laid out at the same time, if that is all right with you."

The three were laid out on the tables. Number one was the John Doe, number two was Joe Decker, and number three was Doris Thompkins. GT saw similarities in the evisceration and claw marks on various parts of the body, but nothing that would solve the cases. He put his hopes on the combined knowledge of the two doctors.

Simpson did a complete visual inspection of each. His examination took about fifteen minutes per body, and he made a couple of notes on each one on the autopsy copy Dennis had provided. GT, Allen, and Dennis stood off to the side to avoid being an interruption.

With the overall exam completed, Simpson studied a small section—the head and shoulders—of the first body. He went to the second body and examined the same area, and finally to the third. He did this more times than GT could count as he slowly moved down the bodies, front and back, looking at a section at a time. No one spoke as Simpson did his study. This comparison continued for over twenty minutes.

With a small flashlight he retrieved from his coat pocket, Simpson carefully looked deep into each empty abdomen. His face contorted as he looked at the third body. He quickly moved to the first and looked into the same area of the cavity, then the opposite side. Then with another jump, he moved to the second body. After a moment he let out a deep sigh.

"Dennis, may I have a couple of small pathology containers, please," Simpson asked mildly as he lifted a scalpel from the tray of instruments. "I know you sent various samples to the lab, but I just found something that wasn't in the lab results and shouldn't be here."

"What did I miss?" Dennis asked.

With a chuckle, Simpson said, "Edward Lowe's wonderful creation: a tiny piece or two, I do believe. The lab will verify that, I'm sure."

"Damn."

GT was confused. "Who's Lowe and what does that mean?"

Dennis started to answer, then pointed to Simpson. "Your find, sir. Take the lead."

Simpson nodded acknowledgment. "Lowe invented a clay-based, extra absorbent cat litter in the forties. Now it is used to absorb almost any liquid. Unless our crazy bear has a house cat living with him, the abdominal mutilations were probably done by a human—a human who was probably using cat litter to soak up the blood. The stuff gets everywhere when dumped on the floor, and I found small amounts in each of the abdominal cavities."

Dennis added, "And I'll wager that clay the lab found mixed with mud in the third body's hair is the same. I'll flag it to check for a match."

"So we can rule out a bear attack?" GT asked.

Simpson frowned. "Not completely, Godfrey. Body number one shows clear teeth marks on his upper left shoulder where a bear probably dragged the body. And it was covered in the woods the way a bear would do. I suspect the body was dumped in a known bear area in hopes that a bear would feed on it and cover the human intervention. But I cannot absolutely say it was not the other way around."

"But no bear marks on the second or third body?" GT pushed for a concise answer.

"Yes, and no. Look here, my man," Simpson said as he shone his light into the claw marks on body number two. "Here, here, and here, we have obvious claw marks. But I believe they were made with the paw of a dead bear. Notice how the spacing between the marks is always the same? A live bear would be moving his toes as he tore at the flesh and the marks would vary in spacing and depth."

No one spoke for a few minutes as they absorbed the new information.

Simpson continued, "And we have similar marks on body number three."

Dennis walked over to body number one and checked the marks.

Simpson came over. "Dennis, I didn't see many fake marks here. If you glance over to the right side, you can see claw marks that are varied. That indicates a live bear, as well as the dead one, was involved."

"So did a bear kill them all, or only the first one?" GT asked.

Simpson shrugged. "I doubt that any were killed by a bear. The bodies were clawed to make it look so."

Dennis shook his head. "That means we don't have a cause of death on any of them."

"And the cases are getting colder by the moment. Anything else to share to further ruin my day?" GT asked.

Simpson said, "And we have another anomaly. Note the wounds on the shoulders of all three victims. Body number one has a pair of puncture wounds on both the front and back left shoulder, typical of a bear jaw grasping. However, bodies number two and three have a pair of puncture wounds only on the front of their bodies, and they have a pair on each shoulder. It looks like the bodies were pulled by whatever caused the punctures. The punctures were not made with a mechanical device."

GT frowned. "Okay. So what caused them?"

Simpson scoffed, "Well, of course a creature with two claws on each foot, my boy, both pointing in the same direction."

GT shrugged off the slight rebuke. "I don't know of any animal like that around here."

"Very true; there are none here. The two-toed sloth is in South America. There is a bird in Australia that has only two claws on the front of its foot, but there is a third on the back. Of course, the Tyrannosaurus Rex only had two claws on his short forearms, but I doubt one of those is running around West Virginia," Simpson replied with a chuckle.

Dennis said, "If it was done by a bear with broken incisors on one of his jaws, there would still be evidence of bruising, and probable impressions from the other teeth. Do we have any bears around here in that condition, possibly from a freak accident?"

"None that I have seen or heard reported, Dennis."

Allen Chambers had been unexpectedly quiet during this examination and subsequent discussion. He cleared his throat to get attention. "We do have one two-clawed creature here. I read an interesting article in the National Geographic last year and remembered a weird fact: a moth has two claws on each leg."

Dennis laughed. "It would take a huge moth to move a human body, Allen."

GT knew where the conversation was going. And he dreaded the results.

Allen said, "When we got the report on Doris Thompkins missing, from her husband, he mentioned quote-unquote *something big* flying over his house when he discovered her gone. Could be the Mothman has returned."

GT frowned. "Or perhaps a big owl."

16

THE COLTS HAD DECIDED TO drive from Alexandria to Princeton. The early fall weather was perfect for the views provided by the Blue Ridge Parkway, which meandered southward through Virginia down the spine of the Blue Ridge, a major mountain chain that is part of the Appalachian Mountains. The Parkway was one of the projects created under the New Deal by President Roosevelt in the 1930s. It took advantage of the wonderful scenery to provide a relaxing drive from northern Virginia down through North Carolina.

For Marcus, it was his second trip down the Parkway. His parents had insisted he and his younger sister, Eleanor, or "Elle," see the sights years ago on a family vacation. Kelly was enjoying her first visit; her father's duty stations saw her growing up in exotic ports of call, so there were many places in America she had not seen. Marcus was determined to make sure she enjoyed those places and built memories, as he had done.

They had left home a few minutes before dawn so there would be plenty of time to enjoy the Parkway. The Mustang with top down provided the best platform for the trip. Granted it was chilly, but that was better than sweating. The scenery helped take Marcus's mind off the reason for the trip. His parents' ashes were riding securely inside a valise resting on the back seat. It would be their last trip down the Parkway.

As Kelly enjoyed the various vistas, Marcus tried but failed to keep his mind off the reason for the trip. As they had so many times recently, the memories took control. The upcoming memorial service in Princeton would be the final piece of the sad short story that started on a normal Monday morning in August. The phone call had been from the sheriff of Hardee County, Florida. For the umpteenth time, Marcus failed to stop the replay of events in his mind.

"Naval Investigative Service, Internal Affairs. Commander Colt speaking. How may I be of assistance, sir?"

"Commander, this is Sheriff Hank Battle from Hardee County, Florida. No easy way to say it, sir, but your parents were killed in an auto accident over the weekend. Sorry for your loss, Commander."

Marcus had been on the other end of that notification process too many times. But this was his first time receiving the call. Like others had told him, it was as if time stopped. He heard the words, but his brain refused to accept the news. *No way. Couldn't be. Has to be a mistake. You've got the wrong number. Gotta be a sick joke.* On and on, the denials zipped through his mind until he blinked and returned to real time. While it seemed like an hour, he knew that no more than a second or two had passed.

Marcus sighed. "Sheriff, does my sister know?"

"Yes, sir. Fact is, Commander, she called us on Sunday afternoon. Her call led to the positive identification. Miss Colt had came home at noon from a long shift at Morton Plant Hospital and found the house empty. She knew they came over here to Wauchula on Saturday to get some produce for canning and visit a friend. Since they had not returned, she was worried that the car might have broken down ... or worse. We contacted the friend and pieced together the events that lead up to the crash."

While he was surprised Elle hadn't called him yesterday, Marcus knew her strength and confidence had blossomed during the three-plus years she had been attending the University of South Florida. Deciding to follow Kelly into the psychology field, Elle had landed part-time work at the local hospital to start building her medical resume, all while carrying a full course load at college. She was a go-getter who never shrank from a challenge or hard work. Knowing Marcus had a lot of stress from his assignments, she did her best to take on the family challenges and buffer him from the trivial odds and ends. This was beyond trivial, but another case of her doing her best to protect her big brother.

"She is never one to sit around and wait, Sheriff. What exactly happened?"

The sheriff's verbal report was similar to ones Marcus had delivered over the years. It laid out the specifics and avoided speculation.

Twenty minutes past sunset on Saturday, his parents were heading north on Route 17 out of Wauchula. They had just passed the town of Fort Meade when a Ford pickup truck traveling south crossed the centerline and hit them head on.

The pickup driver was one of the thousands of migrant Mexican farm workers who followed the crops around the country. He had spent too many hours in a bar south of Bartow that afternoon and was far too drunk to be driving. All three died on impact. Both vehicles were engulfed in fire. The Colts were identified initially by their vehicle and later by the female's medical alert bracelet and the male's WWII dog tags. Marcus asked pointed questions, and the sheriff answered.

"Again, Commander, I am truly sorry for your loss."

"Sheriff, it you don't mind, let's go with Hank and Marcus. I'll be seeing you in a few hours and a less formal atmosphere will help. Guess I need to call Elle next."

"Marcus, Elle is here beside me. She drove over yesterday and refused to leave. We put her up in the local motel overnight, and she insisted on being here when I called you."

Elle tried to keep her voice strong, but Marcus could hear through the façade. It was mostly bravado. "Marcus, I'll be here waiting for you. We have some decisions to make."

After talking with her for a few minutes, Marcus put his emotions on hold and shifted into automatic, doing all the things he had to do. Calling Kelly was rough, but getting emergency leave, flying to Orlando, then driving down to Wauchula and walking into the sheriff's office was the easy part of the day. The rest of that day, and most of that week, were difficult. Fortunately, his parents were efficient and had their wills and last wishes well documented.

Marcus was brought back to the present when Kelly asked, "Any chance you will be feeding your starving spouse soon, Sailor?"

Smiling at the beauty sitting next to him, Marcus said, "Anything for you, Princess. Think you can hold on for about half an hour?" She nodded and squeezed his hand that rested on her knee.

They bailed off the Parkway onto US Highway 460 a bit north of Bonsack. 460 would take them west to Princeton, but a quick exit onto Williamson Road led them into downtown Roanoke.

Roanoke had changed since the last time Marcus had been on these streets in 1957. At that time, the Norfolk and Western Railway was the last major railroad in America to depend on steam locomotives. They designed and built them there in Roanoke and took pride in their efficient motive power. The railway also owned the coal mines that provided fuel for the locomotives. They built the coal cars that carried their main source of income from the hills of West Virginia to the docks in Norfolk for shipment to waiting customers. It was a closed business environment.

But one big negative was the coal smoke that lingered over the city. Many a housewife mumbled curses as they surveyed the coal dust on their once-clean laundry drying on lines in the backyard.

That problem was gone. Like the steam locomotives that caused it, the smoke was history. The railway dropped the fires in the last steam locomotive in May 1961, and all but a few were scrapped. The Norfolk and Western had joined the rest of the country in relying on a diesel locomotive fleet.

Marcus parked on Campbell Avenue near the Roanoke Weiner Stand, across from the old city market. He looked around and listened for a fond memory now gone; no steam locomotive whistles or smoke filled the air. *Progress*, he thought with a sigh, then perked up on seeing their destination.

"This is one of Dad's favorite places in this town. Well, this place and Archie's Lobster House, which isn't open for lunch." Marcus grabbed the valise from the back seat and ushered Kelly into the oldest hot dog stand in Virginia. "Figured Mom and Dad would appreciate one more visit to a restaurant that opened before they were born."

Their hunger satisfied by several hot dogs, the drive west got underway. Marcus shared his knowledge of the area as they left the Shenandoah and Roanoke Valleys and started climbing up and around the many humps that were part of the great Appalachian Mountain range. The ninety-mile drive took well over two hours, including a quick bathroom stop near Blacksburg. There were too many twists and turns to make decent time.

As Marcus pointed out the "Welcome to Mercer County" sign, a loud siren and a flashing red light from the bubblegum machine on top of a beige sedan pulled his attention to the rearview mirror.

"Are you speeding?" Kelly asked.

Pulling to a stop on the side of the road, Marcus checked the mirror again and laughed. "Never speed on these curvy roads, babe. Looks like it's the local welcoming committee."

As Sheriff GT approached the rear of the Mustang, he sang out, "Marcus Aurelius, it's about damn time the Roman legion allowed you time to come home, boy!"

Marcus was all grins as he jumped out of the car and placed the officer in a bear hug. "Godfrey, My Man! Good to see you again!"

GT pulled away, a dark shadow crossing his face. "So sorry about your Mom and Dad, Marcus. Their deaths hurt the whole town, man. Elle doing okay? You?"

Marcus simply nodded. His friend's emotion hit him hard. But the happiness of their reunion swiftly pushed it away, at least for now, as laughter and back slapping commenced.

Kelly watched the reunion with pleasure, as she hadn't seen this thoroughly delighted side of Marcus in a while. She knew the loss of his parents was still heavy on his shoulders, no matter how hard he tried to hide it. She was glad to see it lift, if only for a few moments. Walking around to where the men were exchanging physical and verbal jabs, she asked, "Is that some secret greeting between West Virginian males or can I get a hug also? Hi, I'm Kelly." She gave GT her best smile and extended her hand.

GT took both of her hands in his and stepped back. He looked her up and down saying, "Kelly, your wedding photos were great, but they failed to capture your true beauty. Welcome to West Virginia, darling!" He pulled her into a soft hug.

A radio call for GT interrupted the pleasure of the reunion. He stuck his head into the car window and listened to the message. A short response of "on the way" was all he needed to add. He turned to the Colts. "Y'all will be staying at Aunt Maude's, right?"

Marcus nodded and GT rapidly continued, "Marcus, don't be mad at Aunt Maude. It was all the mayor's doing. I'd fill you in, but I gotta problem, so we'll catch up tomorrow after the memorial. Welcome home, Marcus. Kelly, good to finally meet you." He slammed the cruiser door before either of the Colts could respond and fired off the engine.

As GT spun his rear wheels and sped away, siren blaring and lights flashing, Kelly looked at Marcus. "And what do you think you're not supposed to be mad about?"

Marcus shrugged. "Haven't a clue, dearest. At least it's only about ten minutes to Aunt Maude's house, so the anticipation will be short."

17

THE DRIVE WAS LONG ENOUGH for Marcus to summarize his relationship with Sheriff Godfrey Timmons and their strange greeting. Their families had been friends forever. Growing up, GT and Marcus, who was only four months older, were as close as brothers. With GT's dad being sheriff and his mom working weird hours at the hospital, their only child was a frequent overnight visitor to the Colt residence. And on Friday night sleepovers, that meant the boys, including the senior Colt, would watch old movies on the late, late show while munching popcorn and sipping on Dr Pepper.

The three enjoyed those old movies, and on one particular night the 1936 comedy *My Man Godfrey* was shown. Before it was over, Marcus had taken to using the phrase "Godfrey, my man" when addressing GT. GT was frustrated that he didn't have a comeback until Mr. Colt told him about what he'd wanted to name his son. Marcus James Colt was almost named Marcus Aurelius Colt after the Roman emperor from 161–180 AD. The senior Mr. Colt, the local high school history teacher and a Roman history buff, thought it would be a great name of a great man. But his wife won the argument, and the middle name of Aurelius was dropped in favor of her father's name, James. With that, GT had his comeback, and the two nicknames stuck.

"Is that why he used 'Aunt Maude' so easily? He's family?"

"Yea, pretty much, but we haven't been close these last ten-plus years. You know, my family's move to Florida and me not getting up here too often sort of dampened the closeness. It's nothing like what I have with Doc, but it's good to bring a piece of it back to life just now."

Kelly was quiet for a couple of minutes, then she softly asked, "And how many old girlfriends will I be meeting tomorrow? Any need to worry about, Sailor?"

A snort preceded his response. "Only one, and you'll meet her tomorrow ... or sooner."

"What? Did you send her a special invite or something?" Kelly's smile started to kick up to the right, and Marcus knew things were getting too serious.

"Kelly, I was in junior high when we moved to Florida. I had been interested in only one girl up here, Sally Steinman, and we went to exactly one Sadie Hawkins dance together before we both realized we were better buddies than dating partners. I haven't seen or talked with her in years."

"And yet you're sure she will show up. Exactly how does that work?" Kelly asked somewhat stiffly.

Marcus laughed. "Stay cool, Princess. Since she's been married to GT for the last seven years, I'm pretty sure she will be with him tomorrow."

Before Kelly could come up with a reply, Marcus turned onto Hale Avenue and drove north a couple of blocks. The asphalt was wearing in places, allowing the original brick pavers to show. Parking the Mustang in front of the house gave Kelly a chance to take it all in before the top dropped into place, blocking her view. She climbed out and stood looking at what Marcus had always called a mansion. And, she had to admit, he'd been right. "Wow," she softly murmured.

It technically wasn't a mansion, but would be considered a large two-story home by anyone's definition. Kelly studied the lines and guessed it was built around the turn of the century, and had undergone a couple of major updates since then. The overall package projected that mansion feeling.

The old cut-stone curb bordered several feet of well-maintained grass, complete with ancient oak trees, before reaching the sidewalk. A few feet past the front of the Mustang sat a couple of cut-stone blocks that, in bygone days, were steppingstones into the horse-drawn carriages. The sidewalk butted against an aged cut-stone wall that was nearly four feet high. Stone stairs were set into the wall, allowing access to the higher manicured yard and walkway leading to the house. Large cast-iron planters with small generic evergreens, perhaps arborvitae, accented each side of the stair opening.

A ten-foot-wide set of curved wood stairs rose six feet to the huge, covered porch that wrapped around both sides of the house. The porch had a depth of at least a dozen feet, and someone had covered the deck boards with a medium gray paint. The decorated layered eaves on the porch roof accented the columns that held it up without being too frilly. The huge double doors, painted black to match the window sashes and shutters, were centered with a couple of balanced pairs of windows on each side.

That balance carried through the entire house, from the matching windows on both floors to the matching chimneys on each side. Kelly decided that it would fit into a simplified Italianate Victorian style if she had to find a right set of words to describe it. The gleaming white paint provided a simple elegance that no other color would have. *Yes, this is a mansion*, she thought.

The porch was so large that the pair of matching three-seat swing gliders placed on opposite sides of the door did not cramp it at all. Kelly noticed that one glider was moving, and as she focused on it she saw a woman stand and walk toward the stairs.

"Marcus Colt, you get up here and give me a hug!" Aunt Maude cried. "You too, Kelly!"

Maude Eadden was pushing eighty years on this planet, but she looked closer to sixty. Her black and silver hair was cut in a short style and accented a nearly round face. Standing a little over five feet, she maintained an attractive petite figure. Her eyes automatically squinted when she smiled, as round cheeks pushed up against them. Were she a tad shorter, she would fit the part of one of Santa's elves. Her place on the family tree was younger sister to Marcus's paternal grandmother. Technically she was his great-aunt, but that mouthful was never spoken. Aunt Maude had always been simply Aunt Maude, to just about everyone.

Welcoming of kinfolk in West Virginia is a long process. Hugs and kisses are exchanged, everyone tries to recall the last time they were together, somber remembrances of those who have passed on since then are shared, and another round of hugs happens. It being Kelly's first visit, Aunt Maude also added compliments on Kelly's beauty and wishes that those who had passed on were there to meet her. The welcoming was something Marcus had warned Kelly to be ready for, as it would happen many more times at the memorial service. "It's a family thing."

Once the welcoming had concluded, luggage was moved into the house and Aunt Maude started the tour. Marcus excused himself to prepare a round of drinks in the kitchen. He was well versed on the layout of the house and could safely travel around it in the dark.

Maude and Kelly were left alone in the huge foyer. A massive heat radiator was against the wall on the left, with five varied-length brass chimes of the door bell hanging above. Ornate stairs against the right wall led to the second floor. The entire foyer was open to the second floor ceiling, with a balcony visible on three sides of that floor. Maude pointed to the door on the right at the foot of the stairs.

"This way, honey. This was Ray's study," she said with reverence.

Ray and Maude shared nearly forty years together before a stroke ended his life in 1953. Maude always believed the stroke was a direct result of losing their youngest son in Korea. The telegraph from the Army had arrived three days before his death. Their oldest son was killed in action on the beaches of Normandy on June 6, 1944. Two gold star flags were still displayed in the front window.

Kelly took it all in quickly. Three walls were lined with filled floor-to-ceiling bookshelves, and the fourth wall hosted a huge fireplace done in a dark, rust-colored brick. The mantel was large enough to hold a well-detailed large model of the ocean liner SS United States. An oil painting of Ray and Maude from decades ago filled the wall above the mantel. She could imagine Ray sitting in the dark leather easy chair, feet resting on the ottoman, as he finished reading Doyle's *Hounds of the Baskervilles* for a third time. Ray Eadden had created a warm, inviting room.

Maude led her across the foyer to the living room. It was larger than the study, and like the study, it featured a matching fireplace. Large, comfortable furniture filled the room, and Kelly could imagine the large Christmas tree that would overpower the front windows in a bit over a month.

The back of the living room opened into the music room, filled by a grand piano and a harpsichord. Maude told her that her sons had taken lessons on both through high school. She told her how much she missed hearing them play. Kelly gave her a quick hug as sad emotions came to the surface, and they left the living room.

A walk through the foyer took them into the dining room. The bulk of the back wall of the house was an enormous picture window looking out across the backyard. The yard was immaculate, and several areas were at different heights, with short stone walls supporting the edges. Concrete walks bordered the tall hedges on all three sides. Gleaming, brightly colored Japanese fishing floats, glass balls about a foot in diameter, rested on short concrete columns in strategic locations. A rope swing hung from a huge branch of an old oak near the rear of the garage. Kelly thought it looked like a place any royalty would enjoy. It was neat and private.

The sound of ice bouncing into glasses pulled the ladies from the dining room into the kitchen. A chrome-edged breakfast table with a dark red Formica top was in the back corner of a large kitchen; the room would be the envy of many professional chefs. Plenty of counter space surrounded a huge gas range. Duel ovens and a massive refrigerator rounded out the equipment.

Marcus had found the bottle of Maker's Mark bourbon in the same cabinet Maude had always used for alcohol storage. He had poured two fingers-worth into each highball glass when the ladies entered the room.

"Perfect timing, I do believe," Aunt Maude said as she gave Marcus another quick hug.

Passing the glasses to the ladies, Marcus held his up. "Absent family."

They lightly touched glasses before draining them.

A moment passed as Maude said, "Your mama and daddy are happy that you are carrying out their wishes. I just know it. I had hoped Eleanor would have changed her mind and come up for the service."

Marcus slowly shook his head side to side. "She needs time. Elle handled so much that week of the accident, and she did it well. 'Stiff upper lip,' as the Brits would say. But she has two good reasons for not being here. First off, she has already said her goodbyes. No need to reopen a wound that is starting to heal. And second, she was five when we moved away. She may be Princeton born, but she has no special memories of the place or the people."

"And she has a full class load this semester," Kelly added, "with exams coming up soon."

Maude nodded. "I understand. But still …"

Marcus changed the subject. "Oh, by the way, we had a welcoming committee consisting of GT stop us on the way into town. He had to rush off, but said something about me not being mad at you about tomorrow. Care to fill me in on what I shouldn't be mad about?"

Aunt Maude pointed to the Maker's Mark bottle. "After you pour us another round." And with that, she pulled Kelly over to the breakfast table and took her usual place at the head.

After a quick sip of liquid courage, Maude laid her hand on Marcus's. "Honey, I know you wanted a small private service, and I talked to Preacher Dave about it. I thought it was all settled, us and about twenty of your folks' closest friends, but then you know how this town gossips. Well, your daddy was Mayor Clarkson's favorite teacher, and after he heard about the service, and talked it up with others who loved your parents, they impressed on Preacher Dave that it would need more room. So it is to be held at the high school auditorium. There are a lot of people who want to pay their respects, and after they laid out all the facts for me, I had to agree."

Marcus let out a huge sigh. "Okay. I understand." He was not happy, but he hid his frustration to avoid hurting Maude's feelings.

To lighten the mood, Kelly interjected, "And I get to meet all of your old girlfriends at the same time, right?"

Maude laughed. "There was only one, Kelly, and it was a short romance. Godfrey whisked her away right after Marcus moved to Florida."

Kelly nodded. "I heard a bit about her on the way into town."

"Oh, Sally is a good one. Cute, smart, and so full of life. I just love her," Aunt Maude said.

To change the subject, Marcus asked, "So, how many folks will be attending tomorrow?"

Maude mumbled something as she raised her glass to her lips.

"How many?" Marcus asked again.

"Probably a little over two hundred," Maude said softly.

18

DINNER WAS A WEST VIRGINIA staple: baked steak. It's a simple recipe. Seasoned, cubed steak is dredged in flour and pan fried to a golden brown. The fried steak is then placed in a dutch oven with beef stock, mushroom soup, chopped onions, spices, and a bit of milk. Baking at a high temperature lasts well over an hour, resulting in a tender piece of beef swimming in wonderful gravy. This step allows the cook ample time to prepare the rest of the meal.

On that late October evening, tossed salad, mashed potatoes, and green beans with mushrooms rounded out the meal. Kelly found the conversation about past family events the best part of the meal, as she learned more about her husband and his family through Maude's many stories. Kelly realized Maude thought of Marcus as a grandson, not merely a great-nephew. And she also discovered that Maude and Elle now comprised the extent of his living blood relatives. That thought hadn't occurred to her before.

The three also went over the schedule for the next couple of days. With the memorial service starting at eleven, they would need to be there around ten-thirty. A finger food reception was planned in the school cafeteria; Aunt Maude had paid for the catering and flatly refused Marcus's offer to cover the bill. Sunday afternoon was designated for a private gathering on a parcel of wooded land his parents owned outside of town. That was where they wanted their ashes sprinkled.

Monday afternoon they would meet with Aunt Maude's attorney to get all the land deeds and other West Virginia assets officially transferred to Marcus. There were two land parcels comprising several hundred acres of undeveloped woodland, though the Colts' Princeton home had been sold when they retired to Florida years ago. And unknown to Marcus until they read the wills several weeks ago, there were several brokerage accounts with hefty balances in both West Virginia and Florida. The Colt children were well taken care of by their parents.

While the brokerage accounts were unknowns, Marcus and Elle were already aware of the property distribution. They both thought it was perfect. When Marcus was home on his first leave in 1969 and Elle was looking forward to starting high school, his parents sat them both down and outlined their wills. Assuming the children agreed, they wanted to leave the Clearwater house and other assets in Florida to Elle since it was the home she remembered most. And Marcus would inherit the property and other assets in West Virginia. Dollar wise, the inheritances worked out about equal. The elder Colts knew that their children would work out any issues when it came to mementos, photos, and such. And that is exactly what happened.

All the talk about the service wore Marcus down. He wasn't looking forward to speaking in front of what he thought of as half the town. The stress alone was tiring, and total fatigue set in before the grandfather clock in the foyer chimed midnight.

Maude had settled them in the guest room. As they snuggled in the soft warm bed, Marcus whispered, "Tomorrow, after the service, I'll show you the best part of this house—the basement."

Kelly giggled. "Oh, dusty basements with spiders are always high on my list."

"Then you'll be disappointed. When prohibition started, Uncle Ray finished off the basement into his personal speakeasy. And he upgraded it over the years. This basement—how can I describe it, Kelly? It has knotty-pine paneling, thick wall-to-wall carpet, a built-in record player under the bar with hidden speakers around the room, and a full wet bar complete with mirrors behind it. There's rumored to be a secret entrance, but GT and I could never find it."

"Cool. That should be interesting! Got any other surprises about this place?"

Marcus was quiet for a moment. "Only other one I know about is that one day this place will be ours. On my last visit, I had tried to get Maude to sell and move to a smaller place, but she refused. With her getting up in age and this place so big, I figured it was a wise choice. She refused to consider it and said she was taking care of it for me. When I told her I didn't understand, she told me her will leaves it to me."

Kelly was at a loss for words. So much had happened over the last couple of months with the passing of her in-laws, and now this announcement about the "mansion." She finally whispered, "I'm praying that document will not be read for many years. Maude is such a sweetie, and I can't wait to bring our children here to wallow in her love."

"Sounds like a great plan, Princess."

A couple more moments of silence passed before Kelly said, "Ya know, we never talk about life after the Navy. Our jobs are so encompassing right now, it seems that retirement is so very far off. Yet it isn't."

Marcus let out a sigh. "True. I'll be up for retirement in less than thirteen years. Of course, they could let me stick around for thirty years assuming I get promoted to captain in about ten. But honestly, I haven't thought much about life after I hang up the uniform. Guess in the back of my mind I thought something would pop up when time gets closer."

"Something about a memorial service brings this stuff into focus, Marcus. But right now, just hold me close and let tomorrow happen."

19

MARCUS WAS GLAD TO SEE the house. He needed some quiet time to decompress; it had been a stressful, busy day. His dress uniform had attracted everyone's attention, and even GT was impressed by his buddy's fruit salad with the Navy Cross on top of several rows of ribbons, and several clusters on the Purple Heart ribbon. GT wasted no time in letting others know his buddy had "been there and done that" in the service of his country. For West Virginians, military service was high in importance.

The service went well. The three-hundred-plus attendees—Maude's count was a bit understated—expressed their condolences and love for the Colt family. Marcus, Kelly, Maude, and Preacher Dave formed a receiving line to greet each one as they entered the auditorium. Preacher Dave said all the right words of comfort to start the service. Marcus was able to get through his eulogy with his voice breaking only once. The mayor said a few words and read a statement from the governor, and the senior senator and local congressman both shared a few words of remembrance about the Colts. There were few dry eyes.

Marcus was glad GT was there. Except for during the eulogy, GT was by Marcus's side every moment. He whispered to Marcus that he was doing "crowd control," preventing any one person from monopolizing his buddy's time. The reception would have gone on all afternoon and into the evening if GT hadn't been there.

GT's wife, Sally, had latched onto Kelly like a long-lost sister while performing the same people control task for her. She also made sure Kelly knew the names and stories of everyone as they approached. Kelly immediately recognized what Marcus saw in Sally years ago; in a few moments she saw beauty, kindness, warmth, and a great sense of humor wrapped up in an extremely sexy package.

Kelly tried not to let the huge kiss Sally had planted on Marcus color her judgment about the ex-girlfriend. It gave her something to tease Marcus about later when the receiving line thinned out; she whispered in his ear to ask if he had gotten his tonsils back from Sally. That tease added some much needed levity to the gathering.

The crowd finally started leaving a little before three o'clock. Before the bulk left, Aunt Maude made sure that the folks she knew needed a helping hand got an ample share of the leftovers from the reception. Marcus and Kelly also spent some private time with the politicians before their handlers hurried them out the door. Marcus was happy to introduce Kelly to his friends, and she quickly became accepted by all.

Preacher Dave had enlisted the ladies of the church to help with cleanup. He quietly pushed Marcus, Kelly, and Maude out the door and sent them home. Maude started to argue, but Kelly pulled her into a hug and told her it was time to leave.

Now at the house, Marcus changed into his standard oxford button-down shirt, a dark maroon one, plus blue jeans and highly polished work boots. Since he was technically "home," he rolled up the sleeves, exposing his forearms, and left the jacket, shoulder holster, and Colt 1911 pistol in their bedroom. Kelly came into their bedroom as he started to leave.

"I convinced Maude to take a short nap. She is exhausted, Marcus. The emotions of the day wore her down. So try to be quiet as you thunder down the stairs," Kelly said with a chuckle. "I'll be down shortly. Time to get comfortable. Make sure you hold on to your tonsils, Sailor; Sally's here with GT." Kelly winked and kissed him seductively.

Sally and GT were in the kitchen, the normal gathering place for family. The living room is reserved for non-family guests. GT had poured the drinks and Sally had put some of the leftover finger food on a platter and moved it to the breakfast table. Marcus took the offered glass of bourbon and drained it.

GT replenished it. "You did good today, Marcus. You said all the right things, and in that uniform with as many metals as General Patton, you were a super imposing figure. Overall, it was a nice service, buddy." He touched glasses and both men took a quick sip.

Sally nodded in agreement and sipped at her glass.

Marcus said, "Thanks. It was nice, and again, please pass my thanks on to the mayor. But ya know, I think, well at least emotionally for me, tomorrow will be more difficult. It will be the closing chapter of my parents' life, so to speak. You two will be there, right?"

"Of course, Marcus." Sally laid a comforting hand on Marcus's arm.

"Sorry, with all the stuff going on, I forgot to ask where your kids are hiding?"

GT laughed. "They don't hide well, but Sally's mom knew what we had to do today and tomorrow, so she drove up from Wytheville on Friday and took them home for the weekend. She'll bring them back on Monday afternoon."

Sally said, "You and Kelly should come over Monday evening for dinner."

Kelly walked in right then wearing her comfy college sweatshirt—Georgetown University's logo had replaced Old Dominion's when she got her doctorate there—white sneakers, and slim jeans. Her hair was gathered into a ponytail. She looked exactly as she did the first day Marcus met her in 1971. She smiled at her new friends. "You betcha! Can we bring anything?"

Sally jumped up and gave her a quick hug. "Just bring your beautiful self, Kelly, and Aunt Maude. Guess we need to include old what's-his-name over there, too." Sally said as she tossed a thumb toward Marcus. "Oh, I really like your outfit!"

Kelly smiled at the compliment and nodded bashfully.

GT pointed toward the counter. "Your glass is there, Kelly." He turned toward Marcus and asked, "Okay, Marcus Aurelius, time to level with me. Based on your medals, you do a lot more than count battleship-gray paperclips. What is your real job?"

"Hey, I forgot to show Kelly the basement. What say we move this party down there like old times?" Marcus stood and pointed toward the foyer.

With his face twisted up in frustration, GT said, "Marcus, we can move, but you still need to answer my question."

A staircase under the main stairs in the foyer accessed the basement. Kelly was anticipating a unique place, but her expectations were blown away. In the soft lights, the place was impressive. The bar was in the corner of the longest wall, with leather-covered stools positioned in front. Stemware hung in wood racks above the bar, and liquor bottles lined the shelf in front of the mirrored wall. The warm gold of the polished knotty-pine paneling was gorgeous.

Marcus turned on additional lights, and the bar was accented in the soft glow. An alcove across from the bar held a large console television, and two thick-cushioned sofas faced it. All around the rest of the room, large easy chairs were grouped in small, intimate clusters. Coffee and end tables were within easy reach of every chair. Walls were covered with a combination of paintings depicting West Virginia scenes and a smattering of family photos from over the years. Twenty people could feel comfortable in the basement and still have some privacy.

He dropped down behind the bar, and quickly the smooth voice of a young Frank Sinatra filled the room from the hidden speakers. Marcus turned down the volume to allow a friendly discussion, and he led the group to a cluster of chairs.

"So, Kelly, what do ya think?"

"Marcus, I love it! I want to stay here forever!"

A new voice filled the room. Maude said, "That's the plan, honey. Ray wanted people to feel so happy here they never wanted to leave."

Kelly put on a fake frown. "Thought you'd agreed to take a nap, Aunt Maude."

With a slight shrug, Maude replied, "I did get a quick one. Hell, I can sleep when I'm dead. I don't want to miss a moment with you and Marcus here. So, what are we discussing?"

GT pointed at his buddy. "Marcus was about to tell us what he does for the Navy. And how he earned all those medals."

"My job is simple," Marcus said. "I head the Internal Affairs Division of the Naval Investigative Service. We keep the NIS agents honest, and help out on cases where others have hit a dead end. Most of it is boring stuff. For example, two members of my team are looking into a strange accounting issue at a base in Illinois this week. Last week we had to make sure an agent had a justified shooting of a sailor who opened fire in a bar. It's like most of the stuff you do every day, GT."

GT gave a knowing smile. "Perhaps. But Marcus I don't get the nation's second highest military award for catching speeders. Or a Purple Heart for getting a paper cut."

Marcus smiled. "And you remember from your time in the Army that some things are classified and need to stay that way."

"Yea, I remember. But obviously our senator, that old guy you met earlier, and a few others in D.C. aren't up to speed with need-to-know regs. He told me the Secretary of State was always talking about how you saved his butt a couple of years ago in 'Nam. And a senior congressman is still going on about your work in Italy against a KGB agent." GT lowered his voice. "And because of my Army training, I don't run off at the mouth about my older brother's exploits, but that doesn't stop me from being proud of him. Guess you and James Bond are buddies."

Kelly watched Marcus for any signs of anger. So far he was calm—maybe because he was with family.

"True, from time to time my unit is given some unique assignments. I've been on several. But I cannot go into any detail, so please don't ask. Okay to leave it at that?"

The silence was deafening, as they say, until GT finally said, "Okay. But Marcus, since you're a super-secret special agent, I need your help. Would you be willing to swing by the office on Monday morning and look over a couple of case files? I could use some fresh eyes. Especially eyes that have the experience yours have."

Marcus shrugged. "Sure. What are the cases about?"

Aunt Maude jumped in. "It's about those sick murders, right?"

GT said, "Yes, ma'am, it is. Marcus, we have three bodies in the morgue that look like they were savaged by a bear. We don't have any clues, and not much of anything looks normal. I could use your help."

Marcus glanced at Kelly and saw her head give a quick affirmative shake.

"What do you mean by that 'not much of anything looks normal' comment? What do you have that isn't normal, GT?"

"You need to see for yourself, Marcus," GT said. "I want you to see it all cold, with no preconceived notions." He turned toward Kelly. "And as you're a doctor, I would appreciate your input also, Kelly."

Kelly shrugged. "I'm a psychologist, not a medical doctor. But I'm willing to help."

"Thanks. Since this might be the work of a crazy man, your input may be more helpful than you think," GT said solemnly.

Maude, deciding a change in conversation was needed, said, "That was a really nice service today. I think Preacher Dave hit all the right comments, don't you?"

20

IT WAS AMAZING: THE WEEKEND had been calm, at least, crime wise. No more bodies had been reported, no robberies, and no assaults. There were a couple of DUI arrests from their check point roadblock near the Be Happy Bar and Grill, but no accidents. An arrest was made Sunday night in a domestic violence event. With no new big cases dumped on their desks, it was the kind of day any officer of the law enjoyed. At least so far.

GT was happy for his buddy Marcus. The small ceremony on the Colts' property had gone smoothly. Both Marcus and Kelly said a few words before they scattered his parents' ashes. Everyone shared a remembrance or two, and by the time it was over, the mood had changed from somber to joyful as each one realized how much the Colts had positively influenced their lives. Two wonderful people were gone, but their legacies would last.

He knew he needed the help, but he hated to dump on Marcus. GT rationalized away his reluctance, thinking that perhaps it would distract Marcus from his loss, or at least reduce the pain. Besides, Marcus was the smartest man he knew—well, smartest in terms of crime investigation and getting into the minds of the bad guys. His investigative experience might see something GT was missing. Being a Navy man, he would appreciate GT's position of taking any port in a storm. Marcus was that nearest port.

The thin black hands of the office wall clock had marked nine a.m. when the Colts pulled the entrance door closed. GT chuckled at the thought that some married couples really do start to look alike. Or in their case, dress alike. Marcus and Kelly both had on dark jeans, yellow oxford shirts, and medium gray sports jackets. They even pulled off their sunglasses with their left hands simultaneously. *Wonder if they practiced that*, GT thought as he noticed the slight bulge under Marcus's left arm: Marcus was armed.

GT glanced around the office as he walked toward the door with his hand extended. He raised his voice and announced, "Listen up, people. Most of you know them, but for the others, the fashion twins who just arrived are Navy Commander Marcus Colt of the Naval Investigative Service, and his spouse, Dr. Kelly Colt, a shrink at Walter Reed Hospital. They are here to hopefully give us some insight on our Crazed Bear cases. Any requests they have should be handled as if they came from me."

"Fashion twins?" Kelly asked with her smile kicked up to the left.

GT shook hands with both. "Y'all do look good, that's for sure."

"Since you're in uniform, I figured Marcus and I should follow your lead and have one of our own. I think we look cute," Kelly said with a smile that would stop male hearts.

Marcus rolled his eyes and snickered. "Yea, cute is high on my to-do list. Got any bourbon handy?"

"No, but I have semi-decent coffee, an assortment of fresh donuts, and a short stack of files in the conference room. Right this way, consultants."

GT was right. Marcus found the coffee barely semi-decent, but it was better than no coffee. The conference room also held two other members of the Mercer County Sheriff's Department: Detective Allen Chambers and Sergeant George Walker. They'd met the Colts at the memorial service on Saturday.

"So how do you want to proceed, Marcus?"

Marcus pointed to the stack. "Before any of you offer any comments, let us read through the files on our own. Go do whatever it is you do on Mondays. We'll call ya. Oh, before you vanish, we do need a stack of index cards."

"As you wish, Marcus Aurelius—we'll be doing normal cop work until you call us. I'll get your cards."

Allen chuckled. "For us, that means getting more coffee. Come on, George."

When the conference door clicked shut for the last time, Kelly asked, "Where do you want me to start, *boss*?" Her smile kicked up to the left.

"Autopsy reports. I'll glance through them quickly, then pass them to you. You'll probably find more there than I would. Doc always does. Do you remember Doc and me talking about the index card method?"

Kelly nodded. "But that's been a couple of years, so a refresher course would be helpful, boss."

Marcus put on his instructor hat. "Rather than keep looking at a single sheet of paper with a list for each case, I use the index cards. We write each item of evidence on a separate card in bold letters."

"Okay."

"Next step is creating a row of cards for each case, which are then sorted alphabetically. It probably sounds strange, but looking at things from a different angle or direction is the easiest way to see something that is there but often hidden in the usual format. Then a second set of cards for each case is created that lists the cause of death on one card, location of the body on a second one, et cetera. These are also placed on the table in rows separated by category."

Marcus paused for a quick sip of coffee. "I then read down each row one time, and then across the different cases. I know it sounds weird, but it works. It helps find connections."

Kelly took a small stack of index cards. "We have four hours before meeting the attorney, and I'll need lunch, so we need to get busy, Sailor. Any other pointers?"

"Create a card for each interesting thing you find in the reports. I'll do the same with the base reports."

An hour-plus later, the dregs in Marcus's coffee cup were stone cold, and the large conference table was filled with index cards.

"We need a cork board."

"Probably two or three, Marcus. We have this table covered. Do you see any links?"

His sigh was frustration, weariness, or both. "Nothing yet, but—and this is just between us—these files are not as detailed as what we do at NIS. I suspect that for the bulk of the cases they see here, this level is more than enough. Any concerns about the autopsy reports?"

"I thought it strange there were no toxicology reports. Perhaps with the COD being rather obvious, they didn't think they were needed. It would've been nice to know about any drugs in their systems."

"Agreed. I suppose at first glance the cause of death was obvious: missing innards by crazed bear. Anything else?"

"Doctor Wallace is sure most of the bear evidence was planted. Guess that means there is not a crazy bear running around the woods."

Marcus shrugged. "Maybe. This is West Virginia and you can never assume things about bears. Could be a crazy one out there. And there could be more bodies in the woods. Time to interview the lead officers and see what they have to add to the mix."

Interviewing each of the three lead officers used up another hour. There were a few points mentioned that hadn't been in the reports. More cards were written and added to the rows.

Then Marcus brought them together in the conference room and instructed the three officers on how the card system worked and why it was a good method. After going over it twice, Marcus could see the lights of understanding click on behind their eyes. George left to get the portable corkboards, and in no time, the cards were attached in the proper order. It was easier to share them that way. They bounced the data between themselves for some time.

As the discussion started to wane, Marcus asked, "Gentlemen, you can see the number of cards we added to the boards based on your comments. Not finding fault, but all that information should have been in the written report. And I suspect you will add it now, right?"

"Sorry, Marcus. Like I tried to tell you the other day, we are somewhat overwhelmed here, and as you can see, there isn't much normal about these cases."

"No apologies needed, GT. Your next step will be to talk with your M.E. and Doctor Wallace again as we did with you. Perhaps they'll say something they didn't write down. Then, when you have all that added to the card list, go back over the rows. Usually for us at NIS, something will click and pieces will start to fall into place. Oh, yea, Kelly was wondering about the lack of any toxicology studies; your M.E. needs to explain that. Knowledge about any drugs in their systems could generate a lead."

"Okay, Marcus, we can do that, unless you want to volunteer. The big question for now is do you see any solution to this mess?"

Marcus took a deep breath and slowly exhaled. He glanced at the boards of cards and saw what was not there. "No answers, buddy, but several big questions. Two bodies were left in strange positions and locations. That works against the perpetrator faking a bear kill. Or it being a real bear kill. Why there? Was there anything special about the locations?

And why the evisceration? Were they hiding something, or looking for something? Organ thieves? Cannibals? Swallowed diamonds or drugs?"

Allen said, "We have been asking those same questions, Marcus. No ideas yet."

Marcus pointed to the corkboards. "Trust me, going over the known factors will help uncover the unknowns. And y'all need to dig deeper. There has to be more information out there. Has Cal Thompkins been looked at as the killer? He could have killed the other two to reduce the chance you would nail him for killing his wife. Did Joe Decker have any enemies, either local or in his Seabee unit? Have any of the local hunters mentioned strange-acting bears? I can keep coming up with questions that aren't in these files."

GT shook his head. Allen and George looked down at their feet; they knew they had missed too many things, and a newcomer had laid that fact wide open.

"And, where the hell is the file on the missing children? Doris Thompkins vanished with her two children and a Buick, right? Where are they? Where's the car? Their case is part of this."

GT said, "Before the mother's body was found, we considered it simply a missing persons case, and with the father's comments about his wife wanting to go to Michigan, therefore crossing state lines, we passed it to the FBI."

"Did you follow up with them?"

"No, we've been covered up with the mutilated bodies. I let them know about the dead mother, but otherwise I dropped the ball on follow-up, Marcus."

"It's damn hard to keep all the balls in the air, buddy, once you get past two. But since the mom is dead, face it—there are three possible outcomes for the children. They are dead, they are being held captive, or they may be subjects of human trafficking. Well, a few more options exist: they are alive somewhere in the woods for the last few weeks on their own. Considering their ages, five and three, the alive in the woods option seems impossible. What do you plan on doing to find them, Sheriff?"

Marcus using his title startled GT, but he understood what Marcus was doing: he was reminding him that he had a responsibility to find the children. And GT realized that his buddy had exposed his failure.

Before he could respond, Marcus continued, "Since mom was still in the area, probably the easiest thing to find will be the car. Have you put out a BOLO for the Buick?"

"We did, but I'll upgrade it to a higher priority," Allen said.

"And I'll call some of the local hunters and ask about bear sightings," George offered.

He glanced at Kelly and she touched her watch. Time for lunch. Marcus stood. "Gents, I have a lady to feed and a lawyer to meet, so time for us to depart."

GT said, "Least I can do is pick up the lunch tab. Let's head over to Pansy's Café right down the street."

21

THE PLACE WAS NEW TO Marcus. Pansy, a transplant from New Jersey, had opened her café a few years after the Colt family moved to Florida. Taking a winter vacation from her restaurant job up north, she had vacationed for a week of snow skiing at Snowshoe one cold January week years ago and fell in love with the area. Later that summer, she quit her job, packed up her belongings, and found a home in Princeton. The café opened the month after she arrived, and shortly thereafter it was constantly packed. Pansy was a dang good cook and an even better restaurant manager.

GT waved as he and the Colts entered. It was standing room only at a few minutes past noon. All the tables and counter stools were in use. A tall woman behind the counter gave off an air of leadership and complete control. Marcus assumed she was Pansy and guessed her age in the mid-fifties, as gray strands were starting to outnumber the auburn brown ones. Her laugh lines were permanent, and her smile was warm. She was a touch overweight, but her once-attractive figure was still visible.

Pansy came out from behind the counter and gave GT a hug.

"It's about time you showed up again for lunch, Sheriff. I was beginning to think you found another place to eat." Pansy welcomed them with a wink. "And you must be Kelly and Marcus. The whole town is talking about you two. Sorry about your folks, Marcus. I heard they were good people."

"Thank you," Marcus said as Pansy wrapped him and Kelly in a hug.

During the hug, Marcus did a quick survey of the café: it fit the mold of the standard run-down eatery. Fading medium green wainscoting covered the walls up to the chair rail, then dingy white plaster ran to the ceiling. This part of the walls was covered with various pieces of local memorabilia, fading photographs, framed Princeton High football jerseys, and the occasional commemorative plate. The carpeting should have been replaced several years ago, and the tables showed at least two decades of hard use.

"Right this way, GT. I have a special table ready for you."

As they strolled through the crowded room, Marcus thought, *this place could use some serious remodeling. Hopefully the food does not match the decor.*

Pansy led them through the swinging metal doors that led to the kitchen. She patted Marcus on the arm and said, "I finally have enough money saved to do a full remodeling of this place in March. That's our slowest time of the year between ski season and camping. I'm thinking of following a French bistro theme. Since you and Kelly are big city folks, I'd love to hear your thoughts."

Marcus was taken aback. *Sounds like she's reading my mind!* "Certainly."

"I think you'll find the food is much better than the décor."

She is *reading my mind!* Marcus decided to focus on iced tea as a safe mental subject.

Several cooks were busy at the stoves, and waitresses were picking up plates piled high to carry to the tables. At the rear of the kitchen was an alcove across from a closed door that displayed "office" in hand-painted lettering. A table capable of seating a dozen or so took up most of the alcove. The alcove was actually the crews' breakroom.

"Here ya go, GT. Private and close to the iced tea refills. Best of both worlds!"

"Thanks, Pansy."

"You want your Monday regular?"

GT nodded. "Yes, ma'am, please."

"And what can I get for you two," Pansy asked as she looked at Kelly and Marcus.

Kelly asked, "What's your regular, GT?"

Pansy answered for him, "Meat loaf, mashed potatoes, gravy, and the vegetable of the day, with lots of sweet tea, of course."

Kelly said, "Sounds good for all of us." Marcus nodded in agreement.

Being in the kitchen, the service was fast. Pansy left them alone as they dug into the food. Marcus was pleased: the meal was great. He was also glad to see the veggie du jour was pan-roasted corn, complete with diced roasted red peppers. It had just the right amount of spice, mostly smoked paprika and a touch of cayenne.

Laying his silverware on his nearly empty plate, GT said, "I appreciate all the input this morning. It was a big help even though it was embarrassing for you to point out some of our flaws."

"No investigation is perfect, GT. You must correct the oversights, learn from them, and move on. The Lord knows I've had to do that way too many times."

"I can't stop thinking about those two children. So sad," Kelly said. "I pray you find them … alive."

GT told Kelly what he knew about the missing children. As GT talked, Kelly noticed Marcus pushing a few stray pieces of corn around his plate, lost in contemplation.

When he stopped sliding his food around, Kelly asked, "Okay, Marcus, what's cooking inside that brain of yours?"

"People. GT, it's obvious that you need more people. You need to start a search for that Buick and those children. We can only assume mama was still in the area all this time, and the children might be too. Only way to do it right is with a lot of boots on the ground. Maybe you could call in the National Guard? Or at least ask the Guard to use choppers and fly over the area. I'll bet that car contains evidence you need. Could you call in all the local hunters to help?"

GT nodded. "What I desperately need is Marcus Colt running this case. I'm a simple sheriff and these murders are out of my league."

"Buddy, I'd like to help, but Kelly and I have a meeting with a lawyer in fifteen minutes, and we've got to get back to our jobs in D.C. tomorrow."

Detective Allen Chambers stuck his head around the corner and announced, "Uh, GT, we got another one."

The conversation stopped as the three looked at the new arrival.

Allen continued, "Ottis Mayhew just called. He found a body in his orchard that looks like a bear attack. M.E. is on his way. Want to go with me?"

"Yea, I'd better. Care to tag along, Marcus?"

"Sorry, GT. Time to meet with the lawyer. We'll still see you tonight, right?"

"Hope so."

22

THE HOSPITALITY THAT SALLY OFFERED Aunt Maude and the Colts would have pleased any admiral's wife. The house was immaculate, the children were mostly well behaved, and wonderful aromas drifted from the kitchen as they enjoyed the drinks and hors d'oeuvres that were properly prepared. The only thing not in line was the simple fact that her husband was missing in action. It was a common occurrence for the Sheriff.

GT had called before the guests arrived to explain why he was running late, which put Sally more at ease, since she didn't have to worry about her husband's safety.

"Sally, Kate and Godfrey the Fourth are adorable. Guess you're looking forward to Halloween. What are their costumes?" Kelly asked.

With a deep chuckle, Sally replied, "Both are going dressed as sheriff deputies. Can't imagine why."

Marcus smiled. "I bet by the time he's in his teens, the nickname of *G4* will be getting old."

With the strut of a commanding officer approaching his staff, GT walked in. "That's a fact. I hope he has a buddy as good as you to bounce his frustration off."

Sally said, "Now that the king has returned to his castle, we can eat."

The meal was a combination of great food and even better memories. Everyone dug into the fried chicken, coleslaw, and baked sweet potatoes. For Kelly, the opportunity to learn more about Marcus's early history and friends was priceless. Aunt Maude was in seventh heaven as she listened to the chatter and added embarrassing details the three friends had skipped over as they relived so many shared memories.

"Marcus, I need to talk with you about this afternoon. Let's go to the den."

Kelly said, "GT, you're just trying to get out of doing cleanup. Help carry the dishes to the kitchen, and we can all quickly join you." She picked up a couple of plates and turned toward the kitchen. "Hurry up, Sheriff."

"Close your mouth, GT, you're catching flies. You need to understand that Kelly is used to taking charge around the house," Marcus said.

GT shrugged. "Okay, but today's find is not pretty."

"Neither were the files this morning. Grab a dish or two, buddy."

Kelly was right—again—and they all settled into the comfortable chairs in the den in short order.

"So, what happened this afternoon?" Marcus asked.

"Another one of those strange deaths. This one looks more like a real bear attack. I have Doctor Simpson Wallace coming in tomorrow afternoon to verify. Ever meet him?"

Marcus shook his head. GT provided an overview of Wallace's knowledge base. "The M.E. will have the autopsy underway by then, but he'll avoid touching the empty abdominal area until Simpson gets a look. Can you stop by and talk with both doctors?"

"Sorry, Godfrey, my man, but Kelly and I do have to get back to D.C. Something about having jobs, bills to pay, et cetera. We should be on the road by late morning. You know I'd like to help, but the Navy keeps a tight leash. Besides, you got this, Sheriff, without outsiders imposing."

"I understand. And I appreciate your willingness to help if the situation was different. I keep hoping it will be. But man, I am not ashamed to admit I feel like a lost ball in tall weeds. I need your experience, Marcus Aurelius."

Marcus shrugged, allowing his reluctance to show.

Kelly said, "I think the hardest part of this case, after finding the missing children, is figuring out how the woman's body got inside a locked building. Nothing about her case makes sense."

Aunt Maude clicked her tongue. "I overheard a couple in the grocery store saying it was the Mothman. They said her husband had seen him fly over the day the wife went missing, and that was an omen of doom. The Mothman probably flew her up to the roof to get into the skylight."

"Who is the Mothman?" Kelly asked.

"Another one of those wild fictitious things people love to use when something is hard to explain logically," GT said as his eyes rolled.

Marcus said, "When the Silver Bridge collapsed, didn't some people blame the Mothman for that?"

"A few did, but most folks thought the Mothman was a warning that something bad was about to happen," Sally said. "And most still do."

"So you're saying that's why he flew over the Thompkins house the day Doris vanished," Marcus said with more than a touch of sarcasm. "It was to announce her impending doom?"

"Why not, Marcus?" Sally asked. "It fits the mold, and I think it has to be considered."

"Okay, but what exactly is a Mothman?" Kelly pleaded with a raised voice and both hands waving over her head.

"Kelly, picture a leather-winged, solid black, man-like creature with large glowing red eyes standing between six and ten feet tall. Reports vary on his height. The color and glowing eyes are pretty constant. According to some—the ones that admit they have seen him—he can fly as fast as a car can drive on our curvy roads. And there's one report that he killed a big dog," GT explained.

"You don't actually believe in that stuff, do you?" Kelly asked.

Sally quickly said, "Kelly, there are a lot of unexplained things going on here in West Virginia. Problem is most don't get national attention. I bet no one outside of the state has heard of the Grafton Monster. Heck, few people in the state have heard about him. We are so rural that none of the big news networks come here, and the local reporters who try to report it don't get any respect from them either. We get laughed at as being gullible hicks."

"And that's why our Bigfoot sightings have been overlooked. They've been seen for decades, hell, centuries—the old folks called them the 'Old Men of the Mountain.' And don't get me started on the Flatwoods Monster," Aunt Maude said.

Kelly shook her head. "What's with all these monsters?" Disbelief covered her face.

"*Flatwoods* Monster," GT said with frustration. "It's a creature that came here from outer space. Or so the speculation goes. Sometime in the early fifties, there was a fiery ball that crashed near the town of Flatwoods.

The Army quickly took control of the area and said it was nothing. But they were slow getting here by a day and several local folks reported seeing a strange beast, about ten feet tall with green armor and glowing eyes, hovering above a crater where whatever-it-was crashed. Naturally, the Army said they were all crazy. The Grafton Monster is even stranger, but can we please return to things that really could happen?"

"Hell, it could be the Jersey Devil, or one of its offspring, that come down for a mountain vacation," Marcus joked.

Kelly rolled her eyes as she shook her head. "Another fantasy beast, Sailor? Give me a break!"

"Seriously, Princess, the Jersey Devil has been reported for a couple hundred years. Like the Mothman, the Devil has bat-like wings, it's large, and has glowing red eyes. I kid you not. Could be they are from the same family."

She deeply exhaled. "If you guys keep talking about all this weird stuff, I will need another taste of this wonderful bourbon. Next thing, y'all will be swapping ghost stories."

Marcus refilled the glasses and smiled. "Well, darling, now that you bring it up. Let me tell you what happened to me a couple of months before we met. Remember I told you about being at NTC Bainbridge for training? Well, while there …"

23

BAINBRIDGE NAVAL TRAINING CENTER, LOCATED north of Baltimore, was built in 1942 as an additional boot camp to handle the basic training of many more sailors to fight World War II. In these boot camps, civilians would learn the Navy way, and eleven weeks later emerge ready for the fleet. By then they knew fore from aft and which end of the mop to use when swabbing decks. The base was named after Commodore William Bainbridge, who commanded the frigate *Constitution* when it defeated the British HMS *Java* during the War of 1812.

Since that conflict, the base has handled non-recruit training in several different schools, including radioman, yeoman, and nuclear power. In 1971, barracks and school buildings had seen better days, and a couple of them were thought to be haunted. But they served their purpose and produced the trained personnel the Navy needed.

A case in Norfolk had required Marcus to go undercover there as an enlisted man. He needed specific training to properly fit in, so the CNO had arranged for him to attend the school to gain the knowledge he needed to pass himself off as a yeoman. So there he was in Bainbridge acting like a junior enlisted man, doing all the things required to fit into that mold. Marcus was accustomed to going undercover to work a case, and relished the challenges that came with it, but there were some things he didn't like.

That night's fire watch was one. Every sailor attending yeoman classes had to pull sentry duty to watch for fires at the school building during non-class times. As the class sizes varied, so did the number of watches each student was assigned; Marcus had noticed he was down for three watches. The buildings were all thirty-year-old wooden structures that had dried out with age and were ripe for destruction by fire. Ergo, there was always someone inside as the Fire Watch to sound the alarm. Marcus had the 2000–2400 watch one night.

"Seaman Williams, ready to take over," Marcus yelled, using his undercover name as he banged on the front door of the Yeoman "A" School building. His watch showed the time of 1940 hours. Technically, he was five minutes early. Standard procedure was to report fifteen minutes before the official start time so instructions and equipment could be transferred from the person being relieved.

The rattling of chains preceded the door being pulled open. A sailor in dress blues with a wild look in his eyes stepped aside. "It's about damn time you got here, Mark."

"Hell, Joe, I'm freaking early, man. What's your problem?"

Joe glanced over his shoulder, looking deep into the darkened hallway behind him. He extended the flashlight to Mark. "You know the drill. Walk the halls and check the restrooms, call in to base security that all is well, and do it again every half hour. Right?"

Marcus looked at his classmate and saw a young man who was totally distressed. "You okay, buddy? You don't look well," Marcus said. "Get out of here and get some sleep."

"I'm damn glad to get out of here. See ya in the morning, I hope."

After Joe had bolted out the door, Marcus returned the chain to the handles, securing the double doors, and clicked the lock shut. He signed the log accepting responsibility for the watch and checked the time: fifteen minutes before his first patrol.

The "A" School building was identical to the other school buildings on the base. It was a two-story structure shaped like a squat "T," with classrooms on each side of the center hallways across the top of the "T." The stubby vertical part of the "T" was a hallway leading to another exit. Stairwells were on each of the two ends of the building and at the center intersection of the hallways. Heads, the name the Navy called toilet facilities, were at each end of the halls. The sentry desk was at the intersection right beside the main front doors, giving sentries views of the three first floor hallways and the main staircase.

Security was paramount at all military bases, including schools. The instructors locked all classroom doors at the end of the day. The entry/exit double doors were locked that night, and each one featured a chain and padlock that secured the push latch bars. Windows were needlessly latched; they had not been opened in years, and multiple coats of paint had successfully sealed them tight. No one could get in or out without the sentry's knowledge.

During off hours, the bright hall lights were replaced with small nightlights that gave off enough light to prevent a trip and fall, but not enough to see well. Deep shadows filled the halls. Hence the need for the sentry to carry a powerful flashlight.

Fifteen minutes passed quickly, and Marcus started his first patrol. He walked the hall to the left, checked that each classroom door was indeed locked, and verified no one was hiding in the restrooms or broom closets. He climbed the stairs at the end to the second floor and did the same ritual. Coming down the stairs at the opposite end of the building, he verified all those classrooms were secure. Then he checked the double door at the squat end of the "T" to see that all chains and locks were in place. All was secure.

He called in to base security and reported that all was well, then settled down behind the desk and checked the drawers. Someone had stashed a two-month-old copy of *Playboy* and a two-week-old copy of the *Washington Post* in the bottom drawer. It was a good way to waste time until the next patrol.

The next few fire patrols went as the first. All the doors were locked and no one was found hiding. He checked the clock and was pleased to see he only had a little over ninety more minutes on duty. With class starting at 0800 hours, his amount of rack time was going to be shorted. Falling asleep in class was never a good thing.

Marcus had finished the 2200-hour patrol. He had called the base security office and settled down to read the editorials in the *Post* when a sound from upstairs stopped him cold.

A door closed. Footsteps walked rapidly down the hall, paused, then continued onward. Another door opened and slammed shut.

With flashlight in hand, Marcus bolted up the center stairs and checked all the doors on the second floor. Every door was locked. He shined the light through the window in each classroom door and nothing was amiss. Restrooms were clear. Wondering if someone, specifically one of the instructors, was playing a joke or testing the sentry, Marcus stood at the end of the hall. He clicked off the flashlight and let his eyes become accustomed to the near-dark environment. He watched and listened.

Nothing. No sounds were heard and nothing moved. It was as it had been most of the night. Marcus went down the staircase at the end and quietly walked back to the sentry desk. He had just lowered into the chair when again a door slammed. This time it was on the opposite end of the building. Two sets of footsteps, one on each end of the building, seemed to come together at the center staircase.

On earlier patrols, Marcus had noted that the center staircase had three steps that creaked when he stepped on them. The same steps creaked now as Marcus stood behind the sentry desk. While the light was dim, he was sure no one was on the staircase. He clicked on the flashlight and pointed the beam of light up the stairs. Nothing.

As he looked at the empty staircase, more footsteps came from the first floor hall to his left. He spun the light into that hall and verified it was empty as a door slammed somewhere down the opposite hall.

The rest of the watch followed the same ritual, with lots of door slamming and footsteps upstairs. As the crown on all the spectral festivities, right as he hung up from his latest call to base security, the large radiator right behind the desk let out a loud bang-bang-bang. In a normal world, one would realize an air bubble had gotten trapped in the line, but this night was far from normal. Marcus took it as a "get out now" message.

He was glad no one was around to see him leap out of the chair when the radiator started. It took a while for his heart rate to come down. It was his first time being completely scared as an adult. And the worst part was, he had no idea what was scaring him.

Marcus could not remember who said it, but the phrase "discretion is the better part of valor" came to mind. Granted, discretion at a time like this could be considered cowardice. But as he sat at the security desk staring down the empty halls, he realized he would be happy to confront any living, warm-bodied person. But none were there. He decided to skip the next couple of patrols and continued his watch from the desk.

When his relief arrived, Marcus smiled and reported all was well, "No problems." He passed the flashlight, what he now thought of as the "baton of power," to his relief and jogged to his barracks for some sleep—assuming his heart would ever slow down to a normal rate and the sounds in his mind would go silent.

Finding his buddy Chuck at breakfast, Marcus quietly mentioned the events of the previous evening. It was embarrassing, but he needed to talk to someone about it.

Chuck laughed. "Glad you got to meet the Bainbridge Ghost. I had a similar experience my first week here. Everyone knows about it, but few ever mention it."

24

"… AND THAT WAS MY first real experience with the supernatural. I kid you not—it was weird, and more than a bit unnerving," Marcus said. No one spoke for a moment or two.

Kelly shook her head and let out a huge sigh. "You should know that old buildings constantly settle, and as the temperature drops at night, boards contract, often making strange noises. I doubt it was haunted."

"Make excuses all you want, Kelly, but you weren't there. The sounds were not a building settling. It took a few hours for my goose bumps to calm down, and that's a fact!" Marcus shrugged. "I was glad my next watch was midday on a Saturday. Spooks are quiet during the daylight hours."

"Marcus, that was *not* your first experience with ghosts. Don't you remember when we rode our bikes out Route 19 to the old Ricketts house?"

Marcus nodded. "Oh, yea, what were we—eight or nine? I had forgotten about that adventure."

Maude said, "I remember your daddy grounded you for a week for riding that far out of town."

"True. That place was scary, at least for a kid. Hey, we did see something in that upper window."

"Probably just a hobo rather than a ghost." GT chuckled. "But it has gotten scarier over the years. More broken windows, bigger holes in the roof, and so on. Amazing it's still standing. We still have to run kids out of there frequently. Especially at Halloween."

Kelly laughed again and rolled her eyes. "Can we return to reality here? Enough of the fantasy and ghost stories."

"Today's fantasy can become tomorrow's facts, Kelly. Remember the mountain gorilla was a myth until a live one was discovered in 1902. And the coelacanth, the fish they found alive in 1938 off the African coast, was considered extinct for the last sixty-five million years. Who knows what myth will become reality next," Marcus said.

"Fine. Can we at least rule out pterodactyls moving the bodies?" Kelly snapped.

"Maybe not. Did you ever see that photo shot in the late 1800s showing a bunch of cowboys holding up a dead one? It took about a dozen guys to lift him," GT snickered.

Marcus quickly followed, and in short everyone was laughing. Even Kelly.

"Okay, settle down guys," Marcus said as he got serious. "Was this latest body dropped into the orchard, or were there tracks around it?"

"No tracks. No drag marks. And there were no signs of blood except a small amount of drainage under the body. It was simply lying there between the rows of apple trees. Looks like it was gently lowered, but the owner didn't hear any chopper sounds."

As his face twisted into a look of discomfort, Marcus said quietly, "So the questions we have for three of the bodies is why and how they were moved. If we can get the answer to one, the other will probably fall into place."

No one said anything as GT shrugged.

Marcus continued, "Let's not rule out the absurd. Throw some thoughts out. Why would the Mothman—if he exists—get involved with moving bodies? Or was he involved in the murders?"

Surprisingly, Aunt Maude was the first. "I don't think he would be the killer. He has always been considered a harbinger of doom or bad luck. Kinda like a black cat crossing your path. Only a few blamed him for the bridge falling."

"So you're saying he might have moved the bodies to use them as a warning?" GT asked.

It was Maude's turn to shrug. "That is more his style, at least as far as rumors go."

"We do have the one sighting at the Thompkins place on the day they went missing, but no others."

Kelly's smile kicked up to the right. "Okay, I'll play this game. Due to his 'reported size,' I assume he would be able to fly carrying a body, right?" Her sarcasm was enhanced by her fingers mimicking the quote marks.

GT gave her a thumbs-up.

"So, what other indicators exist to prove the Mothman was involved? What ya got, Sheriff, besides one sighting from a distraught family member?" Kelly asked sweetly, expecting a negative reply.

Giving a deep sigh, GT said, "Not to leave this room, okay? The first body was found the way a bear would hide it in the woods and had teeth marks on the front and back of one shoulder, where a bear would clamp on with its jaws to drag it."

He paused as if considering whether to press on. After another deep breath, he continued, "When the M.E. mentioned that the next two bodies had marks only on the front of both shoulders, Allen Chambers brought up a little-known fact. Moths have two side-by-side claws on each leg, both pointing to the rear. He put forth the suggestion that the Mothman could have picked them up, leaving the two puncture wounds on each shoulder."

If Kelly had a humorous comeback, she held it. And the other three quietly reflected on this new piece of information.

With a bit more force, GT said, "And again, that does not leave this room. This case is hard enough without the Mothman crazies getting involved."

Marcus asked, "And what about today's victim? Any marks?"

"Sorry, I won't know until the M.E. does his thing in the morning. Like I said, you're welcome to be there."

"GT, do you know the latest victim?" Marcus asked.

"No, he might be a transient. Jesus Cabilla is the name. We tracked his name from the social security number tattooed on his forearm."

"Tattooed? Like the Nazis did in the concentration camps?"

GT shrugged and said, "It is something that some migrants from south of the border do when they get a green card. They think the SSN is useful as an ID. A couple of calls to D.C. got us his name and address in

Chicago. Young guy, age is twenty-four. Dennis gave a quick estimate on TOD to within the last couple of days. He'll be more accurate tomorrow."

"Guess your first move tomorrow is to ask around to see if anyone local knows him, right?"

"If I had more people, we could do a door-to-door. I'll get his picture in this week's paper and see if anyone comes forward."

Marcus glanced up toward the ceiling. His brow wrinkled slightly and he returned his focus to GT. "Does your team know of any Hispanic families or businesses in the area? If so, that would be a good place to start."

GT said, "And that is why I need you to hang around for a while, Marcus. Even after a big dinner and a few drinks, you're thinking. Hey, take some leave and help me out."

Marcus smiled. "Again, sorry, buddy. Oh, there is a bit of good news. While at the attorney's office getting all the paperwork done—we are now officially Mercer County property owners since the folks left me those two parcels—I made a decision. I called my yeoman in D.C. and had him change my home of record from Clearwater, Florida to Princeton. So you'd better be nicer to us: next election we can vote for … or against you."

25

AS FAR AS MARCUS WAS concerned, the morning came much too quickly. It was past time to get moving according to the clock by the bed. A couple more hours of snuggle time with Kelly would have been a better start, but they had to leave for Alexandria before noon. He knew from the aromas drifting up from the kitchen that Aunt Maude was laying out her breakfast feast. If he stayed another day, he would probably not fit into his uniforms: Maude was a stickler for big breakfasts. And big lunches, and even bigger dinners.

Since the other side of the bed was empty, Marcus threw on a robe and went down to join Kelly in the kitchen. Maude's coffee was a bit stronger than he preferred, but it sure got the day started fast. And after the extra alcohol last night, he needed a jump-start.

"Mornin' honey, you ready to eat?" Maude asked in her singsong voice.

He gave her a quick hug. "Only after a couple of cups of coffee, Aunt Maude."

Kelly was already enjoying the bacon, eggs, and pancakes Maude had laid out. She giggled at Marcus. "It's about time you graced us with your presence, Sailor."

Reaching for a piece of crispy bacon, Marcus gave Kelly a quick kiss on the top of her head. She was too busy forking in syrup-laden pieces of pancakes to get a kiss on the lips. He dropped into the chair beside her. "You know I need more beauty sleep than you do, Kelly. Besides, all that talking yesterday and last night wore me out."

"Your friends certainly had some weird things to talk about, that's for sure. But how much do we, or rather you, believe, 'cause I find it all totally weird and unbelievable?"

Maude carried the coffeepot to the table and placed it within Marcus's reach. She gave out a short sigh as she looked at Kelly. "Sweetie, a bunch of weird things is always happenin' around here. Welcome to West Virginia!" She gently laughed at the local comeback joke. "One day I seen a …"

The loud ring of the phone hanging on the kitchen wall stopped that story. Maude answered and listened for a moment. "Yes, sir. He's right here." She waved at Marcus and extended the phone in his direction. She whispered, "It's an admiral."

"Colt speaking, sir," Marcus answered.

Admiral Chance's voice came across the wires sounding more friendly than usual. Being unusually informal, Chance said, "Marcus, glad I caught you before you left Princeton. You have a new TAD assignment."

He didn't want to look at Kelly, so he closed his eyes and frowned. "We're leaving in about an hour or two. What new assignment is that, sir? Where is the CNO sending me now?"

Chance couldn't hold in a laugh. "For once, Admiral Gallagher is in the clear. This request comes directly from the Secretary of Defense. You're sort of TAD to the Governor of West Virginia, who is attaching you to the Mercer County Sheriff's Office effective today."

Marcus stammered, "Excuse me, sir? The governor? The sheriff? Sort of TAD? What the hell, sir?"

Marcus could almost hear Chance's smile, probably because Marcus was surprised. It didn't happen often. He continued, "Agreed, it is unusual. But according to SecDef, here's what happened. You should remember meeting the state's senior senator and the congressman from the Third Congressional District Saturday at your parents' memorial service."

"Yes, sir. They both were there. They knew my parents and wanted to pay their respects. Nice guys. I basically just said a quick hello, chatted for a few minutes, and thanked them for coming. What do they have to do with this?"

"You know you have a strong supporter in Congress in the form of Representative A. Jackson Allen. He constantly brags to others on the hill about your splendid work on finding the missing scientist in '71. The way SecDef explained it, your local sheriff complained to his congressman Monday afternoon shortly after you told him you couldn't help with his strange murder cases. The congressman remembered Allen's comments about you and called the senior senator begging for assistance. He said it could be considered a Navy case since one of the dead men is in a Navy Reserve unit."

"Sir, we usually don't get involved with what looks to be a civil issue with reservists," Marcus injected.

Chance sternly harrumphed. "Be that as it may, Commander, the senior senator from the Great State of West Virginia saw all your decorations on Saturday, remembered Allen's comments about you, and jumped on the phone to SecDef late yesterday. I then wasted too much time last night explaining to SecDef that we were covered up with cases, et cetera, to which he ordered, and I quote, 'make it happen, John.' So Commander Colt, you are now working with your local sheriff as of high noon. Do not forsake me, Marcus." The admiral let out a rare chuckle.

"Ha! Thank you for the movie reference, Admiral. But I'm no Gary Cooper and you should know there is not much to go on … just several mutilated bodies and some weird sightings."

"Your mission is to solve those murders. Do whatever you need to do, but I hope you do it quickly."

"Aye, aye, sir. I'll give it my best."

Softening a bit, Chance said with a lighter voice, "Marcus, you have had a lot less to work with on other cases. Oh, and the request included Dr. Colt. SecDef talked with her boss at Walter Reed, and she is likewise now working with the sheriff, and she also has privileges at the Princeton Community Hospital if needed until you close this case. Since it sounds like the work of a crazy person, Kelly now has full authorization to issue psych holds at that hospital."

"Things are getting more strange, Admiral."

"Frankly, I'm not sure what can of worms you opened with the sheriff, Marcus, but let me know if you need anything. I spoke with the CNO, and he said to call David if you hit any snags and need some big league help. Just tell us what you need. See you when you get back."

The dial tone was Chance's standard goodbye. Marcus hung up the phone and stared at it for a moment. He turned to face the two women, who were both wearing faces of bewilderment.

"Okay, Marcus, what has Dad done to us now?" Kelly somehow asked through clenched jaws.

Marcus smiled. "He's innocent this time, babe. Seems the Secretary of Defense is the one who has sent us—yep, both you and me—on temporary duty with the local sheriff starting at noon. Short version: GT was not happy with my refusal to help him with these murders, so he called his congressional representative, who called the senior West Virginia senator, who then called SecDef. Chance tried to stop it, but he got a direct order, so here we are. Okay if we hang around for a bit, Aunt Maude?"

Maude's smile lit up the room. Aunt Maude was thrilled to have the two "kids" hang around for a while longer. She'd never admit it, but Marcus felt she did get lonely in the "mansion."

Speculation about the assignment went on during breakfast and for a while afterward. With breakfast over, the Colts showered and dressed to go meet with the sheriff. They were putting on jackets when the doorbell chimed regally, right before 1100 hours. Marcus got to the door first.

A stern, young-looking sheriff's deputy was standing there with garment bags draped over his arm. His nametag read *Bonner* and his light brown, closely cropped hair gave him a military look. He smiled and gave a quick salute. "Commander Colt, good to see you again, sir."

Marcus quickly remembered him controlling traffic in the school parking lot on Saturday. Glancing at his last name on the standard-issue nametag triggered a recollection of his first name. "Well, hello Josh. Since I'm in civvies, you can drop the rank and call me Marcus. How can I help you?"

"Comm … uh, Marcus, GT sent me to drive you and Mrs. Colt to the office. And I have your uniforms."

Uniforms, Marcus thought. "Come on in and give me more details. What's this about uniforms?"

Josh handed the garment bags to Marcus. "Norma Kissing, our office manager, is pretty good at guessing sizes, but she included a larger and smaller set also just in case. We'll take back the ones that don't fit and get you more that do. GT said the boots y'all wore on Sunday will work okay with the uniforms."

"Okay, Josh, go on back to work. We'll change and get to the office soon as we can."

"Sorry, Commander … damn it, sorry … Marcus, GT insists that I drive you. Shall I wait in the car?"

Marcus chuckled. "I suspect a cup of coffee would be a better choice. Right? Follow me."

After Deputy Josh was settled in the kitchen sipping coffee and chatting with Maude—of course, she knew him and his family—Marcus took the bags to the bedroom. Kelly was just leaving the room when Marcus pointed her back inside.

"Seems GT wants us in uniform."

Kelly had a confused look. "Why?"

"My guess … having a couple of new deputies around town would generate fewer questions than *civilians* riding around with the deputies. And our driver waits."

Marcus gave Kelly all the details that he knew as they changed. She absorbed it without comment.

She looked at him inquisitively. "You okay? I sort of expected you to be a bit upset by the way GT shanghaied us. I'm not happy because of two patients who need me this week, but you seem okay with it."

For a moment Marcus quietly rounded up his feelings. He finally said, "How can I find fault with a man who did exactly what I would do and actually have done? You use whatever tools you can find. Let's use all our energy solving the case so we can get home."

Josh was right: the middle size was a perfect fit for them both. Marcus looked Kelly up and down as she buttoned her shirt. "I like seeing you in uniform. Downright super sexy!"

"Hold those thoughts, Sailor. We have a new job to complete before you can unbutton anything."

As the final accessory, Marcus slid his Colt 1911 .45 pistol into the cross-draw holster GT provided. Pouches were already on the belt for his two extra magazines. The utility belt included a pouch with handcuffs and another with a flashlight.

Kelly had a questioning look. "And where is my weapon?" She held up her belt that had cuffs and flashlight, but no holster or magazine pouches.

"I suspect we'll get that oversight fixed at our new office."

They picked up the zipper jackets that matched the uniforms and went to find Deputy Josh to start their new assignment. Kelly thought of an earlier conversation with Aunt Maude. She was right.

Kelly muttered, "… Weird things is always happenin' around here. Welcome to West Virginia!"

26

GT WASN'T SURE WHAT TO expect when the Colts arrived. He felt bad about the way he got them to stay, but his mind kept playing that *desperate times call for desperate measures* saying, over and over. He rationalized that times were pretty desperate, with two missing children and four mutilated bodies. Marcus would forgive him … eventually. Well, maybe, at least he hoped.

The two newest members of the sheriff's department walked into GT's office. "Okay, GT. You got us. We're here. Now what?"

"Are we okay, Marcus?" GT came from behind his desk and extended his hand.

Marcus held a stern look for a few seconds to give GT some grief before grasping the offered hand in both of his. "Yea, buddy, we're good. Kelly is a bit on the 'can I shoot him' kick, but her loyalty can be bought with food and drink."

GT winced in her direction. "Sorry, Kelly."

She made a deprecating gesture. "No problem, GT. I'm just worried about those two children and my patients in D.C.—let's get this case solved quickly."

"Right, I totally agree, Kelly. Marcus, the state's attorney general talked with the U.S. attorney general. They decided that since you're on temporary duty to the governor, and you're officially West Virginians, it would be all right for me to swear you both in as deputies. It falls into the category of that 'additional duty' thing since you, Marcus, are also serving in the Navy. Similar, in reverse I guess, to National Guard service for full-time police officers. Kelly doesn't have any such duty issues, but she needs a quick session at the firing range to qualify for carrying a sidearm."

"She's ready to go in that area, GT. I've trained her. You can trust me that she shoots 'expert' every time."

Kelly held out her hand, palm up. "I'll take a Colt Combat Commander in .45 ACP, please," she said with a wide smile.

In a short time, the two Colts were officially Mercer County Sheriff Deputies, legal documents had been signed, and Kelly had a Combat Commander tucked on her side, which made her feel more comfortable. They both selected ball caps with the official county logo to complete their uniforms. As Marcus noticed earlier, Kelly was even sexier in her complete uniform, as her blonde ponytail swung freely below the ball cap.

GT tossed a set of keys to Marcus. "Your vehicle for the duration of your stay is a four-wheel-drive Ford Bronco; it's parked out back. So, where do we start, Deputy Marcus?"

"It's your circus, GT—we're only a couple of the monkeys. You tell me."

"All right. Time to put all the cards on the table so we can all get on the same page. Mixing metaphors is so much fun since I know it drives you crazy," GT said as he motioned them to follow him into what police movies called the squad room. He rapped loudly on Norma Kissing's desk. The two clerks and several deputies looked his way as he announced, "By now, y'all should know Kelly and Marcus Colt. They are now officially deputies and they are in charge of the Crazed Bear case. Any orders or requests they have should be considered coming from me. Any questions?"

Several heads shook and a couple of people gave a thumbs-up.

"All right then, make sure those units on patrol understand."

Marcus and Kelly looked at each other and shrugged.

"Again, where do we start, Marcus?" GT asked as the crew looked on in surprise.

That also surprised Marcus, but he quickly rose to the occasion. "GT, you and the two detectives join us in the conference room. I assume the cards are still there."

New cards had been added to the boards providing the details on the latest body found. Marcus quickly read them and the old ones. He was already somewhat frustrated that nothing jumped out. It was a frequent frustration for him, especially on new cases.

"GT, you serious about me leading this case?"

A quick nod was all GT offered in response.

"So be it. George, get us another corkboard in here and a huge map of lower West Virginia. And some of those colored push pins. Allen, round up the files on the latest victim."

The two men left to handle their assignments.

"GT, what time will your 'bear guy' be at the morgue?"

"1330 hours. I'll try to stick to military time to keep you happy, Marcus Aurelius."

"I appreciate that, GT. Okay, soon as George gets back with the map, I need you to use the pins to mark some critical locations. Red for the body locations and green for involved sites like the Thompkins house. Identify them with a note card showing the deceased name, date, et cetera. Then we five need to grab lunch at Pansy's before we go to the morgue."

27

DUTY AS WELL AS PROFESSIONAL courtesy required that they check in with the hospital administration. After all, Kelly was now an accredited doctor with hospital privileges, so taking time to make their manners with the chief of staff was appropriate. Pansy's lunch service having been exceptionally fast, they arrived at the hospital a good twenty minutes before the scheduled meeting with Doctor Wallace.

The meet and greet went well; the senior staff was happy to welcome Kelly. The chief of staff, Dr. John Macon, was especially pleased. With his one psychology doctor home sick with the flu, Kelly might come in handy, he told her. After a few minutes of chat, they were all on a first name basis and jabbering like long-lost friends. As the clock hands moved toward 1330 hours, the five members of the Crazed Bear Task Force took the elevator down to the morgue.

Doctor Simpson Wallace was running late. With his relaxed attitude about most things, promptness was not one of his virtues. Today he had actually tried to be on time, but a truck accident south of Beckley had disrupted his schedule. He strolled in at 1405 hours to find six living and one covered dead body waiting. The living beings were not as patient as the deceased. Frowns, crossed arms, and sighs welcomed him.

However, his face lit up when he spotted Kelly. Ignoring the men, he darted toward her with hands extended. "Dear lady, please forgive my delay. Had I known you awaited me, I would have tried to be more prompt."

"Down boy," GT ordered as he stepped in front of Kelly. "Simpson, let's get the intros done and get down to business. The 'dear lady' is Doctor Kelly Colt, a psychologist from Walter Reed now serving as one of my deputies. The deputy with his hand resting on his weapon and giving you the evil eye is her husband, Navy Commander Marcus Colt, from the Naval Investigative Service, also in D.C. They're here to take over this case."

Simpson showed a bit of shock, but rapidly recovered as he reached around GT and took Kelly's hand in both his. "A true pleasure to meet you, Doctor."

Kelly gave him her best disarming smile. "My pleasure, Doctor Wallace. Let's talk bodies and bears, eh?"

He lost his voice for a moment as Kelly's smile turned his brain to mush. Finally he came back into focus. "Of course, yes, Doctor Colt. And it is nice to meet you, Commander. But I dare say seeing you Washington bigwigs in those uniforms is most unusual."

Marcus shook the extended hand. "Simpson, call me Marcus. And as for the uniforms, it was decided that Kelly and I would fit in better looking like the rest of the local force. So, if there are no other observations or comments, where do you want to start today?"

Simpson paused as a quizzical look crossed his face. "Colt? Any relation to Mr. Colt, a history teacher at Princeton High in the fifties?"

"My father."

In an unusual display of emotion to a stranger, Simpson pulled Marcus into what could only be described as a bear hug. "Dear boy, I am so sorry for your loss and apologize for missing the service on Saturday. Your father changed my life when he kindled the desire in me to learn. Prior to his class, I was just getting by, drifting along gathering wool as they say, but his passion for history and … and um … one might say his unique method of *sharing* knowledge made me want to do better. I am here for you."

"Thanks, Simpson. That means a lot," Marcus said. *Great job, Dad! Your legacy is far reaching, and because of it, this guy just joined our team in earnest.*

M.E. Dennis Bassett was the first to speak after that emotional display. "Simpson, this is the latest victim. Do you want all the other bodies out?"

"Much depends on the Colts. Do you need to see them all?"

Marcus spoke up first. "Due to the decomp, and since you've already certified the live bear marks on the first victim, let's go with the last three."

Simpson nodded. All were respectfully quiet as Dennis and his assistant moved the other two bodies to the tables. Simpson briefed the Colts on the concerns he found on the two older bodies before he started his analysis of the latest one. He went over the new body as he did with the previous one. Everyone was silent for the twenty or so minutes Simpson spent on his analysis.

"We have some good news and some bad. This new body shows the same evisceration as the others. And the same faked claw marks; I checked the spacing on the claws and they all match. No variations in spacing as expected from a live bear."

Several of the observers nodded. Marcus made a hand motion for him to continue.

"However, as I suspect Dennis has already spotted in his initial work, there is trauma to the back of the skull. One or two x-rays will prove, one way or the other, if this was the cause of death. And perhaps point to the weapon if it truly was COD."

Dennis said, "I thought the same, Simpson. Might have the toxicology report on him here by Friday. GT, I got the reports on the other bodies this morning and have copies here for you."

"What did they show?" Kelly asked. "I was wondering about their absence."

"Morphine. All of the first three bodies had a large amount in their system," Dennis said as he pointed to the two older bodies. "And I'll wager our new arrival doesn't have any in his system since someone bashed his skull. Waste not, want not, as they say."

"Sounds like you have a theory in the works, Doctor," Marcus said.

"Well, without most of the internal organs or any external trauma pointing to another cause of death, I can only speculate that these two, and the John Doe, were knocked out with morphine and then died either from a huge dosage or when their organs were removed." Dennis grimaced and slightly shuddered. "Oh, Lord, how horrible. Gutted alive." He mumbled the last as his eyes squinted closed.

GT was concerned the M.E. might pass out. "Dennis, any chance the organs were harvested for sale on the black market. Or do you have any other guess?"

"Maybe. I just don't know, GT. Anyway, unless the tox screen shows otherwise, that means this new guy suffered blunt object trauma, then was gutted in the same manner. Presumably by the same people."

"That's as good a speculation any of us can make, at least at this time, Marcus," Simpson said.

Marcus shrugged. "Yea, but it would be nice to have a firm COD. And we're still missing the whys, wheres, and whos."

Rapid shuffling of paper and a muttered curse turned everyone's attention to Kelly. "What is it, Kelly?" GT asked.

"I think we're dealing with heroin deaths. The reports do show morphine in the blood, but 6-acetylmorphine—it's usually simply called 6-AM—shows up in the urine."

"Okay, where are you going with this chemistry lesson?" Marcus asked.

"Pay attention, Sailor. Heroin has a short half-life in the blood; it converts to 6-AM in about five minutes. And 6-AM has a half-life of around twenty-five minutes before it metabolizes into morphine. So heroin evidence in the blood is hard to find an hour or two after the injection. However, 6-AM stays in the urine much longer, hours in fact, and studies show it can be detected up to twelve hours later. Sometimes days. That's why my psych patients must provide urine samples frequently so we can watch for drug abuse. It lasts much longer in a dead body."

GT's face tightened in confusion. "But the bodies didn't have bladders or kidneys."

Kelly's grin kicked up to the left. "Our excellent medical examiner pulled enough urine from the urethra for analysis, right Dennis?"

Dennis gave a quick nod. "Sorry I didn't catch that 6-AM. I was too focused on the blood parameters."

"Doc, that's why it's best to have more on the team," Marcus said. "We get enough eyes to watch each other's backs."

"Thanks, Marcus. But it's my job to see these things. Guess I'm a bit overwhelmed with all the bodies stacking up. Uh, GT, when can I release the two we have identified?"

"That's up to Marcus. He is in charge of this case now."

Marcus started to answer, and then held his tongue. Lost in thought, he bit his lower lip before saying, "Hold off for another day or so. I'll let ya know."

He turned to Simpson. "Do you have any speculation on the puncture wounds on the front shoulders of these three?"

The big man moved surprisingly fast to again look at the wounds. He measured the spacing and compared it between the bodies. His lips puckered as he shook his head. He finally said, "Definitely not bear related. Doesn't look mechanical, but I have no idea what could have caused them."

"So do you consider them to have been made by the same unknown creature?" Marcus asked.

"Indeed. But they don't have to have been made by a living creature. Someone could have cobbled up a two-claw paw like they did with the fake bear paw. But I will state that the punctures do not match bear claws or teeth."

With a glance and shrug toward Kelly, Marcus asked, "Anything else to ask the good doctors?" Shaking heads of task force members was all he got.

Simpson rubbed his hands together. "Well, if there is nothing else, my friends, I shall dash up the road to my Beckley office. Dare I say there is a ton of paperwork awaiting me."

Marcus shook his head. "Sorry, Simpson, you're coming to the station with us now and for the duration."

"I beg your pardon?"

"GT, call whoever you need to call to make sure Doctor Wallace is assigned to our task force. We can get him a hotel room, right?"

GT failed miserably to keep a straight face. "Aye, aye, sir. As the leader wishes, it shall be done." He turned to Simpson. "And yes, he has the authority to make that happen. Good news is your room at my house is still ready for you."

With hands raised in surrender, Simpson asked, "We still have some bourbon to consume, right?"

28

ALLEN ADDED THREE CARDS READING "COD Heroin?" to the boards. One more piece of information was good, even if a question mark followed it. "Blunt Force Trauma?" was added for the fourth victim. A probable, even a possible, beats a *nothing* every time. Another straw added to the extremely small pile of disjointed straws.

One member of the team was missing. George had spent most of the last twenty-four hours calling hunters, scout troop leaders, and VFW commanders to solicit volunteers for search parties; they were now meeting at the high school gym to break into teams with assigned search areas. Finding the Thompkins children and car were their goals.

Simpson was at the large map with a handful of yellow pins and a small ball of string. He mumbled under his breath as he ran string from one yellow pin to another to outline the known bear habitats. As Marcus watched from across the room, he realized a lot of land had been marked.

Kelly had been on the phone with associates at Walter Reed. Her first call was a conference call to the head thoracic and abdominal surgeons. She explained the case and rattled off question after question. In short order, she had a better understanding on what tools and expertise were needed to surgically eviscerate a body. And she also knew how long it would take, and what precautions were needed if the organs were to be harvested for transplant purposes.

Her second call was to the hospital's transplant coordinator. From him, she garnered information about how long each organ could be stored and what storage parameters were required. And which organs were in highest demand. Kelly filled out and posted more index cards to quickly share the knowledge she'd obtained.

Before concluding the call, Kelly asked the coordinator to nose around and see if any quantity of organs were suddenly becoming available. Granted it was a long shot, but it could be another straw to add to the small pile.

Marcus decided to check in with SA Doc Stevens to make sure all was well in D.C. As he reached for the phone, Norma stuck her head into the conference room and announced, "Deputy Colt is needed on line two—the doctor deputy. Doctor Macon is calling."

Pressing the correct button, Kelly answered, "Kelly Colt."

"John here. Hate to bother you so soon, but we need you stat. Come directly to the ER."

"On the way."

Dropping the handset onto the cradle, Kelly noticed all eyes were focused on her. She shrugged. "I'm needed at the ER. Sounds like I've got a patient."

Marcus tossed her the Bronco keys. "Drive careful. Need a map?"

A wink and a stuck-out tongue were all the answer she gave as she caught the keys and dashed out the door. It wouldn't be a difficult drive to the hospital.

After seeing her off, Marcus again tried his call to D.C. He was successful this time.

"Naval Investigative Service, Internal Affairs Division. Carl Freeman speaking. How may I be of assistance, sir?"

"Afternoon, Carl. I'm checking to see if all the mice are busy while the head cat's away."

"Well, sir, from what I hear, Deputy Dawg is probably a better name than head cat. You know we need photos of you guys in uniform, right? How's it going over there in the 'almost heaven' of West Virginia?"

Colt snickered; the cartoon reference was not lost on him. "As the sheriff said, 'we are all balls lost in the tall weeds.' Too many bodies and too few clues. Did Wendy and Brad get back?"

"No, sir. Their latest ROI says they're shadowing a bunch of people who may be the ones acting suspicious around the base hospital. No hot leads yet. Doc and the Marines are handling the small amount of issues here very well."

"Okay." Marcus paused to gather his thoughts. "Give me the numbers where I can reach Wendy, and cut TAD orders like mine for Lieutenant Gardener to come here. Let Doc and the admiral know I've shanghaied him for this project. And please transfer this call to Rick."

"You got it, boss. Take care and hurry home."

The silence on the line lasted for nearly a minute. Either Rick was in the head or getting another cup of coffee. He finally came on the line.

"Lieutenant Gardener, sir. How may I help you, Commander?"

"Rick, I need you here. Check out your favorite sniper rifle from the armory, pack a lot of gear you might need for traipsing around the snowy woods, and get your butt over here. Bring your sidearm. And a couple of uniforms in case we need to get fancy. Carl will have your orders. Pack what you think Rattler would recommend. Come to the sheriff's office when you get to Princeton. I've got you a place to stay."

"Can do, sir. I'll plan on leaving here at 0500, so I should be there around noon."

"Thanks, Rick. I'll be happier knowing you have my back. See ya tomorrow."

GT gave a look as Marcus returned the handset to the cradle. "And who is Rick?"

A cat-that-ate-the-canary grin covered Marcus's face. "Rick Gardener is a young Marine officer, an excellent sniper, and a member of my IA team. I worked with him in the field couple of years ago and trust him with my life. Have Norma dig out a few more spare uniforms; Rick is about two inches and fifteen pounds smaller than me."

"You're dang good at building empires and issuing orders, Marcus Aurelius. And I'm damn glad," GT said quietly, with respect.

"Godfrey, my man, juggling chain saws is my main talent. Getting the right people to do the job comes as a close second. Make sure we have a fresh pot of coffee on while I call in a resource in Chicago."

Dialing a few numbers got the destination he needed. "Naval Investigative Office Great Lakes, Supervisory Special Agent Todd Burke speaking, how may I be of assistance?"

"Marcus Colt calling, Todd. I need to speak with Lieutenant James. Is she around?"

"Yes, sir. Hold one and I'll get her on the line."

The silence on the line gave Marcus a moment to gather his thoughts. The moment didn't last long, yet his inner contemplation did.

"Lieutenant James." Wendy paused before adding, "Marcus, are you there?"

"Hey, partner. Yea, I'm here; sorry, I was lost in thought for a moment. How are things on your end?"

A long frustrating sigh preceded the words. "Damn slow, boss. We keep following trucks, and none have led to the mother lode. We did lose track of one that seemed to be heading your way or at least south-eastward on Friday morning early. Even without some great results, I want to keep the surveillance going a bit longer … if that's okay."

"Your lead, your decision, Wendy. Just don't let desire overpower logic. Especially if thou art thrashing an expired equine."

"Ha! I hear ya loud and clear. Guess your gut has rubbed off on me 'cause there is something here, Marcus, but it's not obvious yet."

"We see that too often. At this point, I'll be happy to trade cases." With that, Marcus gave her a quick rundown on the Princeton situation. He concluded, "And have you cultivated any contacts with the Chicago police?"

"I met with the chief of detectives on Saturday. Why?"

"Check with him to see if Jesus Cabilla has a record. He has a Chicago address and is the latest victim here. Let me know what you find." Marcus provided all the information they had on Cabilla, then they traded thoughts on both cases for a few more minutes before concluding the call.

Seeing the phone call ended, GT asked, "Okay, what do you want to do now?"

Marcus held up his empty coffee cup to indicate his next action. "Walk with me, GT."

As they entered the empty breakroom, Marcus turned to GT. His voice was low and serious as he asked, "How sensitive is Doctor Bassett's ego?"

"What do ya mean?"

"GT, as soon as I get a refill, I'm going to call in a second M.E. to look at the bodies. He's a sharp Navy doc I met in Norfolk couple of years ago with a lot of experience handling murder cases. Will Bassett be highly offended, which might lead to attitude issues in the future, or will he accept that more eyes are always better? Since he missed the urinalysis point, he might have missed others, but we don't need ego issues right now."

"Dennis is as overwhelmed as I am, Marcus; he'll appreciate the help. He should be okay, but I'll have a private chat with him to prevent ruffled feathers. So, what else can we do today?"

Taking a sip, Marcus nodded toward the door and started walking. "Prep work. Tomorrow is going to be busy. Call Mr. Thompkins and have him meet us at his house at 0830. Then we need to meet with Bob Ledder at the construction site at 1100. What does your gut tell you about these guys?"

"Their records are clean. Their stories seem solid. No holes in them."

"Yea, GT, that's the obvious stuff, but what does your gut tell you? Is there anything that seems off, no matter how small? Something that doesn't feel right?"

"Nothing so far, but I'll be more alert. Please remember the bulk of my cases are traffic issues, with a few B&Es, drunken bar fights, and domestic violence calls tossed in to break the boredom. You have the advantage, Marcus, of working these challenging cases all the time."

"Multiple murders will pull you out of your comfort zone, GT, and quickly. Now time for yet another call for help." Marcus dialed a string of numbers from memory as he returned to his chair at the head of the conference table.

"Chief of Naval Operations Office. Master Chief Bartow speaking. How may I be of assistance, sir?"

"Of assistance, you may well be, David. How are things in Foggy Bottom this fine day?"

"Marcus, things were great until this call. Why am I feeling my day has gone down hill in a big way?"

Marcus laughed. "Because you grouchy old men are always negative. And yes, we're still in West Virginia, thanks for asking, so you know how my day is going."

"The admiral was not happy to hear about that. Seems he has a special mission lined up for you, but that was trumped by the SECNAV. And you know how he hates second place." Bartow lowered his voice as concern showed through. "I've been read into your case over there. What can I do to help, Marcus?"

"Since you're asking so nicely, I need a doc here tomorrow. Name is Sidney Wentworth, and he's the M.E. at the Norfolk Naval Base Hospital. And tell me what my favorite father-in-law has planned for me."

"We have an issue in Iceland, but it will hold until you wrap up your current assignment. And your doctor will be on the way as soon as we hang up. Anything else?"

Marcus tapped his near-empty coffee mug with a pencil for a second. The momentary pause was all he needed for the next plan to solidify. "David, check around and see if any SEAL teams are in need of some wilderness training. One of the victims has left a car and two small children out there somewhere. Since her body turned up here, we are now assuming she never left the area. Originally, it was passed to the FBI as a possible out-of-state abduction heading to Michigan. We're getting more involved and additional searchers with warrior skill sets would help here now. We've got volunteer foot patrols doing ground searches leaving from the high school in the morning."

"Damn. I didn't see the part about the children in the overview we received. I'll get with the admiral ASAP. That all you need?"

"A few eyes in the sky would be appreciated. Know anyone in the West Virginia Air National Guard with access to a few helicopters?"

"Ya never know what info the old Rolodex has to offer. Let me work on it. Anything else on your wish list of demands, Commander, sir?"

"That's it for now." Marcus chuckled at the sarcastic formality. "Oh, one other thing; you might as well send me the parameters on the Iceland case. I can use the three spare minutes I have per day to look it over."

"Can do. And Marcus, the admiral and I are sorry we missed the service on Saturday; I heard it went well. The president sends his condolences. Give my love to Kelly, and you both take care."

"Thanks, David."

GT tilted his head inquisitively as Marcus hung up the phone. "Who's your father-in-law?"

"You mean Aunt Maude kept one thing to herself? Amazing! Kelly's dad is Admiral William Gallagher. Also known as the Chief of Naval Operations."

"No, shit! Yea, Aunt Maude failed to mention that interesting tidbit. No wonder you get all those wild assignments."

"Actually, he started using me for nasty stuff long before I met Kelly. Fact is I was on one such mission when I met her. She didn't know I worked for her father, and I didn't know she was the CNO's daughter until after we fell in love."

"You do have some interesting times. And what's that about Iceland?"

Marcus shrugged. "Another special project he wants me to look into. Don't mention it to Kelly; seems every one of her dad's projects ends up getting me more scar tissue. We all need to focus on this case and there's no need to upset her."

"Got ya. So you think there's a chance he'll send some SEALs over to help search?"

Using his hands as a balance scale, Marcus said, "Sixty–forty that he will. We should know shortly since the CNO is not known for taking long to decide. Biggest issue is if they're on a mission, or prepping for one, they may not be available. Assuming he gives it a 'go' order, what do we have in the way of motel rooms handy? Around ten doubles should do it."

GT carried a quick note about the needed rooms to Norma. When he returned, Marcus was reading one of the case files: Joe Decker's. He didn't look happy.

"What's got you troubled?"

Marcus looked up and shrugged. "I'm not seeing what I need to see here. I'm used to seeing more background info on the victim. Aside from a clean apartment and one friend—that guy Ledder who found his body—Decker is a blank slate. No girlfriend, no wife or ex-wife, or family. No financials. No list of associates. No job history. And what do we have on Ledder?"

"Just his interview comments, Marcus. He was not considered a person of interest. Should he be?"

"Right now, I consider everyone in West Virginia and most of the bordering states a person of interest. He may be as pure as a new West Virginia snowfall, but until we dig into him, we won't *know* that. Family and coworkers are frequently the perpetrators. So we dig. Allen, please see what you can find out about Mr. Thompkins and Mr. Ledder before we meet with them in the morning."

"Yes, sir," Allen said as he left the conference room to start a series of phone calls.

Again Marcus dialed the CNO's office. "Me again, David. I need a copy of service records for two gents. Both are reservists with a Tidewater-area Seabee unit, and both were on active duty before that. Names are Robert C. Ledder and Joseph A. Decker." Marcus provided the social security numbers for both men and again thanked Bartow for his help.

Marcus smiled at GT. "That's a start."

Simpson had outlined all the bear areas on the map and joined Marcus and GT at the table. "What's next, Marcus?"

"GT, do you have a deputy available who knows the location where the first victim was found?"

GT nodded. "Sure. Harvey Wilson's on patrol, but I can radio him in."

"Do it. I know it's not a fresh crime scene, but perhaps Simpson can see an anomaly or two."

"Splendid idea, Marcus. Give me a moment to change into field clothing," Simpson said as he left the room.

GT watched Simpson leave and looked at Marcus. "What do you expect him and Allen to find?"

"Not a clue, GT. I don't know what they will find and neither do you … or them. The mission is to keep looking until we find whatever is there to be found. Therefore, they will check all the body dumpsites. Sure it's grasping at straws, but think of it as crossing each *t* and dotting each *i*."

"Okay, I get it. Marcus, you're good at moving chess pieces around the board. So where do I go next?"

"You need to interview the boss at the construction company to get some background on Decker and Ledder. Ask some of the coworkers what kind of guys they were both on and off the job. Uncover their hangouts, associates, and hobbies; build a file of info on those men. Since it is only 1530, I suspect they are still on site, right?"

"Probably. I'll drive on over—it's about ten minutes away. Want to ride along?"

Marcus shook his head. "First off, I need more coffee. And since I have two admirals wanting me to get this solved quickly, I'm getting on the phone to pull in more NIS resources from Michigan, West Virginia, and Virginia."

29

Sergeant George Walker looked around the gym, relieved. His calls for hunters, scout troops, and VFW members had actually worked, and the gym was filled with volunteers ready to help find the missing children and their vehicle. People come together to help those in need in this part of the country.

George had already explained to the various team leaders the overall plan and what was going to happen in the next few hours. With their help, he divided the county into workable sections and assigned groups to those sections. The team leaders then spread the word about their assignments.

The folks at the FBI had generated a single-page data sheet that showed photos of the children and the auto. They had been passed to all volunteers. George felt he spent too much time drumming the importance of haste to them, but the facts were clear: each hour the children were missing increased the probability of finding bodies instead of living beings. Granted they may already be too late; they had been missing too long.

He climbed up a few rows on the center bleacher and used his whistle to get everyone's attention. "Like they say in the old western movies, we're burning daylight, people," George announced to the volunteers. "You know we only have a few hours of daylight left today, but we are going to use every bit of it. Drive all the roads in your assigned areas looking for the white Buick Electra. Tag number is on the data sheet. Since it hasn't been reported as an abandoned vehicle, we know it's not parked on the side of a main road. There's a good chance it went off the road; keep an eye on the areas down slope or in heavy brush areas. Or it might be hidden off a side road somewhere. So look in the places you wouldn't expect to see it. You know what I mean—go down those gas-well roads, check behind every abandoned barn, or look for a car hidden in plain sight among other abandoned vehicles. We'll meet back here tomorrow morning at eight o'clock to start the walking field searches."

A hand rose in the middle of the crowd. "Deputy, I arrived late, so my question might be silly. But what do we do if we spot the car?"

"Bill, you're always late, but not silly. It can't be expressed enough. Do *not* touch the vehicle. Look inside for the children—if they are there and alive, get them out, but wear gloves and try not to touch too much of the car. Otherwise, don't touch the car period. We need print evidence that might be there. Then get to the nearest phone ASAP and call it into the sheriff's office." George hid his personal belief that the children had been dead for some time. No need to be negative.

A second hand shot up. "Do we have an official quittin' time tonight? I got me some high-powered spotting lights that will help after dark."

George smiled. "Harv, it's a good thing those lights know not to light up deer, right?" That got the expected chuckles, then George continued, "When's quittin' time? When you have covered all your assigned roads is the obvious answer. Unlike Harv, most of us cannot see in the dark. But remember … there are two small children missing. I cannot force any of you to keep at it, but what if they were your kids? Okay, get moving, people!"

Jerry Masterman, the *Princeton Bugle* editor-in-chief, stood off to the side as the crowd drifted out on their mission. He was a short man with thinning brown hair. Even with his black-framed glasses, he wouldn't stand out in a crowd.

As George gathered his paperwork in preparation for the next day's search, Jerry glanced around to make sure they were secluded. "George, glad to see this underway. Can you answer a quick question?"

"Sure, Jerry, I'll try."

"Why did the sheriff wait over a week to start this search? I hear he's brought in some big shot from D.C. to run the case. Was he the one who pushed for the searches?"

"You need to ask GT those questions, Jerry. But off the record, and I mean way off, the big shot is the guy you met on Saturday, Marcus Colt. He works for Navy intelligence and he's a childhood friend of GT. GT felt his expertise might help."

"But why the wait?"

"There was no waiting. We turned the case over to the FBI on 'day one' when we thought she and the children had gone to Michigan. They are more equipped to handle presumed kidnappings, and the FBI folks are still working it. GT decided to put more local effort on it. But you need to get official comments from him."

"With the new guy in charge, it looks like our sheriff can't handle this case."

"Bull. It's a messy one and we need all the help we can get. And we sure don't need you badmouthing the one guy who cares more about this county than anyone I've ever met. Keep out of the way and let GT do his job."

Masterman didn't look happy, but he nodded. As he walked away he muttered, "I'll be nice … for now."

30

FOR THE UMPTEENTH TIME, DOC Stevens looked at the growing piles of paper on Colt's desk and wondered how the man ever got through the mess. Chuckling to himself, Doc contemplated shredding half of it: the modern form of hiding something under the rug, in those days of wall-to-wall carpeting. It was tempting. Instead he picked up the NIR on the top of the closest stack and started reading. His concentration was destroyed by the ring of the phone. The outside line light was lit.

"Commander Colt's office. SA Stevens speaking. How may I be of assistance?"

"Let me guess. The paper piles are about a foot high, right?"

"Hey, Marcus! Damn straight they are. But I'll have them under control by the time you return … unless you need me to come down to West Virginia with Rick."

"Sorry, Doc, you're needed there."

"Yea, we who suffer papercuts also serve."

Marcus laughed, then described the situation he faced and outlined what he needed Doc to handle. "I need you to write up three NIRs and get them on the wire. Here's the requests."

It was a concise synopsis, and he concluded by saying, "Get the NIRs out ASAP. Tag NISRA Charleston WV as the lead office with the SSA reporting to me. Then brief the admiral."

"I'll get it done, Marcus, but you know I should be there helping on this weird case."

"I would agree, but as my XO, you get stuck there when I'm gone."

Before ending the call, Doc had a couple of questions on pending cases he faced. Marcus pointed Doc in the right directions, then promised to call Doc if he ran into problems.

After dropping the three NIRs off at the computer center, Doc went to brief Admiral Chance. The admiral's gatekeeper sent him right in.

"What do you have, Doc?" the admiral asked.

"Mr. Colt is asking for BIs on a couple of the West Virginia victims, as well as some of their friends and family. He said the local sheriff was focusing only on the victims' COD due to the unusual circumstances of the deaths, and not looking deep at them or their associates. Marcus is helping him to expand the net a bit. I just sent NIRs to Norfolk and Great Lakes NISOs and NISRA Charleston—West Virginia not South Carolina."

The admiral nodded. "Lieutenant James is still at Great Lakes, right?"

"Yes, sir. She feels they are getting close, but needs a little more time."

"By involving Great Lakes, is Marcus seeing a connection between her case and his?"

"Not that he has told me. All I know is his latest victim is from Chicago, so he wanted a BI done on him."

The admiral started to say something, then paused. He picked up a folder from his desk and passed it to Doc. "Read this over and let me know your thoughts in the morning."

Doc took the folder and asked, "Anything else, sir?"

"Oh, that one will be enough for now. See you tomorrow."

Leaving the admiral's office, Doc spied Rick Gardener talking with Hank Bates in the coffee mess. They quieted as he approached.

"Saying nasty things about me, eh?" Doc joked.

"Not this time, Doc," Hank said with a shake of his head. "Just discussing concerns about whatever Marcus is facing. Glad Rick will be there, but I wonder if that is enough manpower."

Doc shrugged. "Hard to say at this point. I know he has asked for a Navy M.E. to examine the bodies, and a SEAL team might be heading that way to help search. Hell, he's only been on the case one day, so let's see what tomorrow brings."

The two Marines silently nodded in the affirmative.

As Doc poured another cup of coffee, he looked at Rick. "When you finish here, let's talk. You'll find me under the mess of papers on our fearless leader's desk."

"Aye, aye, sir."

Flipping through the file he'd received from the admiral as he walked, Doc saw that it was a special case requested by the CNO. Looked like Iceland was heating up.

31

MARCUS WAS SATISFIED WITH HIS call to NISHQ. He knew Doc would handle the NIRs quickly and deliver information that might help solve this case. Draining his coffee cup while going over the cards of data one more time, he searched his mind for what he had missed. Nothing jumped out.

Simpson and GT leaned in the door. "Marcus, we're heading out. Any last changes to our orders?" GT asked.

Before Marcus could reply, Norma's face appeared between the men blocking the door. "Deputy Colt, Deputy Colt needs you on line three." She chuckled. "I think I'll start calling her 'Deputy Doc,' if that's okay with you gentlemen?"

"That will work fine, Norma," GT said.

Marcus grabbed the phone and stabbed a finger into the blinking light of line three. "What's up, Kelly?"

"You, GT, and Simpson need to get over here right now. Weird just got weirder. Come to the ER. Now!" The dial tone prevented Marcus from asking questions.

"Gents, we are needed at the hospital. Simpson, ride with Harvey, and I've got shotgun with GT."

"What's up?" Simpson asked.

Marcus shrugged as he led them out the door. "No idea, but since she wants all of us, it must be case related. She sounded stressed. Guess we'll find out in a few minutes."

On the drive to the hospital, GT asked, "You got any thoughts you haven't shared, Marcus? I know your brain is two or three steps ahead of the rest of us."

"Sorry, nothing yet, buddy. Too much disjointed information right now. We need the BIs on the victims and their associates. Maybe then we'll see something connecting. Right now, we're looking for that famous needle without knowing where the dang haystack is."

"Glad I'm not the only one feeling lost."

Marcus cleared his throat as he became serious. "GT, keep positive. We're not lost yet; we just started the journey. We are in the initial data gathering stage. You now have more eyes on the case, and fresh eyes usually see things tired eyes have missed. No disrespect intended."

"As I keep telling you, this mess is not my normal workload."

"Yea, think I've heard that from you a few times." Marcus was quiet for a second as his thoughts turned more harsh. With a louder and more commanding voice, he added, "And this time needs to be the last. GT, you are the freaking sheriff, and whatever comes your way *is* your normal workload. Otherwise, pull that badge off your shirt and go pump gas down at the Gulf station!"

GT's jaw clenched as he focused on the road ahead. Nothing else was said as the hospital came into view, and he pulled past the ER entrance and parked outside of the unloading area. Switching off the ignition, he turned toward Marcus. "You're right. Sorry. Won't happen again."

Marcus gave a quick nod. "Your team needs to believe you have things under control. You may not know all the answers, but make sure your people know you will find them. Instill confidence."

"I understand. Let's go find out what's upset your cute wife, eh?"

"Right beside you, Sheriff."

Kelly was waiting inside the entrance. A lab coat covered her uniform and shock and frustration engulfed her face.

"About time you boys got here. Come with me." Kelly turned and double-timed down the hall.

Catching up to her, Marcus put his hand on her shoulder. "Slow down, Princess. What's going on?"

She frantically looked around, then pulled Marcus over to a storage room. The other three followed.

"Okay, the city police pulled over a car that was driving erratically. The older female driver started ranting about a huge bear. The officer said she was hysterical, fighting him and acting crazy. That's when he cuffed her and brought her here. Doctor Macon was called to the ER when the staff had trouble calming her down. He then called me after hearing her rant." Her stressed-out words ran together in a verbal blur.

Simpson jumped in. "What exactly did she say about the bear?"

Kelly held up a hand. "Best you hear it directly from her. Her blood work was clean. No drug overdose. I've given her a mild sedative that has helped get her under control, and she is in restraints. She is mostly coherent, somewhat less rambling, and no more screaming." Pointing to a shelf containing stacks of fresh scrubs and lab coats, she added, "I need you to wear lab coats. Seems police uniforms are upsetting to her."

As they buttoned their white coats, Marcus said, "Kelly, why don't you and Simpson go in first. Pull the drape around her bed, and then GT and I will quietly come in and listen out of her sight. Too many people might upset her more."

Kelly nodded and led them to the patient.

"Mrs. Cole? Ruth, this is Doctor Wallace. Can you tell him what you saw?"

Her wrists were encased in fleece-lined leather straps that were attached to the bed rails. An IV ran into her left hand. Ruth Cole had a head full of mostly silver hair. She looked at Kelly with a touch of recognition in brown eyes surrounded by deep age lines. "What?"

Touching Ruth's hand, Kelly softly ordered, "Tell Doctor Wallace what you saw on the road a while ago. It's important, Ruth."

A look of concentration came over Ruth. She looked at Simpson. "I was coming home from Sandlick. Guess I was about a mile away from the turn onto Route 20 when I saw it." She turned away and whimpered.

"It's all right, Ruth. Doctor Wallace needs to know what you saw. Please tell him," Kelly commanded, in full psychologist mode.

Ruth rapidly nodded and turned toward Simpson, whispering, "The biggest bear I've ever seen walked across the road in front of me." Her voice became louder and more agitated. "I hit the brakes hard. He had to be ten feet tall since he was walking on his hind legs. He was fast. And he carried something in his arms."

Simpson's face twisted in confusion. "The bear walked all the way across the road on his hind legs? He walked quickly?"

Louder and now fully agitated, Ruth went on. "Yes, he did! I'm tellin' you what I saw. He stayed on his back legs all the way into the woods. And he was running, Doctor, just like you or me. I know what I saw. It was so strange, I tell ya."

Kelly again laid her hand on Ruth's. "It's okay, Ruth. We believe you but want to make sure we get all the facts right."

Simpson was quiet for a moment as he absorbed the information and allowed Ruth to calm. Finally, he asked, "What color was this bear?"

"Cinnamon, it was. And he had some dark streaks in his fur like mud or something." Ruth was becoming more coherent and confident as she talked about the incident.

As Simpson made notes, Kelly asked, "Ruth, could you see what the bear was carrying?"

Ruth shook her head. "It was a light color, blue and white, maybe. I'm not sure."

"And which way was this bear running, Ruth?" Simpson asked.

"Uh, let's see. It was right to left in front of the car, but I'm not sure about the compass direction. That road has a lot of turns, you know. Sorry."

Marcus slowly came around the curtain. "Ruth, I'm Marcus and I have a question, if you don't mind."

"Are you a doctor, too?"

"No, ma'am, I'm an investigator looking into what happened to you."

"You look like a doctor in that lab coat. Sort of like Doctor Kildare that was on TV. He was cute like you."

Marcus failed to stifle a chuckle. "When you braked hard to keep from hitting the bear, do you remember if your tires squealed?"

"Oh, my, yes. My late husband, Oscar, would have told me I left a thousand miles worth of rubber on the road."

"Thank you, Ruth." Marcus looked at Simpson and asked, "Anything else, Doctor?"

"Only one more. Ruth, did you see the bear's face? How long was his snout?"

She bit her lip searching for the right words. "I'm not sure. He had large eyes that looked directly at me as he ran in front of the car, but I can't remember a snout."

Marcus nodded and pointed toward the door. Kelly picked up on the signal and said, "Ruth, I'll be right back. You've been through a lot today, so I will give you something to help you sleep. No more questions for now. Okay?"

Ruth nodded in resignation. "I want to go home and sleep in my own bed, but you're the doctor."

"I know you do, but let's see what tomorrow brings after a good night's rest, eh?" Kelly rubbed Ruth's hand to reassure her.

Returning to the storage room, the men started to ditch the lab coats. GT was the first to ask, "Well, what do you think, Simpson?"

"Doesn't sound like a bear to me. More along the lines of a Sasquatch description."

Kelly rolled her eyes and Harvey couldn't hide a snicker.

GT shook his head. "Please don't go there, Simpson."

Simpson put his hands up in defense. "You asked my opinion."

"She sounded like she believed what she saw," Marcus said.

"Ruth's story matches what she said earlier," Kelly added.

"Kelly, does her medical record list any psychotic events in her past? And dementia?" Marcus asked.

She shook her head. Marcus let out a sigh as he shrugged.

"Okay, we're now looking for a ten-foot-tall bear that can run like a human on his hind legs," GT muttered in frustration.

Marcus held up his hand to stop the conversations. "Let's see what she remembers in the morning. Until then, small change of plans: Harvey, take Simpson and try to find where Ruth hit the brakes. If you find the skid marks, help Simpson look around and see what y'all can find that might identify our unknown creature. GT, head on to the construction site—you know what to do there. I want to chat with Ruth a bit while Kelly does her doctor thing. Then she and I will be at the office until, say, six. Questions?"

There were none. The three men departed to handle their tasks and Kelly left to update Ruth's chart and order the sedative.

Marcus returned to Ruth's room. She looked at him with reluctance. "I'm too tired to answer any more questions."

"I'm almost too tired to ask, Ruth. It has been a long day all around," Marcus said with a chuckle. "You mentioned your husband a bit ago. Was Oscar the man who ran the Western Auto store?"

"Oh, yes. He retired after forty-five years with the company. I lost him three years ago to cancer."

Marcus gently smiled. "Sorry. He was a good guy. He helped me and my dad with my first bicycle purchase many years ago. I remember his smile."

Ruth relaxed. Marcus pulled a chair to the bedside and sat silently for a moment as they both remembered Oscar.

"Ruth, living here for so long, I bet you've seen plenty of bears, right?" She nodded.

"But the one you saw today was different. I know it upset you greatly, but I want you to close your eyes and bring up the memory of this afternoon. I wouldn't ask if it wasn't important."

"I'll try."

"You said the bear was carrying something. Close your eyes now and focus on that image of him in front of your car. Picture the colors and shape of what he was carrying. And on the way he was holding it."

She was so quiet that Marcus thought she had drifted off. Finally, she said, "It was clutched tight against his chest with his arms sort of overlapping in front like an X. Only colors I remember were a blur of blue and white. Like he was carrying laundry."

"Good, Ruth. Now is there anything else about the bear that sticks out in your mind?"

"I'm sorry. Nothing beyond him being big and fast."

"No problem. Sleep on it and Doctor Kelly will talk with you in the morning. Get some rest."

The nurse entered with the meds as Marcus left.

Kelly was waiting outside the room door, leaning against the wall. She looked tired.

"Looks like you need a nap, Princess."

She shook her head. "No, just overwhelmed with all this weird stuff. Guys with nightmares about Vietnam are much easier to treat. Bigfoot shock, not so much." Kelly placed her hand on Marcus's cheek. "What's wrong? You look so sad."

Marcus shrugged. "Hit with a touch of melancholy. Ruth's husband was the man who sold my first bicycle to Dad. I remembered him well because of his first name. At the ripe old age of seven, I thought 'Oscar' was a funny name. Just remembering Dad."

"Oh, babe," Kelly whispered as she hugged him tightly. "Anything I can do?"

"Let's get a shot of caffeine. Is the coffee decent in the cafeteria?"

"I have no idea, Deputy Colt—I've been working since I got here. Dump the lab coat and we'll find out together," Kelly said as she pressed against him.

"Sounds good to me, Deputy Doc. By the way, that's Norma's new name for you: having two 'Deputy Colts' was confusing for her. After a coffee, we can run to the office to update the files with Ruth's information."

Kelly winked at Marcus. "Paperwork? And here I thought you were always out chasing wild women and ducking bullets on these cases."

"The day is still young."

That comment earned Marcus an elbow in his side.

32

IT WAS A LITTLE AFTER five o'clock, and the sun had dropped behind the western mountains. Darkness was starting to take over in earnest. Even so, Doctor Simpson Wallace was still prowling around the woods on the western side of the road. He looked for clues—any would do—but footprints and hair samples were paramount. The beam of his flashlight and flash of his camera gave his portion of the woods a mystical look.

Someone, or something, had come through the woods recently. The doctor had tracked bears through similar environments. Underbrush was trampled flat, clearly marking the trail. Simpson had to hurry since nature would not allow the brush to stay down for long. Most of it would spring up to normal by morning. With a touch of desperation, he followed the trail looking for an indicator. There had to be a print or something, but no luck yet. He pressed on.

Deputy Harvey Wilson was checking for the same on the other side of the road. He had found Ruth's skid marks easily; she was right, there was a lot of rubber left on the road. At least one part of her story had proven true. But his side of the road was otherwise void of evidence. Too many rocks and too little underbrush covered the dry areas on his side, reducing the chance of trapping a footprint or two.

Wilson had searched into the woods well over a hundred yards off the road. He checked for anything that shouldn't be there. His flashlight made short sweeps ahead of his feet as he trudged onward. But ignoring a couple of empty beer bottles that had been tossed into the drainage ditch paralleling the road, he came up empty. But the importance of the case drove him to keep looking.

With the natural light gone and the batteries in the flashlights fading, Simpson came from the woods and yelled, "Harvey, I think we've done all we can do tonight. Time to get to the office and update Colt."

Harvey climbed out of the ditch and walked toward the car. "You got my vote, Doc. My shift is over shortly, and I promised to take the wife to the movies. *The Longest Yard* is playing at the Lavon and I can't keep her away from a Burt Reynolds film."

Simpson chuckled. "Well, we must not disappoint your lady. Want to use the siren to get back faster?" Harvey shook his head as Simpson continued, "Just kidding, Harvey. I've heard that movie's not that great, but at least the theater has great popcorn."

On the drive to Princeton, they compared notes. Harvey's side was a dry well, but Simpson had finally found a couple of strange footprints and one broken branch that had snagged a few strands of hair. The interesting part about the branch was its location at his shoulder height: too tall for a normal bear to have snapped.

33

"I GOTTA SAY ... GETTING this NIR from NISHQ so soon after you were asked—sub-rosa—to check on this same man with Chicago PD ... it makes me curious as to what happened in these last couple of hours," SSA Todd Burke muttered as he pulled the paper off the ASR-35 Teletype. His muttering was loud enough to get LT Wendy James's attention across the room. He handed her the fresh NIR when she came to his side.

She read it as a knowing smile spread across her face. "Marcus Colt has a tendency to get himself into unusual situations. Looks like West Virginia is going to be another one of those." After a moment, her pencil eraser tapped the paper rapidly, and the smile became a look of deep concern.

Todd did a double take. "Are you okay?"

"My gut is telling me there's a lot more here than just a dead Chicago boy. Todd, we need to get on this BI request ASAP. By now, Chief Montgomery has had time to copy whatever exists on Jesus Cabilla. I'm running to Chicago to pick it up, maybe have a nice chat with our brother in blue, and you need to get an agent or two doing some deep background work."

SA Bradley Neil entered the office as Wendy was frantically pulling on her purse, which was snagged in the desk drawer, and reaching for her coat at the same time. Todd was on the phone, and from the sounds of things, something had happened. He looked at Wendy. "Hey, I was gone for less than fifteen minutes. What happened here?"

"Let's go to Chicago, Brad, and I'll fill you in while you drive. I need more time to focus, and the traffic here requires more attention than I have to offer. Hold your questions for a couple of minutes while things gel in my mind."

"Aye, aye, ma'am. I'm still sailor enough to know when the skipper needs silence." That caused Wendy to pause and let out a short laugh as she pulled Brad toward the door.

The drive south was quiet. Brad held his questions and kept the road and traffic forefront in his attention. Quick sideways glances showed Wendy's brow knotting, relaxing, then knotting again as she bit her lip and her hand worked a pen. The small notepad she kept in her purse was out as she made notes on clean pages and rapidly flipped back to consult previous jottings. Brad had seen her mind at work in the past and knew to stay out of the way.

Shortly after passing the "Welcome to Chicago" sign, she stopped writing notes and her face became calm. She let out a deep sigh. The drive continued a bit longer in silence. But before she could start the explanation, Brad pulled into one of the visitor parking slots at the police headquarters and shut off the engine. He continued to stare out the windshield. He knew when to wait.

A deep breath preceded Wendy's cheeks expanding like Louis Armstrong's when playing his trumpet, then the breath escaped in a soft whistle. She gave a quick nod as if telling herself she was right.

"Okay, Brad, here's the deal: facts first. You know Marcus called for us to get some background on his latest victim, Jesus Cabilla, from Chicago PD. You were there when I called Chicago PD. While you were getting your coffee, Doc sent an NIR for us to do a complete BI on Cabilla and get it to Marcus via the Charleston, West Virginia NISRA. Todd's working on it with his agents, and we are here in Chicago to get a copy of the police records from Chief of Detectives Montgomery. That is all firm and documented."

Brad gave a sharp nod. "Marcus must have discovered something else, since he called you."

"Agreed. And he wanted more info on Cabilla, thereby generating the NIR. Now here's what I think is happening. My gut feelings—nothing we can take to the bank, okay?"

"Yes, ma'am. But your gut is pretty sharp."

"Thanks, but I'm still an amateur compared to the boss. What if, and I know I'm grasping here, *what if* the truck we lost on Friday night was driven by Cabilla. Suppose he went home to West Virginia for whatever reason. Maybe to pick up a load or drop some off. Or he missed his mama."

Brad raised both hands, palms up, with a *so what* gesture. "That's not such a wild idea."

"Now take it one step further. Since we believe he might be involved with our theoretical drug ring, perhaps he did something that soured his relationship with 'Mr. Big' of the druggies. Marcus told me Cabilla suffered blunt force trauma, and not the drug overdose of the other victims in Princeton. Result of a fight?"

"Could be. But where's the truck?" Brad asked. "We know each truck coming on the base had only the one driver. And we lost the truck as it was heading southeast from Gary, Indiana. If he drove it to West Virginia, where is it?"

Now it was Wendy's turn to gesture, with a hand signal and facial expression that both communicated a simple *don't know*. "It's been four days since we lost track of that truck, so someone else might have driven it back to Chicago, or on to another destination. Since we have to start somewhere, we need to send out a BOLO to all the regular law enforcement agencies, and include the truck's description in the ROI to Marcus."

The visit with Chief Montgomery had been efficient, but somewhat frustrating. Once they got past the handshakes and introductions, he handed Wendy a rather thin nine-by-twelve manila envelope and wished the NIS agents a good day. He was not willing to chat. No offer for coffee or interagency chatter, just the insincere smile and a push out the door.

They sat in the quiet car for a couple of moments before Brad broke the silence. "Ignoring that fake smile, do you feel like we have had a door slammed in our faces?"

"Oh, yea, big time. And the virtual slam was hard enough to make me wonder if Montgomery is involved with whatever Cabilla is doing."

"Maybe he hates sailors." Brad smiled as he pointed to the envelope. "You can read that to me as I dodge traffic getting us safely to Great Mistakes."

"Be nice, Brad. Great Lakes NTC doesn't deserve that nickname."

Smirking, Brad fired up the engine as he mumbled, "You didn't spend eleven nasty winter weeks in boot camp there."

34

MORE CARDS HAD BEEN ADDED to the boards. As Marcus always said, new cards were a few more pieces of straw grasped and documented. Still, the board was keeping secrets: no solutions were revealed and even small patterns were elusive. It was like working a jigsaw puzzle with all the pieces face down.

Kelly and Marcus finished proofing their typed reports on Ruth's comments, to add to the slim files. And with nothing else for them to do in the office, it was time to find some dinner. Maude was having fun with her bridge club that night and had told Marcus she wouldn't be fixing dinner.

As Kelly clicked off the conference room lights, Doctor Wallace came charging in.

"Hold right there, Marcus! Might I have a word," Simpson exclaimed, his question an order.

Marcus hit the light switch again and winked at Kelly as he whispered, "Dinner is delayed, Princess." He raised his voice as he shook Simpson's hand. "Okay, bear guy, what ya got? Be quick 'cause hunger is foremost in our minds right now."

Simpson pushed past them and stopped at the map. He grabbed more colored pins and marked Ruth Cole's skid marks, then used a black marker to indicate the movement of the creature she'd described. "First off, I sent Deputy Wilson home—he has a date with his wife. Domestic tranquility is important, so I hear. Anyway, Mrs. Cole was being factual, at least to the degree we could prove. The tire marks were in the road, and I found unusual animal tracks and a cinnamon-colored hair sample."

"You can compare that sample to regular bear hair, right?" Kelly asked. "We need to know if we're dealing with a real bear.

"Of course. I have a reference set of various West Virginia bear hair secure in my truck, so I'll set up my microscope tonight and be happy to take a deep look."

"What was unusual about the tracks, Simpson?"

A grin and a wink of twinkling eye preceded Simpson's response. "The three I documented and photographed were right at fifteen inches long and a little over six inches wide at the front." Silence hung in the air, then Simpson finally said, "Dare I say it?"

Kelly placed her hand over Marcus's mouth as he started to speak. "Sailor, we will not use that name you were just about to dump on us."

"Well, Princess, it *is* a damn big foot," he mumbled between her fingers.

Fortunately for Marcus, GT entered the conference room and his laughter stopped Kelly from reacting to the leaked big foot comment.

"Finally, we have a lady who tries to keep Marcus Aurelius under control. I assume Simpson found something." GT winked at Kelly.

"Indeed I did, GT, and it's a rather large something. I'll have the photos in the morning." Simpson gave a brief overview to GT.

"Glad someone had a bit of success. My trip to the construction site was underwhelming. The owner, Gene Brockholder, was full of praise for both the victim and his buddy. There were not many coworkers around, but all save one provided positive comments. One gent, Leroy Stormer, had a negative comment about the two guys taking off on Fridays for their Navy training weekends. He felt it wasn't fair. So much for supporting our troops, eh?"

Marcus grimaced. "Nothing there to add to the board."

"Not yet. I'll need to go back to interview six other workers and check Stormer's whereabouts for the weekend before we found Decker's remains," GT said. He glanced at the wall clock. "Time to call it a day, people."

"Quick question, GT. Was Bob Ledder working this afternoon?"

GT shook his head. "No, he was off this afternoon ... and tomorrow. Something about his dozer needing a repair."

"So he won't be there to meet with us tomorrow?"

"He said he'd be there, Marcus. I called him before I left the construction site. While using the phone in the office trailer, Gene gave me a roster of all the workers with addresses, phone numbers, et cetera."

Marcus nodded. "Good. We might need that later. I think we need to adjourn to Pansy's for chow and kick some ideas around. Anyone game?"

Her hand shot up as Kelly quickly said, "You had me at chow, Sailor. Let's go."

35

THE NOISE LEVEL WAS STANDARD for this time of day. The clatter of silverware against china, the rattle of ice in tea glasses, the bustle of wait staff, and pleasant conversation among satisfied diners—all were expected in a successful diner. Even for a Tuesday, the reported slow day of the week for restaurants, the house was full. And like the last time the Colts visited, Pansy was behind the counter supervising her domain.

Before GT could wave his hello, Pansy intercepted them and looked Marcus and Kelly from head to toe. "Looks like the Navy's loss is Mercer County Sheriff Department's gain. You two look good in sheriff's uniforms. What gives?"

"Just when you think shanghaiing is out of fashion, it happened to us," Marcus said.

"Come on, Marcus, you know you wanted to help, and I used some influence to get your boss to volunteer you," GT offered. "Actually, Pansy, they are temporarily helping me out."

Pansy nodded. "On the Crazed Bear case?" Before GT could respond, Simpson caught her eye. "And who might you be, handsome?"

"Simpson Wallace, at your service, madam," he said as he kissed Pansy's hand.

"Easy, boy," GT whispered as he turned to face Pansy. "Dr. Wallace was shanghaied by Marcus to help with this bear case. His knowledge of bears makes him a West Virginia legend."

Pansy retrieved her hand and used it to point toward the kitchen door. "Let's get you all settled in your favorite spot, GT."

She led them to the breakroom table in the rear of the kitchen, and after Pansy took the food orders, she turned to leave.

"Can you join us for a few minutes, Pansy?" Marcus asked.

Kelly and GT were not expecting that.

"Sure, hon, whatever you need." Pansy sat across from Marcus and locked her hands together on the table. A slight smile crossed her face as she waited.

Taking a small sip of tea, Marcus gathered his thoughts.

"I bet you see at least half of the folks in Mercer County each week. Am I right?"

She snickered and shrugged. "Sounds like you want insider information about my business. Thinking of opening some competition if that deputy thing doesn't work out?"

Marcus shook his head. "No, ma'am, I love to cook, but have no desire to run a restaurant. My goal is simply to help GT solve a few murders and get on to our lives in D.C. To do that, I'm looking for information. I need your help."

"Not much I can tell you, Marcus, except what I read in the paper."

Marcus chuckled as he shook his head. "You have what, fifteen tables, holding sixty people, and twenty or so seated at the counter, right? And with three breakfast seatings, three or more at lunch, and probably four dinner seatings, you could see over five hundred people per day."

"Yea, something like that." Pansy nodded cautiously.

"I see where you're going, Marcus," GT quickly said. "And Pansy knows probably ninety-five percent of them personally."

"And she chats with most of them, I'll wager," Marcus interjected.

"And hears more gossip than anyone else in Mercer County," GT said.

Marcus gave a thumbs-up and returned his attention to Pansy. "And because of that, Pansy, you might hear something that would help our case. For example, any regulars who haven't been around lately? Or one or two newcomers who just don't feel right? It could be as simple as someone not acting right. Would you be willing to keep your eyes and ears open?"

Pansy rubbed her chin as her eyes settled into a faraway look. After a moment of silence, she said, "Well, anything for GT, I guess. Come to think of it, there was a guy acting strange a couple of weeks ago, but I'll need to think about it and hopefully recall the details."

Nodding, Marcus smiled. "That's what I need, Pansy. And it could be something small. Just keep alert and let us know if you hear anything. Call the office anytime."

"I can't promise you anything, but I'll try, hon." With that, Pansy left the area and went back to work.

Kelly and Simpson had been paying rapt attention to the conversation. Kelly was the first to respond. "Slick way of getting a confidential informant, Sailor. Well done."

"I'm still a bit lost here, Marcus," Simpson said. "What are you expecting to get from Pansy?"

"Don't know. But perhaps Pansy will hear someone mention how strange it is that a cousin suddenly has money for a new truck, or a friend stopped returning calls. Is the cousin involved and getting paid? The friend might be another victim. I admit I don't know, but right now, we're grasping at any straw in the hope that some valid piece of information will come our way. I'll take any source."

His face took on a look of concentration. Simpson finally said with an appreciative nod, "I can see where that might work. Jolly good show!"

Changing direction, Marcus glanced at GT and asked, "When can we expect to hear from the car search teams?"

"Probably some time after nine. Sergeant Walker is probably at the office now, and the teams will call him when they either find something or finish their search area. With only a few hours of light, I'm not expecting much."

"Guess we need to eat up and head back to the office for a couple more hours."

GT shook his head. "Marcus, you are running this operation, but I have a strong suggestion. You and Kelly head on to Aunt Maude's, relax, sip some bourbon, and let your brains digest all the input from today. Maybe you'll hit upon the solution. Ditto for you, Simpson: Sally is expecting you. If the search turns up anything, I'll call."

36

AUNT MAUDE'S HOUSE, PRINCETON, WEST VIRGINIA
TUESDAY NIGHT
28 OCTOBER 1975

THEY TOUCHED HIGHBALL GLASSES AS they snuggled on the leather sofa in the basement. The small amount of bourbon took the edge off the stress of the day. Lighting was turned down, and Andy Williams was playing on the stereo. Kelly and Marcus were in their favorite place: together on a soft sofa. Any secluded sofa would do.

Kelly let a sigh escape listening to Andy's version of "Three Coins in the Fountain." She kissed his cheek and said, "After this case, Marcus, we'll need another trip to Rome to recover. I know this is only the first day, but I'm so overwhelmed."

Marcus chuckled. "Welcome to my world, Princess. That is pretty much the standard of every case I've touched. It takes a couple of days for things to start to come together. There is still a lot of information we need to put on the board. Hopefully, tomorrow's interviews will give us more."

"Yea, but this case is already several weeks old. Shouldn't there be more progress?"

Marcus chuckled. "It's been several weeks for GT. But until last week, they were separate cases, mostly unrelated save for the possible bear attacks. And no disrespect to GT—the reality is he has never faced anything this unusual."

Kelly shrugged and snuggled closer.

"We are getting him up to speed, Kelly. And tomorrow he'll help me interrogate a couple of people, and hopefully we'll learn more from them. Then we might also have some info from the teams out looking for the missing auto."

"I got ya. We're grabbing elusive straws and hoping to build something from them."

"We haven't even put in a full day yet. It will come together; it always does."

"What will come together?" Maude asked as she entered their basement sanctuary.

Marcus said, "All the parts of the Crazed Bear case, Aunt Maude. How was your bridge game?"

She dropped into the chair facing the sofa. "Whew! It was a strange night. Instead of our normal gossip about neighbors and chitchat about television shows, everyone wanted to talk about the murders. Not pleasant, if you ask me."

"Did you hear any interesting theories?" Marcus asked.

Maude laughed. "Honey, everyone had a theory. Pour me a glass of Kentucky's best numbing agent, and I'll spill all the beans."

Having fixed her drink, Marcus returned to his seat next to Kelly.

"Thanks! Well, deputies, the theories were wild. They ranged from a rabid bear all the way up to alien invasion. Two people claimed to have seen the Mothman, and Fred Sanders said a Bigfoot came through his yard this afternoon."

Pausing a moment, Marcus sat up and leaned forward, elbows resting on his knees. "I need the names of those who saw the Mothman. GT will want to interview them and Fred Sanders tomorrow."

"You can't be serious, Marcus, it was only nonsense talk over a card game."

"Oh, you bet I'm serious, Aunt Maude. Right now, everything is important. At this stage of the investigation, we take everything in and will sift out the junk later."

With a look of surrender, Maude said, "Claudia Burton and Delores Janson were the ones with the Mothman comments." Then she quickly added, "But don't tell them I mentioned their names!"

Marcus chuckled. "One of the first rules of operation for my team is that information is a one-way street. We take it in, but rarely give anything out. So your secret is safe with me, Aunt Maude. Anything else you want to add to your report?"

"My, aren't we sounding official, Deputy," Maude said with a snicker.

"Sorry. Some days it's hard for me to turn off the investigator especially when the case is so frustrating."

Maude nodded her understanding. "Your dedication is showing, Marcus. It is a good thing, and I know you'll solve those murders."

The silence that followed was finally broken by Kelly. "Aunt Maude, do you know Ruth Cole?"

Maude nodded. "It's strange she wasn't at bridge club tonight."

"How well do you know her?"

"Why? Is she all right?" Concern rapidly covered her face.

"She's okay, but I have her in the hospital tonight. She had an encounter with a strange bear this afternoon, and was a bit hysterical. So the police took her to the hospital and I was called in," Kelly quickly explained.

"Oh, my word! I've known Ruth for years. She's normally levelheaded, so for her to get hysterical about anything is a big surprise."

Marcus realized where Kelly was going. "Kelly, I like that thought you have, and maybe tomorrow afternoon will work, but Aunt Maude needs to be here tomorrow morning."

"Aunt Maude, I need you to visit with Ruth tomorrow after lunch. Will that work with your schedule?" Kelly asked.

With a snicker, Maude replied, "My time is your time, darling girl. But what do you want me to do besides hold her hand?"

"I'll see her in the morning and tell her you'll be by after lunch. Have her tell you about her experience today. Maybe she'll mention something she didn't tell me or Marcus."

"That I can do. Okay, Marcus, what have you got scheduled for me in the morning?"

"Aunt Maude, we have some company coming, and you're the welcoming committee of one."

"Company?" asked Kelly.

Nodding, Marcus shared who he expected to arrive in the morning and why. He turned to Maude. "When they get here, give me a call at the station. I'd like Rick and the doc to stay here, if that's okay."

Her face gave a strong *don't ask silly questions* look as Maude said, "Of course, honey."

"Thanks. GT is holding rooms at a motel for the SEALs ... if they show." Marcus gave a shrug of uncertainty.

Kelly winked. "You had a busy afternoon getting all that lined up. Don't worry. David will make sure Dad gets a couple of teams here. Great thinking on your part, Sailor!"

"My next great thought is I wash these empty glasses, and we all call it a night. Dawn comes early around here."

37

THE COLTS INDEPENDENTLY AND CONCURRENTLY decided that the night had been way too short. The annoying buzz of the alarm drove that point home as it pushed them out of a comfortable sleep state. They had a status meeting scheduled for 0730, so it was time to get moving.

After a good morning kiss, Marcus said, "I'll get a quick shower while you start the coffee. We have miles to go before we sleep again, Princess."

"Oh, you are so encouraging, Sailor. Thanks for the pep talk—now go get wet and I'll join you shortly." Her grin kicked up to the left in anticipation.

The pelting of hot water on the back of his neck helped relieve the headache that was starting. His head had too much scar tissue from previous assignments, and the slightest amount of stress kicked off a headache.

The hot water also helped his brain to focus on the details of the case as the noise of the water provided a mental blank slate. As if he were studying the cards on the boards, his mind flashed them behind his eyes. Still no eureka moment.

With his eyes shut tight and water filling his ears, Marcus realized he had company only when hands started rubbing his chest.

"Nice," Marcus moaned.

Kelly pulled him into a tight hug. "Yes, it is. I know we have a lot on our plates right now—seems like we always do—but we must reserve a few special moments for us."

"You're the smart one in the family, Kelly. And the more I think about it, I love your previous suggestion. When this case is over, we do need to take a vacation to Italy. I have a few places in Naples and along the Amalfi Coast I want to share with you," Marcus whispered seductively in her ear.

Before either wished, the morning ritual was over, uniforms had been donned, and the two newest Mercer County deputies were heading down to breakfast. By the aromas drifting into the foyer, Aunt Maude already had a spread laid out for them.

As they passed the door chime, it sounded an arrival.

"I'll get it, Kelly," Marcus said as he reversed course to the front door. He was surprised by the man standing outside. Decked out in typical West Virginia hunting wear, complete with a John Deere cap, stood his newest officer.

"Hope it's okay for me to be here, Commander." Rick Gardener added a shrug to his sheepish grin.

"Of course, Rick, come on in. I didn't expect you until around noon. What gives?"

"Well, sir, I got everything done at the office by 1600. After getting my truck packed, I realized it was a waste of time for me to sit around, so I drove down to Blacksburg last night and grabbed a room there. This morning's drive here was an easy one."

"You're just in time for breakfast. Follow me."

Introductions were handled over plates full of eggs, bacon, and hash browns. Aunt Maude was thrilled to have another guest and promised to show him his room right after breakfast.

With the plates emptied and removed, Marcus brought Rick up to speed on the situation. He finished, "And as soon as we get to the station, we'll get you into uniform. Congrats on your temporary duty as a deputy. Comments?"

"Only one, sir. I agree with Doctor Colt that the CNO will be sending a SEAL team. Aside from it being good training, if they find the missing children, it will be good PR for the Navy."

Marcus considered that for a moment and agreed with a nod. "By the way, this is one of those situations where military manners and formality go out the door. Skip the titles and stick with first names unless you hear me get formal with someone. Then switch to 'mister' or 'doctor' as needed. You'll pick up on the need should it arise."

Maude laughed. "My title stays—Rick, you call me 'Aunt Maude' always!"

"Okay, unless anyone has something else, time to get moving," Marcus announced, "as we have an early team meeting at the station."

Kelly stuck a finger in the air. "I had a thought … you and Rick head to the station now. I'll stay here and wait for Doctor Wentworth to arrive. Then, unless I hear differently from you, I'll take him to the hospital. After I introduce him to Bassett, I'll check on Ruth. Okay?"

With a slight head shake, Marcus said, "No, I want you at the meeting. You can come here right after, but everyone needs to be up to speed on whatever happened overnight."

"Aye, aye, sir," she responded with a quick salute as her smile kicked up to the left.

Rick chuckled. "Guess it's time to sound 'Boots and Saddles,' if I recall that bugle call name correctly."

38

HE WAS ACCUSTOMED TO ARRIVING at work early, but today Marcus got to the station right as the clock marked 0730. Kelly and Rick followed him to GT's office, nodding to Norma as they passed her desk.

"Mornin,' GT. I have our latest recruit, who is in need of a uniform and swearing in. Give a big West Virginia welcome to Lieutenant Richard Gardener, USMC. If you're nice, he might let you call him 'Rick' like the rest of our unit does," Marcus said as he leaned against the wall.

"You have my sympathies, Lieutenant, having to work with him." GT jerked a thumb towards Marcus before extending his hand to Rick. "I suspect you have been read-in to what's happening around here. Call me 'GT' and know I am extremely happy to have you here."

"Thank you, GT. I'll do my best."

GT nodded, then yelled, "Norma, get this gent decked out in a uniform, please."

Norma stuck her head in the office and quickly got Rick's sizes.

"Sorry I don't have an extra vehicle for you, Rick. The Colt's got my one spare."

Rick chuckled. "Guess their Mustang isn't the best choice for backwoods travel around here. Not a problem: I drove my 1973 Ford F-110 supercab, four-wheel-drive vehicle. It's only got the 360 V8, but I think it will do."

"Oh, yea, that'll work." Turning to the Colts, GT asked, "Shall we get things going, bossman?"

"Everyone here?"

"Waiting for you in the conference room."

The room was nearly full after they arrived. Gathered around the card and map boards were Doctors Wallace and Bassett, Detective Allen Chambers, Sergeant George Walker, and Deputy Harvey Wilson. Introductions to the newest member of the team were handled quickly, and Marcus got down to business.

"Everyone grab a chair. The goal this morning is to get everyone up to speed, which is something we will do daily. So we'll start with a quick report from everyone. George, what's the result of last night's search for the missing vehicle?"

"Struck out, sir. We didn't have much daylight, so that hampered the search. The teams are continuing this morning. I'm meeting with them at the school gym at eight o'clock."

"Okay, I've got a request in to rustle up some air support. I'll let ya know." Marcus looked at the M.E. "Dennis, we're expecting Doctor Wentworth to arrive from Norfolk any time now. I appreciate your cooperation on this. You still okay with it?"

"Not a problem, Marcus. I'm damn glad to have another set of eyes on this mess. I really am."

Marcus gave him a thumbs-up. "Thank you, Doc."

"Regarding Wentworth, Kelly will bring him to you before she checks on her patient. And speaking of that patient, or at least her report— Simpson, did you get a chance to compare that hair specimen with your standard bear collection?"

Simpson stood and cleared his throat. "Indeed, I did, Marcus. The sample that Harvey and I found does not match any bear I have seen. With your permission, I want to send a sample to the Smithsonian for their take." Simpson related the print sightings.

Marcus nodded, then looked at GT. "We're going to work in three more interviews today. Aunt Maude did some covert work at the bridge club last night. Two people, Claudia Burton and Delores Janson, claimed to have seen the Mothman recently, and Fred Sanders said a Bigfoot came through his yard yesterday afternoon. We need their reports on record."

GT rolled his eyes. "I'll have Norma let them know we'll be by later today."

A look of confusion came over Rick's face. But he held any comments or questions.

"All right, unless there's something else …"

Nothing was said, so Marcus continued, "Here's the plan for this morning. George, hang around for a moment after the meeting. Then go get the search teams underway. Happy hunting. Simpson and Harvey, head out to the first body drop site as we planned yesterday, then on to the others."

Simpson asked, "After all this time I'm not expecting to find much."

"Agreed, Doc. But you *are* a set of trained-for-bear eyes, and I want your analysis of all the body drop locations. Collect samples if there are any, shoot photos … whatever you do out there. Be meticulous. Maybe you'll spot something the deputies missed." Marcus smiled. "Think of it as one of those Hail Mary passes."

Simpson shrugged. "Okay. Wild geese chasing here we come."

"Allen, since you still have some work to do on the background checks, I need you to contact the NIS office in Charleston. SSA Chad McHenry received a request yesterday to do BIs on Ledder and Decker. He might need your help, or he might have some info that you do not. Team up with him."

Chambers smiled. "You got it, Marcus."

"And finally, orders for the cutest member of the team. Kelly, head on to the house to wait for Wentworth. Then you two go do your doctor stuff."

"And unless you have other plans for her, Marcus, I plan to release Ruth at the end of the day. Assuming she is acting rationally, that is."

Marcus chuckled. "Acting rational is in the eye of the beholder, right?"

"Of course, Sailor! And I *am* that beholder. Where will you be if I need to talk about Ruth's status?"

"I getting to that," Marcus said. "Shortly, GT, Rick, and I'll do follow-up interviews with Cal Thompkins at his home and Bob Ledder at the construction site. Right this minute, I have *not* taken them off the suspect list."

Allen Chambers shook his head. "I don't see the motive for either of them."

"Nor do I, Allen. Hence the need for another chat or two. Maybe they'll share one. Or better yet, they'll share enough information that we can safely take them off the list."

Allen and several others nodded.

Marcus continued. "And I'm hoping to get us more help with the searching. Most of us have radios in our vehicles, so keep Norma apprised if something changes and GT is out of contact. Oh, one more thing, people. As I told GT yesterday and just insinuated, right now everyone within a huge atom-bomb-blast radius is considered a suspect, so act accordingly. Thank you all!"

With the room emptied, Rick started to study the cards on the boards. Deputy Walker waited for whatever Marcus had to tell him. GT excused himself to check for messages with Norma, leaving Kelly and Marcus alone right outside the conference room.

"Stay safe. Shoot straight. I need you, Sailor."

"Always for you, Princess. And this time I get to say it to you, too."

It was hard to hide his smile as he watched Kelly walk away. Marcus returned to the conference room and picked up the phone. He dialed the number from memory.

"Good morning, Petty Officer. Commander Colt calling for Master Chief Bartow, assuming he's not tied up with Admiral Gallagher."

Seeing Rick's surprised look, Marcus covered the mouthpiece of the handset and said, "I'll explain later."

Back on the phone, Marcus said, "Yea, David, life is still good here in the Mountain State. You sound way too chipper for a Wednesday—the Boss must have the day off."

After a slight pause, Marcus got to the point. "Anyway, I hate to be in a rush, but any word on those National Guard units? Does your Rolodex have a contact I can call to get some help?"

It didn't take long for the admiral's most senior yeoman to tell him to be patient and that help was on the way. David concluded the call with a wish for good luck.

Marcus turned to George. "Head on to your meeting with the teams, but stay close to your car radio. Air cover is on the way."

39

THE THOMPKINS HOMESTEAD WAS THE first stop for the sheriff and his two newest deputies. Neither Marcus nor Rick made any comments about the place as GT pulled in behind Cal's pickup. The two-story frame house was a design frequently used by mining and lumber companies for building a number of employee houses without spending a fortune on design or materials. It had been a "company house." While cookie-cutter, the structure was well maintained, as was the yard. Cal's fishing boat looked showroom fresh. The man wasn't a slacker when it came to maintenance around the house.

"Can we make this quick, Sheriff? I need to get to work," Cal yelled from the porch.

GT's frown became deeper. "The amount of your cooperation will determine the speed, Mr. Thompkins. Can we go inside?"

"Yea. Guess you want coffee and donuts also." His sarcastic reply resulted in negative expressions on the three men in uniform. Cal realized he had overstepped. "Sorry, Sheriff, guess all the stress of this mess is getting to me. Sure, let's talk inside."

Marcus noted the inside of the house was as neat as the outside. He also noticed how interesting it was that a husband and father, distraught over his missing children and murdered wife, would be such a good housekeeper. After all, it had been several weeks since his family vanished, and nothing was out of place.

"Cal, we have a few more questions to ask. And talking with you will help my two new deputies get up to speed faster. That okay?"

Cal nodded. "Sure, Sheriff, anything to help find my kids."

GT pointed to Marcus. "Deputy Colt is an experienced investigator used to dealing with unusual cases from Washington. He'll be asking the questions."

Again, Cal nodded.

Marcus let a slight smile cross his face before it became serious. "Mr. Thompkins, we are all sorry for your loss. And everything possible is being done to locate your children."

"When can I bury my wife, Deputy?"

"Soon, sir. This has been a difficult and unusual case for the sheriff, and in addition, to us." Marcus pointed to Rick Gardener. "We are bringing in, today, a medical examiner from out of town. When dealing with issues such as this, getting more input helps to solve the case. After his analysis, she should be released to you. Do you need any help making arrangements?"

Cal shook his head.

"Okay, Mr. Thompkins, please take me through the days before your family went missing."

It was a quick remembrance. Cal detailed the events of the day before, his night at work, and the scene that he found returning home that morning. It jibed with the report GT had shared.

"Thank you. Now Mr. Thompkins, I've got some tough questions, but they need to be asked. Were you and your wife having any difficulties? Any arguments or bad feelings?"

"Only the normal money issues, and her always wanting to spend Christmas with her family in Michigan. You know … typical stuff that families go through, Deputy. We loved each other."

Cal got emotional on that last statement and his eyes started to water. Marcus lowered his voice and asked, "Do you or your wife have any drinking or drug problems?"

Cal shook his head. "We have a beer or two at night, but don't get drunk. No drugs."

"Were either of you having an affair?"

"Hell, no!" Cal barked.

Rick Gardener looked like he wanted to say something, so Marcus nodded in his direction.

Rick cleared his throat. "Sir, how much life insurance do you have on your wife and children?"

With noticeable tension, Cal jumped up, nearly yelling, "What the hell? Do you think I killed my wife for money?"

Rick held up both hands in a defensive position but kept his voice stern. "Not at all, sir, but when we catch the guilty parties and go to trial, information like that will be used by the defense attorney to throw doubt at the jury. We need to know all this stuff up front so we can be ready for them."

GT placed his hands on Cal's shoulders and gently pushed him back into the chair. "Sir, you need to keep cool. We are all here to help you through this. Just answer the questions."

They talked for nearly twenty more minutes before Marcus thanked Cal for his time, promising to keep him up to date on progress. Cal looked relieved as the three officers left his property.

As GT pulled his car onto the two-lane, he asked, "So, what ya think?"

Marcus took a deep breath and blew it out. "As far as I'm concerned, Cal is a bit further from the list of possible suspects, but not totally removed. Good push on that insurance thing, Rick. It was good to watch him under stress."

GT's face took on a look of confusion. "Why not removed from the suspect list, Marcus? He seemed clean to me."

"Just a feeling he is holding something back. Hiding something. Might have something to do with the Mothman he thinks he saw. Or something else. Not sure what, but maybe something will pop from the BI Allen is running. Then we can make a second visit and bring up the Mothman."

It was Rick's turn to look confused. "He saw the Mothman? What's this creature's history?"

Marcus chuckled. "Best to have a glass of bourbon in your hand when we get into more details about that later tonight."

"That's a fact," GT said, leaving Rick more confused as he changed the subject. "Feelings don't hold up in court, Marcus, no matter how many medals you have."

He was quiet for a moment, ignoring the jab. Then Marcus asked, "But seriously, GT, he didn't seem too concerned about the missing children. Think he has decided they're already dead and come to terms with that?

Or could he have killed all three? What are your father genes telling you? How would you be acting if your kids were missing for a month?"

His face took on a nauseous look. GT swallowed hard and said, "I'd be out searching every day and not going to work. That's for damn sure. But in his defense, for most of that time, he believed, as we and the FBI did, that the wife and children were in Michigan or somewhere out that way."

"Yet the FBI couldn't reach her through her mother. So how much has he worried about the kids since hearing they never left the area? When we get back to the office, call his boss and find out how much time he's taken off since you told him about finding his wife's body. When was that … on the twenty-first?"

GT nodded. "Yea, nine days ago."

Following another deep sigh, Marcus muttered, "If I was a dad, I'd be searching 24/7." He rubbed his forehead as the caffeine-shortage head-ache grew. "Do we have time for coffee before meeting Ledder?"

With a slight smile, GT said, "We pass by Pansy's on the way, boss."

40

Sergeant George Walker rubbed his eyes as he grimaced. The gesture did not relieve the pain throbbing in his head, but at least he was doing something. The volunteer turnout had been larger than expected, and George silently and sincerely thanked God. The teams were already out the door, heading to their assigned areas.

Some of the volunteers didn't like their assignments and were vocal about it. But their complaints fell on deaf ears. At least the weather was cooperating today: bright sun, no clouds, and temps in the sixties. It was a good day for what could be a sad task.

The teams left to cover pretty much the same area they had the previous evening. Hopefully, in the light of day, at least the car would be found. George was praying the children would be found alive, but deep down, he knew that was a long shot. An extremely long shot. Too much time had passed and the weather was not their friend; it had snowed last week with temperatures well below freezing for a couple of days.

George was gathering up his paperwork when the door of the gym closed with an echoing bang. Boots marched across the basketball court sounding like gunshots. A deep bass voice sprang from the tall soldier wearing the silver oak leaves of a LT colonel. "Sergeant Walker?"

Walker looked up. "That's me. How can I help you, Colonel?"

A smile spread across the solemn face. "Actually, sir, I'm here to help you. I have eleven UH-1s and crews from the West Virginia National Guard standing by in Bridgeport ready to start an air search. Give me the search area parameters and we'll get started." He looked at the map pinned to the portable board. "Point out the most difficult terrain areas, and I'll have Hueys over them in an hour."

George couldn't hide his surprise. "I'm damn glad to have the help, but how did you get it together so fast. I thought we were still waiting for approval for air support."

Colonel Sam Wesson again smiled. "Actually, the request originated in the Chief of Naval Operations' office yesterday. Guess when Colt called and asked the admiral's yeoman about some SEAL help, he thought some air cover would be nice also."

Wesson had met Master Chief David Bartow years ago while still on active duty and considered him a trusted friend. Even if he was a swab jockey! Wesson considered a request from Bartow as an engraved-in-stone order right down from the mountaintop.

"Okay. Here are the areas you need to search," George said as he approached the map. "No ground vehicle access and searching on foot is a true bitch."

Wesson took notes for fifteen minutes as George indicated the areas and described the challenges of each. "Okay, Sergeant, I got it. That's a lot of territory, but we can handle it. You staying here until the ground troops return?"

"No, sir. I was packing up to go back to the station when you arrived. Care to join me?"

"That'll work. Wait until I radio this data to my crews so they can get in gear. How good's your coffee? It's going to be a long day."

41

"**AND THAT'S WHERE WE ARE** this morning. Marcus and GT are interviewing the dead woman's husband, and the friend of the man found at the construction site." Kelly sipped more of the second cup she was sharing with Maude. "And I'm here awaiting the arrival of the Norfolk M.E. before visiting my patient at the hospital."

Aunt Maude reached for another piece of leftover bacon. Between bites, she asked, "Do you think Marcus will solve this case?"

"He always does," Kelly said with a soft smile. "I'm just glad I'm here and involved. Maybe I can keep him out of a hospital bed. He has a tendency to get more scar tissue on these weird assignments."

The melodic chimes of the doorbell interrupted Maude's next question about Marcus's past injuries. Kelly motioned for her to stay seated and headed to the door. "Probably the M.E."

With the front door opened to greet the expected doctor, Kelly was surprised to see an older gent in a tweed jacket and herringbone Deerstalker hat: the preferred attire of the famous detective Sherlock Holmes. Her shock was increased by the large assortment of men in hunting attire that stood around him.

"I had planned to start off by saying, 'Doctor Colt, I presume' but I was warned by your father that your mood might not appreciate my attempt at humor. Suffice it to say, Doctor Wentworth and two SEAL teams at your service, madam."

Regaining her voice, Kelly extended her hand, and with a laugh said, "Dad will never admit it, but he's occasionally wrong: that touch of humor falls into the 'really needed' category. Welcome, gentlemen, please come in."

The first man to follow Doctor Wentworth in wasn't the tallest of the group or the one with the most muscle, but his handshake was firm as he announced, "Lieutenant Commander Barry Jackson, ma'am. I was ordered by the CNO to report to a Deputy Colt, but he failed to give a location beyond this town. We were on the same flight as the doctor, and he knew to come here to find a Doctor Colt, so we tagged along. Based upon your uniform, I suspect you're that deputy."

"No, I'm not … exactly. I'm a deputy and also the doctor. But after a quick update meeting, I'll take you to him. Or at least where he will be sometime in the near future," Kelly said. "He's my husband, Marcus."

"Skipper?" Boatswain Mate First Class Kevin Brown called to Jackson from the back of the group.

"Yea, Boats?"

"It just hit me. Doctor Colt is married to one of us: Commander Marcus Colt," Brown said as he glanced at Kelly. "Sorry I didn't recognize you right off, Kelly, but the sheriff's uniform, this location, and lack of sleep threw me off."

Kelly looked hard at the speaker and laughed. "And you're in a good disguise too with that facial hair, Kevin. It's good to see you again." A second glance at the men brought another familiar face into view. "Larry, you look as scruffy as Kevin, but I'm glad you're here!"

She turned to Jackson and continued, "Kevin and Larry were with Marcus in 'Nam in '70 and then helped him with a NIS case in Norfolk in '71."

Aunt Maude stuck her head around the corner and said, "Come on, boys. I got a pot of coffee hot and more's brewing. I think the dining room will be big enough for your quick meeting. Anyone need food?"

Chrome chairs with vinyl seats were pulled from the kitchen table, and folding chairs from the closet, providing enough seats in the dining room. Verbal chaos filled the room as introductions were done all around. As everyone settled down with a fresh cup of coffee, Kelly stood and got started.

"Okay, this will be quick. The doctor and I are needed at the hospital. On the way, I'll lead the rest of you to the sheriff's office where Marcus will be soon, or at least be reachable via radio. Have you SEALs been briefed on the situation here?"

Jackson stood. "Vaguely. I understand two small children are missing, and Deputy, ah, Commander Colt has the power to suggest we do some field training here that might prove helpful in a search."

Kelly took and exhaled a deep breath. "Yea, that's pretty vague. The children and their mother left the area, we assume willingly, about a month ago. The case was passed to the FBI, thinking after a family argument they were heading to the mom's parents' home in Michigan. The concern was the mother might be kidnapping the children. None of the three were heard from again until eight days ago, when the mother's body showed up here in extremely unusual circumstances."

"What all has been done to find the kids?" one of the SEALs asked.

Again, Kelly's face showed her frustration. "Not enough and not fast enough. One of the deputies put together search teams made up of hunters, scouts, et cetera, who drove around looking for the car yesterday afternoon and evening. Nothing. Today, they are back out doing walking searches for the children and the car. Marcus feels the car might hold evidence that will help with the case."

Jackson held up his hands in frustration. "Why the damn delay? Sorry, ma'am, for the profanity, but why not start when the mom's body was found?"

"Not a problem—I've used that word about this situation also. Small town, small law enforcement footprint, Barry. And their limited resources were overloaded. There were two bodies found in unusual circumstances that same day, and the local M.E. already had a similar one in his cooler. Then Marcus and I showed up for his parents' memorial service shortly thereafter, which turned into a bigger social event than we expected, disrupted most of the town this past weekend, and put a further strain on the local law enforcement. And finally, a fourth body appeared this past Monday. While the sheriff and his team are good people, saying they are overwhelmed in this situation is an understatement. That's why Marcus and I were ordered to help out."

"Okay, I get it. But what are the unusual circumstances you keep mentioning?"

"That's why we brought in another M.E. All the bodies have been eviscerated, and it was made to look like the work of a bear. Not pretty."

A few more soft utterances of profanity punctuated the silence that followed Kelly's explanation.

She continued, "Marcus will give you more details and cover the housing issues. Doctor Wentworth, bring your bags in; we have your room upstairs. Finish up your coffee, gents, and then it's time to sound 'Boots and Saddles,' as Marcus always says."

42

SHE ALWAYS HAS A KNOWING *smile like she's reading minds*, Marcus thought as he waved to Pansy. She nodded to three stools at the end of the counter. Hanging up the phone, she picked up a coffee carafe. Marcus noted a few faces he had not seen in previous visits. He logged them into memory.

Three steaming mugs of coffee were quickly placed in front of the men in uniform.

"Good morning, gentlemen," she said as she extended her hand to Rick. "I'm Pansy. And who might you be, handsome?"

Marcus mentally chuckled at Pansy's standard greeting for a strange man. He wondered what she used for ladies.

"Rick Gardener, ma'am. I work with Marcus in D.C." Rick took her hand.

Pansy nodded and looked at Marcus. "Drink fast, deputies. That was Kelly on the phone looking for you. She guessed right that you might show up. You're needed at the office, but it is not an emergency."

"Okay, at least we have time for this cup. Thanks, Pansy," Marcus replied.

Pansy smiled big as Marcus took a sip and gave her a thumbs-up.

"A little bird told me both cardamom and cinnamon, and a dash of sea salt, were necessary additives to keep a special deputy happy. I'll keep a carafe handy for you."

"Keep this up and I'll have you working for me in D.C. Thanks again."

She winked and walked away to take care of other customers.

GT asked, "Looks like the next stop is the office. Any clue as to why?"

Marcus shrugged. "Could be a problem with getting the M.E. out of Norfolk. No clue, really."

"Better not be another body; we have enough on our plates right now. And I hope it's something we can handle quickly. We need to be at the construction site in about an hour."

They sipped their coffee silently for a few minutes, lost in thought. Marcus used the moments to scan the crowd. It was part of his routine when in a public environment. His habit might have paid off—a customer seemed more interested in the three deputies than his plate.

He nudged GT's arm and quietly said, "Don't be too obvious, but do you know the Hispanic guy at your eight o'clock? Plaid shirt, red ball cap, sitting alone. He seems to be more interested in us than anyone else in here."

GT was a professional. He didn't immediately spin around. But after a couple of minutes he excused himself and headed to the men's room. It so happened that allowed him to walk past the table of interest.

Being the sheriff, GT had to stop and talk to people on the short trip to the rear of the building; he knew most everyone in the county. He nodded at the Hispanic gent, a man he recognized but whose name was slow coming to the front of his mind. But it did: Carl Marks. Carl gave an abbreviated smile in return before taking another bite of his food, as he'd developed greater interest in his plate.

Upon his return, GT didn't sit down as he drained his cup. He dropped a couple of bucks on the counter and gestured toward the door. As they got into the car, GT filled them in. "That's Carlos Marcano. He prefers to go by Carl Marks—anglicized version fits better into the local environment. His family has owned a place outside of town for years. Used to be a decent vegetable farm, but the last few seasons haven't been so good for him. Older brother died a few years back. He didn't even plant a crop last year, and the house needs repair. No known family and few friends."

Marcus puckered his lips in thought. "Any guess why he would be so interested in us?"

"Carl's a bit skittish around law enforcement. City police picked him up for drug possession about a year ago. He served couple of months in the city jail and just finished the community service part of his sentence."

Rick asked, "Since he's not farming, what does he do for a living?"

GT had a quizzical look as he dug into his memory for the answer. He was silent for more than a moment as he drove to the office. Finally, he said, "He does a bit of this or that. Mostly light auto mechanic work. Off the books stuff mostly. I hear his tune-ups are nice."

"Any chance he's returned to the drug business?" Marcus asked. "Is that what you were thinking during that long pause?"

"Don't know," GT said. "But it is possible. I'll check with the police chief and ask him to keep an eye on him."

"Maybe you should have asked him if he knew Jesus Cabilla," Marcus said.

43

THE DRIVE TO THE SHERIFF'S office was a short one. Pansy's was easy walking distance from the office. As they came in the back door from the parking lot, Marcus was happy to see a crowd in the conference room that included some familiar faces.

Kevin Brown stood quickly when he saw Marcus and popped to attention. The others, through a combination of Pavlovian training and high respect for Commander Colt, started to follow his lead. He was about to yell *attention on deck*, but Marcus spoke first.

"As you were, men. Boats, you're a sight for sore eyes. You too, Larry Hanes. I heard you made chief—congrats! And I'm damn glad to see the rest of you gentlemen." Marcus and the old friends and warriors with shared history briefly embraced.

"Mr. Colt, glad we could be here to help. Kelly gave us a quick overview and said you'd fill in the details," Petty Officer Brown said. "She took Doctor Wentworth to the hospital."

Marcus nodded. "Okay, let's get to it as we have a full plate today. Who's in charge of this motley crew?" he asked with a chuckle.

"That would be me, sir. Lieutenant Commander Barry Jackson."

Marcus quickly got the introductions out of the way, and they settled in for an update. Most of the SEALs took positions leaning against the walls.

Pointing to GT, Marcus said, "Okay, Sheriff Timmons is the ultimate authority in the county for this operation. He has placed me in charge of the cases, which include four murders made to look like bear attacks and two missing children. I need you to focus your efforts on finding the children, or at least finding their missing vehicle. Allen has an info sheet with photos and the car's description."

"Show us where to start, sir, and we'll get it done," Barry said. "And as for the bears, what problems can we expect?"

GT said, "The state's black bear population is somewhere around five hundred, and they can be found in every county. At this time of year, the females, or sows, are usually heading to hibernation, and the males, called boars, are still foraging for food before they settle down later next month. So the probability of confrontation is lower than summer."

"Good to know, Sheriff," Barry said.

The conference room door opened; Deputy Walker and an Army officer interrupted. "I can provide you with starting points if ya give me a minute to hang this dang map," Walker interjected. "Marcus, say 'hello' to Lieutenant Colonel Sam Wesson, who has eleven Guard Hueys in route to search the areas I've noted on my map."

The meeting immediately degenerated into noise and confusion for a moment as George hung the map. Several SEALs clustered around it, and Wesson tried to introduce himself to GT and Marcus. After no more than thirty seconds, Allen let out a shrill whistle and yelled, "Enough, people! Let Marcus finish the briefing!"

"Thanks, Allen. Colonel, we're glad to have you and your assets with us. Before we send the SEALs out to the field, and Colonel, you will need to relate this to your teams, we have one other complication."

"Call me 'Sam' please," Wesson interrupted.

Marcus nodded and continued, "Gentlemen, there is a lot of doubt surrounding what I'm about to tell you. Frankly, I'm vacillating somewhere between 'might be true' and 'ain't no freaking way' but it needs to be a consideration. In addition to what might be a rogue bear, we have two Bigfoot sightings, and at least one gent seeing the Mothman."

Silence overpowered the room as the men accustomed to fighting armed enemy humans heard what many consider fantasy. A couple of snickers came forth as the men looked at each other, weighing their associates' responses. Sam let out a sigh.

"Yea, that's my immediate reaction also. I'll ask GT to give you the details we know for now."

GT provided a concise overview of the creatures, the sightings, and all speculations. He hid his personal doubts and provided "just the facts," as Joe Friday required in the TV show *Dragnet*. The more info given, the more the faces of the SEALs changed into serious consideration. Barry was the first to comment after GT finished.

"So what are our rules of engagement if we spot either of these two things? Assuming they exist, that is."

Marcus fielded the question. "SOP, Barry. Defend yourself, if attacked. Otherwise, take no offensive actions. Under the assumption that they do exist, they have been in these woods for many years, so they know how and where to hide. And since we have little proof of their existence, they must hide very well. Furthermore, to date, we do not have any proof of either being a threat to persons or property. So keep your fingers off the triggers, and your cameras handy. Photo proof would be great to have."

"Aye, aye, sir," was Barry's only response.

Marcus pointed to George Walker. "You have the floor. Show us where the Hueys will be searching and where you want the SEALs."

Ten minutes later, the SEALs were on their way to their search areas. George and Sam had found five areas where searching would be difficult for the amateur teams and nearly impossible for the Hueys. The SEALs had tactical radios that could contact the Hueys, if needed. Plans were being executed.

"What now, Marcus?" GT asked.

"We have another interview to conduct, right?"

"Yea, time to visit with Bob Ledder. Just you and me or all of us?"

Marcus shook his head and pointed toward Rick. "We three head out for the chat. Sam stays here with George to coordinate air cover and keep in contact with the search teams."

"Do you think there's a chance of finding the children alive?" Sam asked.

Marcus shrugged. "There's always a chance. I keep praying."

"Ditto," Sam said. "Just so you know, my guys will be in search mode for about two more hours before needing refueling. I'll stagger the refueling so we have some air coverage at all times. There will be enough daylight for two sorties. That will give them each about five hours over their grids. Bad news is the weather for tomorrow will probably not allow us to participate."

A grimace showed Marcus's feelings. "I've been so focused on today I have not looked at the weather for the next few days. What's coming?"

"Thunderstorms on the leading edge of a cold front. They should be here by morning tomorrow, maybe sooner, then heavy rain and high wind rest of the day. Temps dropping down to below thirty degrees over-night. If it clears, and you still need us, we'll be ready. We can do a couple of hours in the morning if the storm slows from its current speed. But I don't believe we can do anything in the afternoon or evening. Hell, it might even turn to snow as the sun starts to set."

"All the luck we've had so far has been bad, so why break the trend?" GT added.

44

BY THE TIME KELLY HAD left the SEALs at the sheriff's office and driven Doctor Wentworth to the hospital, titles had given way to first names and they were chatting like long-lost friends. Comparing notes about mutual acquaintances in the Norfolk area solidified their new friendship.

The chief of staff, Dr. Macon, had been notified of the visiting specialist, and was waiting with Dennis Bassett in the morgue when they arrived. Always on top of who would be in his domain, Macon had done some quick research via phone calls to associates in the Tidewater area of Virginia. He quickly discovered that Dr. Sidney Wentworth had been the medical examiner on the Navy base for many years. He was well respected in both the medical and legal community for his expertise and ability to find things others missed.

As they were shaking hands, Macon quickly wondered if Wentworth having the air of a detective from old movies might have something to do with the respect he received. Pleasantries were exchanged and the doctors got to work. Reports were laid out on the counter. Bodies were pulled from the refrigerated lockers. Macon left to handle other hospital issues, and Kelly excused herself to check on Ruth.

The room was quiet and Ruth was sitting up, finishing a breakfast tray. Kelly had ordered her arm restraints and IV removed the previous night. She looked more rested than she had the day before.

"Good morning, Ruth. How's the food?" Kelly asked.

"Oh, hello Doctor. Not bad considering the comments you always hear about hospital food. Except for the lime Jell-O they gave me last night. Whoever invented that slop should have their neck wrung! Can I go home now? I've cleaned my plate." Ruth had a twinkle in her eye at her joke.

Kelly put on her best smile and chuckled. "Later today should work. You know, you were so wild yesterday that it scared the police officer that stopped you. That's why he brought you here. Honestly, he thought you were more than a bit nuts—his words and not my professional analysis. So it's my job to make sure you're calm and rational before we let you go home."

"Do you think I'm nuts because of what I saw?"

Kelly shook her head slowly. "No. But I do think you were greatly upset, somewhat bewildered by it, and that can make the sanest person behave like a nut ... at least in the eyes of someone who has not seen what you saw. And being upset can make you see things differently. Not like you normally would. But bottom line, I don't think you're nuts."

Ruth sarcastically snapped. "Well, thanks for that!"

"You have a wonderful sense of humor, Ruth. How about you tell me again what all happened to you yesterday. Start from when you left Sandlick, okay?"

It took Ruth about twenty minutes to go through the ordeal again. She was slower this time as Kelly injected questions to get more clarification. Kelly again documented the entire report. Looking back at the previous day's notes, she saw only one variation: today Ruth said the bear frowned at her when she hit the brakes. *Bears snarl, but do they frown?* she wondered.

They chatted more about the incident, then she spent nearly an hour listening to Ruth talk about her life in Princeton and gossip about the people she knew. It allowed Kelly to observe her more, and reinforced her belief that Ruth was ready to be released.

"Ruth, I've got to run to check on another patient right now. I'll be back later today to get you out of here. Good news is you can look forward to a visitor after lunch. Be on your best behavior, okay?" Kelly's nose scrunched up as she said the last part.

"Who's coming?"

"Maude Eadden said you were missed at bridge last night. She'll be by to chat and make sure I'm taking real good care of you."

Walking toward the elevator, Kelly ran Ruth's comments around in her mind. The lady truly believed what she saw. And the consistency of her statements added validity. But psychotic behavior is like mercury: hard to hold on to. A psychosis can result from major stress, but considering Ruth's health and mental state, it didn't seem likely that the bear event was a major stressor. *No*, Kelly thought, *she was not separated from reality.*

As the elevator door opened to the basement, Kelly was still mulling Ruth's comments. Concluding that Bigfoot did exist, and that one was living happily in West Virginia, was still hard to accept. Nope, it had to be a big bear. Ruth saw it on its hind legs and that scared her. Period. Nothing more. No doubt about it.

The closed door to the morgue blocked out most of the words, but Kelly heard enough to know a heated discussion was going on inside the place. "Oh, boy," she muttered as she pushed open the door.

"Nope, it had to be a wrench. Look at the x-ray again, Dennis. It's clearly the lower jaw of a pipe wrench!"

"Come on, Sid. Any rounded object would cause fracture lines like we see here," Dennis responded.

Putting on her best smile, Kelly asked, "What's up, guys?"

Doctor Wentworth returned her smile. "Oh, hi Kelly. Only a friendly disagreement between new friends and colleagues. Nothing serious."

Giving her a thumbs-up sign and a nod, Doctor Bassett agreed. "Trying to narrow down the weapon that took out Jesus Cabilla. So far, we know it was right at three-eighths of an inch wide, round on the bottom at least, and had a rounded end. It could be a fireplace poker or a length of pipe."

Sid shook his head rapidly and gestured frustration with his hands. "No. No. No! Pokers have slightly pointed ends. And pipes are cut off square. It has to be a pipe wrench. Second justification for a pipe wrench is, the mass of a decent wrench would help create that amount of trauma."

As Dennis started to respond, Kelly moved between them and placed a hand on each chest. "Enough! Put each of your suggestions in the report to Marcus. Include justifications for both, please. Now, what else have you found, Sid? Anything new?"

Sid paused, looked at Dennis, then said, "Mercer County should be proud of their wonderful medical examiner. Dennis did an intense and accurate postmortem on each body."

"Therefore, nothing new?"

"I didn't say that, Kelly. We spent some time on the COD for number four. You heard part of the discussion. I didn't find anything Dennis had missed. But we need to look deeper into the wounds on the shoulders of the last three. Those two puncture wounds intrigue me."

Dennis jumped in. "We need to take a sample from those areas, freeze them so we can slice thin cross sections, and do a microscopic examination to see what we can see. It will take a few hours."

Sid nodded. "And I want to check for foreign substances in those small wounds. Perhaps your sheriff can put some pressure on the lab to get us faster results. Dennis said it usually takes a couple of days."

Kelly was lost in contemplation for a moment before she asked Dennis, "Where is the nearest FBI lab?"

"Closest one is in Richmond, Virginia, then Cincinnati."

Again she was silent for a moment. "Get your samples ready for analysis, and I'll get back to you about where they need to go. Okay?"

Both M.E.s nodded and Dennis said, "Of course. Right away."

"Is there anything else you gentlemen are going to look into? Marcus will want to know when I see him shortly."

45

HE USUALLY WORKED HARD TO avoid jumping to conclusions, but this morning Marcus was ready to hang Bob Ledder for all of the murders and any other crime he could find lying around. The man was being difficult; no, that wasn't quite true. He was a solid stone wall. An arrogant, frustrating stone wall.

The four were sitting around the small meeting table in the comfort of the construction trailer. The supervisor had made a pot of coffee, then excused himself to take care of issues outside. Bob was smoking one cigarette after another as he ignored the questions or gave some weak answer. GT was fifteen minutes into a 'no comment' interview with Ledder.

"You realize that refusing to answer our questions makes you look guilty," GT offered.

"Guilty of what?" Ledder asked.

"Murder of your friend, Joe, would be a good start."

Ledder scoffed. "You people sit on your hands for a week then order me to show up here. You stroll in with two new guys and accuse me of killing my buddy. I told your deputy everything I know last week. Nothing to add, and I don't have to talk to you."

Marcus held up his hand to stop GT from responding. "Mr. Ledder, you're a lieutenant in the Navy Reserves, correct?"

"Yea, so what?"

"Then I assume you understand a direct order, and the consequences of not following one," Marcus said.

"Yea, but that only applies when I'm on duty during a drill weekend or my two weeks training in the summer." His smirk increased GT's stress.

Marcus smiled at Ledder and mildly added, "I'm just a reserve deputy. My full-time job is that of a Commander assigned to the Naval Investigative Service. I strongly suggest you answer any and all questions put to you by the sheriff."

"Suggest all you want. This ain't a drill weekend, and I don't need to follow your orders."

With a chuckle, Marcus walked to the construction boss's desk and picked up the phone. He dialed a string of numbers and said, "Good morning, Master Chief Bartow. Commander Colt calling. Is the CNO available?"

David chuckled. "Why do I think you're in a situation where formality is required? FYI, the boss is at the White House. What can I do to help, Marcus?"

"Master Chief, you are on top of things as always. Pass to the CNO that in conjunction with the investigation the Secretary assigned to me, I need a reserve officer, who happens to be a murder suspect, recalled to active duty immediately—for a period of no less than ninety days. He's a reserve lieutenant who drills with the Construction Battalion Unit 207 assigned to Little Creek. Have him assigned to me here in Princeton." Marcus pulled out his notepad and provided David with Ledder's full name and social security number.

"Anything else, Marcus?" David asked.

"No, Master Chief, that will be all. If you can get that done today, that would be greatly appreciated. Send the recall notice via telegram to Ledder, using the Princeton sheriff's office address. He'll be locked up there within the hour. Thank you for your help, Master Chief, and pass my warmest regards on to Admiral Gallagher. Good day."

As he hung up the phone, Marcus displayed the grin of a shark, which he'd learned from previous commanding officers. It was rather intimidating.

Ledder looked ill as he yelled, "You can't do that!"

"Yea, I can, and I did. GT, cuff him. For now, we can hold him twenty-four hours for suspicion of obstruction of justice under West Virginia criminal code, and when the telegram arrives, I'll change that to an Article 131b obstruction charge from the UCMJ."

Grabbing the trashcan from beside the table, Bob Ledder vomited his entire stomach contents. Most went into the can; some splattered on his work boots. GT quickly applied the cuffs. Following GT's hand signals, Rick led Bob, his head hanging, to the backseat of the sheriff's car.

With GT and Marcus now alone in the office, Marcus shared his plan. "I don't think we can make the obstruction charge stick for long, but based upon his reaction, it might make him more talkative when we get him to an interrogation room. Thoughts?"

"I think you put the fear of God into the ol' boy. Or at least the fear of Marcus Colt. Agreed, he'll probably open up back at the office. Or maybe on the way. Let's roll."

46

DETECTIVE ALLEN CHAMBERS WAS ON the phone when Bob Ledder was led into the office. If he was surprised to see Ledder in cuffs, he held it back with his stoic expression. It was just another day in paradise as far as he was concerned. Good guys go bad overnight. The sun rises and sets. Same ol' stuff. He returned his attention to what SSA Chad McHenry from NISRA Charleston was telling him.

The portable radios that had been moved to the conference room were manned by Sergeant George Walker. Colonel Sam Wesson was at Pansy's for a quick lunch. Deputy Josh Bonner was manning the phones and watching the front door, since Norma had accepted Sam's invite to join him. Aside from the few comments that Allen spoke into the phone, the office was quiet.

"Josh, take Mr. Ledder to interrogation room one, please. Keep him company there," Marcus ordered.

"Anything new?" GT asked as he strolled into the conference room, getting George's attention.

"No, sorry. Quiet so far. Pilots are staggering their refueling now so there will always be a couple of choppers in the air. Sam ran out for a quick lunch 'bout ten minutes ago."

Rick and Marcus dropped into chairs before the map board when Allen slid a piece of paper toward Marcus. "Here's the first part of the BI on Ledder. Interesting stuff." He left without any further comments.

Sliding it over the Rick without a glance, Marcus said, "Give me your comments, Special Agent-slash-Deputy Gardener. No rush, but remember lunch is calling."

Rick didn't need much time to analyze the BI report. "I have no idea how much construction workers make, but those are some mighty big numbers in both his bank account and investment account. Sorry, make that investment accounts—there are several."

"Did Chad put down a total net worth?"

"Yes, sir. Right at $550,000 and change. No history of inherited family wealth or records of big gains from a lawsuit settlement."

GT started to say something, but Marcus held up his hand. "And what does that suggest to you, Mr. Gardener?"

"Damn lucky or damn dirty, with dirty being the greater probability, sir."

Nodding, Marcus stood up and said, "GT, why don't you and Rick handle the interview. Good ol' Bob didn't seem to like me too much after my phone call to D.C. Perhaps he has a reasonable explanation for having so much money. Since it wasn't hidden very well, I wager that it is legit. Find out the names of his accountant and broker. I might need his broker's services one day." He finished the last with a chuckle.

"Any suggestions on how to go at him if he hesitates?" Rick asked.

Marcus shrugged. "You might consider dropping your special agent title into the conversation if it starts to drag. Keep your rank private, but with him knowing two NIS agents are on his ass, that might help. Excuse me while I find more coffee."

Marcus made a mental note to quietly improve the coffee as he poured a cup of what he was beginning to think of as "Double S," a.k.a. Sheriff's Sludge. He kept that comment to himself, of course. The essence of the roasted beans started to do their magic on Marcus's brain on the stroll into the conference room. He ran down the lines of index cards again. Then he wrote a few more to add to Joseph Decker's short list.

As for Bob Ledder, unless the rest of the background work or a confession to Rick showed some form of ill-gotten gains, Marcus was starting to believe Ledder's bankroll was a combination of frugal lifestyle and luck with investments. While it had only been two days ago—it felt like a month—the attorney showed him that his father had been lucky with his investments too. Maybe good ol' Bob used the same broker as his dad. At least the recall to active duty might dampen the fires of disrespect, leading to better answers.

Again he scanned the row of cards for Doris Thompkins. The old real estate slogan "location, location, location" popped into his mind. *Why the hell was that body dumped inside a locked building? And how?*

Obviously someone or something, if you believed the Mothman theory, wanted the body found. Unlike the other bodies, that location ensured it would be found quickly. Did that indicate the dumper was pointing to someone in that building as the murderer? Did he have a beef against the railroad? Again, Marcus had many more questions and too few answers.

And where the hell has Doris been for the last month? Marcus glanced at her row of cards; she left on 26 September and her body showed up on 21 October. Did she have friends in the area that would hide her and the children? A boyfriend?

Marcus remembered he had not asked for a full BI on Doris. With her husband alive and in the area, he expected to get all the info he needed directly from Cal. Wrong assumption. He jumped up to find Allen and get the BI ball rolling on Doris.

Allen agreed with his logic and started to pull the information together. He scribbled some notes before looking at Marcus. "One problem is she ain't a local. Her folks live in Michigan, Marcus."

"Start with her parents, Allen. Ask if she mentioned any close friends here. I'll try to call Cal and ask him."

Reaching Cal was a dead-end street. No answer at home and a call to the mine ended in frustration. According to the three people Marcus reached, Cal was there, but not where anyone could find him. They all agreed to give him the message to call when they saw him.

Allen had better luck. "Marcus, her mom said Doris was always talking about Anita Colbeck. I know her from church. Tried to reach her at work, but she's out to lunch. Left a message."

"Good. Keep plugging on the BI. Anything else from Chad?"

Shaking his head, Allen said, "Nada. Said he'd call soon as he had more. He has three agents digging."

The crackle of life from the radio in the conference room grabbed their attention.

47

"I'M NOT SURE HOW MUCH we can snoop around the chief of detectives without him catching on, Wendy," SSA Todd Burke muttered as he reread the skimpy ROI they had prepared for Marcus. Not much about Jesus Cabilla had yet been found, but the feeling Wendy got from Chief Montgomery was concerning.

She knew he was right. But she felt she was, also. Montgomery was hiding something, and perhaps it was something related to Cabilla. The link was well hidden; the file he had given her contained a smattering of minor arrests: a couple of shoplifting charges and one DUI. If Cabilla was into anything else, Montgomery had kept it out of the file. At least the file contained the names of two other individuals, known associates of Cabilla, and Burke was already checking into them.

"We send Marcus what we got so far," Wendy said, "and quietly dig into Montgomery. Maybe that digging will uncover more about Cabilla." She shrugged. "The only easy day was yesterday."

Todd nodded. "Okay, fine. And you know we cannot keep up surveillance on the hospital much longer. Something has to turn up or we need to shut it down. Other cases are getting behind."

"Understand. However, tonight is the fifth night since the last delivery. My gut says tonight is the night to catch a visitor."

"Got anything special planned? Or just the standard teams?"

"Standard teams. But Brad and I will be driving around the base starting before midnight. If all goes well, we can follow the truck off base, and the regular surveillance teams can then hit the hospital as soon as the truck drives away."

"Okay," Todd said. "I'll send in a couple of agents dressed in hospital garb in hopes they can see where the stash is being hid, and who all is involved. I'll run two shifts: 1600–2400 and 2400–0800, with two agents per shift."

"Through the photos we took last week, we know that Chief Hospital Corpsman Hugo Diaz is probably a constant supervising the deliveries. And the BI work we've done on him shows there are problems. Biggest being money problems since his wife dumped him a couple of years ago. While he might not be the head guy in whatever's happening, we need to catch him handling whatever is being moved to cement a firm case," Wendy added.

"Let's see what our BI on Jesus Cabilla shows. Montgomery's help was near worthless, but we can probably find more on our own. Rodney Carth should be back from Cabilla's neighborhood soon."

"Anyone available to start on Montgomery?" Wendy glanced at the surveillance schedule posted on the board.

"Sorry, no. I'm running out of available agents even with those extras Marcus sent. Rodney can start it when he returns, and I'll work with him."

Wendy nodded. If tonight was a bust she would have to call it off completely, or at least scale things back greatly. Her surveillance was burning a lot of man-hours, and cases here and at other NIS offices were falling behind because of it. She said a silent prayer that her gut was right.

48

A SMALL AMOUNT OF STATIC preceded the clear voice. "Eye Socket, this is Eyeball Two. Come in."

Colonel Sam Wesson, just returned from lunch, listened as George grabbed the microphone. "Go ahead, Eyeball Two. This is Eye Socket. Over."

"We might have found the missing vehicle. It's nose down off the side of a single lane road under some trees. We almost missed it. Luck held and we caught a reflection. Looks to be off an old logging road. No visible signs of life. And no possible landing site. Over."

"Understood. Give me the location, drop red smoke, and then follow the logging road back to an identifiable paved road. Over."

Hearing Eyeball Two give the location, Deputy Walker marked it on the map. It would be considered the middle of nowhere even by West Virginia standards. Next he checked the location of the nearest vehicle with a radio. Another of the sheriff's men, Deputy David Frost, was on patrol in that area.

"Car Five, come in."

"Hey, George. What's up?" Frost replied in a laid-back attitude, then gave his location.

"Air cover might have found the car, Dave. Drive north on Beckley Road to Roger's Gulf Station. One of the choppers will meet you there and lead you to the location. Might be some walking involved. It's about twenty minutes from Roger's to the logging road. Over."

"10–4. I'm about eight minutes south of Roger's now."

Wesson relayed the plan to Eyeball Two. They would be over Roger's in a couple of minutes and would circle, waiting for the deputy. He looked over at Marcus, who had been quietly observing. "Good news is that Two has already refueled, so they are good for a couple of hours. Three other birds are refueling now. What else should we be doing?"

Marcus shook his head. "That's the hard part: nothing. We wait to hear what Frost has found. *If* it is the car, then we move air and ground assets to that area for a wider search, fanning out from there. You might want to start plotting that out. And if it is the car, then more than a few of us will descend on it to gather whatever evidence we can find."

"Do you want me to start moving some additional search teams to that area, Marcus? There are several about fifteen miles away, and one of the SEAL teams should be near there soon," George said.

"No, hold off until we know for sure. Notify the closest SEAL unit by radio and have them look for the red smoke so they'll know which way to head. But have them stay on their area for now. Might be a wild goose chase. If Frost can drive up that road to the vehicle, then we should hear from him in about thirty minutes, right?"

George nodded. "At least thirty; maybe longer if the logging road isn't open. We've had some nasty storms over the last couple of weeks, and a tree or two might be down."

"Well, keep your fingers crossed and say another prayer for a clear road." With a shrug Marcus added, "I'll be at Pansy's. Send GT and Rick over when they finish with Ledder. And Kelly, if she shows up here." Marcus turned and left.

Wesson watched the door close as he smirked. "Kinda cold. I expected him to be a bit more excited."

George laughed. "I thought all you professional military guys were cool, calm and collected until the guns opened up. From what GT says, I wouldn't want to be in his way when Marcus gets excited."

"I've known that type, and it seems you're right, he is one of them."

49

PANSY HELD UP THE "SPECIAL blend" coffee carafe when she glimpsed Marcus entering. His nod affirmed her offering as he pointed to the kitchen. She returned the nod and followed him to the break room table. He had barely dropped into a chair when Pansy slid the full cup toward him. "I took the liberty to doctor the pot with cream and sugar. Figured it might save you a couple minutes a day."

The first sip delayed his response. "If I wasn't married, Pansy, you would be in my sights. I totally needed this," Marcus replied appreciatively.

Her look went from appreciation for the compliment to concern for the case. "Any progress you're allowed to share? Today's newspaper paints a grim picture of incompetence." She laid a copy of the paper next to the carafe.

Marcus grinned over the rim of the cup. "There is always progress, but sometimes it is not as fast as you'd like." Quickly changing the subject, he said, "A couple of the crew should be joining me soon—send them on back. You might as well rustle up three lunch specials: surprise me. And leave the carafe, please. I might need it as I read this paper."

Pansy attempted a salute and said, "Aye, aye, sir." Her wink showed that it was intended as humor. "Three beef stews on the way."

With fingers interlocked and elbows planted firmly on the table, Marcus glanced at the headlines, then rested his chin as he thought through the latest pieces of straw that had floated his way. *Car being found was still a maybe. Children were still missing, but more people were now looking. Finding no new bodies was a positive. Local girlfriend of Doris might have some answers. Perhaps the day was generating a few positives. As usual, waiting was the hardest part of any case.*

Marcus was lost in thought, running the parameters in his mind. He was brought back to reality by a familiar voice.

"With you eating here so often, you'll soon be as fat as me," GT said as he and Rick slid into place across from Marcus.

With a shrug, Marcus said, "It's a nice change of pace from the official office spaces. Less regimented stress gives my brain a bit of clarity. Mental fresh air, so to speak."

Rick gave a thumbs-up. "So, got the case figured out yet, boss?"

"Not yet, but hey, this is only day two, Marine. I see Doc's impatience is rubbing off on you already. So, gents, what did Ledder give up?"

"He was quiet until Allen delivered the recall telegram. Then the lieutenant became a bubbling fountain of information even before I mentioned that I was also a NIS agent. But nothing was related to drugs," Rick replied.

GT nodded. "Nor any other nefarious things. He never married, so he didn't have big expenses. His stash of money came from cheap living, sharp investments, and uncanny luck at poker, he said. Seems the boys in any unit where he has served knew of some friendly poker games off base, and Ledder usually came home with more money than he had in his pocket when he left."

Marcus took another sip of coffee as he mentally filed the new information. "What about Decker? Did our now-active-duty lieutenant have any insights to offer?"

Both GT and Rick shook their heads. Conversation stopped while a waiter placed a large, piping-hot bowl in front of each man. A communal plate of cornbread sticks was lowered into the center of the table. He provided glasses of iced tea before he departed.

After Marcus led a blessing for the meal and the trio sat quiet for a moment, Rick said, "Marcus, Ledder did send you an apology for his attitude this morning. Said he was short tempered due to lack of sleep, anger over Decker's death, and the perceived lack of progress. And he's sorry he took it out on us."

"Did it seem earnest? Or was he looking to garner favor?"

"He sounded on the level," GT interjected.

"That would be nice if it's true. Let him stew a bit in holding while we devour this bowl of stew."

Not much was said as they ate. Each man took a turn reading the article in the paper. According to the writer, Masterman the editor-in-chief, the law enforcement agencies were close to worthless. No suspects had been arrested, nor had the missing children been found. To make matters worse, Masterman believed the heavy hitter called in from D.C. to save the day, and the sheriff's butt, had failed.

As the guys were nearing the bottom of the bowls, Kelly slid in beside Marcus and gently slugged his upper arm. "Thanks for waiting, my love!"

Marcus smiled. "There are no set schedules when working a case, Princess. It is catch as catch can. Good news is the beef stew is better than mine."

"Then it must be outstanding. Anything new to share, Sailor?"

Rick pushed the paper over to Kelly. As she quickly read the headline and skimmed the article, her face showed the frustration the others felt.

"Ouch! That guy is not a happy camper. What does he expect?" She posed the rhetorical question they all felt.

Kelly's bowl was delivered as Marcus shrugged and said, "Status reports. You first. How's your patient?"

"I authorized her release after she chats with Aunt Maude, who offered to drive her home. Ruth is even more convinced of the creature she saw. I'm still not."

"Anything else, Kelly?"

"Our two M.E.s are getting along well. They will have some samples that need analysis soon, and Dennis tells me the local lab is usually slow. I said you'd look into using an FBI lab. Now, what do you know?" Kelly asked.

Pushing back his emptied bowl, Marcus rested his elbows on the table. "Big picture. The SEALs are out having fun. Our air support might have found the car. A deputy is on the way now to check it out. We arrested Bob Ledder for being a pain in the butt, and I had him recalled to active duty, so I'll have more options with him. Cal Thompkins was not much help earlier, and suddenly he is not available to chat."

Kelly looked at him with surprise. "Whoa, Sailor—air support?"

"Eleven Hueys are currently in the air, courtesy of the West Virginia National Guard, probably at the suggestion of your godfather. We should know if it is the missing car any time now, so eat up, and we'll get back to the office."

As the last of a good lunch was consumed and everyone was up to speed, a new face appeared around the corner. The newspaper man, Jerry Masterman, had found their hidden lunch location.

"Sheriff, I heard you were here, but couldn't find you in the dining room. Figured this was a possible spot for you to hide," Jerry said sarcastically.

GT snorted and avoided looking at the man. "Not hiding, just finding a quiet spot for a quick working lunch without the usual interruptions. Now that you have interrupted us, what do you want?"

Masterman put his hands on his hips and demanded, "An interview with your hotshot from D.C." Glancing at Marcus, he continued, "I assume that's him. Right?"

Holding up the newspaper, Marcus asked harshly, "And I assume you're the guy who wrote this? And the hit piece in last week's paper about the Sheriff? Right?"

Masterman retreated slightly. "Yes, that's my work. I reported the facts."

Marcus stood and looked down at Masterman. "Sorry, Gerald, but opinion pieces should never be on the front page above the fold. The true facts were overwhelmed with your wild opinions in both editions of the paper. And who in law enforcement did you contact to get your information?"

"I stand by my reports. Yes, I did talk to a member of the sheriff's office. And I prefer to be called Jerry."

"Well, Gerald, I prefer to have a quiet lunch; sometimes, like now, neither of us get our way. But back to this issue of your reporting. Deputy Walker told us of your 'digging for facts' last night. Sounded like a quick dig for back stabbing info."

"So?"

"So, instead of slamming the sheriff, you could have been helping. Nowhere in either issue did I see photos and descriptions of the missing children. Seems to me, journalistic ethics would've required you to encourage your readers to be on the lookout for these missing babies. Hell, you didn't even mention their names."

Masterman grunted. "Finding them and their mother's killer is the job of law enforcement. Not mine."

Marcus paused for a moment, then coolly said, "So you see no reason to help? Is that right?"

"Not my job," said Masterman. "I inform the masses."

Marcus simply stared at Masterman for a moment before grabbing the handset from the wall-mounted phone. Dialing a series of numbers from memory, Marcus finally said, "Hi Cheryl, Marcus Colt calling. How's my favorite executive assistant today?"

"Excellent. Does he have a minute for a quick question?" Marcus smiled at the responses and said, "Thanks."

Masterman started to speak, and Marcus held up his hand to stop him.

"No, sorry, Tommy, I'm not calling to set up another match. No time for tennis right now, but we need to hit the courts soon. As I recall, you're hosting the next time. I'm looking forward to you buying my winner's dinner at Bookbinders!" Marcus snickered at the response he got.

Kelly's face showed she knew what was about to happen. She winked at GT and Rick.

"Here's the deal. I'm working a murder and missing persons case with a local sheriff here in Princeton, West Virginia, and we were discussing journalistic ethics. Is there some sort of rulebook that reporters follow? And what is the newspaper's responsibility to the community in a sensitive case like kidnapping?"

GT muttered, "Journalistic ethics sounds like an oxymoron to me—like jumbo shrimp."

Marcus smiled at GT's remark and listened intently to his phone call. After several minutes, he said, "Okay, I understand all that ... You're pulling old memories from our Intro to Journalism class at Tech from dark reaches of my mind, buddy. Yea, true ... Uh, yea ... So in summary, you're saying that in something like missing persons or a kidnapping case, the paper has the responsibility under journalistic ethics to help law enforcement by posting photos and information about the victims. And a good reporter would be asking law enforcement what information he should or shouldn't put out in the news before he does, right ... Yea, like a doctor, the reporter should do no harm. Got it."

Masterman had dropped his hands from his hips and was now more interested in his shoes. One was scuffing at something on the floor.

"Oh, there's no problem here in Princeton, Tommy. We're looking forward to working with the local paper staff on this case."

GT let out a loud cough that sounded more like "bullshit," to which Rick gave a quick nod.

Marcus swallowed the laugh that was starting and said, "Tell ya what, Tommy. If this case becomes super interesting, I'll write a book and let Garrett Publishing have first crack at it. Yea, I'll do that … Y'all take care also. Love to Heidi. Bye." He hung up and smiled at Kelly as he added, "He sends his love."

The room was silent. Masterman, who seemed to have shrunk, finally stated the obvious: "You and Mr. Garrett were college friends."

"Indeed, Gerald, and I was best man at his wedding to Heidi. But like I told him, we're looking forward to working with you. I hope you feel the same."

Nodding, Jerry mumbled, "Happy to, Deputy."

GT stood. "Well, super. Now that we're all friends, let's head on to the office. Care to join us, Gerald?"

50

GT GAVE MASTERMAN AN OVERVIEW of what was happening on the case. He skipped over the possible find of the Buick since it wasn't confirmed. However, the briefing did include the positioning of the SEALs and the areas being covered by the Guard's Hueys. He also provided detailed descriptions and photos of the two missing children.

Marcus stood by quietly as GT handled the briefing, then said, "Jerry, I hope we can count on your cooperation. A lot of what the Sheriff has told you we do not want everyone to know. It might signal the bad guys to change their way of doing things, and that would put us back at square one. As we say in the military, if you tell anyone, we'll have to kill you."

His look of confusion changed to concern as his mind grasped the last statement. Jerry stammered, "Say what?"

"Actually, the standard line is 'if we tell you, we'll have to kill you' but a slight modification is fine for this situation." Marcus paused for impact. "Okay, I'm kidding about the killing thing; well, sort of. But we need to keep people a bit in the dark about specifics. Frankly, I loved that you tagged this case as the 'Crazed Bear' thing. That's a perfect distraction. And I want people to continue thinking along those lines and a few other things I'll get into shortly. But in reality, we have unknown persons committing these murders and not bears, crazy or otherwise."

"Are you sure?" Jerry interjected with a look that shouted disbelief. Marcus nodded.

"How can you be so certain?"

"Easy answer, Jerry. Bears do not remove all of the clothing from their human victims. Tear some off, of course, but not every stitch," GT said. "And they don't clean up the bodies."

"I had not heard any of that," Jerry quietly said.

"One of those bits of info we keep under wraps, Jerry, and you need to also."

"Do you have any leads as to who is doing this?"

"Short answer is 'no,' Jerry." Marcus tried to hide his exasperation. "But I'm hoping the bad guys will feel confident with you pushing the crazy bear scenario and the lack of progress from the sheriff's department. And not telling everyone, and especially the bad guys, everything you heard and saw this afternoon. If they don't think we're getting anywhere, their confidence will lead to a mistake. And GT and I will be there to make them pay for their arrogance."

"Marcus, I will not lie to my readers."

"I don't expect you to. But I'm asking you to leave some things out of your articles. Especially avoid anything about the SEAL teams and the other M.E. Suppressing critical evidence that can aid the perpetrator is not a lie. It falls into the journalistic ethics category of helping solve a crime. Police do it all the time when they do not release all the information about a crime to avoid tipping off the suspects or creating copycats. Some things getting out can cause more harm than good. I'm telling you all this because I think you're one of those reporters who will dig until he gets the answers. We don't want your enthusiasm and expertise helping the bad guys."

Jerry's facial expressions jumped between confused, concerned, and finally committed. "I understand," Jerry resignedly said as he gave a quick nod. "What should I not say in the next issue?"

GT and Marcus quickly covered what they needed to get out and what was considered classified.

"Jerry, there is something else I want you to run in this next edition. You heard about the Mothman sighting, but there were two Bigfoot sightings yesterday. One looks to be a highly probable, and the other is yet to be looked at carefully. Mention both vaguely in your article. The more we can get the bad guys thinking we are looking in the wrong direction, the better.

"Guess a bit of misdirection wouldn't be too bad a thing. Anything else?"

Marcus opened one of the case folders on the conference table. He pulled a drawing of the face of the first victim, which the FBI had created from the remains, then handed it to Jerry. "And run this, asking if anyone has information about this gent. He was the first victim found, and there was no ID on his body."

Jerry left after promising to get a special edition on the stands by dawn—with emphasis on finding the children and little else. In turn, GT had promised to keep him apprised of the developments.

"Think we can trust him, Marcus?" Rick asked as the door closed.

"Yea, we can. He knows that one phone call will end his career on this newspaper and blackball him across the industry. But I don't think I'll need to play that blackmail card; my gut tells me Jerry has seen the light and is a firm member of our team."

"I agree," Kelly added.

GT raised both hands, palms up, with a *not sure* grimace on his face.

Rick pressed the issue. "So that guy you called could do that?"

"Oh, for sure—that and more. Tommy Garrett inherited Garrett Publishing from his father. Tommy owns our local paper as well as at least thirty more across the country," Kelly said.

"Okay, Marcus, what's next on the list?" GT asked.

Marcus stood. "Right this minute, another cup of coffee is my highest priority while we wait to hear from Deputy Frost. Well, coffee and planning our next moves."

As coffee was being poured, Norma stuck her head into the break room and said, "Deputy Doc, you're needed on line one."

The call was a short one, and Kelly returned to the break room with a look of concern. She sipped her cooling coffee before saying, "Our forensic team has samples ready for analysis. How can we get them to the FBI lab?"

Sam Wesson said, "I can pull a UH-1 off the search and they can get it to Richmond. With the storm coming in from the west, Cincinnati wouldn't be a good choice."

Marcus shook his head. "No, keep those choppers searching. GT, call your FBI contact and tell him we need a rush job from the Richmond lab. I'll go have a chat with Lieutenant Ledder."

Ledder popped to attention when Marcus entered the interrogation room.

"As you were, Lieutenant," Marcus ordered, projecting the senior officer persona.

Still standing, but a little more relaxed, Ledder said, "Sir, please accept my apologies for my actions and attitude earlier, Commander. No excuse, sir."

Marcus looked hard at Ledder for a moment before his expression softened. "Accepted, Bob. Now, take a seat."

"Sir, what can I do to help you find Joe's killer?"

Chuckling, Marcus answered, "Since you asked, we do need your help. Is your plane available for a quick trip?"

Ledder nodded.

"Good. I need you to fly a deputy and some evidence to the FBI lab in Richmond. According to my sources, there is a storm front coming from the west tomorrow, but you should have clear skies for the round trip. Gas will be on the sheriff's card. Can you handle it?"

Again Ledder nodded. "I can be in the air in less than an hour, sir."

"All right," Marcus said, "Let's join the rest of the team in the conference room."

As Marcus led the newest member of the team there, he motioned for Deputy Josh Bonner to join them.

Rapping the table to get everyone's attention, Marcus announced, "Bob Ledder is now part of the team. With GT's permission, he'll fly Josh Bonner and the M.E.'s evidence to Richmond and bring back the results."

"Works for me," GT said.

"Fine. Kelly, call the boys in the morgue and tell them to expect the pickup shortly. Josh, we should have priority at the lab, but there's no telling how long it will take. Stay until you get the results."

Allen Chambers leaned into the conference room and interrupted the discussion. "Marcus, I just heard from Anita Colbeck. She's pretty upset about Doris's death, so I think a face-to-face chat will be better than a phone call. I'm heading over to her office now."

Marcus nodded his agreement. "Hurry back, Allen. I think things are about to heat up around here." He returned his gaze to the group and said, "Fly safe, gentlemen," then he dismissed Bob and Josh.

After everyone had departed on their assignments, those remaining used the wait time to look over the evidence boards again and study the now-updated map. Marcus hated the waiting, which added stress and frustration, but knew it was part of the job.

Less than ten minutes later, the wait was over. The radio call from Deputy David Frost relieved the stress, but not the frustration. He reported that it was, in fact, the missing car, but there were no signs of the children. There was damage to the right front fender which looked like a deer strike.

Marcus took the mike. "Dave, look around the scene and check for trash, footprints, clothing, et cetera."

"Did a quick check after looking into the car for bodies. Sorry to say, the area has gone through at least of week of rain, wind, and a ton of falling leaves. There might be something under the forest clutter, but it will take a bit of looking."

"Understand. Anything obvious on the vehicle?" GT said, taking the mike from Marcus.

"Sorry, boss, nothing obvious. The car seems too clean and was probably completely wiped down after dumping. Did a quick dusting of the door handles and areas commonly touched, and nothing was there."

GT grimaced. "Okay, hold one," he said, seeing Marcus hold up an index finger.

Marcus asked, "Where is the nearest FBI office that can do a complete analysis of that car?" GT provided the information, so Marcus continued. "Tell him to call for a wrecker and get the car to the FBI in Beckley."

David responded quickly, "Got ya covered, Marcus. I brought the tow truck with me, figuring it would be needed eventually."

Marcus smiled. "Good thinking, Dave. Stay with the Buick until the FBI receives it; maintain the chain of evidence, okay?"

"10–4. Out."

51

THE HOUSE HAD A RUN down, deserted look. That made it perfect for their needs. It had been built around 1880, and maintenance the last couple of decades had been sparse, so it was *extremely* run down, but far from deserted. The location was good, hidden behind a small hill that kept drivers on the two-lane from seeing the house, barn, or other structures. A locked gate secured the rutted excuse for a gravel drive. The gate matched the local gas-well gates, so it looked like it belonged. And it kept people out.

One of the two people in the old house was having a bad day. He tried to hide his impatience, but it was difficult. The more he needed to get moving, the more the doc delayed to perform more tests. *Experiments* was a better term, he thought, but since the doc was paying the bills and calling the shots, he could apply whatever name he desired. The man sucked up his frustration and entered the room they called the lab.

"Doctor, we gotta get the truck back to Chicago with the next load. And since you killed Jesus, I need to make the run myself."

The doctor snorted. "The bastard was being difficult. We don't have time for him to take a week or two off. He was weak, so no great loss."

"Yea, right. As for the delivery, if we had another driver handy, it wouldn't be a big loss. For now, it is. At least the barn keeps that truck out of sight."

Writing quickly in his spiral notebook after a glance into the microscope, the doctor said, "Hold off until the weekend. Otherwise you'll be missed in town. I need another subject immediately. Leave me, Hans, and go get me one."

"You know damn well that's not my name. And I'm sick of hearing it!"

The doctor chuckled. "That was the name of my father's favorite assistant, and I think it wears well on you. Now leave me!"

The assistant quietly left the lab, knowing the verbal battle had been lost. "Glad to be out of there," he muttered to himself.

Since the doctor had started storing body parts in glass containers lined neatly on shelves against the back wall, the room was becoming more disgusting by the minute. And if the sights were not repulsive enough, the odor of the chemicals—the assistant thought of it as a nauseating pickle smell—gave him headaches and turned his stomach.

Now he needed to find another subject: not an easy task. Tomorrow would be soon enough, he decided. He needed to stay out of the doctor's vision so maybe he'd forget about it for a day or so. After getting to the house and grabbing a beer from the fridge, he decided it was time for a call he didn't want to make. He dialed the numbers anyway.

"Hey, it's me."

Talking with the big boss was always unpleasant, almost as bad as chatting with the doctor. Both acted like he was beneath them and didn't try to hide that opinion.

"No, the truck's not heading back yet; I might get it there over the weekend or first of next week. We ran into a snag here. Jesus is dead. The doctor got pissed and crushed his skull with a wrench."

He grimaced as he was read the riot act.

"I'm sorry, Sir, but there was nothing I could do. Hell, I wasn't even in the lab at the time. I did dispose of the body quickly … well, at least a day or so after the doc had his fun with it."

A deep sigh almost escaped as he rolled his eyes in frustration. The big boss didn't appreciate insubordination in the form of such noises.

"No, Sir. I'll make sure that doesn't happen. I've got the truck well hidden. Say, I've got an idea. Could you send the next truck down with two drivers? That way we could get the truck here back to you."

The dial tone told him that the boss had hung up, but he suspected the handset had been slammed down hard. It was obvious he was pissed. His final order was to not let the doctor down and get him whatever he wanted, when he wanted it.

He slowly hung up the phone and picked up the beer. Several more sips gave him time to think about his situation. He felt caught between two ticking time bombs with no idea how long was left on either counter, wondering when his body parts would end up in a glass container. As his old man used to say, life sucks and then you die.

And while his life currently sucked, he hoped he didn't die anytime soon. He finished off the beer and headed into town. Perhaps it would be a good hunting day.

52

GT UPDATED THE BOARDS WITH the vehicle's location and sat down in front of his empty coffee cup. The only good news about the discovery was the lack of bodies, blood, or other indicator that the missing children were dead. There was hope they were still out there somewhere. At least they had the car. He said a silent prayer that the SEALs heading toward the area would have better luck. They needed a few more clues and needed them quickly.

Marcus stood by, quietly staring at the boards. Rick, Kelly, and GT glanced between themselves, then shifted their gaze to Marcus. Sam and George were busy updating the map with the search areas the ground crews had covered.

GT stated the obvious. "Since the exterior of the car was clean of any prints, and based upon the isolated location ... it was a dump job."

Most people in the room nodded, agreeing.

"Here's hoping the Bureau's forensic folks will find a clue or two on the inside. Lord knows, we need a break," Marcus solemnly said as he raised his near-empty coffee cup.

"Will we hear anything back from them today?" Rick asked.

Marcus shrugged.

Shaking his head, GT said, "Probably not. They normally need a day or two to issue the report. That being said, since they know the importance put on the case by some extremely powerful people, perhaps they'll have a bit of incentive."

"Okay, Marcus. What now?" Kelly finally broke her silence.

Marcus took a final sip of his now-cold coffee. "Kelly, I need you and GT to go talk to Sanders, Janson, and Burton. Perhaps your expertise at reading people—combined with his knowledge of the locals—will tell if they're on the level about what they saw."

Kelly laughed. "Sure thing, Sailor. Talking about mythical creatures is always high on my list of things to do."

With a slight smile, Marcus replied, "Well, do try to keep a proper positive demeanor during the interviews as you don't want to embarrass GT. And we need those folks to tell us everything they *think* they saw."

"Sounds like you have doubts."

"No, my mind is open with regard to the creatures' existence. I'm more concerned that we'll alienate the good people of Mercer County if we're not careful talking about these sightings. Some of them have strong feelings about these creatures and don't appreciate being thought a fool," Marcus said. "So no laughing at them. Treat them as you would Aunt Maude."

Kelly nodded. "Seriously, I plan to sit quietly and let GT do all the talking. I'll take copious notes, and if something sounds off or needs clarification, I'll proceed with the same level of care I give all my patients."

"My problem is I can't see what these creatures have to do with the murders," GT said sharply, his mouth twisting into a grimace. "We might be wasting a lot of time on nonsense."

His head slowly moved side to side as Marcus put his hands on his hips and turned to face GT. "Godfrey, my man, the one thing to keep in mind on the vast majority of these weird cases is that there are no coincidences. So far, we have five people saying they saw something. They might all have alcohol dependencies or be total nut cases, but we won't know that until you've had your chats. Cross every *t* and dot every *i*, please."

"It might be some of that mass hysteria stuff created by the comments in the paper. I'm ready to believe in enormous bears more than that other guy," Rick interjected.

"Possible, but we need to investigate," Marcus said.

GT stood, hiked up his belt, and tossed a sloppy salute toward Marcus. He turned to leave and lobbed a response over his shoulder. "Aye, aye, sir. Come on, Deputy Doc, we've important interviews to conduct."

"Into the valley of the shadow of monsters we go," Kelly said as she pulled the conference room door closed and hurried after GT. Marcus let out a long sigh.

"He didn't seem happy," said Rick, stating the obvious.

Marcus chuckled. "That's GT showing his frustration and not his anger. Cases like this will generate a hell of a lot of frustration. I'm used to it, but GT isn't."

"I'm in GT's camp right now," both Rick and Sam said over each other.

"Lightweights," Marcus said through a short laugh. "You can always expect the unexpected from this Mountain State."

53

BEFORE LEAVING THE OFFICE, GT had Norma make three quick phone calls. Two of the people they needed to interview were now expecting them. The third, Delores Janson, was not answering. GT asked Norma to keep trying and radio him if she made contact.

Kelly had a local map on her lap as GT zipped along the highway. She knew GT didn't need help navigating, but she checked street signs as they drove toward their destination. Since Princeton was her new hometown, she wanted to learn the layout as quickly as possible. Reading the map while riding shotgun was a good way. The intersection they passed caused her some pause. "Uh, GT, we have passed the road that leads to the Sanders place," Kelly said.

With a knowing smile, GT said, "Yep, that was the plan. Ya see, Claudia Burton saw the Mothman fly-over, and we might get some good info from her. But just words—no hard evidence. However, Sanders said Bigfoot came through his yard. There might be physical evidence there in the form of footprints, hair samples, and so on. Much better than words."

With a quick nod, Kelly understood. "And we can quickly wrap up with Claudia, then spend more time with Fred Sanders."

"That's true, but the real reason is the road to Burton's place will have too many school buses on it slowing traffic down if we go there later. She's first so we can avoid the traffic delays. And the office will only be fifteen minutes away when we're done with Delores."

"I can see you and Marcus are cut from the same cloth with your multi-dimensional thinking. Good use of time."

The visit with Claudia Burton went as expected. Claudia was a retired high school math teacher. A silver–gray had replaced the bulk of the medium brown in her hair, and a few extra pounds inhabited her middle and her face. At the age of sixty-seven, her health was still good and her vision was excellent: GT did a quick vision test as they stood in the backyard. Asking her to identify the type of bird on a tree about forty yards away was less conspicuous than asking how many fingers he was holding up.

She explained why she was outside before dawn—her dog was an older beagle with a weak bladder—and what she saw. Kelly's notes logged that the creature was flying about fifty feet above ground level and heading in a west–northwest direction. The moonlight allowed her to see the creature.

Claudia emphatically reported that the creature was black, or at least a dark brown. Huge wings flapped slowly, yet the creature moved across the sky quickly. The only sound was a whooshing noise from the wings. And no, she had not seen its eyes. It was flying alone and didn't seem to be carrying anything.

After Claudia seemed talked out, Kelly said, "Claudia, as a doctor as well as a deputy, I have a couple of questions that need to be asked. Please know that this information will help flush out the report.

"Ask away."

Kelly nodded. "Are you on any prescription medications?"

"No."

"Your sighting was around six a.m. Were you drinking any alcohol the night before?"

"I wasn't drunk, if that's what you're asking. And for the record, my first cocktail this entire week was a sloe gin fizz when we sat down to play cards later that night," Claudia said in a huff.

"Wasn't implying anything, Claudia. Just getting all the facts in place so we'll have a complete picture. And the more information we get now will help reduce our speculation. So continuing, is it possible you saw one of those big cranes or owls? Some have a large wingspan, ya know," Kelly said.

Claudia slowly shook her head. "No way. Cranes have long necks, and this Mothman didn't. Rather obvious difference. And owls in this area are not that big."

"Anything else either of you wish to add?" GT asked. A sharp head-shake was the answer from Claudia. Kelly rolled her eyes from her position behind Claudia as she stifled a sigh.

They again thanked Claudia for her report, and the patrol car was soon heading toward Fred Sanders' place. Initially, neither spoke as they contemplated the new information. But as the first few miles rolled past, that quiet didn't last.

"Okay, Kelly, you're the shrink. What's your thinking?"

"I'm not a psychiatrist, so officially not a shrink, but I think she's on the level about what she *thinks* she saw, GT. But unlike Marcus, I'm not ready to believe these creatures exist unless I see one directly in front of me."

GT chuckled. "Guess I'm more in the Marcus camp on this. They might exist. We've had so many stories, sightings, and interactions over the decades here in West Virginia—it's hard to completely dismiss it all. Maybe we can find some hard evidence at Fred's house."

Fred Sanders had about ten heavily wooded and desolate acres; most were up the side of a steep mountain. They turned off the highway and traveled west on the narrow lane about six miles, to his place. The gravel driveway had been carved into the mountainside and was barely wide enough for the cruiser. Kelly said a silent prayer that no one was coming from the other end. There was no room to pass: one side of the driveway was pressed against the upslope of the land, which was a shear wall of rock at least ten feet high, and the other side dropped off sharply. It was a long way down to whatever was at the bottom.

Rounding one final curve gave them a view of the house. A typical two-story frame farmhouse was set back from the driveway by about fifty feet. The driveway ended at a two-car garage that matched the style of the house. The gray shingled roof looked good, and the wood sported a recent coat of white paint on the walls and medium green on the trim. Well-maintained shrubbery bordered the wide porch. Thin smoke curled from the chimney, finishing the Norman Rockwell look.

"Nice place," Kelly offered.

GT nodded as he killed the ignition. "Fred retired last year after a career as VP of the Princeton First National Bank. Jane, his wife, is visiting the grandkids in Cincinnati for a few weeks. Solid citizens, as the old saying goes."

"Come in, Sheriff," Sanders said as he stepped back from the open door. He waved them toward the living room. To Kelly, he seemed nervous.

"Thanks, Fred. By the way, this is Deputy Kelly Colt."

Sanders turned to her and grabbed her hand. "Welcome, Deputy Colt. Very pleased to meet you."

Kelly was surprised that Fred Sanders was much younger than she expected. He probably had yet to see his fifty-fifth birthday, and his grip was firm. His eyes sparkled as he nodded to Kelly in what could have been a sophisticated bow.

"Thank you for seeing us, Mr. Sanders. I'm anxious to see where the creature went through your yard," Kelly said as he released her hand.

"No time for coffee, Sheriff? I just made a fresh pot."

GT nodded. "Sure, always time for coffee. As long as we can drink it while visiting the creature's path."

The coffee was much better than that at the office, so Kelly understood GT's desire to have a cup. She needed a shot of caffeine as well, to balance the stress, and it would also give her a chance to observe GT with Fred. Their conversation showed they weren't close friends, but had spent time together at various civic and social functions. Fred relaxed some as GT chatted.

Sitting the quickly emptied cup on the kitchen counter, GT asked, "Where exactly did you see this Bigfoot guy? Tell me about the sighting as we walk that way, Fred."

It was a short walk out the back door to the edge of the woods behind the house. Fred pointed to a path leading into the woods. "He came from there."

"Was he moving fast or slow?" Kelly asked.

"He was running. He cut across the yard through here, and ducked around the back of the garden shed over there." Fred pointed for emphasis. The garden shed was about thirty feet from where they stood.

"And how tall was he? Color?" GT asked.

"Kind of a cinnamon color, you know, reddish brown, but he had streaks in his hair. Maybe dirt. And I know he was right at ten feet tall."

Kelly looked up from her notebook. "How can you be sure about the height?"

"That's an easy one. The garden shed is eight feet high at the lower edge of the roof, and when he ran around it, I could still see his head and part of the shoulder."

"Okay," Kelly said, adding another note to the page. "You don't seem upset by this sighting. This wasn't your first, was it?"

Fred grimaced. "I usually don't talk about it; I don't want people to think I'm a nutcase. But you're right—this was not the first time I saw one of them. Last time was when we had that late April snow. Remember that, GT? Anyway, one was in the yard late one night. The dogs barked and I caught a glimpse of him as he dashed into the woods."

GT pushed his cap back a bit and ran a hand across his forehead. "Where were you when you saw this thing, Fred?"

Pointing toward the house, he replied, "At the kitchen window. I was cleaning up my lunch dishes when the pups, Daisy and Beau, started growling looking out the sliding glass door. Their carrying on caused me to look up in time to see him."

"GT, being a city girl, I'm no good at looking for tracks. Why don't you check the path while I ask Fred a few more questions?"

GT nodded and walked toward the garden shed. Kelly smiled as she said, "Fred, I have a couple of questions that need to be asked. Please know that this information will help flush out the report. And I'm not insinuating anything by them. Okay?"

"Not a problem. Ask away."

Kelly nodded. "Are you on any prescription medications?"

"No."

"Did you have any alcohol with your lunch?"

"Sadly, no. I'm trying to drop a few pounds, and the doc said to skip alcohol or exercise a hell of a lot more than I am now. Easier to skip the booze."

"I understand that. Is there anything else you want to add to the report?"

Fred stroked his chin as he searched his memory. "No. I think that's all."

"Please give us a call if you remember anything else," Kelly added. "You can go on inside and I'll see if the sheriff has found anything."

GT was heading toward the woods when Kelly caught up to him. They scoured the ground, but the dry soil was hard packed. No tracks, no scat, and no hair samples were found. They bid farewell to Fred Sanders and headed off to check with the last witness.

Back on the highway, Kelly quietly studied her map, then finally broke the silence. "What is located west–northwest of here?"

"Mountains, valleys, and lots of trees. Why?"

"Our witnesses mentioned that was the direction the creatures were heading."

GT's face twisted in thought. He knew where she was headed with this.

After a pause, Kelly cocked her head towards him. "Do we have any ground patrols in that area?"

54

RICK SAT AT THE OTHER end of the conference table, glancing between the boards and Marcus. His boss was at the other end, sipping coffee and making notes on a yellow legal pad. Not sure if he should interrupt Marcus and ask if he should be doing something, Rick tried to focus on the boards in hopes of seeing what he hadn't the last twenty times he'd read through them.

Marcus looked up. "Guess you're wondering what you should be doing, right?"

Rick blushed slightly at having his mind read. "Yes, sir. That thought did cross my mind."

"Give me a rundown on the status of things right this minute," Marcus ordered. "Including who is where doing what."

Rick stood, then after a moment walked to the map board. He pointed to several areas. "We have civilian search teams covering these areas indicated by green pins. SEAL teams are here, here, and in these other three areas marked with the white pins. This group is moving to the car dump location. Hueys are searching the areas designated by the blue pins and string outline. Forensic evidence is in route to the FBI Richmond lab in the hands of Deputy Bonner, who's being flown by Lieutenant Ledder, and the Thompkins' Buick will soon be on its way to the FBI staff in

Beckley under the control of Deputy Frost. The sheriff and Deputy Doc are out interviewing people who claim to have seen unusual creatures. Detective Chambers is interviewing Anita Colbeck, who is possibly the last person to see Doris Thompkins alive … except for her killer. Doctor Wallace and Deputy Wilson are checking the sites where bodies were dumped, in hopes of finding some bear or creature evidence. Deputy Walker and Colonel Wesson are coordinating the search teams here. And M.E.s Bassett and Wentworth are in the morgue checking for more evidence on the bodies."

"And what about you and me?" Marcus expected and received a deer-in-the-headlights look from Rick.

"Uh, well, sir, we are … well, waiting to hear from the teams out in the field, sir, as we, uh, go over the existing evidence one more time," Rick stammered uncertainly.

Marcus chuckled softly. "Calm down Marine, and sit. You're right: we're waiting to get more info. Face it, we're on unfamiliar ground and have no suspects, so with all known bases covered as you succinctly stated, being here going over the known data again, and again, is the best we can do."

Rick nodded his comprehension.

"And as part of that procedure, we also need to go over the six basic questions of any investigation: who, what, when, where, how, and why."

With a shrug, Rick said, "And we don't have answers to any of those questions. All we have is four unrelated bodies in somewhat unusual conditions."

"Rethink that last statement, Rick."

His brow furrowed deeply as Rick searched his mind for the answer. After a few seconds, which to him seemed much longer, he said, "They are related by their post-mortem condition. All have been eviscerated. All have been doctored to insinuate a bear attack. And three of them have drugs in their system."

"And?" Marcus made a come-on motion with his hands.

Rick glanced at the board, paused for a moment, and finally said, "I got nothing."

"All four bodies were killed and mutilated somewhere else than where they were found. And with the cat litter residue found on the bodies and the similarity of the fake bear claw marks, they might have been gutted at the same place. So for this discussion, let's assume that's a fact and throw out some ideas on why they were gutted."

"Money is always a good place to start. Kelly's research on organ donation ruled out the legitimate avenues and left the black market open, where five-digit prices are common. But logically, it seems they would want to be near faster transportation since the organs need to be implanted quickly. Face it, we're a bit isolated here in the sticks," Rick said.

"Unless they have access to small aircraft." Marcus turned to Sam Wesson and asked, "Can you pull a list of locally owned or operated craft? Local pilots also. And how about flight plans for the last two months?"

"I'll see what I can do. Excuse me, I'll go find a quiet place with a phone and get busy," Sam said as he walked out of the conference room.

"And with that, we are back to waiting," Marcus said with a laugh.

Rick smiled at the quip. "Could our *vampire* be a sick collector of body parts?"

"Possible." Marcus wrote a note on his legal pad, then chuckled. "I like the vampire name."

"It's not as impressive as the 'viper' title you used in Italy, but it's fitting with all the missing blood."

"Missing blood … you know, we've focused on the missing organs, but not so much about the blood. Keep thinking along those lines," Marcus said as he grabbed the phone. "Hey, George, what's Dennis's direct line at the morgue?"

The call was answered quickly. "Dennis, aside from transfusions, how could you, as doctor and/or scientist, use a few gallons of human blood? Ask Sidney for his opinion also."

The answers came quickly. Marcus thanked the doctors for their input and hung up, then smiled. "Both of our M.E.s had the same suggestion for the blood use: transfers and cultures."

"Cultures?"

"Yes, indeed. To grow viruses and bacteria in the lab, they need food. The culture provides that, and blood is a common base material. Granted, it is usually animal blood."

"Marcus, I wonder how much blood the missing organs hold?"

"An adult has between eight to twelve pints total, so I'd guess that some of that has to stay in the organs at the time of death. The liver and spleen probably have the largest amount, but I'll get Kelly working on that when she gets back."

Rick's mouth twisted in contemplation. "And we need to know what machinery and other materials are needed to make these culture things. Another Kelly task?"

Marcus nodded. "She's got the medical vocabulary that makes asking such questions much easier. For me, *doohickey* is my favorite medical term."

Rick glanced at the boards before he asked, "Should I put this on the board? And do you have any other uses for body parts?"

"No, hold off on the board update for now. We'll add it if our speculation becomes more solid."

"Understood."

"As for other uses for body parts, I guess medical schools have well-established providers and wouldn't need bootlegged organs. But I wonder about pharmaceutical companies. Do they experiment with organs? Maybe there are some that don't have high ethical standards and never ask questions about the origin of their raw materials. Time to find out, I suppose."

Rick's face showed confusion. "And how do we do that, sir?"

"Put on your best authoritative NIS special agent voice and call the Center for Disease Control in Atlanta. See if they have a list of companies that use the body parts we're missing," Marcus said. "And while you do that, I'll get more coffee."

Finishing the fresh cup before the coffee got cold, Marcus stared at the map of lower West Virginia. He massaged the bridge of his nose as he contemplated the large amount of wooded area in the county, and softly muttered, "Our isolation works both ways for the Vampires. While the vast amount of wooded areas makes body dumping easier, when someone local gets taken they are missed faster than, say, a homeless guy in a big city, and it becomes a higher priority. So the 'where' comes into play. Where do they get the victims?"

That question hung in the air.

55

LOST IN THOUGHT ABOUT WHAT the witnesses had said, Kelly and GT had gone quiet as the cruiser neared the city limits. GT suddenly slowed as they went by a man walking down the road. The man had started to stick his arm out and thumb for a ride when he glanced over his shoulder and saw the light on top of the cruiser. He quickly shoved his hand into his jacket pocket and hunched down under the weight of the backpack.

GT whipped the cruiser around and pulled up short of the hitchhiker. "Stay here, Kelly."

"What's wrong, GT?"

"Probably nothing. I try to keep an eye on people passing through. Most are good people, just down on their luck. But from time to time, they're trouble."

GT radioed in where he had stopped and why. The man with the backpack stopped walking and stared at the cruiser. His expression said he knew he was about to be hassled.

"Is there a problem, officer?" The man asked politely when GT approached.

GT looked the man up and down as he stood in front of him. His hair was in need of a trim, and he hadn't shaved in several days. His clothing looked like well-worn Army–Navy store stock and needed a wash. A surplus Navy peacoat a size or two too big and a knit watch-cap pulled down to his brows kept him warm. Sternly, GT asked, "What's your name?"

"James, sir."

"First name or last? And where are you heading?"

"Full name is Roland James, and I'm passing through on my way to Beckley. Got an old Army buddy there who said he can help me find a job whenever I get there."

"Where ya comin' from, Roland?"

"Nashville."

Nodding, GT continued the interrogation, but his voice had softened. "When and where did you serve, Roland?"

"I was drafted in the summer of '65 and got to 'Nam in the fall of that year. Medically sent home in December, same year. Spent the rest of my time at Fort Hood, some of it in the hospital there."

GT heard the bitterness mixed with sorrow in the man's voice. "You were at la Drang Valley, right? I heard it was rough."

Roland nodded as a faraway look descended over his face.

GT said, "Come on, trooper. Get in the car and we'll get you to Beckley."

"You don't need to do that, Sheriff. I can make it on my own. There's no set schedule, so time ain't critical."

"Yea, you could make it, but us draftees with 'Nam scars need to stick together. I was an MP in 'Nam about a year or so before you got there. Come on."

With introductions out of the way, Kelly quickly slipped into her psychoanalyst mode and chatted with Roland as GT drove back to town. She turned from the front and rested her left arm on the top of the seat so she could look at their passenger.

"Roland, I'm a temporary deputy. In my regular life back in D.C., I work at Walter Reed Medical Center counseling vets. Some are seeking help readjusting to civilian life, others are fighting memories of the time in 'Nam. So I'm always trying to get perspective from other vets who are not on my patient list. If you don't mind my asking, how have things been for you since your discharge?" Kelly's smile was both sincere and useful in relaxing her patients.

A mixture of disappointment and anger flashed across his face. Roland snapped, "I'm fine." After a moment of reflection, he winced. "Sorry. That was uncalled for, ma'am."

Nodding, Kelly said, "Not a problem. After three years of counseling vets, I really do understand. If it hurts to chat, I'm the one who's sorry for opening wounds. But I might be able to help, if you're willing."

"Rocky is the best term, I guess. I was getting into construction before I went into the Army, but the shoulder wounds make it hard to do that work now. So I've tried to get into restaurant work, but so far, dishwasher is about all I can put on the resume. I'm a pretty decent cook but haven't had a chance to show off my skills."

Nodding, Kelly asked, "And your friend in Beckley runs a restaurant?"

"No, ma'am, but he knows people who know people, as the old saying goes. I'm just hoping for a shot. I'll sling hash at any greasy spoon so I can get experience."

"Any family back home in Nashville?" GT asked.

Roland was quiet for a moment; GT wasn't sure if from pain or embarrassment. Then Roland said, "Not any more. Dad died while I was over there, and Mom remarried last year and moved to California." He let out a deep sigh. "And my ex-fiancée married one of my draft-dodging buddies while I was still in the Army. They live somewhere in Canada where he ran to when the draft notice arrived."

Kelly said, "Looks like life dumped a lot of negatives on you in a short period of time, Roland. If you don't mind me asking, how are you handling it all?"

Roland shrugged. "It's life, ma'am. Some days are great and others not so much. I'm glad I didn't get a worse wound over there. A lot of my buddies paid the full price, ya know."

"Too many, that's for sure," Kelly sighed. "I lost a good friend over there, and my husband carries both physical and mental scars from his time in country."

They rode in silence, each lost in private thoughts, for a few minutes. As the city limit sign passed, GT broke the silence. "Trooper, when did you eat last?"

"It's been a bit. But I'm okay until I get to Beckley. My buddy will help me then."

"Kelly, do you think Pansy might help a vet?"

"If you're thinking what I'm thinking, I suspect she'll help in more ways than one," Kelly said as her smile kicked up to the left.

GT was surprised at the amount of information Roland shared with Kelly; her methods of getting people to talk impressed the hell out of the sheriff.

At a Gulf station farther up the road, but within viewing distance of the sheriff's interaction with the hitchhiker, a man had sat quietly in a dark green pickup. Parked on the restroom side of the gas station, the pickup didn't stand out and wouldn't make anyone think twice about why it was there.

As the cruiser with his lost target sailed by, the man's frustration grew as he realized he needed to look for another. That transient was perfect, since no one local would miss him, but the appearance of the sheriff's car had messed that up big time. He pulled his red ball cap down a bit to shade his eyes, turned the ignition key, and pulled out onto the road. The hunt was back on.

56

DEPUTY DAVID FROST'S FIND KICKED off another action. A radio call on the SEALs' network went out to one of the teams, call sign Charlie, which was closest to the logging road. They were told to move to the car's location and start an outward search. It wasn't a full team, as LT Commander Barry Jackson had split the twenty men into five groups of four. But a group of four SEALs is equal to at least eight normal men: just ask a SEAL.

The final group, Team Charlie, actually consisted of five men. Jackson had attached himself to this team since they had the nastiest terrain to cover. He wasn't going to miss out on any of the fun.

Jackson signaled the team to form around him. They had been spread out, searching the woods. "Okay, people, quick minor change of location. The car has been found, but no sign of the kids. The boss wants us to do a radial search from that point. It's about three klicks to the north. You saw the smoke they popped. Maintain our established spread, and we'll swing north so we'll have a portion of the area searched by the time we get to the car. Questions?"

Team Charlie was professional, so questions were a waste of time. Their response was an assortment of quick nods and thumbs-up signals.

Jackson's responsive nod spurred the men to spread back to their search positions and swing from an eastward direction to north.

The men made sure nothing was overlooked in the fifty-foot-wide swatch they checked, moving toward the target vehicle. It wasn't easy. The area was dense with a variety of trees. Spruce, maple, tulip poplar, locust, and others ranged in size from one-inch-diameter bases to nearly four feet. The canopy was tight, allowing little sunlight to filter down, even with the bulk of the autumn leaves now under the men's feet. The early afternoon in the West Virginia forest seemed closer to dusk, due to cloud cover from the leading edge of the front moving into the area. And the forest floor was an obstacle course, as the sharp thorns of greenbriers latched onto their legs and fallen trees slowed their progress. It also took time to check for anything hidden by the thick carpet of multicolored leaves. There was not a path, beaten or otherwise, to follow through this mess.

Even with the challenges of the vegetation, they'd quickly covered about one-third of the distance to the target when BM3 Kevin Brown signaled everyone to halt in place. He motioned for Jackson to join his location.

"What ya got, Boats?" Barry Jackson asked quietly.

"Not what we wanted to find, Skipper, but probably related," Brown said in a hushed tone as he pointed toward a spot on the ground. While mostly shoved under a fallen tree, parts of a human body were visible.

Jackson squatted for a closer look. The body was in the early stages of decomposition and showed it had been food for some local critters. Not much blood was on the body or around the dumpsite. And like the others, this body was naked. Due to the positioning, Jackson could tell it was an adult male. "At least it's not one of the children. That is definitely an adult."

Brown said, "Yea, I'd hate to find a child in this condition. As for this guy, based on the smell and look of the skin, it's been here for a while. Two weeks, maybe longer."

"Agreed. Time to call Home Base." Jackson got on the tactical radio to Marcus and reported the find.

Following back-and-forth chatter, Brown was left standing guard on site to await the M.E. and his team. Although he wasn't in favor of leaving a man alone, Jackson agreed with the logic, and the rest of the team continued on to the target.

Even with the delay caused by the body find, vines, and other issues, they made good time. The remaining four men arrived at the scene as the wrecker was pulling the Buick onto the road.

Focused on the vehicle and hoping to find a clue or two, Deputy Frost didn't see the SEALs until they were literally a few feet away. He tried to hide his surprise. "Good to see you, Navy. Find anything?"

Jackson nodded sharply. "Yea, Deputy, we found another adult body about two klicks back. Naked and gutted like the others. I let Marcus know. Left one of my guys there to wait for the M.E."

Frost slowly shook his head. "This shit is getting old. At least we have the vehicle, and hopefully the FBI techies will find something to help the case. Excuse me, looks like they're ready to get going."

A short nod was Jackson's only response. Frost turned and walked over to supervise the final steps of strapping the vehicle in place and getting underway to Beckley. The deputy waved his goodbye from the cab as the wrecker and victim's car vanished down the hill.

Jackson turned to his three men. "Let's get moving. We'll swing south and see what we can find." He almost smiled while adding, "We have a little over three hours of light, followed by a five-klick jog back to the vehicle. Should be fun."

57

KELLY WAS EXCITED TO SHARE the information about Roland James with Marcus. Pansy was happy to give him a chance as line cook in her kitchen. She had hustled him off to the kitchen for lunch and a tour after GT explained the situation. GT then worked a deal for a room in the old Mercer Hotel a quick walk down the street. Kelly suspected GT paid the rent for at least the first week; she knew vets stick together. At least one good thing happened that day.

With the good news shared, she got back to work and added several new cards to the board. Anyone who looked closely at her face would see her doubt about it all. She knew these three people truly believed they saw what they reported, but logic told her that wasn't possible. Using a vast amount of energy, she forced out the negative thoughts and focused on getting the facts, as they told them, on the cards.

The interview with the last witness, Delores Janson, had been the shortest of the three. Delores refused to let them come into her house and simply stood behind the closed screen door. Her answers were short, and the only thing she added to the case was that the Mothman was flying west when she saw him. It wasn't much, but at least it was another straw.

Marcus looked at the cards. "More info is always a good thing. Did you see or hear anything that just didn't feel right? Or something that generated one of those 'they might be related' feelings?"

"I was trying to restrain my personal doubts about all these weird sightings and keep an open mind. It was difficult. Along those lines, I did have a thought. We might narrow down the Mothman's hideout based upon these sightings. Mrs. Janson saw him flying west from here." Kelly pointed to Janson's house on the map.

"Okay."

Pointing to another spot, Kelly said, "And Burton saw him flying west–northwest from here. The intersection of lines from these points might give us the place he was heading to."

"Logical. Plot it." Marcus handed her pins and string. Pointing to the Thompkins' house marker, he added, "And Cal Thompkins said the beastie flew over his house from the backyard, so it was going in an easterly direction. Might as well add that one also." He was going to add a funny comment about how the CNO would react to them plotting Mothman movements, but noise from the tactical radio got his attention.

"Home Base. Home Base. This is Team Charlie. Over."

"Go Charlie. Marcus here."

The report was disturbing. Another body found, but still nothing on the missing kids. Marcus told them the M.E. and a team would be on the way shortly. He got the location and signed off.

GT was already on the phone to the hospital telling the medical examiners to get their meat wagon headed to the location. He wanted both to go, to make sure nothing was overlooked. Marcus asked Deputy Walker to call Dr. Wallace and get him to join the M.E.s to check for evidence of bear, or any other creature.

"I'm heading out to meet them. Wanna come?" GT asked Marcus.

"Part of me wants to, but considering the expertise in route, I'll be in the way. Kelly and I will hang here rehashing the new info. And I need her to dig up some medical information to back up a wild thought. Rick, follow GT in your truck, and when they finish with the site, you and Sid call it a night and go to the house."

Rick nodded.

"What's the wild thought, Marcus?" GT asked.

"Probably a waste of time. Rick'll fill you in while you traipse through the woods," Marcus said as he shooed them out the door.

After they left, Kelly said, "Okay, Sailor, what's your wild idea?"

The explanation about the uses of blood was quickly shared, and Kelly agreed it was plausible. She called some friends at Walter Reed and took copious notes as they answered her questions. With the calls done, she added a few more notes to the pad, then called Marcus away from yet another study of the map and cards.

"Well, babe, your wild idea isn't so wild after all. Of course, blood can be used for cultures. The interesting thing is that while they said it's unusual, organs could be puréed and would work also. My question is, what could the evil ones be growing?"

With a shrug, Marcus said, "Anyone's guess. Some sort of bacteria or virus."

"Just another thing to throw into the mix, right?"

Marcus nodded. "I hate the idea of a biological weapon being created. But there aren't too many other options if we go down this road. Now we need to find the who, the why, and—as important—the when."

58

KELLY EASED THE NOSE OF the Ford Bronco up to the closed garage door and switched off the ignition. While Maude only had one car, a black '58 Caddie, the second bay held the Mustang, and the last bay of the three held the lawn mower and other standard garage junk and clutter. Good news was, the good folks of Princeton usually didn't mess with police vehicles, so the Bronco would be fine overnight.

"I called earlier and told Aunt Maude we'd be late for dinner. She said she'd leave some leftover meatloaf and veggies in the oven for us. She sounded almost too happy when we talked," Kelly said with a shrug. "Strange she wasn't upset we were missing dinner with her."

"She understands what we're doing. Glad you called—I didn't think about doing it."

Kelly nodded. "Well, deputy, you did have a full plate."

"Speaking of full plates … with Rick bringing Sidney, if he can pull him away from the new body, we should make quick work with those leftovers. I know I'm starving," Marcus replied slowly, his fatigue showing.

"Well, are we going in or what?" Kelly asked as she noticed Marcus lean back, resting his head on the seat back instead of opening the door.

"Yea, shortly, I'm enjoying the quiet for a moment," Marcus said in nearly a whisper. He let his mind wander over the day's events and again ran through the information the team had collected. Although his reverie lasted less than thirty seconds, it was time well spent. "We need to get with Sid and Rick for a short brainstorming session after dinner. Let's get inside."

Entering through the garage brought them into the dining room. They heard noises coming from the kitchen and followed the sound.

Aunt Maude, visible from the dining room, was sitting at the kitchen table and nursing a short glass of bourbon as she listened intently to someone hidden by the wall. They didn't have to wonder about the visitor's identity for long.

"It's about time you guys got home," Elle said. Her smile grew at their bewildered looks as Kelly and Marcus dashed to embrace her.

"What are you doing here?" Marcus said more sternly than intended.

Stepping away from their clutches, Elle said with more than a hint of sarcasm, "Nice to see you too, big brother."

Kelly gave Marcus a playful punch on the arm and kissed Elle's cheek. "I'm glad to see you even if grouch-butt has forgotten how to say a proper 'welcome' to his favorite sister." Quickly becoming serious, Kelly said, "But what about school? Exams?"

"Have a seat and I'll tell you all about it." Elle gestured to the table as she leaned against the counter. "I passed all of the exams last week, and my professors said I could take a week off from class to attend the memorial service." She shrugged and gave an elf-like grin. "Needless to say, I didn't give them the exact date of the service, so if they want to believe it's this next weekend and not the last, that works for me."

Marcus's face twisted in confusion. "You told me that you didn't want to attend. So why come now?"

"That's true, Marcus, and you know the reason why I stayed in Florida. But when I called your office yesterday afternoon to see how things went, and to make sure you were doing okay, Doc told me about the situation here. I had to see you two in police attire. And Doc wants lots of photos, so I picked up several rolls of Kodacolor film."

"I'm tickled pink that she's here, but I will not call her the letter 'L.' She will always be Eleanor to me," Aunt Maude said as she laid a hand on Marcus's arm. "Nice to have the family together. Right?"

"Yes, ma'am," Marcus said. "It is."

As the oven heated the food, the four chatted about the memorial service and the situation that held the Colts in West Virginia. Kelly had only started to share the story about the hitchhiker when the front door chimes sounded.

"Must be Rick and the doc," Marcus said as he stood. "Keep your seat, Aunt Maude, I've got this."

Marcus had guessed correctly. As the two late arrivals entered, Rick threw Marcus a quick salute and hung his jacket and cap on the hall tree. After his trudge through the West Virginia woods, he looked as tired as Marcus felt. As he pulled off his slightly muddy boots, he said, "Sir, we need to talk."

Doctor Sidney Wentworth followed Rick inside and grabbed Marcus's extended hand, quickly pulling him into an embrace. He patted him on the back, and said, "Thanks for including me in this adventure, my friend. Most fun I've had in years! Oh, yea, it is good to be working with you again. And young Rick is right: we do need to talk."

Marcus nodded. "Food first, then we can settle in the sanctuary and chat."

"Sanctuary?" Rick asked.

"That name just hit me. Better than calling it the basement. You'll like it," Marcus answered. "Oh, where's GT?"

"Probably still following Doctor Wallace around the woods. GT said he would drag the doc to his house in an hour or two. He'd call you from there if there was anything exciting to report," Rick said.

"Okay. By the way, another family member has joined us," Marcus said as he led the two to the kitchen.

Introductions to Eleanor were quick, but Marcus noticed she was slow releasing Rick's hand. And Rick seemed at a loss for words once he got past the standard "nice to meet you" line.

Dinner was well received and finished off quickly. As Kelly and Maude cleared away the dirty dishes, Marcus served the pumpkin pie and said, "Finish this and we'll head downstairs for a quick update. I suspect tomorrow will be hectic, so we need to get some sleep."

"Am I allowed to sit in on this meeting?" Elle asked as she glanced at Rick.

"As long as you remember that what you hear or see here, stays here. Some of it is not pleasant, but I suspect you can handle that," Marcus said. "And a lot of the information we don't want the public to know yet. Okay?"

"Thanks. I think I can play by the rules … for a change." Elle winked at Rick and got a grin in return.

Rick and Sid were as impressed with the basement, now dubbed the sanctuary, as Kelly had been on her first visit. Matt Monro was singing "Born Free" softly on the stereo as Marcus set up the glasses, each with two small, round ice cubes, and poured the bourbon. Everyone stood at the bar waiting.

Raising his glass, he said, "A quick toast, ladies and gents." They all raised their glasses. "May our team have success in finding the missing children alive and getting the Vampires off the streets."

Everyone muttered agreements, then moved to comfortable chairs after the glasses were refilled.

"All right, gents. What's the word about the latest victim?" Marcus asked.

Rick nodded toward Sid to take the lead. "From all indications, victim five is actually victim one. We tagged him 'Able Doe,' at least until we find an older one. His decomp leads Dennis and me to believe his demise came a week or more before the John Doe in Dennis's cooler. Of course, we'll know more in the morning after the autopsy. At first glance, he is missing the same organs as the others." Sid then pointed to Rick to continue.

"I had a long talk with Doctor Wallace after he did his thing at the site. No bear traces in the area or on the body. He did mention that there was some evidence of bears at the site of John Doe, but none at the others he had visited. He still needs to go over the rail yard site tomorrow, but since it is not in or near the woods, he doesn't expect to find any traces of bear. He'll participate in the autopsy in the morning."

Marcus silently absorbed the new information. He finally said, "Okay. Aside from finding the missing Buick, the air searches didn't find anything. And the volunteer searches had the same bad luck. I haven't heard from the rest of our SEALs yet tonight."

"Neither did we hear from the FBI lab in Richmond or Beckley. Maybe tomorrow they'll call," Kelly added.

"A frustrating day." Rick almost inaudibly voiced the feeling they all shared.

Marcus said, "We got a lot done for the first full day. And I think the possible use of the blood and organs as the food in a culture is a solid maybe. And with the number of victims growing, looks like he needs a lot of it."

Elle raised her hand.

Kelly chuckled. "That's not necessary around here, Elle. Just jump into the conversation whenever you want."

Nodding, Elle asked, "So this vampire kills for his supplies? I mean he's not killing for fun, but for some other reason."

"Yea, Sis, it looks that way. My speculation at this point in time, which is based on absolutely no solid evidence, is he's either a total psycho or growing something for use as a biological weapon. What, why, and where it would be used are unknowns."

Sid jumped in. "My confusion comes from the use of heroin to kill the victims … well, most of the victims. We do have one with a crushed skull. But when you can smash a skull, or in the isolated West Virginia woods fire off a pistol shot or two to kill, with no one hearing or caring, why waste money on heroin?"

"What if you have a good supply of heroin? Then the costs aren't a big deal," Rick offered. "Could these vampires be druggies? Maybe trading body parts for drugs? Or shipping drugs inside people, then gutting them to get it out?"

Marcus gave a thumbs-up and said, "Kelly found that black market organ sales would require major expertise and logistics, making the culture possibility more viable. As for drug trafficking, Sam's already checking on locals with access to aircraft since that would be an easy way to transport organs or drugs. GT mentioned that a guy we saw in Pansy's place had a history of selling drugs. Therefore, we have some checking to do in that direction."

"And we have no idea how he's getting his victims. No connections to each other have been found yet," Rick interjected.

"Could be he's suckering in the victims with an invite to a party where drugs might be, then overdoses them," Elle said.

Nodding, Marcus said, "Could be. But the kids' mother and the construction worker had no record of prior drug use. We don't know for sure, but it is another possibility we need to consider. Detective Chambers interviewed the mother's friend, Anita Colbeck. According to Colbeck, Doris Thompkins and the children had been staying with her. Doris was extremely mad at Cal, but she had calmed down and was going home. Doris left Colbeck's house the Friday before her body was found. She said she didn't alert police because she didn't realize Doris had been reported missing. Could be Cal killed her in a rage after her running out on him."

Kelly said, "But that doesn't explain the missing children."

Marcus shrugged and grimaced.

"Possibly they were victims of convenience—you know, wrong place, wrong time," Sid said.

"That's as good a guess as any. One thing we can conclude is there are at least two people involved," Marcus said.

"How do you figure?" Kelly asked.

"Doris's car was dumped up a logging road a good distance from anything. Whoever drove it there surely didn't walk home."

The group sat silently for a few moments.

"Without any firm links, not much else we can think," Rick said.

Kelly sighed. "Which doesn't make it any easier."

"Marcus, have you heard anything else from Lieutenant James? Doc said she was thinking there's some sort of drug ring at the Great Lakes NTC," Rick asked.

Marcus shook his head. "I'm expecting her update call in the morning. Wendy's gut was telling her tonight was the perfect time to grab one of the drivers servicing the base hospital with the mystery deliveries. Hopefully, she will also have more info on our fourth victim." To keep the new members updated, he continued, "Number four is from Chicago, so that NIS office is doing some background work on him."

"Any idea what a Chicago boy is doing in the wilds of West Virginia?" Elle asked. "Too late in the year for decent camping and too early for skiing."

Marcus shook his head.

Kelly started to add something only to be interrupted by the door chime upstairs. Being closest to the stairs, she said "My turn" and bolted to the door.

Elle asked a couple of pointed questions about the deceased, and Sid filled in her missing knowledge. She absorbed it all and asked, "Marcus, is it all right for me to shadow Sid tomorrow? I know I'll learn a lot watching the autopsy."

"That's up to Sid."

"Not a problem for me, Marcus. I welcome the company."

"Well, Sis, you are now assigned morgue duty."

Kelly returned to the sanctuary. "Ah, Commander Colt, you have a visitor." She stepped aside and allowed LT Commander Barry Jackson to enter.

"Sir, hope I'm not interrupting, but I felt an update was due."

Marcus escorted Jackson to the bar and said, "Drop the *sirs*, Barry. Bourbon okay?"

"Yes, sir, thanks. Sorry."

After waving off the comment, Marcus poured and said, "Barry, you know everyone here except the cute young lady over there. That's my sister, Elle, who will be helping us the next few days. So anything you have to say is okay for her ears."

Barry took a long sip of his drink. "Don't know if you've been watching the weather reports, but that storm is moving faster than expected. Temps have already dropped lower than projected, and the forecast rain will probably give us a decent layer of snow by dawn. An inch or two, maybe more. I pulled the teams out of the field and back to the motel."

Marcus nodded. "Yea, I got the weather update from Sam as I was leaving the office. He ceased air ops at sunset and will be on call for late morning tomorrow. He expects the front will have passed by then. Good move getting your team to shelter."

"My plan was to keep all my guys in the field overnight, but the weather changed my mind. It's hard enough to see anything in those woods without a snowstorm, so the inclement weather kills the search. We did complete the radial sweep around the vehicle out to over three hundred yards. Nothing found. Looks like the car was dumped there and the victims elsewhere."

"Logical thing to do," Marcus said.

"The other teams completed about ninety percent of their assigned areas, and there was nothing to report. We've got enough cold weather gear, so it's possible for us to head out at first light."

His face twisting in frustration, Marcus muttered, "And the way my luck goes, any decent clues are waiting in the last ten percent." He paused in thought, then commanded, "Barry, have your other four teams finish their areas starting around 0930 hours. That will give the snowplows enough time to get the roads cleared and them a couple extra hours of rest."

"Can do."

"Send three men from your team back to your assigned area. You and the leftover guy need to be at the sheriff's office at 0900. How do you feel about working with Marines?"

Barry chuckled. "They're usually trainable, and might not slow us down too much." That generated laughter from everyone except Rick.

Winking and tilting his head toward Rick, Marcus said, "I've found that to be usually true, but there are some exceptional ones. Anyway, unless y'all have something else, I think it's time for one last round before we call it a night."

59

Headlights from oncoming traffic were causing a true bitch of a headache. LT Wendy James was starting to think her great plan was a monumental flop: one of the most disastrous wastes of time and personnel assets in NIS history.

It had been nearly a week of nothing. No trucks making strange deliveries, no other leads. She needed to find and follow another truck in hopes of getting to the bottom of this case. Sure, she could raid the hospital and discover what they were moving, but she wanted to cut off the head of the snake, not just shut down a single distribution point. That's what she felt the hospital could be—a distribution point—or even the headquarters of the entire operation. Time would tell. So with high hopes of finding another truck, she'd been driving around the base for hours, waiting and watching.

Agents were undercover inside the hospital, and one was assigned to watch the loading dock from outside the building. Other agents were watching for possible trucks at all the base gates.

She slammed her hand against the steering wheel, frustrated. The silent radio indicated that Brad's luck had been as bad as hers. He was working the north side of the hospital as she patrolled the south. SSA

Todd Burke was positioned in a parking lot across from the loading dock, ready to go wherever he was needed.

"This is Campbell. We have a twenty-foot white box truck coming in the South Gate. No markings on the box. Small lettering on the cab door. Can't read it from where I am. Tag is an orange Illinois truck plate. Number is 2736H. Should I follow? Over."

Wendy grabbed her mike. "This is James. Hold your position. I see it and will follow."

The truck, as anticipated, slowly backed up to the hospital loading dock. As also expected, Chief Petty Officer Hugo Diaz walked to the rear of the truck and shook hands with the driver. Wendy watched as they chatted for a moment, then the driver rolled up the truck's rear door and both men vanished inside for a couple minutes. When they came out, the driver was pushing a hand truck full of boxes as he followed Diaz into the hospital.

Since this was the second delivery they'd witnessed, Wendy figured they had about ten minutes before the truck left. Maybe longer if the driver went inside for coffee. After all, his goal was to not look suspicious, and sipping coffee with the chief is a good way to look cool.

"Brad, hit the gas station, top off your tank, and grab some food and drink. Get whatever will keep you alert for twenty-four hours; I think we have a long night ahead. Over," Wendy said into the mike.

"Aye, aye, skipper," came the response from Neil.

Wendy added, "Todd, I'm going to tank up as well. Keep an eye on the truck. Over."

"Roger."

With full gas tanks, bags of snacks and drinks on the front seat, and empty bladders, Wendy, Brad, and Todd had a quick planning session. Figuring it would be the three of them tailing the truck, they agreed upon the switch-off method of a tail. This involved one or two vehicles falling back but staying in visual contact, and the third speeding ahead to await the truck, dropping in behind him when he passed.

The planning session abruptly ended when the radio came to life with Todd's voice. "All units. Subject vehicle is on the move. I'm on it."

Wendy slightly smiled as she keyed the mike. "Stick with the plan, people. Everyone hold positions until Todd, Neil and I find the subject vehicle's nest." Her order received numerous affirmative responses. The game was afoot, as Marcus had frequently said in the past. Wendy silently wished he were with her tonight.

The three-car version of the fall-back & speed-up tailing method worked well as the truck drove south, past downtown Chicago. But when it slowed to worm its way around the industrial area of the south side, it got a little more complicated. Traffic was nearly non-existent at this time of night. Todd knew the area and took a wild guess on the direction the truck was heading. He darted down a street two blocks over and positioned himself where he hoped the truck would go. The other two cars swapped positions around the truck, whose driver seemed unconcerned about any possible tail.

The truck nosed up to a run-down warehouse that had a single light fixture hanging over a rusty freight door. After a brief tap on the horn, the door quickly rolled up and the truck drove inside. The door slammed shut and all was quiet. As Todd watched this from his position in a dark alley up the street, Neil and James were positioned in a secluded area near the entrance to the complex. They settled down for what might be a long wait.

60

His headlights weren't that great, and the left one was slightly out of alignment, but they were enough to highlight the solitary man walking down the side of the road as he turned and extended a thumb. The driver immediately thought that maybe, just maybe, his luck had changed.

The pickup drifted to a stop, and the hitchhiker ran to it and stuck his head into the open passenger window. "Thanks for stopping, buddy. With the temps dropping, I thought I was going to freeze to death tonight. How far are ya goin'?"

"I'm heading up to Elkins, but plan on a late dinner stop at a place north side of Princeton. How 'bout you?"

"Pittsburgh is my home, so if you're willing to haul me along, Elkins is a lot closer than where I am now. Name's Hank."

The driver nodded and waved the hiker into the truck. "Call me Roy and get in." Roy was not his name, but if all went well, Hank would never know that.

It was a short twenty-minute drive to the far north side of Princeton. The truck nosed into a parking spot on the dark side of what most people would call a run-down shack, with a crappy neon sign flashing "Jim's lace" since the capital P that started the second word was burned out.

There were a couple of backlit signs pushing popular beers beneath it. They both needed a good cleaning.

As the now-quiet V-8 ticked as it cooled, the driver asked, "You got any money for some chow, Hank?"

Hank nodded and slid out the truck door. "Yea, I'll even cover you since you're driving. Hope the food's better than the sign."

After two bowls of chili and more than half a dozen beers, Hank and Roy were chatting like old friends. Roy had the gift of gab and was able to make strangers feel comfortable. Comfortable people open up. By the end of their third beer, Roy knew that Hank was not married, hadn't seen his parents in at least five years, and had spent those years hitchhiking around the country. He took odd jobs when he needed money, and hit the road when he didn't.

Back in the truck, Roy said, "Thanks for picking up the check, Hank. That wasn't necessary. Least I can do is tell you there is a bottle of tequila under your seat. Help yourself." Hank did.

They were about halfway to Beckley, the shared bottle now empty, when Hank said, "Man, I gotta sleep. Tequila always gets to me."

"No problem, I got a buddy who can put us up for the night. Hell, after a good night's sleep, I'll take you to Pittsburgh tomorrow before I head to Elkins, okay?"

"Sure. Wake me when we get there."

When Hank's head flopped back and the snoring overpowered the rattles of the old truck, Roy eased into a turn-around usually used by the highway patrol and pointed the nose of the truck toward Princeton.

After too many miles and way too many road changes, the headlights of the stopped truck showed the gate was closed and chained. Roy shifted into neutral and set the hand brake. He reached under the seat and pulled out a small case. The liquid was drawn into the syringe and Roy reached over and injected it into the side of Hank's neck.

Hank roused, looked around, and said, "What was that?"

"Nothin' man, I stopped at my buddy's house. Go back to sleep."

No response came from Hank. His eyes were closed and his breathing started to get ragged. Roy exited the truck and went to open the gate. By the time he got behind the wheel, Hank's breathing had stopped. Time to get him to the doctor.

61

LT WENDY JAMES GREW MORE frustrated by the minute. She had been sitting and waiting for the suspect truck to leave the warehouse for nearly an hour. This was her last chance to follow the truck to its next destination, but it wouldn't happen if the damn truck stayed in the warehouse. And SSA Todd Burke and the backup agents couldn't raid the warehouse until the damn truck left.

Wendy slammed her hand against the steering wheel again to relieve the frustration. Noise from her radio pulled the veil of irritation from her eyes.

Burke's voice was hushed. "We've got movement. Truck is heading your way."

"Copy," Brad Neil replied as Wendy grabbed her mike to do the same.

"Take the lead, Brad. I'll hang back. Burke, give us ten minutes to make sure he doesn't turn around before hitting the place," she said.

"Happy hunting. Stay safe," Burke replied.

The hours passed quickly as Wendy and Brad swapped positions while tailing the suspect truck. The chase led Wendy and Brad south and east, leaving Gary and Indianapolis, Indiana in their rearview mirrors. They swapped gas breaks and kept the truck in sight. Heading south from Dayton Ohio, they crossed into West Virginia on the Silver Memorial

Bridge at Point Pleasant on Route 35. Continuing south, they connected with the interstate in Charleston and continued on toward Beckley.

On the unexpected long-distance drive, one impediment was the lack of radio repeater stations. Car radios have a distance of ten to twenty-five miles under good conditions. Illinois had repeater stations installed statewide, but like many other states, Indiana and West Virginia were only starting their installations. As a result, Brad and Wendy were in communication with each other, but not with the team back in Illinois. When time allowed, they'd need to find a phone to provide an update.

Making matters worse, the surveillance became more difficult south of Beckley. The snow had started several hours ago, and now the amount of traffic was severely reduced due to the weather and late hour. The dashboard clocks were rapidly approaching 0600. It had been a long drive, on the tail end of a long day.

The lack of other vehicles reduced the opportunity for them to hide from their subject. The only positive was that the reduced traffic allowed them to follow the truck tracks in the fresh snow. And since they frequently lost sight of the truck due to the hills and curves of the West Virginia roads, the snow gave them a needed edge.

Brad had passed the truck as it slowed down to take an exit onto a county road. He keyed his mike. "Subject exited at Camp Creek onto Route 19 and headed south. I'll turn around and take the tail position. Might be difficult to keep passing him on that side road."

"I see the road. Catch up when you can." After making the turn, she continued, "Truck tracks are the only thing on this side road. Will make the tail easier. I'm holding back and letting him out of my sight."

Five minutes later, Wendy expected to see Brad's headlights in her rearview. It was still dark behind her. While she reached for the mike, her eyes left the road for the briefest of moments. Her gaze returned to the road in time to see part of a large black shadow fly across the road slightly above the car.

"What the hell?" Wendy muttered as she looked in the mirror, hoping to see whatever that was. Distance, dark, and snow hid it from her … if it even existed.

Getting her mind back on the surveillance, she keyed the mike. "Brad, what's your status?"

Silence filled the car as she squinted to see the tracks through the falling snow. It was coming down faster and heavier.

"Brad, come in."

She slowed to let Brad catch up and continued on for a few minutes before trying to contact him again. Again there was no response. If his radio was out or blocked by a mountain, he should have caught up with her by now. Her gut was screaming that there was something wrong.

Marcus had taught her on their first assignment that you never leave your partner behind. Wendy still vividly remembered Marcus ignoring his own wounds as he carried her down the side of a volcano to get help for her broken leg. With that in mind, she slowed and started scanning for a place to turn around.

The road was typical of many in the state. Bulldozed from the side of a mountain, the road featured either a rock wall or steep upgrade on the uphill side, and a sharp drop off on the down side. Roadside parking was not standard on most of West Virginia's back roads. On this one, a stream was at the bottom of the drop off. But a road named Wolf Creek came up on her left and provided the perfect place for a three-point turn. She picked up speed as she retraced her path in search of Brad.

It was only about eight miles to the exit, but travel on the road was slow even in pleasant weather and daylight. Night and heavy snow further slowed the travel time.

Wendy was nearing the last big curve before the exit when she saw Brad's car. It was mostly off the road, with the crumpled front nosing down toward the creek below. Had a two-foot-diameter oak tree not been there, it would have been a rough fifty-foot ride to the water. Luckily, Brad was standing at the edge of the road waving both arms above his head. Wendy stopped with the headlights pointing toward him and the wreck behind him.

"Damn glad to see you, partner! I was just getting ready for a long walk back to the exit."

Wendy looked him over and noticed blood on his forehead. "You okay?"

"Yea, I'm better off than the car."

"Your forehead isn't. Give me your handkerchief and bend down into the light," Wendy ordered.

The cut on his forehead was minor, but since head wounds bleed profusely, Brad's face was becoming a mess. As she put pressure on the wound at his hairline, she asked, "What the hell happened?"

Brad shrugged. "Three deer jumped down from the bank right in front of me. I swerved too quickly. That saved the deer but killed the car on a tree. Car's radio is totally dead, so I couldn't let you know. My head hit the steering wheel even though I had stiffened up."

"Well, glad you're not hurt worse. I wonder where the closest hospital is located?"

"I'm good, Wendy, really I am. After this long drive, we need to find that truck."

"Okay, Brad, your call. Grab your stuff while I leave a note on the car. We can still follow this guy if we hurry."

62

KELLY SNUGGLED CLOSE TO MARCUS. She admitted to herself that these few moments before they fell asleep, wrapped in each other's arms, were some of the best parts of the day. The comfort, protection, and love formed a cocoon that locked out the day's evils. It was like Superman's Fortress of Solitude, she thought, but without all the ice.

"Any unspoken plans for us tomorrow, Sailor?" Kelly whispered, her reluctance to open the cocoon trumped by her concerns for the case.

He blew out a deep breath of frustration, then chuckled softly. "I'm counting on my subconscious and dreams to provide those plans. All we can do is what we have been doing, and adding more data to the boards. It will come together. We have a good team in place."

"This situation has showed me that when working with my patients, I only get a glimpse of some of the issues they experienced. It is nothing compared to what we have here. War causes pain and death, but this evil here is different. It's more personal, I guess. And I'm seeing it firsthand."

"The thing is, you are seeing it closer to the source. The evil is fresher by being closer. It's more alive. Imagine how it would be if you worked with those soldiers while they were still in 'Nam."

"Yea, I get it."

They lay quietly for a time, then Marcus asked, "So, based on all you've seen, what's your guesses about the main man behind all this evil? Have you worked up any kind of psychological profile?"

Kelly rolled away from Marcus, on her back, and looked at the ceiling. "No. I can't grasp how anyone could do that to people. What was done to those bodies is horrible."

"You're probably falling into the trap that catches many new intelligence officers—you're looking in the mirror."

"What does that mean?"

"It's simple, Princess. You're assuming your enemy thinks or believes as you do. They don't. You see him as a reflection of yourself, so it's hard to grasp that level of evil because you can't conceive how anyone could do it. I've seen enough evil over the years that I can usually avoid that trap."

Turning on the nightstand light, Kelly rolled onto her side and looked at Marcus. She traced the aging scar of a gunshot wound on his arm with her finger. "You carry a record of the evil you've seen on your body. I hope it hasn't scarred your mind the same way."

"Not that I've noticed. Besides, I suspect my live-in head shrinker would spot any problems before I would. In reality, my experiences have given me a way to get into the heads of the bad guys. Makes it easier to catch them."

"Okay," Kelly whispered. "So what does your vast library of evil tell you about our Vampire?"

"Not enough … yet. The Vampire is probably male. He's driven. Not working alone, but doesn't have too many associates. He's intelligent, with training as a scientist or doctor. That shows in his meticulous approach to removing parts from the bodies. And working on the assumption he's educated, that puts his minimum age in the mid-to-late twenties. But without any solid evidence or logic, I think he's older."

Kelly said, "Impressive."

"Not really. Just educated guesses," Marcus said. "And he probably has a trigger that started his collecting body parts a couple of months ago. If we knew that trigger, this case would be easier to solve. Something started his actions, unless he's been doing this for years in other areas of the country. But a crime spree this evil would've eventually made the news. Like it will here, in the near future."

"What leads you to believe he isn't working alone?"

"Of the five bodies, the last three were moved to areas where they would be found. To me, that comes across as whoever is moving the bodies is showing remorse. Maybe the assistant is feeling guilt and wants to be caught or—"

Kelly interrupted, "Maybe the Vampire is showing off?"

"Possible, but doubtful. It's another thing to keep in mind."

With a soft giggle, Kelly asked, "Sounds like you're giving up on the Bigfoot and Mothman involvement."

"No way, Princess. I want to see your father's face when the *Washington Post* headline reads 'Navy SEALs Capture Bigfoot.'"

"That's almost enough for me to want to believe!" Kelly reached to turn out the light.

Marcus chuckled. "Yea, it would be great, eh? But the thing we have not uncovered is how the three bodies were moved to the places they were found. No tracks, no footprints, nothing. That opens the door to the Mothman making deliveries—as crazy as that sounds, even to me."

"It will be hard to prove that Bigfoot is telling Mothman where the bodies were dumped," Kelly said with more than a hint of sarcasm.

"Don't let your doubts cloud the facts, Princess. Let those fair winds of doubt blow the fog from your eyes. Someone, or something, lowered three bodies into place and left no tracks. And on that thought, I think it's time we get some sleep."

"You're right again, Sailor," Kelly whispered as she pulled tight against Marcus.

63

HE CHECKED HIS WATCH AGAINST the dashboard clock. Wendy had stipulated a ten-minute wait, and both timepieces told him the wait was almost over. The truck had not returned, and no one had come or gone from the building. As he waited, SSA Todd Burke thought back to the meeting with a lawyer earlier in the week.

Most of Monday morning had been spent speaking with a JAG officer. The meeting's purpose was to clarify the legal ramifications of unannounced popping in, so to speak, on a company providing services or materials to the Navy base. This Judge Advocate General attorney was a serving naval officer whose specialty was contract law. He assured the NIS agents that a surprise "inspection" was authorized in all military contracts, ergo no warrant was necessary. And any evidence of wrongdoing would be admissible. All of the boxes were checked to make sure they stayed legal.

SSA Burke again consulted his watch and radioed his agents. "Time to hit the warehouse. Stay in your zones. Breach in two minutes. You know the drill. Move!"

Six NIS agents moved swiftly and silently to their assigned entry points.

The building had one vehicle door, the one the suspect truck had used, and three thirty-six-inch-wide steel entry doors. Two doors were on the ground floor, one at the front and one at the rear of the building, and the third was on the second floor, providing egress to the metal fire escape stairs on the side of the building.

One agent was assigned to keep that door under tight surveillance while three agents breached the entry door in the front, and the other two did the same at the rear.

Security was lax on the part of the bad guys. All doors were unlocked, so when the moment arrived, the agents simply opened the doors and entered quietly. Lighting was minimal, and at first glance, only a small section of the ground floor was visible. Low voices came from that area as the agents slowly worked toward them.

With weapons drawn, three agents stepped from the darkness as SSA Burke announced, "Federal agents! On your knees! Hands on your heads!"

Four men at one of several workbenches covered with various pieces of laboratory equipment froze, with deer-in-the-headlight looks. They slowly raised their hands as ordered. But none of those three agents saw the fifth man, who was at the edge of the lighted area. Ducking down and backing into the darkness, he soundlessly moved away from the agents.

He crept deeper into the shadows, heading to the rear door. Logic told him there would be an agent stationed there, but he had heard no activity in that area. Perhaps the agent's rear guard was not as sharp as he needed to be. He paused and listened. Nothing.

The two NIS agents who'd breached the rear door had positioned themselves in strategic places, as ordered: a storage shelf directly across from the door concealed one, with the second concealed in a similar location a few feet deeper into the warehouse. The darkness hampered their surveillance of the exit, but careful listening picked up a soft noise. It was a noise of someone moving toward them.

Reaching the door, the man looking to escape was suddenly blinded by the flashlight of one NIS agent as the second grabbed his arms and pulled them behind him.

His escape attempt ended with an agent yelling, "On your knees!"

As they were leading their cuffed captive back to the group, all the overhead lights came to life—one of the agents had found the electrical panel. With the large warehouse bathed in light, the agents saw that it was hardly used. A few loaded shelving units were strategically placed to block the view of the interior, should someone glance in as one of the doors opened. Other than that, a couple more storage shelves and several workbenches were centrally positioned so the trucks could unload near them.

Two large rectangles rested side by side behind the workbenches. Burke recognized them as walk-in coolers; he found both unlocked and in use, with small boxes stacked neatly on wire racks running down both sides of the coolers.

But it was the workbenches that held Todd Burke's attention. Set up like an assembly line, the extensive set of benches contained open cases of small glass medical vials with rubber stoppers, an open box of pre-shaped aluminum caps, and a small machine designed to crimp the caps around the necks of the vials. Stacks of pre-printed labels covered the last bench in the row. Most of the names on the labels were alien to Todd, but he quickly recognized an illegal medication-packaging operation. Crimp vials were standard for liquid medications given by injection.

As the suspects were being led out the door, SSA Burke found a phone and called for backup from the NISO office. The forensic teams would have a field day with this warehouse.

The radio connection was spotty at best, but Todd was able to tell Wendy that there was evidence of stolen Navy property in the warehouse. And as the JAG officer had clarified, the truck was involved in the crime and NIS had every right to stop and inspect it.

64

THE SNOW WAS DOING A decent job of covering tire tracks by the time they retraced Wendy's journey. Passing Wolf Creek Road meant new territory for Wendy, and the urgency to find the truck before the snow obliterated its trail pushed her to speed up. But not too much, since darkness, unknown roads, and snow make for a dangerous drive.

A sign told them the community of Spanishburg was right ahead, but as they slowed in anticipation of congestion, Brad said, "Not much to see here, is there?"

Shaking her head, Wendy replied, "These woods and mountains could hide an aircraft carrier. Right now, they're doing a good job of hiding a box truck, and we now have another set of tire tracks, so it's getting challenging."

"Look there," Brad nearly shouted a moment later as he pointed to large truck tire tracks in the snow, which turned right at the upcoming intersection. "Nubbins Ridge Road. Take it."

After what seemed like an hour of twists and turns in deepening snow, but was only a couple of miles on the odometer, Wendy saw the tire tracks turn onto a narrow driveway. She slowed slightly to scope out the place on the drive-by. There wasn't much to see, as the driveway quickly vanished into woods and over a small hill. No lights were visible from the highway.

"Not much to see from here either," Brad said.

"True." Wendy slowed more once they were around another curve, hidden from the driveway. "Looks like there might be a place to stash the car ahead. Are you up for a bit of infiltration of the farm? Can your wounded head handle it?"

"My butt is numb from all the driving. Slinking around in snow-covered woods sounds like fun," Brad replied. "Even with my growing headache. At least the bleeding has stopped."

They jogged to the driveway, keeping in the tracks from the truck to hide their footprints. Sunrise was coming, and that would make the quick recon more dangerous. Fortunately, the locked gate that secured the gravel drive was easy to scale. The "driveway" beyond it was more of a deeply rutted gravel cattle path.

They hugged the trees that flanked it as they quickly moved to find the truck. As they reached the crest of a small rise, a house came into view.

The run-down, deserted-looking farmhouse was circled by common farm structures including a large wood barn, a modern metal building, and a couple of smaller storage sheds. A pickup truck was visible beside the house, bathed in the yellow glow from a bug light over what might be a kitchen door. No other exterior lights shone.

The box truck they'd followed from Chicago was backed up to the open door of the metal building. Soft light from inside the building leaked out around the edges of the truck's silhouette, and forms of people moving boxes into the building interrupted that light.

The NIS agents eased into the brush on the side of the driveway and approached the building. Their speed was hampered by the requirement of silence, but they were soon positioned out of the sight lines of the door. Wendy whispered, "Stay here. I'm moving closer."

Brad nodded.

Wendy quietly walked in a crouch to the wall around the corner from the open door. She dropped to the ground, knowing the snow had turned the area to mud. Hopefully the area was void of animal droppings. *Another set of clothes killed by the job.*

Keeping as low as possible, she crawled to the corner. Easing her head around the side allowed her to see the truck and hear most of the conversation happening near it.

Her language skills came in handy: two men were speaking Spanish. She recognized the accents and phraseology as being from South America, probably from Argentina, she thought. *Maybe Bolivia.*

The man that sounded older, more gruff, spoke with authority. The younger-voiced man, the one using more slang, was probably the truck driver. Her assumption was confirmed when the second man was ordered to get back on the road to Chicago pronto. His complaints about lack of sleep fell on deaf ears. The back-and-forth continued for several minutes as each man argued his logic. In the end, the driver lost the argument.

Wendy retraced her movements to Brad. She pointed toward the gate and motioned for him to move out. When they were past the crest of the hill, she said in a low voice, "The driver has been ordered to get out of here. I've got a plan, if you're up to it."

65

THE SNOW WASN'T MUCH OF an issue for the morning commute. A total of about two inches had fallen in Princeton, a bit more in the higher elevations, and the plow crews had been efficient on the main roads. Marcus rode to the sheriff's office with Rick. Kelly drove Sidney Wentworth and Elle Colt to the hospital arriving as GT dropped off Simpson Wallace. She tossed the Bronco keys to Wentworth and bummed a ride to the sheriff's office with GT.

"I left the Bronco at the hospital—Sid has the keys," Kelly said as she and GT both reached for the coffee cups Marcus had filled. Norma was on the ball and had brought in a second coffee maker to ensure they wouldn't run out.

"I didn't want to leave them stranded, so I figured with GT's and Rick's vehicles here, we'd be okay without it today. The two M.E.s and Simpson were starting to work on the new arrival. The body is in pretty poor condition, they said. Elle decided taking photos and notes would keep her out of trouble and help them."

"Did they give any hints on when they would have results?" Marcus asked.

Kelly shook her head. "No, they said they'd call when done. I suspect it will be mid-afternoon at the earliest. Like I said, the body's in rough shape."

Marcus smiled through his freshly growing headache. "Okay. By the way, our *Bugle* editor Jerry gets a 'done good' award for today's special free edition. Did you see it?"

"No," Kelly said. "Got a copy handy?"

Sliding the special edition across the counter to Kelly, Marcus said, "He sent a supply to all the surrounding counties, so the word is spread far and wide—at least locally."

After a quick read and a flip through the six-page edition, Kelly gave her nod of approval. "And we need to send a copy to Tommy Garrett."

Marcus smiled. "Norma's sealing the envelope right about now with a copy and a note of praise from the sheriff." He pointed to GT. "Now, before the SEALs arrive, the sheriff here needs to place a personal call to a neighbor."

"Hopefully you will elaborate on that a bit more, Marcus Aurelius," GT said as his brow knotted up. "I got lots of neighbors."

"Sure. Now that everyone is properly caffeinated, walk with me to the war room."

In the conference room that now boasted a military title, Marcus went to the map board. He pointed to each string line Kelly had added Wednesday evening. "These are the reported lines of travel for our cryptid critters: Mothman and Bigfoot. Since the intersection is near the border with Wyoming County, I think GT needs to notify their sheriff that our crew is invading. Don't you agree, Godfrey my man?"

GT couldn't hide a look of confusion. "What exactly are we looking for there?"

"Whatever Rick, Frost, and the SEALs can find," Marcus answered with a shrug.

Rick grimaced and rubbed his temples. He, too, felt a stress headache starting.

Marcus continued, "Perhaps they will find the Mothman's nest ... I guess moths have nests. Or locate a cave full of Bigfoot creatures. Or just maybe they find the missing children. Then again, it might be a total waste of time, but please think of it as another *t* to cross."

GT pointed to the map's junction of strings. "Yea, it wouldn't take much for them to invade Wyoming County when starting there. Maybe I can notify Sheriff Stroud that we'll be in his territory without telling him why. I don't want to be the source of ridicule at the next sheriffs' conference if word gets out I'm chasing the Mothman."

Choking on a sip of coffee and a subtle laugh, Marcus said, "Tell him you got a vague lead about the missing children that needs to be checked. That should keep you off the joke list. Hell, he might want to help."

GT headed to his office to make the call. He saw Deputy David Frost coming in the back door with a man in a three-piece suit, and he directed them to the war room.

"I'm surprised to see you so soon, Frost," Marcus said as he noticed the deputy's arrival. "Who's the guest?"

The man in the suit, an FBI liaison from their Beckley office, introduced himself as Supervisory Special Agent Ken Santoro. He shook the hand Marcus extended. "Someone higher than the director said we are at your beck and call, Commander. After we finished with the suspect vehicle, I decided we might need closer contact. So I'm here for the duration. I followed Deputy Frost, so I have my own transportation."

Marcus nodded. "All that works for me. We don't have time for formalities around here, Agent Santoro, so I'll call you 'Ken' and I answer to 'Marcus.' That okay for you?"

Santoro chuckled. "Damn straight, Marcus. Until I get up to speed, I'll be sitting quietly absorbing information, so please continue."

After a quick round of introductions, Marcus turned to Frost. "So, what ya got?"

"Like Ken said, the FBI boys had orders from on high to get it done fast, which they did. Finished up around 0400 hours. I napped while waiting for the roads to be cleared, then came on home, sir." Frost handed a large manila envelope to Marcus.

Feeling the weight, Marcus knew it would take some time to read. "Give me the executive summary, Frost. What did they find?"

Standing close to attention, Frost said, "Minor damage to the right front fender and evidence of a deer strike. Otherwise, the exterior of the Buick was clean. And most of the interior was also. However, they found a partial print on the seat adjustment lever; they're running it, but that might take a while. Two other things jumped out. The seat was pushed all the way back."

Kelly interrupted, "Why was this concerning?"

"Her height, ma'am. Doris Thompkins was only five-four. With the seat slammed back that far, a driver had to be at least six-two to reach the pedals. Indicates someone else dumped the car."

Kelly nodded. "Makes sense. What was the second thing?"

"They found a small amount of mud on the top edge of the brake pedal. Considering how clean the rest of the vehicle was, I'm amazed it was overlooked. But since it was on top of the pedal, and right in front of the actuating arm, I can see how they did. What made it interesting is initial testing showed it contained traces of blood and clay. They'll send down an analysis report later today about their findings."

"Any wagers as to whether the blood matches Mrs. Thompkins, or the clay is a match to the cat litter found on the bodies?" Marcus asked no one in particular.

"No thanks! That would be a fool's bet," Kelly said.

"True. Please add those pieces of information to the boards, Kelly. Put a question mark behind the six-two height comment about the possible bad guy, since he could be shorter and pushed the seat back to make cleaning the floor easier."

Marcus noticed GT and Detective Allen Chambers enter and grab chairs. He quickly introduced Ken, shared the synopsis of Frost's report, and tossed the envelope to Chambers. "I think this has your name on it, Allen. Frost gave a good overview, but the techies might not have told him all the goodies. Give it a good read, please."

Chambers nodded as he mimicked weighing the package in his hand, then muttered, "There goes my morning."

"Marcus, Sheriff Stroud appreciated the heads-up call and promised to keep an eye out for the kids. And yes, I risked my reputation and mentioned both Bigfoot and the Mothman. To my surprise, he has three reports on his desk about Mothman sightings and one Bigfoot report these past few weeks. Weird, eh?" GT raised his hands in helplessness.

Marcus's face twisted as another thought hit. "Did he mention any missing person's reports?"

"No. Since he knew about our John Doe, he would have mentioned any issues he had," GT replied. The team fell silent in reflection.

Kelly broke the silence. "Marcus, did you hear from Wendy yet?"

Marcus shook his head. "Nothing yet. I suspect they had a long night. I'll call them in about an hour unless they beat me to it."

Norma stuck her head in the door. "Deputy Bonner called just now. That guy Ledder expects the weather to clear by noon, so they'll be here around three."

"Thanks, Norma." GT turned to the map board and continued, "I told George to sleep in this morning. He had two extra-long days this week, and my budget doesn't have room for a lot of overtime. He said his teams covered most of their assigned areas. Nothing found. They'll be back out this afternoon to finish up these areas. Anything else you want from them, Marcus?"

Rubbing the area between his eyes, Marcus looked at where GT pointed on the map. "Yea, have them start searching for the place where the bodies are being gutted. Kelly, what sort of equipment would be needed for organ harvesting or to create those cultures and grow some bugs?"

Her slight smile twisted up to the right in a look of concentration before she said, "Electricity is a must in either case: refrigeration storage for the harvesting and heat for the cultures. For the cultures, they can convert the organs into liquid with simple household blenders, but it would take a while. Restaurant-type equipment would be faster. And to grow the bacteria or virus, a constant heat source is needed to maintain a proper temperature. Heat lamps would do that. Or even some heating pads placed under the containers. And a fairly clean controlled environment, so no open sheds or dirty basements."

"Isolation would be my preference, if I was doing it," Rick said. "Hauling in and out dead bodies is not something you'd do in a populated neighborhood."

GT said, "Yea. We have a lot of abandoned houses, barns, and garages away from the public eye around here. No warrants needed to search them since they're abandoned. George's teams can start there."

"They can search inhabited structures if the owners give permission. And if they don't allow a look-around, that would be a red flag that something illegal might be going on there," Allen added.

"All right. George's groups will start with remote structures. Kelly, I want you and Josh to check out garages, warehouses, any industrial-type building here in town. Stop by the police department and brief Chief Wester first. He might have some suggestions where to start, and ask if he has any officers who might be free to help. Allen will hold the fort here, while GT and I go have a chat with Carl Marks," Marcus ordered.

"Who's he?" Kelly asked.

"A local Hispanic fellow who kept eyeballing us at Pansy's yesterday morning. He has had drug issues in the past," GT offered.

Marcus pointed to the board with all the index cards. "And we have a link, albeit a weak one. Our fourth body was Hispanic, and with less than one percent of the Mercer County population in that ethnic group, it's a good guess they might know each other. Like I said, the link is weak, but with the druggie past, Carlos Marcano—a.k.a. Carl Marks—is a person of interest, and he might know Jesus Cabilla."

"I saw a town called Spanishburg on the map. Guess he might live there, right?" Kelly asked.

GT chuckled. "Sorry, Kelly, no Hispanics live in Spanishburg. It was named after a relative of the first guy to claim land in that area a few years before the Civil War started. His brother-in-law, or at least I think that was the relationship, was named Spanish Brown. Hell of a first name, eh? Good news is I know where Carl hangs out, so let's roll."

"May we have a moment of your time first, Sheriff?" Wendy asked wearily. Mud and fatigue had her looking worse for wear as she led a bandaged Brad into the war room. Both agents looked as if they'd lost a battle. Walking between them was an unknown man, also roughed up, wearing handcuffs.

66

IT SEEMED THE LONG NIGHT would never be over; fact is, it still wasn't. SSA Todd Burke might have looked relaxed as he sat at his desk sipping coffee, but actually he was running on fumes, both mentally and physically. Too much caffeine coursed through his system as he approached his twenty-sixth-straight hour of work. And there was still a lot to do before he could call it a day.

While things looked under control at the NISO, they weren't. Six suspects were locked in holding cells awaiting interrogation, one team of agents and lab techies were scouring the warehouse gathering evidence, and a second team was doing the same at the base's hospital. If anything, they had more to do now that they'd found the warehouse.

Burke had called in help from the base Shore Patrol commanding officer (SPCO) to round up the off-duty hospital staff that worked for or around Chief Diaz. Each was considered a suspect until interviewed and cleared. The SPCO offered to hold them at the brig, separated of course, until the NIS agents could get the interviews underway. Which would happen only after the six suspects currently in the NISO office were handled.

Burke's biggest headache was the lack of communications with the two NISHQ agents. Wendy James and Brad Neil had dropped out of

"

radio range last night as they followed a suspect truck heading south. Whatever they found when the truck stopped was data he had to report to Marcus Colt that morning. He hoped his phone would ring soon with their update.

SA Rodney Carth stuck his head in the door and destroyed Burke's train of thought. "There's something you need to hear, boss."

"What?" Burke snapped, immediately regretting it. "Sorry I jumped on ya, Rod. What ya got?"

"No problem, boss. We're all running on fumes. Anyway, Chief Hospital Corpsman Hugo Diaz finally let something slip. Here he was being all closed mouth for hours, smirking that 'you can't get nothing from me look,' you know the one I mean. Then Josh pushed him about being a total idiot for being involved with this mess. Diaz laughed and mumbled something about letting the games begin."

"Can you elaborate on that, Rod? Kinda vague. Got anything else?"

"Nothing yet. But we'll keep pushing him. Only a matter of time before he realizes the bad spot he's in. I'll get back to it."

Burke nodded. "Okay, thanks. Send Morgan in, please."

SA Morgan Turk must have been in the hall, appearing seconds after Rod Carth left. Leaning against a file cabinet for support, he asked with a tired voice, "What's up, Todd?"

"What's your plan on the interrogations for the warehouse crew?"

"Based on the colors they're wearing, the five we grabbed are members of the Southside Cardinals. They control most of the drug traffic on the south side of Chi-town and are used to being pulled in. Right now, we have each one isolated, and we'll keep them that way. I don't expect the normal questioning routine to give us much, so I'll tell them that one of their buddies is accusing them of being the ringleader. Might shake them loose a bit, but I'm not holding out for a miracle," Morgan said.

"Okay. You might also let them stew alone for another hour or so before you start."

Morgan nodded. "Anything else?"

"Yea, Rod mentioned Diaz let slip a line about 'letting the games begin.' You might be able to toss the word 'games' into the questioning. Maybe that will give them the impression we know more than we do."

"I'll let ya know if that works."

"Hope you get something to work soon. I have to call Colt with an update, and I want to tell him more than I've misplaced two of his people."

67

RIGHT BEFORE WENDY JAMES AND Brad Neil started the debrief on Wednesday's activities, LCDR Jackson and RM2 Waterman strolled into the war room earlier than expected.

"Mornin' deputies, how goes …" Jackson said with a light, cheery voice, halting when he saw the condition of the two new people. He nodded to Marcus and continued more solemnly, "Sorry, sir."

Marcus smiled as he replied, "Navy SEALs Lieutenant Commander Barry Jackson and Petty Officer Andy Waterman, say a quick 'hello' to FBI Supervisory Special Agent Ken Santoro from Beckley, and NIS Special Agents Lieutenant Wendy James and Brad Neil. The last two are part of my D.C. staff and are working a possibly related case in Chicago. They brought us a suspect named Luis Johnson, and are now getting ready to tell us why they are so far out of their assigned territory and looking like they lost a battle."

After a brief exchange of laughter and greetings, Brad extended his hand, palm up, toward Wendy for her to take the lead.

She provided a quick and concise overview of what was happening in Chicago. Some of it Marcus knew, but the info about last night was new information. Brad offered a few detailed comments to complete her report.

Before she could continue about the events of the overnight drive, Norma rapped on the door casing. "Uh, Deputy Marcus, NIS Chicago is on line one for you. He said it is very urgent."

"Thanks, Norma." Marcus pressed the buttons for line one and speakerphone. "SSA Burke, how can the good folks of West Virginia help you today? As a word of warning, you are on speakerphone with Wendy and Brad."

"Thank God they're there. I've got a dozen more gray hairs worrying about those two overnight. What is their status, sir?"

Marcus smiled. "While they both look a bit worse for wear, they gave an overview of what happened last night in Chicago and were starting to tell us about their overnight adventure. You might want to pull in a secretary and take notes, Todd."

"Can do, sir. Give me thirty seconds," Burke replied.

While waiting, Brad laid his head on the table and closed his eyes. Kelly noticed and moved to his side. She quietly asked, "You okay?" as she rubbed his shoulders.

"Fine except for a nasty headache. Think I need more coffee and several aspirin."

"Uh, no aspirin. I think you need a CT scan," Kelly said.

"What the hell is that?"

Kelly smiled. "Computed Tomography. It's a new technology that provides a detailed image of your brain. Think of it as an enhanced x-ray machine. And with it, we can check for issues that might be hiding inside your skull, such as a subdural hematoma. That's a bruise on your brain that can kill you. And aspirin can make it worse, by the way."

Brad nodded. "Okay, doctor, I'll follow your lead, but only after we debrief."

Kelly raised her hands in surrender.

Coming back on line, Burke said, "Ready to go on this end, Marcus."

With a nod from Marcus, Wendy then went into greater detail about the trip down from Illinois and the events at the farm. Reluctantly, she included seeing some large black bird fly over her car before she turned around to find Brad. By the time she was finished, everyone knew the farm was the next stop. Wendy pointed it out on the map, and Kelly added the appropriate pin and tag.

"Wendy, do you recall what direction that 'large bird' was flying?" Marcus asked as Kelly did a quick eye roll.

"Sorry, no. Too many curves on that road, and without the help of seeing the sun, well, I'm at a loss. It seemed to be following the road," Wendy added.

A quick glance at the map board showed Marcus that the road basically pointed toward the intersection of the cryptids' lines of travel.

Looking at Brad, Marcus asked, "Anything to add, SA Neil?"

"Only an apology for wrecking the car, sir."

"That's nothing compared to the pain you'll get telling the admiral why you have a new scar." That garnered light laughter and ribbing, then Marcus held up his hand to regain control. "Okay, based on their overnight finds, we have to make a few changes to our plans here for the day. What can you add, Todd?"

Burke gave a detailed report on the finds in the warehouse and the little information they pulled from the arrested chief petty officer. "I'll let you know how things progress here. We have a lot to catalog between what we found at the warehouse and the hospital. And more than enough people to interrogate."

"Thanks, Todd. And keep pushing to find out what that 'games' comment means."

"Will do, Marcus. Later," Burke said right before the dial tone sounded.

"I'm taking Brad and Wendy to the hospital right now," Kelly said with a voice that let everyone know it was a fact. "Brad needs an exam, which will include a scan of his head and possibly a stitch or two. Then I'll drop them off at the house for hot showers and some sleep. Norma needs to pull a couple of uniforms for them, and while they're sleeping, I'll get their dirty clothes cleaned."

"I'm fine and …" Wendy started.

"Of course you are," Marcus said, hoping he was keeping both sarcasm and condescension out of his voice. "But you've been up for over twenty-four hours and driven a few hundred miles. To be any good to me, you need some rest. Consider Kelly your boss for the next day or so, and follow her orders."

Wendy nodded. "Aye, aye, sir. I have to admit a hot shower sounds good."

"Okay, Kelly, make your hospital run," Marcus said. "Take Wendy's car, and after they're both checked, get the Bronco and let her follow you to Aunt Maude's. They can get some sleep there. Oh, and bring Sid back with you."

Kelly gave a quick salute and ushered the two bedraggled agents out of the war room.

After those three left, Marcus turned to GT. "Do we have a place where we can hide that truck? No need to tip off anyone connected to the farm that their delivery boy hasn't left town."

GT nodded. "Allen, drive it out to Brian's farm. Tell him to stash it in his barn and not to talk about it. Frost will follow and bring you back. Get moving."

The two officers didn't need further instructions. They left to accomplish their assignment.

With raised eyebrows, Marcus inquired about Brian.

"It's all good, Marcus. As Sally's younger brother, he knows not to mess with the sheriff."

After a quick nod of agreement, Marcus looked lost in thought. He turned to Barry Jackson. "Call your people at the motel and tell them we have a change of plan. Have them come here now."

"Yes, sir," Barry said as he reached for the phone.

Rick stood and quietly said, "I'll fetch us more coffee, Marcus, we're gonna need it." He offered to bring some for GT and Ken.

"GT, call Sam Wesson and ask him to join us at his earliest convenience. We'll need him and his air assets again." Marcus walked to the map, again lost in thought, and muttered, "And where the hell are those children?"

68

THE TRIO OF DOCTORS—SIDNEY WENTWORTH, Simpson Wallace, and Dennis Bassett—looked up from the empty abdomen of the cadaver on the table as Kelly entered. Elle stood off to the side with her camera, at the ready, and waved a greeting. The smell of decomposition was strong, even with the exhaust fans humming.

Kelly had excused herself from the emergency room after the chief of staff, Dr. Macon, had taken charge of the care for SA Brad Neil. He had spotted their arrival and stepped in to supervise the two ER doctors under the watchful eyes of LT Wendy James. He promised to page Kelly should anything not look right.

"You're in too much of a hurry, Kelly," Dennis said. "We still have a lot of work to do on this poor fellow."

"Just checking in, Dennis, and looking for a place to hang out for a while. I dropped off one of Marcus's agents in the ER due to a head injury. So, I'm waiting for a CT scan and the radiologist reading; that will take about half an hour. He also probably needs a stitch or two. So I have some time and figured you might have already found something that would interest Marcus."

Sidney Wentworth looked startled. "Who's injured? What happened?"

"On his late-night drive down from Chicago, Brad Neil hit a tree avoiding a deer outside of Princeton. He's got a laceration on his forehead and nasty headaches. He and Wendy James were both following a suspicious truck that seems to be related to our case," Kelly said.

"Have they started the CT scan yet?" Dennis interjected. In a more apologetic tone, he continued, "We installed that machine last month, I, uh … I've not had a chance to watch it in operation."

Sidney grinned and waved toward the door. "Go, Dennis. Simpson and I have got this for now. I met Neil a couple of years ago—nice kid. Give him my regards."

With Dennis gone, the attention returned to the body and Kelly.

"Well, Deputy Colt, you can tell the other Deputy Colt that so far, our victim displays the same parameters as all the rest. He's missing all the same organs, but due to decomp, we might not get any urine for a drug analysis," Sidney said professionally. "And his fingerprints are gone courtesy of the local critters."

"And it looks like the same fake bear claw marks sort of show up. Decomp makes it hard, but it looks like there are a couple of spots I can measure," Simpson added.

"I shot several photos of what's left of his face and the tattoo on his left arm," Elle said. "They might help identification."

Kelly considered that and went to the phone on the desk and made a call. "Norma, Kelly here. Do we have access to a sketch artist? Great, call him in … I have a job for him. Bye."

Elle's face twisted into the obvious question.

"Get your photos developed and we'll give the head shots to a sketch artist, who might be able to fill in the details."

"Got ya. And I'll get multiple copies of the one with the tattoo so the deputies can show it around."

"Good thinking, Elle." Kelly turned back to the body. "Any rough estimates on time of death? Or should it be *month* of death?"

Sid scoffed, "That last question is closer to the truth, Kelly. This guy's been out there for a while. Dennis looked at the temps for the last couple of months, and we came up with an estimate of late August. So tagging him 'Able Doe' was right, since he died before our John Doe in locker eight."

Kelly pulled her notepad out and scribbled a few lines. She went to the calendar that was posted on the wall, checked a few dates, and scribbled a few more things in her notepad. Tapping her pen against her lips as she reread the notes, she then turned to see she was the center of attention.

"What?"

Sidney replied, "You look like you're about to shout 'eureka,' and we're wondering why."

Kelly shrugged. "It might be nothing, but the timeline might be telling us something. Perhaps we have a progression here. We have one death in August, then three weeks later a second. Then three weeks after that two more bodies appeared on the same Monday, and then another one appears a week later. If the theory about using the bodies to grow cultures is true, the Vampire is ramping up his production, and we can expect to find more bodies soon. And these finds will be fresh bodies."

Lost in their thoughts, the four were quiet for a moment, until the door opened and Dr. Macon entered. Dennis Bassett followed.

"Kelly, Neil does have a small hematoma, his laceration needed three sutures, and I'm keeping him overnight for observations. Otherwise, he's okay and can probably get out of here tomorrow morning," Dr. Macon announced. "Lieutenant James is with him as he gets settled. I stuck him in intensive care because it makes it easier on my staff to keep a close eye on him. Anything else you need from me?"

"Thanks for the special care, John. I can't think of anything else right now, but you know I'm not afraid to ask."

Dr. Macon nodded and walked over to the corpse. "Any idea who this gentleman is?"

Dennis replied, "No idea yet. We know our latest victim is male, Caucasian, age estimated in the late forties, height around 5'11", probable old GSW on the right shoulder, and he has avoided dental care for too many years. Teeth are in bad shape like we usually find with a hobo."

"Pass a flashlight, please," John said absentmindedly as he stared at the left arm tattoo.

After looking at the tattoo in better light, John finally said, "This man was a Marine assigned to the 1st Marine Division in November 1950, and he survived the Battle of Chosin Reservoir. I recognize this tattoo."

Kelly asked, "How so?"

John had a melancholy look as he replied in a low voice, "After finishing my residency, I enlisted in the Navy and spent four years in the mid-fifties at the Pendleton base hospital. That base is the home of the 1st Marine Division. Many of the survivors of Frozen Chosin were there and had that tattoo."

"Not an obvious memento of that battle, is it?" Simpson said.

With a soft sigh, John said, "True. They didn't want to brag about a lost battle, but wanted a way to display their grief … their frustration, ya know, and it was a way to remember fallen comrades. Someone designed this simple square housing '1MR' over 'FFC' and it caught on. '1MR' is 1st Marine Division, of course, and the 'FFC' is … well, uh, Fornicate Frozen Chosin but with the less-clean version of the first word."

"John, we're going have a sketch artist use Elle's photos to create a facial reconstruction. Marcus has a Marine buddy who probably knows a contact or two who wear that tattoo. He might know him or at least tell us a place to start."

Elle asked, "I think Rick is too young to help; he was a toddler during the Korean War."

Smiling, Kelly replied, "No—not Rick. I mean Sergeant Major Jasper Railey at Camp Lejeune. He's the senior noncom of the II Marine Expeditionary Force. He's been around for so long I think the Commandant of the Marine Corps calls him for advice." Kelly chuckled.

"Is that the gunny named 'Rattler' that Marcus met in Vietnam?"

"One and the same, and if all goes right, we'll soon get an ID on this gent," Kelly said. "Okay, Elle and Sid, time to get to the war room."

69

"THANKS FOR GETTING HERE SO quickly. Your speed is greatly appreciated," Marcus said to the war room, now filled with several SEALs and one National Guard colonel. "We have new information that changes the battle plan for the day. Finding the missing children is still critical and Mission One, but we might have a lead on the murderer. Here's what we now know …"

After the verbal overview, Marcus directed their attention to a large new Mercer County map mounted on yet another portable corkboard. On it, the suspect farm was highlighted in yellow, and red pins had been stuck in several locations around it.

As Marcus took a seat, GT walked to the front. "The Chicago team followed that truck to this location shown in yellow. It is the old Fogerty farm, and has been a rental place since the old man passed away three years ago. George Fogerty and Douglas, his son, were taxidermists—good ones—and around 1960 they spent a lot of money on a nice building behind the house for their new shop. The guy who built it told me it was decked out with heating and air conditioning, couple of work rooms, and included a large walk-in cooler. Fact is, Fogerty let the house run down because of all the money spent on the shop. That was the building where Lieutenant James saw the truck."

Marcus asked, "So it fits the requirements that Kelly gave. Is the son still in the area?"

Shaking his head, GT said, "No, he died in 'Nam in the late sixties. He's buried in the National Cemetery in Grafton. The old man's sister, who moved to California years ago, inherited the place and uses a local realtor as a rental agent."

Marcus nodded his understanding.

GT continued, "I checked with the realtor, and she rented the place to a middle-aged man in June. He paid his deposit and six months' rent in advance—in cash—so Shirley has had neither complaint nor contact with him since. Man's name is Bruno Perez: a retired surgeon from Miami. I don't recall having met him," GT said.

"Any photos of Perez?" Barry Jackson asked.

"She's bringing in a copy of his Florida driver's license shortly. Looking at the map, you'll see I've added red pins to places where a chopper can land. Each spot is about a quarter mile or so from the building, but separated with a ridge line. I'll let Marcus explain his plan."

Marcus stood and, pointing to Colonel Wesson, said, "Colonel, we need your eyes in the sky again."

Wesson nodded. "Figured sooner was better than later, based upon your call. They're in the air now, heading to the Princeton airport."

"Excellent. Okay, here's the start of a plan; it will probably change as the day goes on. GT, Barry, and I will do a quick fly over the farm for a look-see and snap a couple of photos. Sam, we need a couple of the other Hueys to make some diversion action here." Marcus pointed to an area on the map that was south of the farm.

"Let me guess. Make enough noise and stay in the line of sight of the farm so those guys there will think something's happening down that way. Then, your Huey making a fly-over will not be a concern, right?"

"You broke the code, Colonel. With GT pulling camera duty, Barry and I can start figuring out the best way to approach the place without showing our hand. Then, with the recon work done, the SEALs selected to hit the farm can plan their assault. Sam's Hueys can drop them at the red pin locations for a quick hike over the ridge. And as soon as this meeting is over, I want two unmarked cars with a deputy and a SEAL hidden on each side of the access road to the farm to stop and detain anyone leaving. Okay, GT?" Marcus said.

As GT nodded, both GMGC Larry Hanes and RM1 Andy "Sparks" Waterman stood. Their voices overlapping, they said, "I'll lead the assault team, sir."

"That's yet to be decided, gentlemen," Barry said. "As you were."

Addressing the SEALs, Marcus smiled and said, "So much for never volunteering, eh? Back to the issue at hand: the missing children. The five teams of four SEALs each need to drop a man and finish checking your designated search areas. Your skipper told me you still have about ten percent of the areas to check—and it needs to be done quickly—then come here for the assault on the farm. The men cut from the teams will accompany Lieutenant Gardener and Deputy Frost to check out a special area. They'll fill you in on the way. Any questions?"

Since there were none, the SEALs quickly reconfigured their teams, and all headed out to finish their assignments, leaving GT, Allen, Barry, Sam, and Marcus to decide their next step. The Hueys were not due for another forty-five minutes.

As Barry and Sam studied the map and considered possible access routes, Marcus asked Allen to make some local calls to do a quick BI on Perez. Marcus placed a call to NISRA Miami asking the SSA there to do the same. GT headed out to track down Carl Marks and find out what he'd been up to lately.

70

SHERIFF'S DEPARTMENT, PRINCETON, WEST VIRGINIA
THURSDAY AFTERNOON
30 OCTOBER 1975

THE SMALL NUMBER OF PEOPLE in the sheriff's office were busy when Kelly Colt and Sidney Wentworth came into the war room. Kelly spotted a new face tacked to the board and went to investigate. Marcus concluded his phone call and joined her at the board.

"Brad doing okay?" Marcus asked as he gave her shoulder a quick hug.

"Dr. Macon personally oversaw his exam and is keeping him overnight for observation. Couple of stitches and a small hematoma is the diagnosis. You know from the one you got in Italy that headaches will bug him for a while, but no lasting issues. Wendy is already asleep, under continual protest, in the garage apartment. Aunt Maude is getting their clothing cleaned. So, all is well with the Chicago team, Sailor," Kelly reported as she stared at the enlarged driver's license photo of Bruno Perez, MD.

"Good to know. Ya done good, Princess."

"So, is this our Vampire?"

Marcus shrugged. "Yet to be determined. Maybe. He rents the farm, ergo he's probably involved. New in the area since summer, he hasn't been on the local police radar for any reason. I asked NISRA Miami to check him out down there; that was them on the phone. They reported he was in their area for a bit over eight years. Long enough to take all the required courses and pass the three exams allowing a foreign doctor to practice in the US. He worked at Miami Central Hospital as a general surgeon for a couple of years before deciding to move up here. No family there, none here or reported to be back home in Bolivia. He's fluent in English, Spanish, and German. Well liked, but no known love interests. License says he's forty-three, but he looks older in the photo."

Kelly said, "Sounds like he checks off several boxes on the evil guy list."

"Yep."

"Elle is getting her film developed and will come here shortly. Norma has a sketch artist coming in to hopefully come up with a complete face. Wildlife and decomp took away about half of Able Doe's face, so we thought an artist sketch might help. And Dr. Macon recognized a tattoo he had: Able was a Marine who served in Korea at Frozen Chosin. Rattler might be help finding his identity if we wire him the sketch," Kelly said, finishing her update.

A quick nod acknowledged Marcus's agreement.

"My turn?" Sidney asked. He had been standing over to the side to give Marcus and Kelly time to chat.

Marcus smiled. "You bet, Doc. What ya got?"

"Able is the oldest corpse found, at least thus far. And he displays the same conditions as the others with regard to missing organs, fake bear marks, et cetera. When we left the morgue, Dennis was trying to find some urine, but due to the level of decomp, it is doubtful we can give you a yea or nay on drugs being cause of death. No other obvious causes are displayed," Sidney reported. "Dennis is going to shoot some x-rays to see if that uncovers anything new. Kelly had an interesting thought on the number of bodies."

Marcus looked at Kelly with raised eyebrows.

"Nothing major, just that the number of bodies is increasing and time between their deaths is decreasing. I expect to see more soon. Looking at the dates of death, it kinda looks like the Vampire is ramping up his plan."

Marcus was silent, and that bothered Kelly.

"What?" She asked harshly.

It was like a dark cloud descended over Marcus. He said, "I pray the next bodies are not those of the children."

Kelly sighed, "Yea. Nothing new from the search teams?"

Marcus shook his head. "All but Gardener's team have finished searching their areas, and relocated to the airport to prep for the farm assault. Nothing found. Hopefully, we'll hear from Rick soon." He turned to Allen and asked, "Have you heard from Cal Thompkins?"

Looking up from his reading of the intense FBI analysis of the Thompkins' car, Allen said, "No, sir. Hate to admit it, but calling him again slipped my mind. I'll get right on it." He left to use the phone at his desk, where it was quieter.

GT nearly ran over Allen as they passed in the hall. Dropping into one of the war room chairs, GT grumbled, "We can scratch Carl Marks off our suspect list. When I queried him about our victims, he had no idea about any of them. I've known him for years, and he can lie like a rug. But when he does, his neck breaks out in blotches. That tell of his is better than an FBI lie detector. His clear neck tells me he honestly doesn't know anything about the murders."

Marcus slowly shook his head as he said, "Something still doesn't feel right about him. We'll keep him on the board for now. Returned to the drug business?"

GT lifted his hands in surrender and grimaced. "Sorry, didn't ask."

Colonel Sam Wesson leaned into the war room door. "Marcus—time to roll. Your Huey waits at the airport, and the others are already moving the SEALs into place. The diversion choppers will come with you. Barry is already heading to the car."

"Can do, Sam. We'll be right there. GT, take Barry in your cruiser, and Sid and me will follow in the Bronco."

Looking a bit shocked, Sidney asked, "On a Huey going where, if I may ask?"

"We are heading to the suspected lair of the Vampire. We'll do a flyover to scope it out and pass the info on to the SEAL teams. They'll do the assault after our chopper and the other diversions leave the area. We'll drive to the farm, and I want trained medical eyes with me when we go in behind them. He might have the children there. Okay?"

"Lead on, Marcus! Oh, do I get to carry a weapon?" He grinned with excitement.

With a tight smile, Marcus said, "Your rapier wit is weapon enough, Doc. While you don't get a weapon, a notepad might be useful." Marcus slid one across the table, and he turned toward the door.

"Care to join, Ken?" Marcus asked.

A quick head shake accompanied the FBI liaison's response. "Not now. More reading to do to get up to speed." His attention never left the boards or the open folder in his hand. "I'll join you for the ground assault."

Allen entered and held up a hand to stop Marcus. "Sorry, sir. Wanted you to know that Cal Thompkins has missed two shifts at work and there was no answer at his house when I called a minute ago. Figured I'd run over to his house and check it out."

"Good plan, Allen. Take Kelly with you; if he's sinking into depression, she could be helpful."

71

"DO THE THOMPKINS HAVE MORE than two vehicles?" Kelly asked as Allen turned into the driveway. A dirty white Ford pickup was parked in front of the house. There was room for two vehicles in the gravel-covered parking area.

"Just that truck there and the Buick still residing at the FBI lab. Place looks deserted, so maybe someone picked him up," Deputy Allen Chambers said. "We'll do a quick circle around the house and check the outbuildings. You go that way, and then when we're done, you'll cover the back door while I knock on the front. Got it?"

Kelly nodded and headed off to the right. Allen studied the area as he moved leftward. They met at the rear of the house and shared their negative outcomes.

Nothing was found on the rest of the outside survey. No lights showed from the windows. Mr. Thompkins was neither in the garden shed nor in the medium-sized barn ten yards behind the house. Hood of the truck was cold: it had not recently been used. Nothing was in the boat save for well-stowed boating and fishing gear. Aside from some traffic noise from the two-lane, all was quiet. Allen pointed to the back door, indicating Kelly was to take that position as he walked around to the front.

Heal of his hand pounding on the door, Allen yelled, "Cal, open up. This is Detective Chambers—we need to talk! Yo, Cal!" No sounds came from inside, so Allen repeated the routine with no better luck. He called to Kelly, "Hey, Partner, get around here!"

Kelly came running around from the right side of the frame structure with her weapon at the ready, her head in swivel mode. "What?" she said in a stage whisper.

"Stand down, Deputy, no problems. Just wanted you to back me up as I go inside. But thanks for having my back like that," Allen said with respect.

She shrugged. "Do I get to kick the door down?"

Allen took the stairs to the porch two at a time and stopped at the door. "Best and most logical thing to do is first try the doorknob. A lot of folks around here are lax at locking doors." He tried the door and it swung open.

"Cal, its Detective Chambers. I'm coming in!" he yelled into the dark house, motioning Kelly to follow. With the window shades drawn, the house was dark. A faint odor of feces and spoiled food hit his nose. Allen found a light switch and the living room became visible. The body of Calvin Thompkins was sitting in an easy chair, his bloodied head thrown back with mouth agape.

"Oh, crap."

After a quick check of the house to make sure it was empty, they stood looking at the body. Kelly stepped closer and pulled out her flashlight. Careful not to disturb the scene, she did a quick look at the wound.

"Powder burns in his mouth, hole in the soft palate, and missing a good portion of the right parietal are all good indicators of the cause of death. That"—Kelly shined the light downward—"and the Colt Trooper revolver, .38 Special, maybe .357 Magnum, on the floor below his left hand, screams suicide. The near-empty bottle of Jim Beam bourbon on the coffee table could have eased the decision process," Kelly said as she looked from the body to the ceiling. "And it looks like a good portion of blood and brain matter is splattered up there around another hole. Dennis will have to make it official, of course, as well as time of death. He's cold, so it probably happened last evening."

A deep sigh escaped before Allen quietly said, "And here is the suicide note. 'Blah, blah, can't live without my family, blah, blah, blah, hurts too much, blah, blah.' Damn." He dropped the note on the sideboard, looked at the floor and sighed again. "It's my damn fault. I should have pushed harder to find him yesterday. Maybe if I had …"

"Don't go there, Allen! In a perfect situation where a professional counselor is talking with a suicidal person, there is still a seventy-five-percent chance they will go through with it. This is all on Cal and especially the Vampire, not you," Kelly said.

"Whatever. I gotta call this in and get Dennis here."

"Do you know if Cal was left-handed?" Kelly asked.

"Yea, he was a southpaw, why?"

"Angle of the bullet path matches that of a left-handed shooter. It could also indicate someone right-handed shot him after incapacitating him somehow. Dennis's autopsy will check for drugs or any other physical damages to rule out murder," Kelly said. "And he'll check for powder residue on Cal's left hand."

"You're turning into a great deputy, Kelly." Allen made the necessary calls to the office and morgue, then said, "Let's look around while we wait for the cavalry to arrive."

"Okay. What are we looking for?"

"Signs of a struggle. Any indicators someone else was in the house with Cal. It could also be a robbery after the suicide or murder. We have to be thorough."

72

THEIR VEHICLE WAS STASHED OUT of sight, thirty yards farther down the road from their location, on an old gas-well road. Equipped with a handheld tactical radio, the two-man team was assigned the call sign of Ground One. A few hundred yards to the west, a second team, also consisting of a deputy and a SEAL, was designated as Ground Two. They watched and waited for action from the farm.

"If we had been thinking, we would've brought lunch," Deputy Harvey Wilson mumbled toward BM2 Kevin Brown. "Breakfast was a long time ago." Both were crouched down low behind trees across the road and about twenty yards east of the road to the farm. Wilson was taking his turn watching the gate with the binoculars.

"Quit whining, deputy, the only easy day was yesterday. And you are now part of Colt's Crazies, which means expect the unexpected. Plan for the unplanned. Good news is I hear choppers, so I suspect the wait won't be too much longer," Brown whispered as he passed a candy bar to Wilson.

He nodded his thanks, and between bites asked, "Why the name Crazies?"

Brown smiled. "Marcus Colt has a tendency to do some wild things, but he pulls them off and gets the job done no matter how impossible it seems. Someone said you have to be crazy to follow him, and the name stuck. I was with him in 'Nam a few years ago and wouldn't trade those memories for the world. It was a wild time."

"Hey, we have movement at the gate," Wilson whispered with excitement.

As they watched, a green pickup pulled up, coming from the house. After getting the gate open and driving the truck to the highway edge, the driver went back and secured the gate. Looking around as he walked to the cab, he tugged his red ball cap tighter against his head, slammed the truck door, then pulled out onto Nubbins Ridge Road heading west.

Keying the radio, Brown said, "Ground Two, dark green pickup, one Caucasian occupant, jeans, denim jacket, red ball cap, heading your way from the farm. Follow with caution and we'll hang here. Over."

"Rog, One. Over," GMG2 Glenn Jensen replied.

The radio came to life again. "Ground Two, this is Colt in Eyeball One. We have the vehicle in sight, so hang back about a mile. We'll keep you informed. Over."

"Roger."

Several minutes passed in silence, then the radio barked. "All units. Eyeball One RTB. Eyeball Two handle overwatch on truck. Out."

"Eyeball Two has overwatch. Out."

The green pickup was obeying the speed limit as it continued west on Nubbins Ridge Road for a while. The driver couldn't afford to be stopped for any moving violations, so he adjusted his red cap to block the afternoon sun, checked his mirrors and, seeing a clear road ahead and behind, let out a light sigh.

GMG2 Glenn Jensen was riding shotgun in the patrol car. He turned to the deputy behind the wheel. "Drop back more, man. Eyeball Two has him and will tell us when and where to turn. We don't want to spook him."

Deputy Marty Albertson nodded and eased off the accelerator. As he did, the radio came to life. "Ground Two. Truck turned north on a small side road approximately two klicks from your position. Seems to be slowing, possibly due to road condition. Eyeball Two out."

"Copy."

"That must be the one, at least based on fresh tire tracks in last night's snow," Jensen pointed out a few minutes later. The road was more of a rutted path. It looked like a small amount of gravel lay under the melting snow.

Turning onto the side road, Albertson stopped the cruiser and nodded. "That's an old logging road, Glenn. The farther it goes into the woods, the less gravel and the greater the amount of mud and number of potholes. Okay for a four-wheel-drive pickup, but not conducive for this patrol car. We need to rely on Eyeball Two."

Glenn grabbed the mike and called his boss. "We need a team via air to apprehend the suspect in the green truck. He's heading down a logging road and we can't follow. Over."

"Ground Two. Eyeball Three here. I'll get Team Four picked up while Eyeball Two keeps him in sight. Hold where you are at the main road. Over."

"Roger, Eyeball Three. You copy, Eyeball Two? Over."

"Copy, Ground Two. We have him in sight."

As Glenn and Marty dutifully blocked the logging road, time seemed to slow down for the two men. Glenn kept checking his watch as his ears listened for anything incoming from the radio, but all that did was confirm that he disliked waiting. Marty felt the same way as his fingers drummed the steering wheel.

Finally, after another ten minutes, the radio came to life. "Eyeball Two. Eyeball Three is one minute out coming in low. Over."

"Three. Two has you in sight. There's a clearing one click off your starboard large enough for an infiltration. Suspect has stopped two klicks from Ground Two and exited the vehicle, but doesn't seem to know he is under observation. Team Four needs to move due west about four klicks over a small ridge. Over."

"Copy. Out."

The two men sat quietly in the cruiser awaiting further orders. Waiting was not a strong suit for GMG2 Glenn Jensen, but his training overpowered any idea of striking off on his own. He sat in silence.

The tactical crackled after a few more minutes. "Eye Socket. Eyeball Three. Team Four in place. Bingo fuel. RTB. Out."

Jensen continued to wait, but perked up when the radio came to life again.

"Ground Two. Eyeball Two. Suspect is messing with something in the bed of the truck. Team Four is still three klicks out."

Jensen acted without delay. "Stay here, Marty, and update Eyeball. I'll take care of the suspect." Before Marty could respond, Jensen was out of the cruiser and double-timing it up the logging road.

The two klicks passed quickly, and Jensen switched from speed to stealth as he neared the target. With his weapon at the ready, he slipped into the woods and moved to where he could observe the truck. He had arrived in the nick of time.

The truck was parked in an open area of the woods. It had probably been used as a turn-around place in the past and would be perfect for some high schooler to take his girl for a little secluded petting. Thick woods were on each side, with the ground dropping off sharply in one direction and rising steeply on the other.

The suspect was pulling a rolled-up tarp from the truck bed. With the tarp tied in several places to keep it snug against whatever it hid, it seemed at first to give him a challenge. It finally dropped to the ground with a dull thud as the bulk came off the pickup's tailgate. He straightened his back as if the unloading had caused pain, then bent over to grab the package by one of the rope ties.

With the subject distracted, Jensen stepped from the shadows. Moving into position a few feet behind the suspect, he yelled, "Freeze. Hands on your head!"

Silent for a moment, the suspect slowly moved his hands up as he rose. "Who are you, man?"

"A pissed-off U.S. Navy SEAL with a weapon pointed at your head. Move away from the truck and get down on your knees," Jensen ordered. "What's your name?"

Dropping to the ground, the suspect said, "I want a lawyer."

"Funny name, jackass," Jensen said as he snapped on the cuffs. "We'll try this conversation again when I drag you into your cell. For now, face down on the ground."

"I want a lawyer. I know my rights."

Jensen rolled his eyes as he whipped a small piece of rope around the suspect's feet to keep him from running. "Yea, I've heard that before." Suspect secured, he walked over to the tarp.

The tarp was the common, dark green, polyethylene type that every military surplus store was selling for a couple of bucks. Its past heavy use showed in multiple stains and small cuts and tears. Jensen's K-bar knife made quick work of slicing the four rope ties, and he unrolled it finding exactly what he expected: another naked body.

73

THE POST OFFICE PARKING LOT was empty save for two vehicles; the small town didn't have enough people to cause an afternoon postal rush. One vehicle, a five-year-old blue Ford sedan, probably belonged to the postmaster. The second was a Bronco with sheriff markings. GT's arrival added a third. He got out of his cruiser and walked to where Marcus Colt and Doctor Wentworth were leaning against the Bronco. Marcus was bouncing between checking his watch and scanning the sky.

"Late for a flight, Marcus Aurelius, or checking your record time for getting here from the airport?" GT asked jovially. He punched Marcus in the arm as a friendship greeting.

"Just hoping I don't hear or see the team hitting the truck getting into place. They should be there shortly," Marcus answered. "Barry said the farm was secure, and he sent four men to find out what that pickup truck is doing in the woods. Time for Doc Wentworth and me to join Barry."

As if wishing made it so, the tactical radio came to life. "Eyesocket. Eyeball Three. Team has been dropped off. Bingo fuel. RTB. Out."

GT said, "See? It's coming together. You head to the farm, and I'll join up with the crew at the pickup. Okay?"

Marcus didn't reply, nor did he move from his spot leaning against the fender. GT had seen that look of intense thought years ago when Marcus religiously beat him at chess. Marcus had the ability to think ahead multiple moves while GT struggled to keep an eye on the last piece Marcus had moved.

"Yea, that's fine, GT. Have you heard anything from Gardener?" Marcus said with a voice low and slow as he continued to stare at something GT couldn't see.

Shaking his head, GT replied, "Nothing. But considering the area his team is searching, not being in radio range is expected."

"Do you think they'll find the children?" Marcus shifted his gaze to the ground at his feet as he kicked at a small stone.

GT blew out a breath. "Probably not alive, Marcus. I think their bodies will eventually turn up. Maybe not today, and maybe not in Gardener's search area, but we will find them."

Grimacing, Marcus said, "Of the two of us, you were always more negative."

"I call it realistic, man. Just looking at the facts. Two small children missing for going on two weeks. Too many nights of cold weather, rain, and now snow. It ain't pretty. What else is bugging you?"

"You're still pretty good at reading my moods. Red ball caps are also still bugging me, GT. One is on the driver you're going after. Carl Marks wears one, but you don't think he's involved," Marcus said.

"Remember you are in West Virginia where ball caps are considered part of the standard dress code for everything except worship service and funerals. While John Deere green is the most common color, red ranks right up there. Not much to go on, buddy."

Marcus again looked off into the distance. "Perhaps not, but there might be a message there that we're not seeing. I've often found major clues in the small, weird things that nag at me. Oh, well, time for us to get to our next appointments."

74

DEPUTY HARVEY WILSON NUDGED BM2 Kevin Brown and passed him the binoculars. Watching the gate was about as exciting as watching paint dry or grass grow, he thought. It was boring, but a necessary part of the mission.

Brown took his turn surveilling the gate with the binoculars. "At least someone is having fun while we watch this," he said quietly.

"Wish I was doing more than watching a gate."

"Deputy Wilson, trust me when I tell you that sitting here can be just as dangerous as charging headlong into battle. Boredom will make you careless, so keep your ass awake and watch my back while I watch the freaking gate!" Brown whispered harshly but with authority.

"Uh, yes sir."

Another half hour passed, and all was still quiet at the gate. The sun caused the light snow to morph into mud. Two vehicles had driven past, but neither slowed. A couple of airliner contrails crisscrossed the cloudless blue sky, too high to be heard. The distraction created by the Hueys was long gone, and silence reigned.

Seeing the Sheriff's car zip by heading west, without siren or flashing lights, broke the monotony. Wilson was behind the binoculars and recognized GT at the wheel, but couldn't see if anyone was with him. Then it was quiet again for another few minutes.

"We ready to move, Kevin?" Marcus said in a stage whisper as he squatted behind the two men watching the gate.

Deputy Wilson nearly dropped the binoculars from the surprise of Marcus's sudden appearance.

Kevin Brown smiled. "Glad to see you remembered your training on silent approaches, Marcus. I spotted you at ten feet, but ol' Harv here was taken by complete surprise."

Marcus chuckled softly. "Hell, Kev, I'm still a few years shy of worthless. Anything happening here?"

"All quiet, sir—and, oh yea, we're way past ready to do something else. What's the plan?"

"A lot went down these last couple of hours. We'll cover that later, as it's about time to breach. Harvey, Doctor Wentworth, and a new team member, FBI SSA Ken Santoro, are waiting at my Bronco parked next to your car. Bring both vehicles to the gate. Kevin will have it open shortly, and our assignment is to keep anyone from leaving." Marcus passed a pair of bolt cutters to Brown. After Harvey left on his assignment, Marcus continued, "Barry is leading three four-man groups that the Hueys dropped a bit ago to secure the farm. Let's go join the fun."

They sat in the two police vehicles, blocking the driveway, until the tactical radio crackled. "Commander, all secure." Kevin and Harvey maintained control of the gate, and Marcus, Ken, and Sid drove on to the house.

Barry Jackson shifted his weapon behind by working the sling; a quick tug sent the M16 toward his lower back. He came nearly to attention as Marcus left the Bronco and approached.

"What's the situation, Barry?"

"Entire area secured, sir. We found one older man in the shop building: he's not talking. No other people here, but there are indications in the house that one other person stays there. A burn barrel we found has traces of cloth. Aside from a lot of medical-type equipment in the shop, the most interesting thing is all the blood."

Marcus nodded appreciation of the concise report. "We've picked up the individual who left here a bit ago. That's probably the other resident. Show us the blood and equipment."

The tour of the shop didn't take long. The walk-in cooler contained boxes of jars filled with an unknown liquid. Marcus saw a few labels indicating Navy property. Another room housed tables covered with shallow, glass-covered trays filled with a brown liquid. Heat lamps were suspended over the tables.

The next room was a combination of operating room and slaughter-house. Wood chips and a half ton of cat litter covered the bloodstained floor around a table in the center of the room. Various machines rested on the benches against the wall. A couple of stainless steel tubs contained what Marcus suspected to be entrails; Doctor Sidney Wentworth confirmed that these were parts removed from a human, and recently. Turning away from the disgusting sight to leave, Marcus knew that image would stay with him. Ken was silent as he took in the horrible scene.

As Marcus turned, his gaze fell on something hanging by the door. The claw of a black bear, mounted on a steel rod, was covered in dried blood. Further proof this was the Vampire's lair.

The tour ended in an area that could be called the office, with a couple of desks, filing cabinets, and a wall covered with chalkboards filled with lists written in German. Two large entire-year wall calendars, one for the current year and the other for 1976, hung on the wall facing the main desk; each had various dates circled, and the 1976 calendar had July 17 crossed out.

Most notably, two SEALs stood guard behind an older-looking man who wore a typical white lab coat showing brown stains that reminded Marcus of dried blood, probably resulting from the work in the operating room. A pair of small half-glasses was perched on the end of his nose, and the salt-and-pepper hair made the man look older than what Marcus suspected was mid-forties. A nod and slight flick of the commander's left hand signaled for the two SEALs to move away from the suspect; they relocated to the hall outside the door.

Marcus looked around the room twice before locking eyes with the suspect. He moved to a position in front of him and leaned casually against a filing cabinet. Clearing his throat, Marcus finally said, "Doctor Bruno Perez, you are a long way from Miami. In addition to being a sheriff's deputy here, I am a serving naval officer assigned to the Naval Investigative Service, and you are in trouble with both law enforcement agencies. We have shut down your connections in Chicago."

Perez continued his stare. No movements, sounds, or reactions came forth. He appeared as if in a trance.

"Doctor Wentworth here will back me up, but I guess you missed that ethics class in medical school. I never took it myself, you understand; my doctorate is in criminology, but it seems one of the basic rules for medical doctors is to 'do no harm.' Not sure how killing people so you can gut their bodies fits into that rule. Care to fill me in, Doctor Perez? Why did you kill them? What are you making from the body parts?"

The doctor continued his silent stare, but his eyes came alive with hate.

Marcus slowly shook his head as a slight smile touched his lips. "Now that we have your talkative assistant in custody, along with the body of your latest victim, your conviction will be a quick one even without your confession. My only concern is if I can convince the state legislature to reinstate the death penalty for slime like you."

"Excuse me, Commander, but you need to see this," Barry said as he leaned into the door opening.

"Can't it wait?"

"Uh, no, sir, it cannot."

"Okay, Perez, you have a few more minutes to consider your fate. I will return. Chat with Doctor Wentworth while I'm gone. Let's go, Ken."

They followed the SEAL team leader to the house. As they hurried to cover the hundred yards, Marcus asked, "So, what ya got?"

"Proof that the old bastard is worse than you can imagine."

Climbing the stairs to the second floor, Barry pointed to a small door that led to the attic stairs; it had been kicked down and the casing was splintered. "It was padlocked when my team got here. Guess Perez didn't want the other guy to see his collection."

Marcus smiled. "Little overkill on that door, eh?"

Barry shrugged as he said, "Combination of an enthusiastic SEAL, old wood, and short hinge screws. He only meant to take out the jamb, sir."

The short climb ended in a finished room and not the dusty attic Marcus expected. The room had the pristine look of a museum. Framed photos and bright red flags with black swastikas embedded in white circles graced the walls above glass cases of memorabilia circling the room. The center of the largest wall featured a portrait of a man that Marcus immediately recognized. *Der Fuhrer*, Adolph Hitler, arms crossed in defiance, stared down at them as they stood in the middle of a Nazi museum. No, Marcus realized after a quick look around, it wasn't simply a museum exhibit, it was a shrine dedicated to the National Socialist German Workers' Party. He stopped to study one section of glass-covered photos and papers.

Ken and Barry were checking each display and repeatedly muttering "Unbelievable."

"Barry, look at this." Marcus pointed to a photo. "My German is barely basic, a mixture of 'give me a beer' and 'where is the restroom,' but I think that caption, '*mein toller vater*,' translates into 'my great father'—and do you recognize that man?"

"Sorry, sir, I do not."

Marcus chuckled. "Good news for us is that my father was both a World War II vet and a high school history teacher. I was educated on the war more than the average kid. That man is the Angel of Death. He was a Nazi officer, a captain in the Schutzstaffel,[1] and medical doctor by the name of Josef Mengele. Nazis were generally bad, and SS officers were the worst of the bunch. Mengele went out of his way to be considered the worst of all those evil bastards."

"Him, I heard of. He did some nasty experiments on people in the concentration camps. I thought we hung him?"

"No, he was one of too many bastards that got away. Somehow, he got to Argentina after the war, and the Mossad, the Israeli intelligence agency, tracked him to Brazil last I heard. Yea, he was at the Auschwitz death camp and loved to cruelly experiment on twins in the name of genetic research. If this is true, our suspect might be a love child from Mengele's years at university."

"Why a love child?" Barry asked.

Marcus continued in lecture mode, "Mengele married Irene, can't remember her maiden name, in 1939 when she was only twenty-one. He was around twenty-eight, and their only known son was born in 1944. If the driver's license age of our suspect is accurate, he was born when Mengele was around twenty-two years old. That would be around six years before he met and married Irene. Assuming our suspect is the son, he might be as evil as his father."

Impressed by the history lesson, Barry asked, "So what does all that mean for what we have here?"

Marcus shrugged as he quietly muttered, "Hell if I know. And if that statement ever gets out, I'll have to retake a course or two at Naval

---

1 The SS (*Schutzstaffel*, or Protection Squads) was originally established as Adolf Hitler's personal-bodyguard unit. It would later become both the elite guard of the Nazi Reich and Hitler's executive force, prepared to carry out all security-related duties, without regard for legal restraint.

United States Holocaust Memorial Museum. "The SS" Holocaust Encyclopedia. https://encyclopedia.ushmm.org/content/en/article/ss
Accessed on September 5, 2024

Command College, since senior officers are supposed to know what's going on at all times."

"Your secret is safe with me, boss."

"Thanks. Time to have a go at our suspect again." Marcus led them out of the shrine. "Maybe this room will provide some leverage."

75

THE MORNING HAD STARTED FULL of promise. Deputy Frost's cruiser, crammed with four SEALs, led the way to the starting point of the search area Marcus had assigned. Rick Gardener and the SEAL team leader followed in his Ford F-110. Initially the drive was quiet, but that didn't last.

RM1 Andy "Sparks" Waterman glanced over at Rick and asked, "I hear the lacquer is still on your butter bar, Lieutenant. No offense, but you're older than the standard shavetail, so what's your background? Can you handle a heavily wooded search?"

With a chuckle, Rick said, "I suppose so. My first year in the Corps was with the Third Marine Division in Vietnam as a scout sniper. That gave me some jungle experience. When my tour was up, they decided my manly looks and new corporal chevrons would look good at the embassy in Naples. That's where I met Commander Colt. It was after a mission with him that he and my gunny pushed me into the officer corps. After finishing my degree, of course."

"Good enough," Andy chuckled. "You'll do."

Now, several hours later, the seven men were spread out far enough to cover a decent amount of area, yet close enough to stay in visual contact. The melting snow uncovered much of the forest floor, and after several hours of walking and looking, nothing worth using an evidence bag was found. Rick took the second inbound position on the right with Deputy Frost on the outside. David was the only one with some local knowledge, and Rick wanted him close.

Rick checked the map again to make sure they hadn't missed anything. They were slowly moving west as they walked the search areas north to south. The search area was shrinking with each pass, but as they entered a small valley—Frost had called it Devil Holler—the terrain became steeper and the search became more difficult.

Asked why the name, all David Frost could provide was a vague reference by his grandmother about something evil living in one of the caves that populated the deep end of the holler. Hearing that, Rick immediately recalled a Bible psalm about a valley of the shadow of death that he hoped wasn't this particular valley.

The afternoon was passing fast, as was the light. Fall afternoons in the mountains make for limited sunlight when clouds and ridge peaks overpower the sun, darkening the hollers. Searching became more difficult but the team continued.

Without notice, the quiet was disturbed by a faint knocking sound. Someone in the distance was building something.

"Frost!" Rick said in a loud whisper as he raised his hand for everyone to stop. "Anyone living in this area?"

"Shouldn't be, since this is a state forest. Might be a pileated woodpecker—they're the biggest ones we have."

"Camper?" Rick asked.

David shrugged. "Doubtful. Designated camping areas are to the south, and this is past the usual camping season."

Rick signaled the man to his left to join him. When he did, he told him to pass down the line: "Strive for total silence and listen for the source of the knocking." The SEAL nodded compliance, and once the order was transferred, they returned to their search.

The knocking paused, then got louder. It was random now, coming from two different directions—or perhaps it was one heck of an echo. Rick thought of the old Tarzan movies where the restless natives sent messages using jungle drums. A five-foot-long tree limb dropping in front of him interrupted his reminiscing. It was at least three inches in diameter, capable of doing major damage to a person.

The team froze.

Rick signaled the team to come to him as everyone listened to the silent forest. And as sudden as the first hit, a second limb crashed about ten feet to the right. The team saw no other movement, but another crash occurred deeper in the woods. Spreading out with two-meter separation, they moved quietly in the direction of the noise. More knocking came from the distance ahead of them.

They had to move quickly as the darkness was closing in. Whatever was making all the noise was leading them farther north and upslope. One more crash was heard, and as they approached the location, they found another large limb in front of a small cave.

Brush covered one side of the opening as the rocks extended out over the top of the dark hole. The hole was tall enough for a man to enter slightly hunched over, and wide enough for two men to walk side by side. Limbs the size of medium tree trunks covered the entrance in what looked like a fence to keep something inside. The limbs were braced with others to keep them in place.

The team closed in on the cave. Three men studied the entrance as the rest of the team formed a security circle facing outward.

Rick nudged David Frost and quietly asked, "What ya think? Ever seen anything like it?"

Frost shook his head as he pulled out a flashlight. Shining it between the limbs of the barricade, he said, "Guess we need to look inside. It turns to the left about ten feet in, and I can't see a dang thing from here."

The three men started pulling down a few of the braces and limbs. Getting it clear, Frost pulled his weapon and slid into the cave. Rick and Andy Waterman followed with flashlights on and weapons at the ready. The cave was larger once past the entrance, allowing the men to walk without stooping over. A soft noise was heard in the distance and a faint odor of wood smoke and rot filled their nostrils. A slight breeze drifted by, indicating at least an air vent somewhere deeper.

A few paces down the left-turn path, the cave jogged back to the right. Additional limbs formed yet another blockade that was not as formidable as the first. Past that, the three could see a small fire and bundles of clothing. Someone was here, and something was keeping that someone prisoner.

Signaling the others to take cover to opposite sides of the cave, Rick stood in the middle and yelled, "Come on out!"

One of the piles of clothing moved, and a small head appeared. "Daddy?"

76

DOCTOR BRUNO PEREZ WAS STILL sitting behind his desk when they returned. His one acknowledgement of their presence was a slightly raised left eyebrow. Marcus felt he now had the upper hand in their confrontation.

Sidney Wentworth nodded toward Perez as they entered the room. "He doesn't want to talk to another doctor, that's for sure. Sorry."

"Thanks, Sid. SEALs treating you okay, Doctor Perez, or should I say, Mengele?" Marcus moved a few items and sat on the front edge of the desk, giving him a vertical advantage over the doctor.

Marcus knew he'd struck a nerve when he saw the doctor's face color slightly. He decided on a different direction for the interrogation based on something his father had told him about the senior Nazi officers: their arrogance and belief of superiority was extreme. And they didn't like to be made fun of. Marcus decided to use it.

Using the worst fake German accent he could generate, Marcus said, "Ve know about your *vater*, Herr Mengele. And vith your friends in Chicago and those here in custody, ve vill soon know all of your vorkings here. Ve have our vays of making you talk."

While the doctor remained quiet, Marcus saw his jaw clench several times as he worked to control his temper. The hours spent watching all those old WWII movies with fake Nazis had finally come in handy.

Marcus continued, "Vhat I don't have is much information about your mutter. You are too old to be part of the Schutzstaffel's Lebensborn[2] project: Herr Himmler's SS was desperate to create more of his perfect Germans, ya? Perhaps papa Josef met her vhile at university in Bonn around 1930. Since that was years before Kristallnacht[3], maybe Josef pleasured a nice Jewish girl that would become your mutter. Am I getting close? Are you a closet Jew? Do you keep your yarmulke handy for Shabbat?"

The doctor leaped from the chair and yelled, "Enough! I will not allow you to defame the great name of Mengele!"

A SEAL laid a hand on the doctor's shoulder and guided him back to the chair. Marcus signaled the warrior to step back. As Perez regained his composure, he looked sickened.

Marcus resumed his normal voice. "No problem, Perez. I'll ask the sheriff to order some kosher meals for you." He stood and leaned against the filing cabinet again.

A look of disgust engulfed Perez's face as he looked up at Marcus. His voice was arrogant as he said, "My mother, Amelia, was a dedicated member of the party and often dined with key members of the führer's inner circle. Her father was Field Marshall Ludwig Becker. While she liked my father so very much and they had a short affair, she fell in love with an Argentine army major who was a military attaché at their embassy in Berlin. After a short romance, they married, with him not knowing she

---

2 Nazi authorities created the Lebensborn program to increase Germany's population. Pregnant German women deemed "racially valuable" were encouraged to give birth to their children at Lebensborn homes. During World War II, the program became complicit in the kidnapping of foreign children with physical features considered "Aryan" by the Nazis.

United States Holocaust Memorial Museum. "Lebensborn Program" Holocaust Encyclopedia. https://encyclopedia.ushmm.org/content/en/article/lebensborn-program
Accessed on September 5, 2024

3 On November 9–10, 1938, Nazi leaders unleashed a series of pogroms against the Jewish population, in Germany and in recently incorporated territories. This event came to be called Kristallnacht (The Night of Broken Glass) because of the shattered glass that littered the streets after the vandalism and destruction of Jewish-owned businesses, synagogues, and homes.

United States Holocaust Memorial Museum. "Kristallnacht" Holocaust Encyclopedia.
https://encyclopedia.ushmm.org/content/en/article/kristallnacht
Accessed on September 5, 2024

was already pregnant with me. We left Germany in 1938 when my stepfather finished his tour of duty in Berlin.”

Quiet for a moment, Marcus asked, “Does Amelia know you are pulling a Doctor Frankenstein routine with bodies here in America? Think she would be proud?”

“Typical American playing the fool. I’m not creating life, I’m planning for the destruct …” Perez snapped. He clenched his fists as he realized he was saying too much. He then placed his hands flat on the desk as he stood and quietly said, “It is all about games. You will see. It has started. Ah, yes, you will see.” And with that statement, he pulled a pistol from the top right-hand drawer and aimed at Marcus.

Muscle memory, honed through years of training, took over as Marcus saw the weapon coming up. Without conscious thought, he pulled his Colt 1911 in a blur of movement. He placed two .45 caliber rounds center chest. The two 230-grain, jacketed hollow point bullets expanded into flowers of death as they shredded the heart, punctured a lung, and exited the doctor’s back before embedding in the wall behind him. Perez was dead before his body fell back into the chair.

Two more SEALs ran into the room, weapons ready. Wentworth stood with mouth agape. No one said anything for a few moments. It wouldn’t have done any good, as the hearing of those in the office was impaired from the two intense explosions in a small space. Ken went to the body and checked for a pulse. He shook his head.

And in the seconds that passed, Marcus again felt the anger and frustration that he always did after a shooting. While this was not the first time he fired his weapon against another human, he knew that each time added to the remorse he carried from this part of his job. Just because an evil bastard deserved it didn’t mean it was forgotten; often the images returned to haunt him at the most inopportune times.

As the ear ringing settled down, Marcus was the first to speak, muttering, “Damn it, I needed to get more intel from the bastard.”

Marcus dropped the magazine now missing two rounds from his pistol, pulled a full magazine from one of the two pouches on his belt, and slammed it into place. The thumb safety clicked into position as he slid the weapon into his holster. The short magazine was slipped into the empty pouch, reversed, so his hand would know it was the short one if he needed to reload in the stress of a gunfight. Experience had shown him it was wise to be ready for a gunfight with a full magazine.

Barry said, "You didn't have any options, sir." He reached down and picked up Perez's weapon by the barrel. "Walther P38. Standard weapon of the Wehrmacht."

"And the preferred weapon of those in the SS who knew the sexy-looking Luger P08 sometimes had feed problems, resulting in jamming. I have one. They look nice, but I also find them hard to cock when in a hurry," Marcus added.

Shaking his head, Sidney said as he looked at the body, "At least the cause of death is obvious and witnessed. Do you think we need to put a stake in the heart of this Vampire?"

77

MARCUS STARED AT THE MAIN board in the war room. He felt as if he'd been juggling chain saws all day long, with physical and mental fatigue to match. More data cards and photos had been added to the boards over the last few hours, but there were fewer people there to appreciate them.

"That sums up the events of the day, gentlemen. Any questions?" Marcus asked.

The gentlemen present included Princeton Chief of Police James Wester, *Princeton Bugle* editor-in-chief Jerry Masterman, FBI Liaison Ken Santoro, Sheriff's Deputy Josh Bonner, and Naval Reserve LT Bob Ledder. The latter two had returned from a flight to Richmond only an hour ago. Deputy Marty Albertson was pulling double duty and manning the office for the night; he leaned against the door casing, paying attention.

"Okay, since there are no questions, let's run down the current status. With so much going on, there's a great chance we've overlooked something. Sheriff Godfrey Timmons and Doctor Sidney Wentworth are handling the scene and body at the farm; a rotating team of SEALs will stay there for security. Detective Allen Chambers and Doctor Dennis Bassett are taking care of the suicide at the Thompkins place. We have two men in lockup: the driver from Chicago and the body dumper from the farm, and neither is talking. GMG2 Glenn Jensen has taken the newest John Doe's body to the morgue to await his turn at autopsy," Marcus recited, pausing for a sip of coffee.

"Continuing on … National Guard assets have returned to their home base. NIS agent Rick Gardener, and my wife, Doctor Kelly Colt, are with the two children at the hospital. God smiled down on those kids as, except for being hungry, slightly dehydrated, and confused, they're in fairly good shape. It's a true miracle … just wish their parents were here."

Marcus again paused to gather his thoughts. "The CO of the SEAL teams, Lieutenant Commander Barry Jackson, has taken the rest of his men to search the area around Devil Holler in hopes of finding some evidence as to why and how the missing children ended up secured in the cave. Doctor Simpson Wallace is with them. They will *RON*, remain overnight, to investigate the knocking Rick's team heard. Everyone else is down for the night getting needed rest. Questions before I head home and fall over?"

Jerry Masterman raised his hand. "Marcus, what, if any, of this can be released? I mean, finding the children alive is great news that will relieve a lot of minds around here. But we have another murder, a shooting, Nazis, and a suicide? It's almost too much and nearly unbelievable!"

"Good question, Jerry. I need everyone to sit on this information for now, so no special edition at this time. We have to hold the suicide news until notification of next of kin. The sheriff will release a statement in the morning about finding the children, but aside from the status of their health, it will not go into any more detail. I suspect the hospital staff gossip network has already spread that news. That's the best we can do until we know who else is involved with the evil at the farm. Okay?"

Ken Santoro and James Wester nodded in comprehension. Jerry gave a thumbs-up.

Wester stood and said, "Marcus, you have done as much as possible for one day. Thanks for including me in this brief. All I can add is to suggest we all call it a night. Let me know if you need any of my resources." And with that, the chief gave a quick salute and left.

Marcus nodded to Bonner and Ledder. "That's all for tonight, gentlemen, see you at 0900 tomorrow. You can brief me on the lab report at that time."

After heading toward the door, Marcus looked at Ken and asked, "Staying overnight or driving back home?"

"Considering the hour and my orders to be 'at your service,' I'll find a room and hang around here. I've got my go-bag in the car. Dinner is on my mind right now: Pansy's provided a good lunch, but that was hours ago."

"Follow me to my place, Ken. I know food will be available, and I suspect I can find at least a comfy sofa, if not a bed."

"I'm too tired to politely fake a refusal, so thanks. Lead on."

78

Lights were on in several rooms when the vehicles assigned to Marcus and Ken nosed up against the garage door. Entering through the garage, they heard noises coming from the kitchen and followed the sounds—and the wonderful smells. Wendy James was sitting at the breakfast table while Aunt Maude and Elle were busy at the stove.

"Hi, hon. Glad the children are safe. Since I didn't get an update on when you would be here, Eleanor and I have been keeping busy with prepping for Triple C. It will fill you up. Welcome home! Finally!" Aunt Maude snipped without turning around.

Elle nudged her and teased, "Watch your tongue, Aunt Maude, we have a visitor."

Introductions went quickly, and in short order, Ken and Marcus attacked full bowls of food.

Marcus looked at Wendy. "Feeling better?"

She nodded. "Much. And I talked with Brad a while ago. Aside from a headache, he's anxious to get out of the hospital. Amazing what a bit of sleep will do."

"I'm not familiar with Triple C—care to fill me in?" Ken asked.

"One of Aunt Maude's house specialties for as long as I can remember," Elle said with a laugh. "Triple C is a simple Chicken and Corn Chowder consisting of cream of mushroom soup, chicken breast meat, whole kernel corn, chopped onions, heavy cream, and a few spices. Quick and easy, since most of it comes out of cans stored in the pantry. Aunt Maude is using some of her leftover roasted chicken in place of the canned stuff. The few spices kick it up a level from boring."

"And a handful of oyster crackers add to it nicely," Marcus interjected.

Not much was said while the food was being consumed. Ken asked for the Triple C recipe after his second bowl. Aunt Maude smiled.

"Any idea when the rest of the crew will be arriving?" Aunt Maude asked as she and Elle cleared the table. "We'll need another batch of chowder if they're hungry."

"Sorry, no. But we do need to find a bed here for Ken," Marcus said.

With a sly smile and bouncing eyebrows, Aunt Maude said, "Hotel Maude is always open for family and friends."

Marcus nodded his thanks. "Chowder was great as always. While waiting for the others to arrive, I suggest we settle in the sanctuary. It's a relaxing place to gather thoughts and chat."

"Sanctuary?" Ken asked.

"That's my nickname for the finished basement. You'll like it."

Ken and Wendy were as impressed with the sanctuary as everyone else had been. Fiddling behind the bar for a moment, Marcus soon had Nat King Cole's soft voice singing "Portrait of Jenny" while he set up the glasses, added a couple of ice cubes, and poured a shot of bourbon into each. Raising his glass, he said, "A quick toast, ladies and gent." They all raised their glasses and Marcus continued, "Safe children, and a successful mission, at least so far."

Everyone muttered affirmations, then moved to comfortable chairs with their refilled glasses. The group was silent, each person lost in thought.

Wendy was the first to speak. "You are planning on explaining that 'so far' part of the toast, right?"

Tenting his fingers in front of his lips gave Marcus a studious look. He dropped his hands and said, "Well, it looks like we have stopped the local murders, and your work in Chicago has probably stopped that section of the drug ring, but something else is the end result of both. That's the unanswered question."

Ken said, "Based upon all I read in the case files, you're right—there is something building, but I have no idea what, so far."

"Agree. Perhaps tomorrow we'll have lab results identifying the stuff from the Chicago lab and that growing in the sludge we found at the farm. That might give us a lead. My conclusion right now is that they're cooking up something nasty. If they were only stealing the Navy's meds for resale, then they could simply replace the drugs with water," Marcus said.

Footsteps padding down the carpeted stairs interrupted the discussion. Kelly, Sidney, and Rick looked burned out as they surveyed the room.

Kelly said, "Wasn't sure if anyone would still be awake, so we grabbed a burger to-go from Pansy and slammed it down on the way home. Got enough energy to pour your exhausted minions a nightcap, Sailor?"

As Marcus did bartender duty, Aunt Maude asked, "How are the children?"

Kelly's face filled with concern. "Physically, they're doing okay. Mentally, the jury is still out."

"How so?" Ken asked.

"They're confused about all that has happened. They keep asking for mommy and daddy, which is typical. But it's the story the five-year-old is telling that makes me concerned." Kelly turned to Marcus. "Hold your comments, Mr. Colt."

Marcus grinned as he passed her the glass. "Yes, ma'am."

Regret colored the sigh that preceded Kelly's recount. "The children are telling me a couple of huge bears took them to the cave. And the bears brought them food and more clothing. And the biggest bear started a fire to keep them warm. 'Bears' might be what they thought, but large vagrants living in the woods that haven't shaved or cut their hair in a while seem more probable. That would give them bear-like looks. And to a short kid, tall adults look huge."

Rick slowly shook his head side to side. "You didn't see the materials used to block the cave. It took two well-muscled SEALs to move each log that secured the cave entrance. A four-hundred-pound bear, or whatever huge creature those kids think looks like a bear, could move the logs easily. But not an old vagrant or two."

Wendy looked confused. "Are you suggesting a Bigfoot is responsible?"

"Not you, too," Kelly said.

"Marcus thinks we have some of them here, Wendy," Aunt Maude said, "Helping to move the bodies around."

"I'm so glad I came on this assignment." Sidney Wentworth chuckled. "This is an interesting discussion, but I'll leave you young people to consider the realm of unknown possibilities. This old man is going to bed."

Marcus said, "Before you slide into slumber, Sid, does next July seventeenth mean anything to you?"

Sid shook his head. "That's two weeks after the Bicentennial celebration, but nothing connects there. Why?"

"The Vampire had that date marked on his 1976 wall calendar. Therefore it's something special. Maybe when we dig into his office tomorrow we'll find a hint. I have some of the Beckley NIS agents coming down to help."

"Am I to be a part of that?" Wendy asked.

"No, I need you to interrogate that driver y'all picked up," Marcus replied. "He hasn't said anything to the deputies, but you know the situation in Chicago and that might help drag some info from him. Then you and Brad need to return to Chicago to wrap up that end of the investigation. Assuming Brad is up to it."

"I checked in on Brad before I left the hospital. He's doing okay and should be up to a ride by Saturday. John plans on releasing him tomorrow afternoon," Kelly said.

"I'll make a quick visit to the farm in the morning; it might help with the interrogation. And we need to take Luis Johnson back to Chicago, since that's where he broke the law. He might be good leverage against the men Todd picked up at the warehouse," Wendy said.

"And his truck needs to go back to Chicago." After a short pause in thought, Marcus asked, "Can you drive a box truck, Wendy?"

"Sure. I helped several friends in college move, and the big U-Haul was my vehicle of choice."

"Brad's head will need a smoother ride than that truck; I'll ask GT to send one of his men with you. Brad can ride in the cruiser and help guard the prisoner. You can drive the truck with your car on a trailer behind. We'll worry about Brad's wrecked car once we get the damage report—it might not be worth fixing."

Wendy nodded her approval and drained her glass. "If you will excuse me, I'll walk up with Sid: we're both staying in the same wing of this mansion. I have a few questions about Brad's recovery that he can answer. Good night."

Everyone was quiet for a short while after they left, then Ken Santoro asked, "Going back to that July date. Should I run it by my people in Beckley or D.C.?"

Marcus considered that offer. "Hold off until we know more. We need to keep all this compartmentalized: nothing goes outside the sheriff's office. I'm afraid too much info getting out will cause the rest of their crew to dive into hiding. I want to catch all the Vampire associates. We need to stop whatever they are doing."

"Hopefully before they do it," Rick added.

79

THE OFFICE WAS HECTIC FOR so early in the morning, even though not everyone was there. Marcus looked at the board that held the names and locations of the sheriff's staff and tried to remember them all.

Dr. Kelly Colt had returned to the hospital with M.E. Sidney Wentworth right after breakfast; she would check on Brad and talk more with the children. Sid would help Dennis with the autopsies of the two newest morgue arrivals. Kelly wanted him to determine if the Vampire was using drugs—that might help explain his behavior.

Over that early breakfast, Marcus had asked Elle Colt to photograph the cave and surrounding area, and since SA Rick Gardener knew the location, he volunteered to drive her to the area and lead her to the cave. As far as everyone knew, SEALs and Dr. Wallace Simpson had spent the night in the area looking for bears, or whatever cryptid had taken care of the children.

The tension in the interrogation room was thick. "Luis Johnson, let me lay it out for you so you don't miss anything. Okay?" Wendy James asked the rhetorical question as she took her time shuffling through a sheaf of papers from the manila folder and found the one she wanted. Facing Luis across a small table bolted to the floor, she said, "In Chicago, you're facing a charge of theft from the Navy base, and possibly some drug charges, depending on what was found at the warehouse. And you have to wonder what stories your friends are telling my agents there. Perhaps naming you the ring leader?"

Johnson looked around the interrogation room, nervously avoiding eye contact with Wendy. He quietly repeated his earlier statement: "I didn't do nothin'." He pulled on the cuffs and chain that held him to the table as he leaned back in defiance.

Wendy laughed. "The old double-negative confession. By the way, being at the farm ties you as an accessory to multiple murders here in West Virginia. The sheriff is working with the local district attorney to convince the DA in Chicago to allow the murder case against you to be tried first. Life in a West Virginia prison is their goal."

"I'm just a truck driver. I don't know what's inside or what they did at that farm."

"Nice try. We have witnesses who saw you loading the truck at the Great Lakes Naval Hospital, saw you take it into that seedy Chicago warehouse, and followed you to the local farm here where bodies were being gutted. On top of that, Chief Hugo Diaz is telling my people in Chicago all about your involvement. Bottom line, Luis, is that—You. Are. Screwed." Wendy paused a moment between the last three words to drive the point home. She stacked the papers and tapped them straight before standing. "I'll let you ponder your future for a bit."

Closing the interrogation room door behind her, Wendy blew out a deep breath of frustration and walked to the break room. She hoped a caffeine rush would help with the case-generated headache. She was caught up on sleep and food, but had assimilated stress from Marcus. Working closely with him the last few years seemed to have mentally connected them, allowing them to share feelings without vocalizing them.

Marcus had the same needs and was already in the break room. Turning from pouring another cup—he'd lost count of the number—he said, "How'd it go?"

Wendy shrugged. "He knows nothing, of course. I planted the idea of the murder rap and will let him stew on that for a bit. At least he's too stupid to call for a lawyer yet. How about you?"

Nodding approval of her methods, Marcus said, "I'm letting the FBI handle the body dumper; Ken's got more energy than I do right now. And his freshness, and FBI ID, might give him an edge. By the way, dumper's name is Manny Alvarez. Came to the USA from Bolivia about ten years ago on a student visa, got his degree in business at the University of

Central Florida, and then got his green card. No priors, and he is not on any radar with immigration."

"Think he and Perez were buds either in Bolivia or Miami? Guess NISRA Miami could check on that. But you've already called, right?" Wendy winked.

Marcus again nodded. "Last night. I also wired the military attaché at our embassy in La Paz to see if they could find out any more info about these two. And see if they had any other associates. Of course, I let them know Perez was dead so they could notify any relatives. It's a long shot, but …" Marcus shrugged, then sipped more coffee.

"Usually long shots are the only ones we have, partner. Time to look at the boards again." Wendy pushed Marcus toward the war room.

They had been sipping coffee and quietly looking at the boards for several minutes when Marcus said, "There has got to be something important with that date. Time to call an off-the-wall thinker." Marcus picked up the phone and dialed a direct line number from memory.

After several moments, Marcus pressed the speakerphone button. "About time you answered, Doc, sleeping on my desk again?"

"Hell, no, boss. There are too many file folders here taking up all the space, but your comfy chair works fine for a nap. What's up, oh great one?"

"Wendy and I are enjoying a cup of West Virginia coffee, wondering how things are going back in Foggy Bottom. Having fun yet?"

Doc chuckled. "Tons of fun with a desk full of work that you should be doing. Hurry home 'cause Iceland's getting hotter. And yea, I have read the update from Great Lakes about the road trip Wendy and Brad took. He doing okay?"

Wendy interjected, "He'll be out of the hospital later today. Short-term headaches and a small forehead scar are his souvenirs. And a big hit to his dignity for wrecking his vehicle. He and I will head to Chicago tomorrow to wrap up the case on that end."

"Hi, Wendy! Guess we need to go easy on him at the next Monday meeting. So again, what's up, Marcus?" Doc asked in his easy-going way.

"We'll get you a full update soon, but right now I need you to ask around the office and see if anyone knows anything special about July 17, 1976," Marcus said impatiently.

Doc was quiet for a moment before saying with a touch of sarcasm, "Aside from the opening ceremonies of the *Montréal Olympics* … nothing comes to mind." He knew that while Marcus was an avid tennis player, he ignored other sports save for a few football games during social events. Doc enjoyed pointing out what he considered his buddy's major social flaw.

Face contorting into a painful expression, Marcus said, "That's probably it, Doc."

"It's what, Marcus?"

"I gotta run, Doc, we'll talk more when the thoughts firm up. Ask around and see if anything else big is cooking around that date. Call me when ya got something." Marcus ran the words together in a quick stream and slammed the phone's off button. He muttered, "Oh, crap."

"You're not thinking another terrorist attack at the Olympics, are you?" Wendy quietly asked.

Marcus started tapping his pencil against his coffee mug and looked at the overhead to focus. His memories came flooding back of the horrible events he watched unfold on television a few years ago.

The 1972 Summer Olympics in Munich saw eight Palestinian terrorists invade the Olympic Village, killing two Israeli athletes and taking nine more hostage. They were from a terrorist group called Black September. Sadly, twenty hours later, eleven Israeli athletes and one West German police officer were dead. Five of the terrorists were killed in a gun battle, with the other three arrested. As an insult to law and order and to the memory of those innocent victims, the remaining three pieces of trash were soon released in exchange for hostages taken from an airliner highjacked by similar terrorists.

Coming back to the here and now, Marcus said, "Yea, another Olympic attack is my concern right this minute, unless something else is happening on that date. I'll ask Norma to call Charleston and see if anything big is on the state's schedule. But looking at the Olympic possibility, what makes little sense is the lack of cohesiveness. What is the justification of mixing Nazis, West Virginia, Chicago, and the U.S. Navy with the Canadian Olympics? How do they relate?"

Wendy raised her hands in surrender. She had no idea.

Deputy Josh Bonner and LT Bob Ledder strolled in together. Marcus pointed them to chairs at the conference table. After another moment of contemplation, he turned his attention to them.

"Sorry I didn't have the energy to hear your report last night, gentlemen. As you heard then, it had been a hectic day. So what good news did the FBI lab offer on the wounds? Report, Lieutenant," Marcus said.

Ledder started to stand as he slid two copies of the report over to Marcus, but a quick hand signal motioned him back down. Settling in his chair, Ledder said, "They were extremely thorough, sir, as you can see by this two-inch-thick report that took them all night to create. The two-page executive summary will save you an hour of reading. In a shorter verbal version, the holes on the victims' shoulders were not caused by anything man-made: no traces of metal or plastics were found. They called them 'claws' and said they were about two inches long and three-eighths of an inch thick. The same pair of claws made all the holes, with those on the left matching across all victims, and the same with the right. There are minor differences between the left and right claws that the lab techies thought were due to wear. And with the curve of the claws pointing toward the back of the body, they speculated the perpetrator was behind the victims. Furthermore, tearing of the flesh around the punctures indicates the bodies were pulled or lifted by the claws."

Wendy said, "Were they able to determine the type of animal that did it?"

"No, ma'am, but off the record they told me that none of them had seen anything like these punctures. And they all are avid hunters and outdoorsmen, so they would know the wildlife in this region."

"Did they find anything in the wounds? Any debris?" Marcus asked.

"Yes, sir. There were traces of tree bark. I don't recall the ratio, but it was a combination of oak and spruce," Ledder said.

Marcus was quiet as he processed the information. "So, what you're telling me is that something or someone with a pair of two-pronged claws stood behind each victim and slammed holes into the front of their shoulders. Using these claws, the bodies were pulled or lifted. And before being slammed into the bodies, the claws were holding on to trees."

Wendy finished the thought as she muttered, "Easy to imagine a huge bird swooping down from a perch in a tree to latch onto the victim from behind and carry him off. Maybe that large bird I saw yesterday?"

"Anything to add, Josh?" Marcus asked, ignoring Wendy's bird comment.

"No, sir, Bob covered it well."

"Okay, Josh, report to GT and see what he needs from you. Bob, while I believe we have Decker's killer in custody, I still need you for a bit longer. Okay?"

"Fine with me. I'd like to see this to the end, sir."

"Thanks. Is your airplane ready for flight?"

With a slight head movement, Bob said, "No, sir. When we got back last night, all I did was set chocks and tie-downs. I need about an hour for refueling and fluid checking, et cetera. Then I can wind up the rubber bands for whatever trip you need. Quick enough?"

Marcus nodded. "Nothing planned right this minute, but that can change. If you don't mind being a gofer, please run one copy of this report to the M.E.s at the hospital. You'll find them in the morgue. They might see something that us non-medical types might miss. Then before coming back here, get the *Songbird* ready to fly."

"*Songbird*?"

"Sorry. A reference to my favorite Saturday morning kid's TV show from the 1950s called *Sky King*. A modern crime-fighting western where the good guy, a World War II naval aviator turned rancher, gave up his horse for a twin-engine Cessna like yours that he named *Songbird*. Seems fitting."

"Aye, aye, sir," Bob chuckled as he headed out the door. He stuck his head back into the war room and added, "I'll think about naming my Cessna 310 *Songbird II*."

The morning passed quickly as Wendy and Marcus added information to the boards as it came in. The newest victim of the Vampire was identified as Hank Grant by his ID, which the recently recruited NIS agents from the Beckley office had found; Manny Alvarez had probably planned to burn the ID with the victim's possessions after dumping the body. Grant's ID showed an address in Pittsburgh, so NISRA Pittsburgh was asked to check him out and look for next of kin.

They kept tossing about ideas and scenarios, but nothing jelled, as each theory contained multiple flaws. The missing links would join the known parameters together.

Sheriff GT and Detective Allen Chambers had been in the office all morning, covered up with the Thompkins' family issues. It was a bit of a mess. When GT called Doris's parents to notify them of Cal's death and the rescue of the children, he was surprised to hear that Cal had not told them about the discovery of their daughter's body. The unpleasant duty of telling them their daughter had been found fell on GT. Of course, they would be in charge of her funeral, and since Cal's parents were dead and he had no siblings, responsibility for his funeral fell on them, too.

The parents' emotions were a mess, between the sadness of the double loss combined with the happiness of finding their grandchildren. GT played counselor and sheriff during the long phone call. Allen started planning with the funeral home as a way of helping them. They would come from Michigan in the next couple of days to pick up the children and complete the funeral arrangements.

Thin black hands of the wall clock approached noon as GT came into the war room, dropping into one of the chairs. His moan got the attention of those present. Wendy stopped the doodle that was starting to cover the full page of the legal pad; it was her way of mentally putting information in the proper order.

Marcus turned from the third board. "Well?"

"Ah, hell. Well what?" GT asked. "Please tell me you have all this mess figured out."

Marcus shook his head. "Not totally, but as soon as we hear from Great Lakes, we'll have a better handle on the situation. And that might lead us to the answers we all need."

"Okay. Don't know about you two, but I'm in need of lunch. My treat at Pansy's, if you can spare the time."

80

AFTER INTRODUCING WENDY TO PANSY and getting her congratulatory hugs, the three were seated in what Marcus now considered their private dining room: the break table at the back of the kitchen. A face new to Marcus set them up with sweet tea and gave a quick nod to GT. Dressed in olive drab fatigues under his mostly white apron; the serious fellow wore a camo-colored ball cap. Pansy darted into the office and came out with four shot glasses and a bottle of Maker's Mark bourbon.

"I know you people are on duty, but I hope we can do a quick toast to finding the children alive. The whole town is excited and singing your praises, GT." Pansy poured the bourbon without first getting the okay.

With glasses drained, GT said, "The honor goes to Marcus and his assets: he pointed to the area, and his friends found them."

"Ignore him, Pansy—it was a total team effort. And as the sheriff, he gets and deserves the loudest praise." Marcus then changed the subject. "Who's the new guy?" He pointed to the tea server, who was now flipping burgers on the grill like those guys at the Benihana restaurant flip shrimp. His hands were a blur.

GT said, "Didn't Kelly tell you about the hitchhiker we picked up Wednesday? That's him, Roland James. Ex-Army. Draftee. Purple Heart from Vietnam."

"And a damn good cook," Pansy interjected. "With the upcoming re-model and Roland's skill in the kitchen, I'm excited about the future of this place. Roland is a true godsend and I owe you, GT."

"Yea, Kelly mentioned him, but guess it slipped my mind," Marcus said. "Y'all did a good thing setting him up with the job."

"He'll be cooking your steaks, and his mushroom risotto is second to none. And Marcus, I think you're going to love his fried green beans," Pansy said with a wink, then left the area.

"Sounds like lunch is going to be a high point of the day," Wendy said.

"My high point will be calling the governor to tell him we have stopped the Crazed Bear Killer." GT continued in a pleading voice that kept pitching higher. "Assuming the team leader will allow me. Can I, Marcus? Please!"

Laughing at GT, Marcus replied, "Sorry, not yet. If our Gov is like the rest, first thing he'll do is call a press conference and make the announce-ment a six o'clock leading news item on all three networks. It stays under wraps until we get the entire crew."

GT shrugged. "You always did know how to rain on my parade."

"It's hard enough to keep these things under wraps without getting a politician involved," Wendy added to bolster her boss's position.

"GT, I think it's time for you to get back to being the best sheriff Mercer County has seen. We have people wrapping up the crime scenes and in no time we'll have all the reports done, and so forth. My guess is the next phase of this mission will be out of your jurisdiction," Marcus added.

"I hear ya. But it will be hard to wind down from the excitement the last couple of days have created. Working with you and your people has been a real treat. And I must admit having you around again has been fun, Marcus, even with all the evil things that happened. Like old times."

"Same here, GT. It's been good to be home, and all this stuff has eased the pain of the memorial service by keeping my mind busy: less time to feel sorry for myself. But I need to wrap up this case and get back to my real world."

The conversation was interrupted with the delivery of lunch. Roland sat the plates before each person, and Marcus, impressed by the presenta-tion, passed his compliments to the vet. The three dug into the food, al-lowing the sound of silverware hitting plates to replace the conversation.

Placing his silverware on the plate at the proper 1830 hours position and pushing the empty plate away, he let out a sigh of contentment. Seeing GT and Wendy do the same, he smiled. "Now that we have had a gourmet meal, did it stimulate any ideas on how our bits of data link to Canadian Olympics?"

"Drugs," Wendy said.

"Care to elaborate, Special Agent James? The lab we busted yesterday at the farm seems to tell a different story."

"Okay, boss. I agree there is something else, something nastier going on here, but the foundation is based on heroin, maybe cocaine, or possibly hash and marijuana. And I'll put forth the theory that the Nazi doctor is part of that supply chain, and he's using it, and the drug people and their resources, to further his plan. Possibly funding it, also. Following the drugs in both directions might lead us to that Nazi plan." Wendy's mild southern accent carried authority.

GT asked, "Both directions?"

Marcus answered. "The warehouse in Chicago is probably the midpoint of the supply chain. The drugs come from somewhere to the warehouse, and leave the warehouse going someplace else. My gut tells me the original source is the best place to start. Perez is probably linked to a drug source in South America, and is piggybacking on it to do whatever evil deed he has planned. Maybe drug money is his funding source, or he needs the supply line or people."

Wendy chimed in when Marcus paused for a sip of tea. "And something leaves the warehouse going back to the Naval Hospital, so that might be the link to Canada if we find the Naval Hospital has a link to the Olympics."

Marcus continued, "And all this speculation is in a holding pattern until we hear from the NIS agents in Chicago, who are analyzing the stuff they found in the warehouse, and what they find when they tear apart the supplies at the hospital. And we need the analysis of the stuff at the farm. Maybe knowing what our good doctor was cooking up will—okay, maybe will—point us in the direction of the target."

Slowly shaking his head, GT exhaled. "I'm damn glad I'm the sheriff of a county where nothing that complicated happens. Sure, we get a homicide every year or so, and a frequent moonshine operation, but most of my cases are boring. And I'm glad. Not sure I could handle your stuff, Marcus."

"Don't sell yourself short, Godfrey my man. You are more than up to the task. Let's get to the war room and study the boards until the phone starts ringing." Marcus dropped his napkin on the table and stood.

Wendy held up her hand. "Boss, you sure there is nothing else we can do here? Today? Hanging around the war room is not high on my list."

Marcus dropped into his chair. "Okay, moving from dead bodies to drugs, perhaps we need to talk with GT's buddy, Carl Marks. His red ball cap still nags at me."

GT nodded. "The other day when I talked with him it was only about the bodies. What say Wendy and I chat him up about drugs? He used to be in the game, and might be back involved."

"Happy to, GT, but it might be more useful to set up a sting. Get someone to approach him to make a buy. Then we have some leverage," Wendy said.

"Only problem, Wendy, is finding someone to make the buy. Marks knows everyone around here," GT said.

"I can do it, Sheriff," Roland James said as he approached the table. "Didn't mean to eavesdrop, but you folks are talking loud due to the kitchen noise. Anyway, I helped CID at Fort Hood with undercover work while I recuperated. My wounds convinced the pushers that I'd need more pain killers."

"Your thoughts, Marcus?" Wendy asked as GT gave a thumbs-up.

"Go for it. I'm heading to the war room."

81

"So, what's the verdict, Supervisory Special Agent Santoro? Did you get the truth, and nothing but, from Manny?" Marcus asked as he entered the war room and saw the FBI agent adding notes to the board. Seeing dejection shadow the agent's face, Marcus pleaded, "Please tell me you have something, Ken."

A slight smile replaced the dejection. "Sometimes when a bad guy tries to not say anything, they actually reveal a lot. Manny Alvarez didn't break the way they do on that *Hawaii Five-O* show; however, I did get to see inside his mind."

Making a come-on hand signal, Marcus said, "And …"

"I believe Alvarez is part of the upper management of a drug ring centered in Chicago. His job here was to keep Perez doing whatever he was doing at all costs. He demanded a lawyer."

Marcus chewed his lower lip. "You just told me he didn't say anything—what generated these conclusions?"

"Since the jerk isn't talking, I had to make some educated conclusions. His attitude tells me he's not just a body dumper, but he's involved up to his ears—including decision-making. He carries himself with importance, and he has the arrogance of a boss. While he's South American, his accent has been softened and gained Chicago phraseology from spending most of his time there. And when he asked for an attorney, he pulled a card from his wallet that I glimpsed is from one of the prestigious—and reportedly a favorite of the corrupt—legal firms in the Windy City. A simple worker bee he ain't."

"Impressive. But it sounds like we're dead in the water with this guy," Marcus said.

"Maybe not. His attorney won't be here until tomorrow, so I have more time to try."

Marcus absorbed that thought. "How about you take a stab at Luis Johnson, and get ready for another possible member of the group."

"Who?"

"Local guy calls himself Carl Marks, anglicized version of Carlos Marcano. Not connected so far, but my alarm bells keep going off when I think of him. Drug involvement is in his past. GT says he seems clean now, but ya never know. GT and Wendy are setting up a sting in hopes of having some leverage with him," Marcus said.

Ken nodded. "Drugs keep getting mentioned with all this. Okay for me to call a friend at the Drug Enforcement Administration? She's ex-FBI and owes me a favor or two. I'll make sure it's off the record there and won't get them involved."

"What do you expect to hear?"

"Background information. If I have the names of the big drug people and associated gangs in Chicago, it might give me a wedge to shove in any cracks I hear in their stories."

"Give it a shot. Worst case is we're left where we are. How is working with this new organization? Any problems? I dealt with the Bureau of Narcotics and Dangerous Drugs, BNDD, back in '71, but that was my last contact."

"Overall, things are good. They did have a few management issues after the merger, but less as time goes by. That was to be expected, I suppose. After all, they mixed the Bureau of Narcotics and Dangerous Drugs, the Office for Drug Abuse Law Enforcement, the Office of National Narcotics Intelligence, and the Narcotics Advance Research Management team together with parts of the U.S. Customs Service that handled drug trafficking. Lots of high management egos got trampled."

Marcus nodded. "Yea, I saw something like that in '72 when the Defense Investigative Service came about to merge all military background information checks into one unit. Prior to that, each service branch did their own, and there was a lot of wasted personnel covering overlapping areas. Some didn't want to give up their share of the work because it would cause some downsizing. Anyway, let me know what your DEA mole has to offer."

"Uh, Marcus. If we do find a trafficking connection, we're obligated to bring the DEA on board," Ken said with concern.

"I'll be happy to get their help, once we get a grip on whatever the Nazi plan is. But not one minute sooner. Got it?"

"You're the boss. Let me get another cup of coffee and call the DEA. Then I'll go have a friendly chat with Luis Johnson."

82

DOCTOR SIMPSON WALLACE WAS IN his element; he felt as happy as a clam, assuming one believed a clam could ever be happy. Simpson knew he was where he belonged. Battery-powered lights had been placed around the cave and he was collecting multiple samples from many locations. Elle photographed each sample in its location under the watchful eye of LT Rick Gardener before the doctor did his bag-and-tag routine.

While LT Commander Barry Jackson had assured him the cave was clear, Rick wanted to keep Elle safe. He could not imagine the wrath of Commander Colt if anything happened to her, but he was starting to admit to himself that he was attracted to his boss's baby sister. So keeping her safe was a personal thing.

RM1 Andy "Sparks" Waterman walked over to Rick and quietly asked, "You guys going to be much longer? My boss wants to wrap this up since it has been a dead end finding anything as exciting as bears, big-footed critters, or flying monsters."

"What did you find?"

"Sir, there are a lot of trails around here. We found lots of compressed undergrowth and broken tree branches. Many hiding places too. And the doc found and marked about half a dozen somewhat large footprints before he sequestered himself in this smelly cave. The deputy is converting the prints to plaster castings. But nothing alive has been heard or spotted, and we've been out here over twenty-four hours."

Rick nodded and raised his voice, "How much longer, Doc?"

Simpson stood up slowly and leaned backwards with his hands on hips to get a catch out of his back. He turned to face Rick. "I could continue the collection for hours, but I'm afraid it would be repetitive. And my back has nearly reached its limits, I'm afraid. Give me another half hour, please."

Elle checked her camera bag. "Just as well, Simpson, I'm about out of film."

Rick gave them a nod. "Okay, Sparks, you have the official answer: thirty minutes, give or take."

"Aye, aye, sir. I'll round up the teams and wait outside," Waterman said as he turned to leave.

Rounding up the teams was a relatively straightforward task; one radio call spread the word, and in a short time, a group gathered around their boss at the mouth of the cave.

"Time to pack up. We need to head to the motel in about thirty, so grab your gear. While we had no contact, I consider this operation a success," Jackson said.

"Skipper, we never found the source of that knocking," said a SEAL. "Maybe we need to come back tonight and look around more. We could stake out the cave in case something returns."

"That'll be up to Commander Colt. Our mission was to help find the missing car and the children. We have succeeded in both. But I agree bagging a Bigfoot would be spectacular," Jackson replied with a laugh. "I'll confer with *the man* on our next task while you slobs hit the showers and down a hot meal. Both are well deserved and needed ... especially the showers."

"I could use some help in here," Rick said from the cave. "The doctor has more samples than we can carry."

It was a forty-minute walk out of the woods to where the vehicles were parked. Following their normal methods, the team members walked abreast distanced about five yards apart. Simpson Wallace, Elle Colt, and Rick Gardener followed Barry Jackson, who was following one of the trails.

They were about halfway to the vehicles when a sound came from behind. Someone was beating on trees with stout limbs, creating a knocking sound. It came from several different directions. The teams stopped and listened. The taps varied in loudness and frequency.

Simpson tapped Jackson on the shoulder, and in a stage whisper said, "I dare say that our hosts are signaling our departure."

"Sounds like a code similar to Morse, with varied longs and shorts," Jackson said. He paused to look Simpson in the eye as he asked, "So you believe Bigfoot is in these woods, Doctor?"

Simpson chuckled. "To quote the Bard, 'There are more things in Heaven and Earth, Horatio, then are dreamt of in your philosophy.' So yes, Commander, I believe some form of a Sasquatch exists, perhaps not in these woods, but somewhere. Then again, the fact the children are alive because of 'huge bears' leads me to believe they are here, probably watching us, and they have been a big help directing your men to that cave. If I knew their language, I would be tapping out a big 'thank you' right now."

83

MARCUS HUNG UP THE PHONE and grabbed another index card. Another piece of information had arrived from the Great Lakes office: the red ball cap was a symbol of a Chicago drug gang. The Southside Cardinals selected the red ball cap as their colors rather than the three-peaked Biretta or the skull-cap-styled Zucchetto, both worn by the Catholic cardinals. They didn't want to become laughing stocks in their hood by wearing either.

The gang members arrested in the warehouse weren't talking much, but had said enough to piece together that they were reloading official drug vials from the base hospital with the concoction from the Vampire's lab. While that was good news, the bad was that Marcus was still waiting for the analysis of the materials from the warehouse.

And one of the gang had let slip that some of the tampered vials were making their way to Canada. They didn't know the final destination, but knew they headed north in the direction of Montréal. Another card was written and tacked to the board.

A link had finally showed itself, and a more complete view was slowly forming. West Virginia to Chicago was firm, and at least one person had linked Chicago to the location of the Olympics. Now Marcus was desperate to know what was in the bogus vials. And where the others were going. Each new piece of information generated a couple of new questions.

Ken Santoro dashed into the war room. "Okay, Johnson was a waste of time, but I got a link from the DEA, Marcus!" His smile faded when he saw the cards with Southside Cardinals and red ball caps in big letters. "And my news is obviously old."

"This is hot from the Great Lakes office. What do you have?"

"My DEA contact did a search of their files—off the record, of course—and found that the biggest drug kingpin in Bolivia vanished about a year ago. He is reported to have relocated to the Chicago area. Furthermore, there are unsubstantiated rumors that his dealings in Chicago are through the Southside Cardinals. Who you obviously know wear red ball caps as their colors."

"Did they provide the kingpin's name? Description? Background?"

Ken nodded. "Rodrigo Quispe was born in Sucre in 1930, then moved south to Tarija, near the Argentina border, when he was five. No data on what happened to the father, but his mother was a maid for a family that was big in wine: they had a successful vineyard and extensive distribution network. When Rodrigo reached his teens, the wine king took him under his wing. Taught him about business and distribution, and put him through college here in the USA. Got his MBA in 1955 before returning to Bolivia. But they have yet to find a record of him in any universities."

"Sounds like a rags-to-riches scenario. What got him into drugs?" Marcus asked.

"Sorry, nothing specific on file. After he finished school, seems there were a couple of years of bad grape crops. The wine king died from a bad heart, and Rod took over the business operation. Shortly thereafter in the early 1960s, two American companies moved into the wine business there by buying several smaller vineyards. Speculation at DEA is that wine money was going away and drug money filled the need. The hippies were into drugs more than Malbec, and Rod was happy to satisfy their needs."

"Did they have any idea why he's hiding in Chicago?"

Shifting the papers he held, Ken said, "New attorney general in Bolivia hates druggies, so the DEA has determined Rodrigo sneaked across our southern border and went to the land of the successful mobs and gangs. DEA hasn't had any luck finding the man. Here's the most current photo."

Marcus studied the image. "He looks like that actor, uh, Ricardo Montalban."

Ken nodded. "I'll send copies of all this to your NIS guys at Great Lakes, okay?"

Marcus considered the new information. "Good plan. Maybe they can help DEA find the gentleman. By the way, pass a 'well done' to your DEA friend. Nice to have a name to add to the board, even if it's just a possibility."

"Adding names without me? I'm crushed, Sailor," Kelly said as she led Brad Neil into the war room. "At least I brought you more help."

"Hey, Boss. Sorry my accident cost us a day. I'm ready to work now." Brad extended a hand toward Marcus.

Marcus took the hand and pulled Brad in to give him a brotherly strike on the back with the other hand. He stared with concern at the wound on Brad's forehead and said, "Glad you're here, Brad. Kelly brief you?"

"Yes, sir. But we both need to know what happened so far today."

Ken and Marcus quickly related all that had transpired. The possible connection to the Olympics became the center of discussion for a good ten minutes until they decided they were going in circles. Quiet shrouded the conference table.

Kelly finally asked the question on everyone's mind: "So, what's the next step?"

"While we wait to hear what the labs have discovered in the farm's vats and the Chicago corrupted meds, we have to answer the pending questions about the victims here. And figure out what we can share with the public about the unusual aspects. Those anomalies you don't want to discuss, Kelly," Marcus said.

Rolling her eyes, Kelly replied, "There will be logical answers to all those anomalies, and you know it."

"Hopefully. Then we'll need to wrap up all the points of the case for the local district attorney. Bummer that there will only be one murder charge to dump on Manny Alvarez. Unless the team at the farm is able to find something belonging to the earlier victims, the latest victim is the only one we can connect to him," Marcus said. "The similarities with the victims might hold some power in court, but would probably be considered circumstantial."

"And since I suspect Alvarez is one of the leaders of their plan, he probably has information about the end destination for the tainted drugs," Ken offered. "Maybe we can use some leverage with lessening the murder charge in exchange for more details on the Nazi plan."

Marcus slowly moved his head side to side. "No damn way, Ken. You haven't seen the gutted bodies. He doesn't deserve any leniency. Fact is, I wish West Virginia still had the death penalty, or that the bastard would try to escape when I'm nearby."

84

PANSY STUCK HER HEAD INTO the small office, disturbing Wendy James and Sheriff GT from their heads-down planning session with Roland James. As the three heads turned in her direction, she said in an urgent stage whisper, "GT, Carl just arrived and took a seat at the counter."

"You ready for this, Roland?" GT asked.

"Sure, Sheriff. Excuse me while I go take his order," Roland replied.

Wearing confidence, Roland went behind the counter and stopped in front of Carl Marks. The customer's red ball cap was pulled down, but he finally looked up from the menu and made eye contact with Roland.

"Reached a decision yet, buddy? Pansy got stuck on a phone call, so she sent me out to get your order."

Carl looked him up and down as he said, "Yea, sure. BLT, chips, and iced tea."

Roland turned and prepared a glass of tea from the setup behind him. "Here ya go, sir. I'll be back with your lunch shortly."

The order was an easy and quick one, and Roland carried the plate out in a matter of minutes. As he refilled the tea glass, he asked, "Anything else ya need?"

"I'm good," Carl said. Then he looked hard at Roland. "You're new here, aren't ya?"

Roland nodded. "Got here last week. I decided Chicago was too cold, and I hope to end up in Florida before winter hits. For now, Princeton looks good."

"Where in Chicago?"

"Washington Heights area. Bummed a room for a while from an Army buddy who was going to Chicago State on the GI Bill. Why?"

Munching on a chip, Carl said, "I used to hang around there years ago. Miss it some days."

"Yea, the place grows on ya. Lots of memories. Including a bad one from a run-in with some of the local gangs. There was one group that had red hats like you wear."

"What happened between you and the Cardinals, if you don't mind me asking."

"You know them?"

Carl nodded. "I used to run with them back in the day."

"Well, long story short, I needed some weed, you know, to help get over the memories and nightmares from 'Nam, and a student hooked me up with one of those red hat guys. They were the local dealers. But after a couple of buys, the bastard tripled the price. I argued and a couple of them jumped me. Bruised big time, but no broken bones, so I left town."

Carl Marks looked lost in thought, then asked, "Are you still needing some stuff? For the nightmares?"

His face showed confusion as Roland asked, "You still in that gang?"

"No, man, uh, not really, but my friends up north keep me supplied. I keep on truckin', taking care of some local friends. A Chicago dude is automatically a friend, so will a nickel bag do ya? If so, come out to the parking lot a couple of minutes after I leave."

Roland nodded and walked to the kitchen. GT and Wendy stepped back from the door as he entered.

"Well, how'd it go?" GT asked.

Roland smiled. "I'll meet him in the parking lot for a nickel bag transaction when he finishes his lunch."

"Good," GT said. "Last I heard a nickel bag is running ten bucks. Here is a five, two tens, and twenty, all carefully marked and witnessed. Wendy and I will be nearby, so holler if you need us. If the deal goes down, pull off your cap and shake it as you walk toward the restaurant."

"Sheriff," Roland said, "I can take care of myself, but nice to have backup."

"I suspect you can, but we'll be ready. Wendy, Marks drives a faded red Ford pickup. So position my cruiser down the street, and put yourself where you can watch, but not be seen," GT ordered as he passed her the keys. "Be ready to stop Marks when you see Roland walk away and give the signal. I'll watch from the alley and be ready to stop him if he comes that way."

Wendy nodded and left by the back door.

"Remember, we need Marks to take the money and pass over the drugs. Okay?"

With a quick nod, Roland went back to the stoves.

Pansy looked at GT. "All right for me to resume my position at the counter?"

"Sure, Pansy. As soon as Marks leaves, let Roland know. I appreciate your help with this." GT headed to the back door to find a place of concealment in the alleyway.

They didn't have to wait long. Marks scarfed down his lunch in obvious anticipation of a drug sale and was on the way to his truck in less than ten minutes. From their concealed locations, both Wendy and GT watched Roland leave the back door, glance around, and meet Marks at the driver's door of the pickup. The short conversation ended in Roland passing something to Marks, and Marks reaching behind the seat for a small package.

Roland checked the package, nodded, and strolled slowly back to the restaurant. As he neared the door, he pulled his cap off, shook it, and ran a hand through his short hair. Replacing the cap, he entered the building.

Marks fired up the truck and started to pull out of the parking lot. He stopped to check traffic both ways, and before he could move, Wendy placed herself in front of the truck. Marks tried not to panic as he shifted into reverse, but a sharp tap on the driver's window got his attention.

GT aimed his weapon at Marks as he yelled, "Shut off the engine! Out of the truck!"

By this time, Wendy was on the passenger side with her weapon also at the ready.

Marks shut off the engine and raised his hands. Under his breath, he said, "Busted, damn it."

85

THREE RED CAPS WERE NOW in custody, isolated from each other to prevent fabricating a joint story. The Southside Cardinals' reach into West Virginia was running out of workers. Or at least workers known to the sheriff's office.

GT rubbed his face in frustration. "You know we can only link Alvarez to the latest victim. Unless your boys at the farm can find some evidence to link him or Perez to the others."

Marcus nodded. "At least we have him on one, and he is completely nailed to it since Dennis and Sid have linked the drugs in the victim to the partially filled syringe we found in Alvarez's truck. One is better than zero, but I suspect for the others we need a miracle."

The only West Virginia Cardinal connected to the bodies wasn't talking, so Marcus suggested they focus on the other two in custody. *Look for the weak link* was the plan kicked into gear.

Pushing the interrogation door closed with a soft click, Marcus took the chair across from Carlos Marcano, a.k.a. Carl Marks. Without a word, he opened the manila folder he carried as he leaned back, holding the folder up to prevent Marks from seeing inside. "Interesting," he muttered a couple of times after several minutes of flipping through pages.

"What?" Marks pleaded.

Marcus lowered the folder to focus on Marks over the top edge. His slight smile kicked slightly up to the left as he slammed the folder shut flat on the table, the motion sounding like a gunshot.

Marks jumped in response to the rapid action.

"Carlos Marcano, all I wanted to do was chat with you, but the sheriff lucked out by adding drug possession and distribution to your growing list of charges," Marcus said, his voice carrying authority that Marks was not used to hearing. "If you're planning on staying in the criminal business, you need to learn how to surveil without staring. Your interest in me while we had coffee at Pansy's the other morning piqued my interest in you."

"I prefer to be called 'Carl Marks,' and I don't remember seeing you earlier."

"Too bad—I prefer to use real names when questioning murder suspects. In pursuit of full disclosure, I am Commander Marcus Colt, who happens to be a temporary deputy. In my full-time job, I am a naval officer and investigator assigned to the Naval Investigative Service in D.C. I'm helping the sheriff solve a series of heinous murders because one of them was a Navy Reserve member."

"Man, I didn't do no murders," Marks yelled.

Marcus cringed internally at the double negative, then said, "Perhaps, but I, and the district attorney, don't care. Your red cap ties you to the Southside Cardinals, as does your confession to being from that area. Your associate, Manny Alvarez, was arrested dumping a body, and he has fingered you as part of the team. The DA is as happy to tag you with being an accessory before or after the murders." Marcus paused after each sentence. "The more bastards I put in prison, the happier I am."

"Like I said, I didn't murder nobody!"

A shark-like smile crossed Marcus's face. "Again, I don't care. Since you were caught selling drugs, as far as I'm concerned, you are still killing people, just a bit slower than using a knife or gun. That being said, the sheriff mentioned he didn't think you were involved with the six murders."

Marks looked shocked. "Six? The papers only talked about three dead dudes."

"I suspect one is a Chicago friend you might know, Jesus Cabilla. That name ring any bells?"

Sadness clouded Marks' face, and he paused. "Yea, I know, well, knew him. What the hell happened?"

"Alvarez is saying you bashed in his skull, but either you're a damn good actor, or you didn't know he was dead. I'll go with the latter," Marcus said, sounding apologetic. "Look, Carl, I'm into believing you more than Alvarez, but he talks a good talk. Is there anything you can give me about him, Perez, Luis Johnson, or even Jesus Cabilla that might tip the scales in your favor? Help us out here, and I'll talk to the sheriff about dropping the distribution charge, and the possession charge might go away also."

"Sir, I'm not sure what I can tell you."

"Think on it." Marcus stood and picked up the folder. "I'll be back."

Sheriff Godfrey Timmons, NIS agents Wendy James and Brad Neil, Doctor Kelly Colt, FBI SSA Ken Santoro, and Deputy Josh Bonner were at the boards in the war room when Marcus returned. Marcus hoped that all the talking over each other and the multiple fingers pointing were leading toward something positive. It was chaotic.

But before he could ask, Doctor Simpson Wallace, Elle Colt, and NIS agent Rick Gardener, followed by LCDR Barry Jackson and LT Bob Ledder, joined the melee. Wallace boomed, "Marcus, we need to chat!"

GT put two fingers to his mouth and released a whistle to silence the room. "Thank you! Deputy Colt, this is your circus, so what do you want from your monkeys?"

Marcus chuckled. "Glad to see all this excitement; raise your hand if you've solved the case?" No one did, but several chuckled. "That being the situation, here's the plan. It's Halloween, so GT and his crew need to do whatever they normally do to ensure safety of the children on the streets. The rest of us need to get the hell out of their way. We head to Aunt Maude's for dinner, rest, and most importantly, Simpson's 'chat.' Following that, everyone will share their updates so we're all on the same page. Okay?"

No one spoke for a moment. GT broke the silence. "Best idea I've heard today. We'll reconvene here at eight in the morning. Bonner, go with them as my representative."

86

THE CHILDREN WERE ALREADY OUT trick-or-treating as the caravan of vehicles moved from the sheriff's office to the house on Hale Avenue. Aunt Maude had a card table set up on the front walk, halfway between the house and the sidewalk. Maude didn't want any children climbing the stairs to the porch—Halloween masks and costumes increased the risk of tripping or falling—so her bundling up against the night chill was a small price to pay for the little monsters' safety. Fresh jack-o-lanterns lined both sides of the front walk, providing a warm, candle-lit welcome.

"There's clam chowder and a couple of veggies on the stove and baked steak in the oven. Since I have candy duty, I ate earlier," Aunt Maude said as Marcus led some of the team around from the garage parking area.

"Need any help, Aunt Maude?" Marcus asked.

"No, hun, I'm fine. I'll be in later. And Dr. Wentworth got here about fifteen minutes ago."

Small talk over dinner avoided the case parameters. Sidney gave a quick update while everyone loaded their plates: lab reports should be there the next day. Simpson and Barry Jackson started to talk about the strange events in the woods, but stopped when Marcus suggested everyone retire to the sanctuary and continue the conversation there.

Music was on low, drinks had been served, and everyone found a comfortable seat. Marcus noticed that Elle and Rick were close together on one of the sofas, just as he and Kelly were. Marcus rapped on the coffee table to get everyone's attention. "Before we get lost in Simpson's strange events in the woods, I need to hear from Bob."

"Yes, sir?" Ledder asked.

Marcus paused slightly to gather his thoughts. "Of the six bodies in the morgue, it looks like three were hitchhikers moving through the area with no local connections. One was a member of the Southside Cardinals gang, making deliveries to and from Perez. From all indications of his bashed skull, he lost an argument at the farm; we found blood on a wrench there that matches his blood type and shape of the wound. That leaves Doris Thompkins and Joe Decker. How and why did they become victims?"

Ken jumped in. "Alvarez isn't talking, and he's the one who would know."

"Agreed," Marcus said. "But with Doris we can paint a highly possible scenario. Her Buick had front-end damage from a deer strike and other minor damage, so she may have run off the road resulting in her being knocked unconscious. Probability is that Alvarez was first on the accident scene, took her body for Perez to use, then dumped her car."

Kelly said, "But that doesn't answer what happened with the children."

"True. We'll get into that later, Princess," Marcus said. "Focusing on the dead bodies, we have nothing to build on with Joe Decker. Bob, what were his habits, routines, vices, et cetera. How could he have been in contact with Alvarez?"

Ledder's face contorted as he racked his brain for information. All eyes were on him as he said, "Sir, shooting pool for money was his biggest pastime. Being somewhat short tempered, he had a tendency to start a fight if he thought someone was cheating or insulted him. That got him barred from most pool halls around town. North of Princeton is a rough dive called Jim's Place. Semi-decent food, cold beer, three pool tables … and Joe mentioned going there the week before he died. The farm is north of town, so maybe they connected there."

Marcus nodded. "Anything else?"

"No, sir. Joe didn't do drugs and never hitchhiked. He dated a few women around town, but never got serious. We both worked long hard days and didn't have much energy for sports and stuff."

"All right. In the morning, you and Rick head to Jim's Place. Rick, pick up copies of the photos of Alvarez and the victims first, and show them to the staff. Someone there might recognize seeing them together. Take Ken with you in case you get resistance—his FBI badge might open doors," Marcus ordered.

Both Bob and Rick nodded their understanding.

"Okay, Simpson, what do you have for us?"

"I dare say it was a most interesting day of gathering samples. And the cave was a treasure trove of ..."

The bear guy talked non-stop for about ten minutes. Marcus noted that Elle, Rick, and Barry Jackson quietly reinforced Simpson's report with nods, smiles, and hand signals. The rest of the team focused on Simpson as they tried to wrap their heads around what he was saying.

And when he finished, Barry jumped in with a report on the strange things that his SEALs found in the woods around the cave. He became more animated as he described the knocking they heard as they left the woods. Barry wrapped up his report saying, "And that is why I want to take the teams back out there tomorrow. There is something living in those woods, and I want to find it. If you concur, sir, of course."

Marcus quickly consulted the oracles of the overhead, stood, and walked to the bar. He turned to face the group and leaned against the bar. "Possibly. First, let's get other opinions. Kelly, you first. What are your thoughts?"

"We have reports from people who aren't prone to exaggeration or fantasy. People I respect. But I am still not buying the Bigfoot existence. Especially since I'm now hearing a theory that multiple Bigfoots are running around the area saving children. Granted, some of the samples Simpson collected might, and I emphasize might, *not* belong to a bear, but the Bigfoot theory is way too far out," Kelly said, trying to keep the exasperation out of her voice. "I still believe in some hobos living out there."

The other six, who hadn't been in the woods, were given a chance to express their thoughts. It ended in a tie, with the three West Virginia residents leaning toward the existence of Bigfoot, and the three out-of-staters supporting Kelly.

Marcus smiled. "Since they pay me the big bucks, I get to make the decisions. Here's the plan, Barry; let your SEALs not guarding the farm sleep in and take them to the woods tomorrow afternoon. Stay out playing as late as you want. And take Kelly and Simpson with you. However, I'll need you all at the office at 0800."

Kelly started to protest, but fell silent when the phone on the bar rang. On the sixth ring, Marcus answered. He listened intently for several minutes and responded with an *okay* or *understand* several times. He took control of the conversation and said, "Thanks for the update, Todd. Go ahead and issue the recall, but keep it out of the press for now. Blame it on a possible contamination and the recall is a precaution. Wendy and Brad will be back in Great Lakes tomorrow evening and they'll fill you in on all that has happened here. Thanks again."

The faces all asked the same question.

Marcus cleared his throat. "Anthrax. Anyone getting an injection from the rebottled meds gets a major dose of anthrax. And not the normal version you get from cuts and scrapes, but one that has been intensified for a faster and more deadly reaction like the inhalation version."

"God please intercede and stop any anthrax from getting released." Doctor Wentworth prayed aloud what everyone was thinking. "That inhalation version is almost always fatal without aggressive treatment."

"Amen. We all need to pray for that, and we need to kick our thoughts into high gear. We now know who and what, and possibly where and when, but a why might tie it all together. Don't be bashful, throw out your thoughts. Anyone?" Marcus ordered.

Everyone was quiet as they processed the new information and tried to answer the question. Marcus poured another shot of bourbon into his glass as he waited.

"All right, people," Marcus said. "Following a tried and true process, we go back over what we do know in hopes it will trigger any new thoughts. Six people were gutted over the last couple of months to provide raw materials to generate a lot of anthrax. We have traced the bodies to the farm-slash-germ factory operated by a now-dead doctor who we believe to be the illegitimate son of a truly evil Nazi. That gives us a 'what' and 'who' to at least part of the plan. The dead doctor had the start date of the Montréal Olympics on his calendar, and some evil worker bees on the Chicago end said some of the anthrax was heading to Canada. That's at least one of the 'where' and 'when' items assuming an attack on the Olympics. And both the Vampire and the Great Lakes Hospital chief petty officer mentioned 'games' with some level of importance. Loose connections, but connections still."

Barry asked, "So we ignore the possibilities of Bigfoot or Mothman being involved?"

"Yea, we put them on the back burner for now," Marcus replied. "If they exist, they have been helping us and aren't related to the end use of the anthrax. We need to focus on Chicago and Canada and wherever else the anthrax is going."

Wendy said, "Since it's ending up in the base hospital, it could be used against recruits."

"And the analysis I did of the hospital's records shows they're the central supply for medication going to any ship or station on the East Coast. I would have thought Norfolk or Charleston would've been the hub, but Great Lakes is the spot," Brad Neal offered.

"The FBI continues to search for Nazi criminals in South America," Ken said. "Mengele is one we want for war crimes. Perhaps the dead doctor might be continuing his father's work in hopes of killing more Jews and crippling the U.S. Navy at the same time."

Marcus nodded. "A continuation of the 1972 Olympic attack against Jews keeps bouncing around in my head. I'm not sure how they could pull it off. Sidney, would you assume that since each team has their own medical staff that they would bring their own meds?"

Wentworth replied, "Probably their common medications and ointments. And their kits would be inspected by the medical personnel of the International Olympic Committee to ensure nothing prohibited—you know, those performance-enhancing things—would be brought in."

Marcus absorbed the doctor's comments before inspiration hit. "But what about the medical needs of the spectators? First aid stations? They could be an easier target."

"I have no idea how those are handled, Marcus," Wentworth said.

Everyone was again quiet as they processed the information.

Finally, the silence got to Kelly. "To paraphrase a line from Thomas Jefferson, I know not what course others may take; but as for me, give me sleep or I'll die from yawning. It's time to call it a night, Sailor."

"I second that," Wentworth said as he stood. "What's tomorrow's plan for the rest of us, Marcus?"

After what seemed to be a longer than usual pause, Marcus said, "I failed to do this earlier because most of you understand OPSEC. Josh, Elle, Bob, and Simpson—pay attention. OPSEC is operation security. In our case here, everything you see and hear is classified. No sharing with family, friends, coworkers, et cetera. Should you break that rule, I can and will make your life very uncomfortable. Understand?"

Heads nodded their compliance.

Marcus stared a moment to allow the importance of his statement to set in. "Okay. Barry, you and Simpson will need to be at the sheriff's office in the morning to finalize today's reports before you head back to the woods. Sid, I need you to do the same at the morgue with Dennis; wrap up all the autopsy reports with a neat bow and bring copies to me. Bob, Ken, and Rick will check out the bar. Elle, you will need to be there to document all your photos and set up a photo log. The rest of us will be at the sheriff's office updating status reports and, hopefully, figuring out what to do next. Get a good night's rest, everyone, and maybe your dreams or subconscious will come up with some answers."

87

GT AND MARCUS SAT AT the conference table in the war room contemplating the filled boards behind them. The teams were out handling their assignments. GT had selected Deputy Josh Bonner to drive Brad Neil and his prisoner from Princeton to Chicago at 0900 hours. Wendy James completed their caravan by driving the prisoner's confiscated truck, which towed her own car on a trailer. It would be a long day's drive, but at least the weather was cooperating with clear skies and moderate temperatures.

GT drained his coffee cup and said, "So, what's the plan? Besides staring at that damn board and drinking coffee."

"Just the normal exciting fun of piecing together a major crime, GT, which is the excitement of waiting for more information to get here. We should be hearing from Bolivia soon with background on Perez and Rodrigo Quispe; maybe it will fill in some blanks. Or at least generate more questions. All while I'm trying to figure out what to do about Canada."

"Maybe we should let the FBI handle it. Or dump it on the RCMP."

Marcus shook his head. "Not yet. I talked with Ken, and he agreed that the heavy foot of the FBI might cause the rats to run and hide before we can round them up. And I suspect the Royal Canadian Mounted Police would be hesitant to act without more solid information. We need subterfuge, not a sledgehammer, to find the rats, but I'm not sure how … yet."

"Sledgehammer, eh, nice description of the feds. Hey, how about you go in as part of a construction crew?"

"No, I need to focus on the first aid stations. Too bad I studied criminology and not medicine. Otherwise I could go in undercover as a doctor, inspector, or med tech."

"Send Kelly?"

"No. She could handle the medical stuff but wouldn't know what to look for, and I don't think we have time to run her through the agent training course," Marcus answered with a chuckle.

"Well, as you ponder your options, I'll get us more coffee. And see if a donut or two are still available." GT scooped up the empty mugs as he headed to the door.

The silence in the war room helped Marcus gather his thoughts. He looked at the large calendar for 1976 and wondered about the timeline. When would the teams start showing up? When would the first aid stations be open? Obviously, both would occur before the opening ceremonies.

He needed more information about the Olympics, and a good friend might be the conduit.

His first call, to a number north of Philadelphia, was pleasant but unproductive. Heidi Garrett told him that Tommy was in the office that day, trying to finalize details on a new project. Marcus promised that they would get together again soon before the call concluded.

Marcus next tried the Garrett Publishing office number and had similar luck. Mr. Garrett was out of the office for a meeting that would run through lunch, but Marcus was told to expect a call as soon as the lunch meeting concluded. More waiting.

As he waited, Marcus started scribbling notes on one of the legal pads. What did he expect to find in Montréal? How could he find the Vampire's rats … assuming they were there? Where to start looking? If it was a Nazi anti-Jew plan, why target the Navy? What would be the trigger event that would unleash the anthrax? Why would hundreds or thousands of spectators need an injection? International cooperation needed between bad guys? As usual, he generated more questions than answers.

GT slid the fresh cup to Marcus. "Writing a novel?"

"Just putting thoughts on paper. Often that makes them more concrete, and they become something to build on," Marcus rambled as he continued to jot notes.

GT looked around to make sure no one else was in the war room before he said, "Wanted you to know, I plan to send letters of appreciation to your admiral for Brad and Wendy's help on this case. Those are two excellent investigators. And good people."

"Thanks, GT, they're good people who make my life easier. And there is something else I need to take back to D.C. Since this case is going international, I need copies of all the files. I think it fits better into NIS jurisdiction once I leave here."

GT chuckled. "Be that as it may, you are still my deputy until I release you. So whatever credit gets dished out, make sure a good portion comes to this office."

"There ya go assuming it doesn't get highly classified and buried in the muck of Foggy Bottom. I'm not sure the powers that be will want anything negative to darken the Olympics, so get ready for that part to be a non-story," Marcus said before giving GT his best shark grin.

88

As Tommy Garrett returned to his office, one of his secretaries told him that Commander Marcus Colt had called while he was meeting with an advertiser. That put him in a better mood. He asked her to get him back on the line, which happened quickly. Tommy picked up the phone's handset and pressed the blinking button on the base.

"How can Garrett Publishing help the Navy today, Commander?" His light voice carried his pleasure in talking with one of his true friends.

"My, aren't we being formal for a change, Tommy. Everything all right on your end?" Marcus asked, only half joking. He knew Tommy carried a big load on his shoulders running the company and, when overwhelmed, hid his stress in formality or humor. It was always a challenge to determine which.

"Working on a Saturday helped pull a new project together, so things are good, buddy. But my horoscope said to watch out for a man in uniform. Or maybe it was that fortune cookie at lunch. Ha! Either case, I'll risk it and ask what's happening? I appreciate hearing from you even if it will probably cost me."

Marcus chuckled briefly, then his voice became serious. "Tommy, this is a matter of national security, so I need your promise this goes no further."

Humor was gone as Tommy replied, "You got it, Marcus."

"I assume you have a reporter or two covering the construction and preliminary setup for the Summer Olympics …"

"Sure. Several of our papers have each sent people. Things are coming together nicely up there," Tommy said. "Why?"

"I think, and the key word is 'think' here, that there might be an incident at the Olympics," Marcus started.

"Oh, crap." Then Tommy rapidly threw out questions. "How solid is your hunch? Who's behind it?"

"Slow down, Tommy, and let me finish. Again, it is only a possible scenario and when I get more data, I'll be able to judge the level of probability. Right now it's at less than ten percent, and that's one of the reasons why no one else has been notified. No need to cause an unjustified panic. I need your help to keep it that way and to help me dig deeper."

"Okay. Okay, what do you need from me?"

"I need to quickly and quietly find out how some things are going to work in Montréal … specifically with the first aid stations and overall medical care for the athletes and fans. Who orders the various meds and what is the security on the inventory. And how are doctors and nurses selected and assigned? I figured that a known reporter who's a familiar face at the site could snoop around getting info for an article without raising suspicions. Call it 'Keeping the Five Rings Healthy' or something like that. Hopefully, their questions would be considered standard stuff."

As calm settled over him, Tommy's journalist persona kicked in. "That title is extremely hokey—we can come up with something better. How soon do you need it?"

"Day before yesterday, Tommy."

"You think an attack is imminent?"

"Doubtful. Logic and a few clues indicate that if there is an event, the perpetrators would want the biggest possible audience. Opening ceremonies would be my choice, if I was up to no good," Marcus said. "But now is the time for planning and getting people and materials in place. Those are the people I want. That's the best place to stop it."

"Based on your comments, I surmise that you think someone has tampered with the medications, right?"

"That's where the data is leading me."

Tommy's face twisted into a grimace as he considered the potential of such an event. "Guess they would need some sort of trigger event that would cause a widespread use of a tainted medication. Have you figured that one out, Marcus?"

"I've got some thoughts, but right now, that's not the priority. I need to know … will you help?"

Tommy nearly yelled, "Stupid question from the guy I consider my brother! Of course I'll help! I'll call Sam Bigalow as soon as I hang up from this call."

"Sorry," Marcus contritely said. "Make sure he knows we need in-depth information. But not who it's for or why."

Tommy laughed. "*Samantha* is one of the best investigative reporters I have ever met. She normally works at the paper here in Philly, but she asked for a favor, a well-earned favor. She's working the Olympics full time because her little brother is an athlete, and she wanted to be there to support him. That's the good news. Bad news is that she is one hell of an investigative reporter. Her skill sets are sharp, and she will quickly grasp that there's something going on. But she'll keep quiet if I ask."

"Got ya. Any guess on when *she* will have it done?"

Tommy shrugged. "It will take a couple of days for research, a day or so for writing, and then additional follow-up questions to make sure she got it right. You should have it in your hands in less than a week. Will that work?"

"Sooner would be better, but I'll take what I can get. Ask her to send me the first draft as soon as possible. I might need more info based upon what she uncovers or need to point her in a different direction. I appreciate your help, Tommy, and your—and Sam's—discretion. I can only hope that I have egg on my face, but I'm afraid my gut is right on this."

"I hope you're wrong also, Marcus, but I don't think you are. After the '72 attacks, the nut jobs consider the Olympics a target-rich environment with lots of media coverage. I'll call you back if there are any issues with Sam on this. Bye."

Tommy leaned forward as he steepled his fingers in front of his face. "This could be Pulitzer material," he muttered to the empty office. "Too bad I can't talk about it. And those two seeing each other again would be fun to watch. Ah, to be the proverbial fly on the wall."

He picked up the intercom line. "Cheryl, get me Sam Bigalow ASAP, please."

89

THERE'S AN OLD SAYING THAT when it rains, it pours. Quick translation is that when something hasn't happened for a while, it comes in large amounts when it resumes. The adage, usually negative, holds true with criminal investigations, where hours of total quiet are disrupted by too much information coming too fast.

GT was on one phone line, learning from the garage that Brad's car had been totaled: the old oak tree did a number on the frame. Marcus was on another line discussing Iceland with Doc Stevens, who was still holding the fort in D.C.; both men knew something had to be done there soon. Kelly, Simpson, and Barry came into the war room looking for Marcus, and upon seeing him tied up, took seats at the conference table and quietly waited.

No sooner had they settled down than Bob, Ken, and Rick returned from their interrogation of the bar staff. They leaned against the wall, waiting their turn to share information that needed to go on the boards.

Both phone calls ended at nearly the same time. Marcus looked at Rick and said, "What?"

Rick stood away from the wall and consulted his notepad. "Jim's Place is a dump; I think I need a tetanus shot just for walking in that bar. An older guy runs it, Caucasian, mid-fifties, named Art Bronski. He was neither talkative nor helpful. However, one of the waitresses, Jane Doe—yea, I checked her ID and that is her real name—recognized Alvarez from this past Wednesday night. He was with the latest victim and they both had chili and beers. Acted like friends, she said, but while Alvarez had been in before, the victim was new to her. The other victims were not recognized."

"And one of the cooks knew Joe Decker as a pool shark. He said one of the irate losers to Decker a couple of weeks ago might have been Alvarez," Ken added. "Firm identification was not guaranteed. Probability factor of forty percent."

Marcus paused in thought before he said, "That locks up the case against Alvarez for the murder of Hank Grant. And it somewhat links him to Decker's death, hopefully enough to remove doubt from the minds of the jury."

GT said, "We'll keep digging at the farm and maybe find links to the others. But I have my doubts."

"Soon as we tie up the Chicago-slash-Nazi-slash-Canada mess, we can release more information to the local public, and perhaps someone will come forward with the links we need to tie Alvarez to the other dead bodies," Marcus said.

Rick started adding cards to the boards showing the new evidence and possible links.

Marcus turned to the three across the conference table. "I thought y'all would be scouring the woods all night long. What brings you in while the sun still shines? You first." He pointed to Barry.

"Sir, my men are still out there, but we felt you needed to hear a few things right away. If you don't object, I think you should hear from Deputy Kelly Colt."

Pointing to Kelly, Marcus said, "And?"

With a grin kicking up to the right, Kelly cleared her throat and placed both hands flat on the table. Her action, followed by a deep sigh, told Marcus something monumental was coming. Kelly finally said in a slow, soft voice, "I think, and that's the important word to keep in mind—um, well—I think I saw a Bigfoot."

The silence in the room could be cut with a knife. Kelly was the number one skeptic in the group; even with the "I think" disclaimer, her statement overpowered the rest of the team for a minute or two.

"Kelly, can you add a bit more to that confession?" Marcus asked.

Her apprehension gaining an edge of anger, her voice became stronger and her words flowed faster. "Look. The shadows of the forest made it difficult to see specifics, but again, I think I saw a large, um, well, an enormous creature in the holler. Simpson, Barry, and his men were ahead of me. I dropped back to look at some broken limbs when I looked up the bank in front of me. About fifteen feet above me, a creature was standing mostly hidden behind a tree. I'm sorry to admit that I screamed like a little girl, which scared it away and caused Barry and Simpson to come running to help me."

Simpson laid a hand on Kelly's. "While we were too slow responding to her scream to confirm her sighting, I found hair and tracks behind the tree she indicated. My support is with her sighting."

"And I concur, Marcus. Her demeanor when we got to her showed near shock. She saw something that shook her up … a lot," Barry added. "If there's nothing else, I'll head back to join my team."

Kelly sat quietly twisting her fingers as she heard their support. No one else in the room spoke as this new information was absorbed.

"Princess, are you going back with Barry?" Marcus asked.

Shaking her head, Kelly said, "No, I'll stay here and help Elle with her documentation. Excuse me." She stood and left the room.

Looking intently at Simpson and Barry, Marcus exhaled loudly. "Wow. That's a shocker. Do either of you think you can glean any more information from that holler?"

"Frankly … no, Marcus. These creatures have been hiding successfully forever. I can keep finding tracks and hair samples until the end of time, but I don't think we'll find anything else. Time to move on," Simpson said.

Barry shrugged and nodded in agreement.

"Barry, round up your men, get a good night's sleep, and head home tomorrow. Y'all have done a great job and we all appreciate it," Marcus said. "You might as well take Doctor Wentworth with you."

90

AUNT MAUDE'S HOUSE, PRINCETON, WEST VIRGINIA
EARLY SUNDAY AFTERNOON
2 NOVEMBER 1975

PREACHER DAVE'S SERMON WAS STILL bouncing around inside his brain as Marcus fumbled with the key and finally opened the door to the house. It had been a simple, yet powerful message about how people think they know the Bible, but don't. Little things like that the wise men didn't come to the stable to worship the newborn Jesus. And nowhere is the number of wise men stipulated, only the number of gifts. On the drive home, it had pushed Marcus to think about parts of the case where he thought he knew what was happening but might not.

Aunt Maude, Kelly, Elle, and Rick were in a tight line behind him, hoping to get out of the rain quickly. After three days of dry, warming weather, the rain clouds returned, guided by winds strong enough to blow water onto the covered porch where they stood. Good news is that it was a fast-moving storm, so the afternoon looked to be clear.

Things were getting back to normal in Princeton, as the SEALs had finished their final look at the holler and were heading for Norfolk that morning, taking Sidney Wentworth in tow. Ken Santoro drove home to Beckley the previous night with a promise to quietly do some digging with his FBI contacts; he'd return if needed.

The phone started ringing as they shed their coats and wiped soggy feet. Aunt Maude got to the hall extension on the fifth ring. After the

347

standard greeting and pause, she held the handset toward Marcus. "It's a lady for you, hon."

"This is Colt."

"Commander, Sam Bigalow here hoping you've got a few moments to chat." The voice was sultry.

"Of course. Happy to, ma'am," Marcus replied.

"Stop the ma'am crap. I'm not old enough for that title. Call me 'Sam' and we'll work together fine. Okay, Marcus?"

Marcus chuckled. "Ma'am and sir are terms of respect we use in the military that have nothing to do with age, Sam. With that out of the way, what's up?"

"Tommy was rather vague when he gave me this bullshit assignment. Come on, it has no value for the readers; they care about the games and not the first aid issues. Since he refused to tell me more, you need to fill me in, or this assignment is dead before it takes the first breath."

Trying to keep from grimacing, Marcus silently considered the situation.

"Well, I guess this call and article are over."

"No, it is not, Sam. Tommy said you were good, and my silence was my brain deciding what I can tell you. What I should tell you. This is a matter of national security and cannot be discussed with anyone without my permission. Understand?"

"That's how I work anyway, but yes, I understand and agree. I've heard the military rules before … talk out of school and you kill me, right? So, what's up?"

It took a few minutes, but Marcus shared the drug and contamination parameters of the case, avoiding all the murder issues and the Nazi and paranormal connections. He was still having trouble believing that latter part, and he was afraid wording it to a stranger would make him sound like an idiot. But he believed he got the importance across.

"Wow. How sure are you of contamination?" Sam asked after a moment to process what she'd heard.

Marcus sighed. "At this point, pretty dang sure. Like I said, we know some meds in Chicago have been replaced with a super anthrax, and we've been told some have headed to Canada. And with the Olympic opening ceremony date being the only one circled on a calendar in the germ lab, the dots connect, leading to Montréal. Your research will help prove the theory and help me figure out a way to stop it. But I need to move quickly to keep the rest of the gang from knowing we're on to them."

"I've got an idea. How soon can you get to Montréal?"

"Tomorrow, sometime, at the earliest. What's your plan?"

"Two of us looking around would reduce the possibility of me overlooking something. I'll be conducting the interviews with the staff as you, my photographer, listen for clues that I might not pick up, and then you can nose around on your own taking photos. Who knows, you might get a photo or two that later becomes evidence. You game?" Sam asked. "Tomorrow might be fast enough, right?"

"You bet. Give me your number, and I'll get back with you as soon as I get things organized," Marcus said.

The call concluded, allowing Marcus to join everyone in the kitchen. Aunt Maude and Elle were pulling a quick lunch together as Kelly and Rick stayed parked at the table, out of their way.

"Looks like I'm heading to Montréal. I'll see if Bob can fly me up there so I can fake being a photographer for Sam as she gathers information for her article. Makes sense and wish I had thought of it," Marcus admitted.

"While you go international with a beautiful reporter, what will Rick and I be doing? Kelly asked.

"What makes you think she's beautiful?" Rick asked. "Do you know her?"

Kelly snorted. "No, but you've seen all the Bond Girls in the movies. Can we expect less when Agent 006.5 heads off on a mission?"

Rick laughed. "006.5?"

"Yea, that's what he called himself before the adventure in Naples. Marcus said he was close to a 007 when I had concerns about his safety, later justified by things that went south over there, with him getting involved with international spies."

"006.5. Cute," Rick said. "I'll have to remember that one."

"No worries, Princess. I know how to behave. And while I'm gone, you and Rick can go back over all the case parameters to see if we have missed anything. Or you can spend more time looking for your big-footed friends," Marcus said.

Kelly stuck out her tongue at Marcus's comment. She was still having problems accepting what she saw yesterday.

Elle said, "Sorry I must head back to Clearwater tomorrow. This investigation stuff has been interesting."

"It's been good having you here, Sis, but you need to get back to your real life. Finish that education and start helping people," Marcus said.

With a giggle, Elle said, "Aye, aye, Captain, sir!"

Marcus shook his head as everyone laughed. "It's still Commander, Elle, and will be for years to come. Okay, excuse me while I make a few phone calls to get this next phase started. Don't hold lunch." He left the room for a quieter phone location.

Settling in Ray's study, he called Bob Ledder. "Bob, it's Marcus. We need to make a couple of flights ASAP. Pack a bag with casual clothing, sport coat or two, and a winter coat. We're heading to Montréal after a quick overnight stop in Manassas, Virginia, so remember your passport."

Bob promised to be at the airport ready to take off at 1500 hours. While the Cessna was already fueled, he explained he still had to check the weather, preflight the plane, and file a flight plan.

The second call was to a stately home in the country, outside of Manassas. He gave the SecState notice that he would be there for a short overnight visit later that afternoon. When pressed for information, Marcus said he had to explain in person. Now he needed to pack a bag. Part of him hoped this was a wild Canadian goose chase, but his gut screamed that Canada was where he could stop the deadly virus. If he hurried.

91

FLIGHT TIME FROM PRINCETON TO Manassas, Virginia was a bit under two hours. The Manassas Regional Airport is the largest regional airport in the state, and as expected, the facilities were nice. Having called the FBO before leaving Princeton, Bob Ledder quickly secured parking for his plane, tied it down, and got things set up for refueling. The Fixed Base Operator, called the FBO by all aviators, is basically an airport's super service station: handling parking and hangar space, fueling, and other needs of the pilots. There Bob handled the aircraft's immediate needs, checked weather for the next morning, and picked up the Jespersen chart for Montréal; his Flight Guide was for the Eastern USA only. As Bob took care of the aviation needs, Marcus found the rental car counters and secured a vehicle.

The fifteen-minute drive in the Virginia countryside was restful. The storm had blown through, clearing the air and refreshing the colors of the late fall foliage with the mist of rain. Their destination on the winding two-lane road was a large house some distance behind a brick wall. *Bentwood* was the name on the bronze plaques bolted to the two aged-brick columns that flanked the driveway. Homes in this area had names rather than numbers.

The black metal gate blocking the driveway was secured, and as Marcus stopped the rental car near it, two men appeared near the car. The bulges under their windbreakers indicated they were armed. The one on the driver's side leaned down and said, "Commander Colt, you are expected, but I need to see your identification, sir."

Satisfied with the ID, he continued, "Sir, I understand you are armed, and the Secretary has ordered me not to confiscate your weapon. You may proceed, sir."

"Thank you," Marcus said as the gate opened.

It was a quick trip down the tree-lined bricked driveway, which ended in a circle around a fountain in front of the house. As they exited the car, the front door opened and a trim lady dressed in blue jeans and pink sweatshirt stood on the porch. Her dark pageboy cut framed a face needing no makeup; it was difficult to guess her age, but she projected a combination of strength and compassion.

The wife of the Secretary of State considered Marcus Colt a family member, and greeted him as such with a tight hug followed by a customary kiss on each cheek. Margo's parents were French, so the greeting was natural. Marcus returned both the hug and the kisses.

Margo backed away, holding his hands in hers, and looked him up and down. She finally said, "Marcus, my love, I have missed you; July was a long time ago. I'm so sorry we couldn't attend your parents' memorial service. The president insisted we be at Camp David. Like you, we give up much for our country."

"I understand, Margo. The flowers you sent were marvelous. Thank you. And let me introduce my associate, Bob Ledder."

"Welcome to our home, Bob. Dinner will be at seven, and your rooms are ready. Frederick will get your bags. I understand you both are in a hurry to see Harry. He's in the study. Come."

Margo led them past the foyer to a set of double sliding doors. She slid one open and announced, "Darling, Marcus has arrived."

The two men entered and Margo left, closing the door as she did.

Coming to attention, Marcus said, "Thank you for seeing us on short notice, Mr. Secretary. This is Lieutenant Robert Ledder, my pilot and team member while I'm TAD to the West Virginia Governor's office. I asked him to join us to take notes, since my mind has been overloaded lately."

SecState shook both their hands and waved them to the sofas flanking the coffee table in his study. He took the chair at the head of the table and said, "Well, *Commander,* since we are being so formal, I suspect this isn't just a social call. Forgive me if I slip up and call you 'Marcus' during our chat. No matter the reason, it is good to see you, my friend. Coffee? Beer?"

Marcus chuckled and said, "Not a problem with whatever you call me, Sir. I'll probably drop a 'Harry' or two also. And we'll pass on the refreshments for now. I do truly wish this was a social visit; my taste buds have been missing the flavor of that shrimp you grilled here at the July cookout."

"Like I said, it's always good to see you, Marcus. So, what's up?"

Ledder watched the interaction between the two with great interest. The expected formality quickly dissolved into friendship. He was unable to hide his surprise that Marcus and the SecState were buddies. No, not buddies—more like family. But Colt had been surprising him since day one.

"Harry, we have come upon evidence of a possible terror attack at the Montréal Summer Olympics," Marcus said slowly as he opened his briefcase and pulled out a folder. "What started as a number of highly unusual murders in Mercer County, West Virginia—my hometown of Princeton is the county seat—expanded to include illegal drug importation and distribution. Which quickly morphed into the distribution of tainted medical supplies to Navy units. And perusing these issues, we uncovered the possible terrorist plan."

"Good God! You're not kidding, are you? Has the FBI been notified?"

"No, sir. Not officially. You are the first outside of my team to hear this."

"At least the president must be notified, Marcus!"

Marcus shook his head slightly. "Harry, the key word right now is *possible* with regard to the Olympics. We've already taken action to clean up the Navy supplies, and that will be fully documented. My gut tells me we have rounded up or rendered harmless a good portion of the lead conspirators. I have an FBI liaison, the senior agent from the Beckley office, on my team, and he concurs that the heavy hands of the Bureau might scare off the half-dozen people we think are still in the wind. And I hate to dump speculation on the president. Let me read you into where we started and what we have, and then you'll see why I need your help."

SecState frowned as he asked in a low voice, "Does 'rendered harmless' mean what I think it does?"

Marcus nodded. "Yea, it does. And to answer your unasked question: yes, I did the rendering."

It took nearly half an hour to lay out the situation and answer the questions it generated. After all that, Harry leaned back and let out a deep sigh as he chewed on his lower lip. No words were spoken for a period that seemed longer than it actually was.

"Okay, Marcus, I get it. And while I'm not sure it's the right thing to do, I *will* support your plan. What do you need from me?"

"I know I can jump through some hoops and get permission to be an armed investigator on Canadian soil, but I don't have the time, and I don't want to let too many people get their noses under the tent until I know more. But like you did for me in Naples, if we are carrying diplomatic passports, then we're covered with diplomatic immunity."

Following another deep sigh, Harry finally said, "What's that line you used in 'Nam? Forgiveness is easier to get than permission? I hope so, as we both may need a lot of forgiveness. Okay. I'll get them done for you both even though I suspect I will regret it. Since that task can't happen until early tomorrow morning, I do believe we have time for a round of drinks before dinner."

"While you're pouring, I need to call my reporter friend to update her on tomorrow's schedule," Marcus said. "But only one small round for us flyboys—we're winging north in the morning."

92

As the Cessna lined up with the runway at Montréal–Dorval International Airport, Marcus saw something he'd forgotten: Montréal is an island as well as a city. It's a rather large island, of nearly two hundred square miles and over a million people. *With a hundred thousand potential victims coming to visit in July*, he thought.

"Another flight and landing without dead bodies roasting in a fiery crash; it has been a good day," Bob said as he finished turning off all the switches that gave life to the aircraft.

Marcus chuckled at the gallows humor. "I don't know when we're leaving here, but do your airplane magic with the tie-downs, fuel, and whatever else in preparation, while I see if I can locate our contact. Okay?"

"Aye, aye, sir, captain, my captain," Bob joked as he gave a halfhearted salute. He was enjoying this assignment, especially flying on the state's dime.

Marcus had climbed off the wing when he saw an above-average-looking woman approaching. The lady was tall, at least five-foot-nine, and her khaki hunting jacket and cargo pants did nothing to conceal a nice figure. And while she wore hiking boots, her gait was like that of a fashion model, with a sway that enhanced the movement of her golden hair falling past her shoulders. A large leather bag, dark brown matching her boots, hung from her left shoulder. She looked vaguely familiar, but Marcus couldn't recall meeting her. Whoever she was, she looked ready for safari.

The stone-faced woman stopped right in front of Marcus closer than a stranger would, extended her hand, and said, "I must say the years have been good to you, Marcus Colt. Tommy told me all about Kelly, so I know you're off limits … this time."

A smile broke across her face when she enjoyed his confusion. "Don't feel bad, I didn't remember you either until Tommy mentioned you were his best man at the wedding. I was Heidi's maid of honor. You and I had some great fun together dining and dancing at the reception, and a lot more fun later that night and the next day. At least I hope you remember that." A wink joined her smile.

Marcus took her hand as the memories flooded his mind. He finally said in a low voice, "Longer hair, now blonde, and missing that golden tan … but seeing that smile, I do remember you and that night. Hello again, Samantha Marie Bigalow."

"Hello again, Marcus James Colt," Sam softly said, pulling even closer. "Long blonde hair gets more interviews from the guys, and the last six months in Canada has erased the tan, but it's still me."

Bob destroyed the intimate moment as he jumped down from the wing. "So where do we go from here? Hi, I'm Bob."

Reluctantly reclaiming her hand from Marcus, Sam offered it to Bob as Marcus introduced them. She quickly said, "Customs is right this way, gentlemen. Grab your bags and let's get busy."

Passing through customs was easy with the diplomatic passports. None of their bags were checked, and the agents wished them a pleasant stay in Canada. Bob went off to the FBO office to handle the needs of the airplane, leaving Sam and Marcus alone in a waiting area.

"Tommy told me about you, but nothing about your pilot. What's his story?"

Marcus gave a short laugh. "He's a full-time bulldozer operator from West Virginia, and for a short time was a suspect in my murder investigation that brought us here. He was being belligerent and uncooperative during an interrogation, so since he is a lieutenant in a Naval Reserve Construction Battalion, i.e. a Seabee unit, I had him recalled to active duty, reporting to me. He quickly saw the error of his obstructionist ways and became a big help to our investigation. Good news is, he lets us use his airplane."

Sam also laughed. "I like your style, Marcus Colt. Tell ya what—we'll call him your trainee or assistant, so he can hang around and help look for stuff while doing nothing. Okay?"

"Sure. Perfect."

"I got you a room in my hotel. Only reserved one room, not expecting Bob, but it has two beds."

"That'll work." Marcus looked around, checking for eavesdroppers, and continued, "What's the plan?"

"Quick and simple. We get you checked into the hotel. Grab lunch at my favorite Italian place, and meet with the head of medical services for the games at two o'clock. Once we finish with that interview, I have her assistant lined up to give us a walking tour of the first aid stations. Fast enough for ya?"

"I like your style, too, Samantha."

"I go by 'Sam' when working and save 'Samantha' for intimacy. Remember … off limits," Sam said with yet another wink.

Sam's safari look extended to her vehicle. She led the men to a medium green 1974 Land Rover complete with the spare wheel mounted on the hood. It was a short couple of miles to the hotel—the classy Ritz-Carlton Montréal, with fast check-in—and then a quick walk to the Italian restaurant. A quiet booth in a deserted back corner provided the seclusion Marcus preferred.

Over a superb lunch of *Cacio e Pepe*, favorite pasta of the Colt family, Sam outlined what would be expected from a staff photographer and his trainee. In detail, she explained how and where they should stand, when to take photographs, and when not. She concluded by handing press passes to both Bob and Marcus. Marcus noticed they had an "anywhere at anytime" access level.

In return, Marcus explained what he was hoping to find, such as boxes of meds with Navy markings that could be traced to Chicago. He joked, "Maybe we'll find a guy in a red cap wearing a Southside Cardinal nametag and looking nefarious—that would help."

"What's your knowledge level on the Nikon F2 SLR? I have two in the camera bag along with all the goodies," Sam said.

"I've got one, so no problem. How about you, Bob?"

"I still use a Pentax Spotmatic, but I can act like I'm carrying the back-up for Marcus."

Sam nodded. "Okay, you carry one with a telephoto lens and keep a light meter hanging around your neck. You'll look exceedingly professional."

The meeting with the chair of the IOC Medical and Scientific Commission went well. She was happy to share information about all the work that went into keeping the games safe. Marcus saw that Sam's methods were top notch, and she was able to keep the director talking—even about issues and procedures she'd initially shied away from.

Marcus shot a couple of photos of the office, and several that included Sam and the director chatting. But he spent most of his time leaning against the wall, absorbing all the data the director offered. He was happy that Sam was covering all his areas of concern, and some he hadn't considered. The speculation in the sanctuary had been correct: each team brought their own medical supplies, which were carefully checked by IOC staff. The only areas of concern for Marcus were the IOC-operated first aid stations.

As the interview was winding down after nearly an hour, the director's assistant knocked on the door.

Sam stood and said, "Thank you, Director, for your time and information. I'll send you an advance copy of the article as you requested. Time for the tour, it seems."

Following the lead of the assistant—"Call me Henri," he'd said—they stopped at a first aid station right inside the village. Henri unlocked the door and fumbled to find the light switches. Their faint clicking bathed a large, relatively empty room with light.

Inside the door, an empty new desk was backed with portable partition walls forming a reception area. Beyond that, multiple gurneys were parked in the middle of the large room. Privacy pull-around curtains, as used in a typical ER, were pushed against the walls on both sides of the room. Wall areas between the curtains were studded with connections for electrical and gas needs. A door centered on the back wall was closed.

Marcus shot a few photos around the area as Sam questioned, "Storage in the back room?"

"Oh, yes. Well, but like most, this one is empty now. The bulk of the stations won't be stocked with supplies until a few weeks before the opening ceremonies. We do have three stations of the eighty-three in use for the construction workers. They are stocked with supplies needed for construction injuries and such. Not as fully stocked as these will be on opening day. Would you like to see one?"

Nodding, Sam said, "Yes, please. Photos of shelves filled with supplies will be a big asset for the article."

The functioning aid stations offered better photo subjects, including medical staff doing what they do best. Marcus and Bob surveyed the stockroom and shot photos of many of the box labels. Nothing looked out of place.

As Sam and Henri finished up the interview of one of the nurses, Marcus joined them. He turned to Henri and asked, "I would assume you have a warehouse or two stocked with the medical supplies." Seeing Henri nod, Marcus continued. "Could I get some shots of those stockpiles?"

"They're not much different than what you see here."

Marcus smiled. "True. But from an impact viewpoint, more is better. Just like two cars in a parking lot can make for a good photo, a shot of a thousand lined up in the factory lot will carry more impact. Right?"

"Oh, yes, I can see that. Well, the warehouse is not here in the village, and I'm pressed for time right now. Would you be available for a quick tour in the morning? Say, around eight o'clock?"

Marcus pointed toward Sam. "That's up to the boss."

Sam gave Henri her best smile as she did a slight toss of her blonde hair. "Perfect. Where shall we meet, Henri?"

93

SSA Todd Burke had spent most of Sunday afternoon going over the case file sent up from Marcus Colt. The photos of gutted bodies and the blood-stained lab were many times worse than he expected.

The written reports from LT Wendy James and SA Brad Neil about their truck chase were concise, at least. He had given them the ROIs and photos of the Chicago-based part of the case. They needed to get up to speed on the five people in custody and what the agents had found at the warehouse. He was glancing at the photo of the missing drug kingpin Rodrigo Quispe on his desk when the two Internal Affairs agents knocked on the casing of his door. Todd waved them to the chairs in front of his desk.

Wendy said, "Interesting stuff at that warehouse. Shame the bad guys are so tightlipped about it all."

Nodding, Todd said, "Aside from drug paraphernalia, stolen Navy drugs, and some deadly anthrax, we are facing a blank wall."

"Well, there's that." Wendy gave a slight chuckle at their stalled situation. "I'm sending Brad back to D.C. today. I'll hang around until we tie up this mess up with a bow."

Burke slid the photo aside and pointed to the data sheet on Quispe. "Does wrapping up include finding this guy?"

"Marcus believes he's the Chicago-end boss, so he is in our sights. I'm not sure where to point the weapon," Wendy said. "He's one of those needles Marcus is always trying to find."

"Seems to me, the best place to focus our efforts is with Chief Hospital Corpsman Hugo Diaz. We've got the most leverage with him. Caught him stealing Navy property, bringing a deadly substance onto a military base, contributing to the distribution of said deadly substance, and obstruction of justice. Wish I could charge him with being a jerk, but the world ain't perfect," Burke said as he tapped a case folder at the corner of his desk. "Maybe a new, and very pretty face, will get him to open up about his chain of command. You game, Wendy?"

Wendy picked up the folder. "Give me a few minutes and I'll see if I can make him cry." As she stood, another thought hit. "No, let him sit and consider his bleak future for another day. I want to hear what Marcus has found in Montréal, and perhaps that'll give me a shovel to slam on his head. Okay."

"My effort failed, so I'm open to whatever you think is best with the crooked chief. So what do you want to do now?" Todd asked.

"I hate to leave this brainstorming session, but I have two hours to get to Midway for the flight to Washington National. Anything you want me to take home?" Brad Neil interjected.

Wendy shook her head. "No. Have a safe flight, and tell the admiral I'll be home as soon as I can." She thought a moment. "Tell ya what—Todd and I will drop you off at Midway before we go to the warehouse. I want to see the place."

Todd asked with a touch of anger, "And what do you expect to see that's not in my people's reports?"

She held back her instinct to respond in kind, brought on by the general fatigue of the case. Everyone involved was on edge. As an Internal Affairs investigator, she frequently felt resentment from other agents when their work was questioned. To calm the churning waters, she shook her head slightly and politely said, "No offense intended, Todd. I need as much ammo as I can get before I chat with Diaz. I don't believe anything was overlooked; however, my firsthand knowledge of the place might give me an edge."

Calmed by that answer, Todd nodded. "Okay, I'll drive."

Brad made his flight, and before his plane graced the takeoff runway, Todd pulled in against the garage door at the warehouse. Two armed men in uniform with Shore Patrol armbands approached the car from either side. Having spotted SSA Burke, they backed away and resumed their watch.

Inside the warehouse, several agents and technicians continued the work of cataloging and processing the scene. All of the anthrax had been removed by Thursday afternoon, so unless something else turned up, the place was safe to search.

Wendy did a quick 360-degree look at the warehouse, then turned to Burke. "Okay, Todd, take me through Wednesday night step-by-step, please."

Talking Wendy through the evening's events took longer than the actual assault. Todd made sure she knew who was where, and doing what. Then Wendy started looking at the equipment on the various workbenches.

One machine caught her eye: a manual label printer. She studied the device and figured out it printed an adhesive-backed label using a rubber stamp. A side-mounted hand crank, which moved the stamp from an inkpad onto the blank label and back, automated the machine. As the stamp moved to re-ink, the next blank label moved into position and the process continued.

She cranked the machine and saw that the label printed was a standard label for the small glass vaccine vials. It contained the usual information: manufacturer, lot number, dosage, expiration date, and vaccine name. It looked official, but the criminals had access to great forgers. The stamp installed was for the tetanus vaccine. Other stamps on the bench were for other meds, including the H3N2 influenza virus, commonly called the Hong Kong flu, from the late 1960s, and the relatively new measles, mumps, and rubella combination vaccine. There were several she didn't recognize, but one that caught her attention was for anthrax.

As Wendy studied the labels, something not mentioned in the reports jumped out at her. Each label had a small ink smear at the lower left corner. It was less than a sixteenth-inch in size, however her accounting mind was geared to notice small things out of place. Since most people focused on the printed data, few if any would see the smear. She checked, and all of the printed labels from this machine had that same flaw, so the machine—and not the rubber stamp—had generated it.

"Todd, did you see this?" Wendy pointed to the smear. "Is this the only label printer here?"

"Yea, we documented all the different stamps for this one printing machine. Guess they didn't see the need to create two of them, just change the stamps," Todd said.

"But did you see this small smear?"

Todd looked again at the label. "Where? Oh, that … it looks like a small heart."

Wendy tried to avoid rolling her eyes as she said, "Yes, right here!" and pointed to the smear with the tip of her pen. "I think we found the key."

94

BOB LEDDER HAD REQUESTED FRENCH for dinner, and Sam selected the restaurant; it turned out to be a good choice. Sam ordered the beef bourguignon, Bob wasted no time picking the coq au vin, and Marcus yearned for the bouillabaisse. Marcus tried to pick up the tab, but Sam explained she was under orders from Tommy that the publishing company was covering all their expenses. Not debatable.

Discussion over dinner was light and limited to the work Sam had seen as the IOC built the village and game locations. After finishing the meal with Crème Brûlée, they thought ending with the hotel bar would be a good idea. But seeing the large crowd, Sam said, "Gents, let's move to my room for drinks and quiet. Doubt that Marcus will want to chat in this place."

Sam's eighth floor "room" had become her home-away-from-home for the last six months. Since she was both an ace reporter and a personal friend of the publishing company's owner, expense was not an issue, and her room was a suite with a separate bedroom, efficiency kitchen with small dining table, and sitting area with several easy chairs, a sofa, large color television, and coffee table. In addition, a desk against a wall had become her Montréal office. Bob and Marcus were invited to the easy chairs.

She opened the refrigerator. "Labatt's okay with you guys? I know Molson is considered the local brew, but I like the fruitier taste that Labatt's offers." Without waiting for an answer, Sam pulled three cold bottles, popped the caps, and passed them around. "Glasses are in the left cabinet if you prefer," she added as she dropped onto the sofa, pulled her feet under her, and took a pull on the beer.

After taking a sip, Marcus asked, "So, what do you want to discuss?"

Sam paused to gather her thoughts. "Assuming you trust ol' Bob, I need to know more about this Marcus Colt fellow."

"Why?"

"I've got the feeling I'm either boosting or risking my career hanging around with you, and based on things I've heard about you, I could be risking my life. So the more I know about you, the more I can trust you. I've heard some rumors, but want you to confirm them. Understand?"

Marcus shrugged as he said, "Yea, I get it. Know that the trust thing goes both ways. Feel free to chat, since Bob knows the penalty for spreading my secrets."

Bob nodded vigorously and said, "The short version: don't talk out of school."

"Well said, Bob." Marcus chuckled and continued in a stern voice, "I normally don't let anyone outside my team get their nose under the tent, but there are exceptions to every rule. And I suspect you know that if you break my trust, the only position available to you will be obituary editor for whatever paper they print in Goose Bay, Labrador."

Sam saluted and said, "Aye, aye, sir. I understand and agree. Moving on, our buddy Tommy refused to tell me more than you are a Navy Commander working at Naval Investigative Service. Knowing that the usual age of commanders is in the late thirties and usually early forties, I wanted to know why a thirty-one-year-old guy who looks like he's in his twenties holds that rank. I made a few calls to track down some members of your fan club. And one fellow who owed me is an ex-assistant secretary of defense with an interesting tale of rescue."

Marcus tensed up, but held his comments as he sipped the beer and cut his eyes over to see Bob's expression.

"All I'm saying, Marcus, is that I'm glad we're family, or at least at a pseudo-brother/sister-in-law level. Nice work over there … assuming what I've been told is true. And any and all secrets I know about you are safe, until you let me write your biography … which would probably get me another Pulitzer based on that one rescue," Sam said.

Sam noted Bob's confusion and clarified, "My boss, Tommy, is like a brother to Marcus. And Tommy's wife Heidi was my college roommate and is my sister as far as I'm concerned. This guy and I first met at their wedding in '66, but haven't seen each other since. Hence the 'family' comments about Marcus and me."

"Uh, Marcus." Bob cringed, wondering if he should talk. "While you were on the phone last night, Harry showed me photos of you guys in 'Nam and told me about how you rescued him there, and then saved his daughter the next year in Naples. You've got family there also. He also showed me a photo of you getting another medal added to a chest-full of decorations. Impressive, sir."

Sam leaned forward with surprise, "Harry, as in SecState? That Harry? Naples? Do tell!"

Marcus held up his hand as the standard stop indicator. "Uh, I've nothing to say on that one, Sam. Here's the deal. While the bulk of my work is handling Internal Affairs for NIS, a few times I have been handed assignments outside that scope, like this one dealing with murder, drugs, and possible terrorism, and I've been lucky that I've had good people backing me up. Yea, I was in 'Nam, met SecState and others—like your contact, there—and I came home with them and some scars. Aside from that, let it rest, okay?"

Sam said, "Okay, for now we'll skip both 'Nam and Naples. Let's talk about murder and terrorism since those two words didn't come up when we talked about this assignment."

Marcus nodded and gave her the *Reader's Digest* version of the case. "And none of that goes further. I'm telling you this because I want you to understand the importance and the far-reaching repercussions if we fail. When we go to the warehouse tomorrow, I need two things from you. First, distract Henri long enough for me to do an in-depth examination of the med stockpile."

"Easy. He was visually appreciating my assets, so I'll toss my hair a bit to get his attention, take a deep breath to seal the deal, and ask to see his records. After all, my article needs to know how many bandages and aspirin they plan on stocking. To get numbers like that, we'll need to go to the warehouse office. Maybe I'll take Bob and he can shoot some photos there. What's the second?" Sam asked.

"You being near the records might make number two easier. Find out the names of the companies supplying the liquid medications. I don't care about the aspirin and bandages, only the injection stuff that will have a shorter shelf life. I suspect the IOC won't stock those items until a month or so before opening ceremonies due to shelf life, so I need to know who owns them now and where they are warehoused."

Sam peeled off a corner of the beer bottle label as she focused on the request. "Okay, I can do …" Before she could finish her response, the phone on the coffee table rang.

"Yea?" Sam said rather brusquely, frustrated at being interrupted.

"Miss Bigalow? Sorry to bother you. I'm Kelly Colt, and Tommy Garrett gave me your contact information."

Casting a grin towards Marcus and switching to a friendly voice, Sam said, "Call me Sam, Kelly. Nice to meet even if it is only over the phone."

"Thanks, Sam. I'm trying to locate Marcus, and Tommy thought you could help."

"He and Bob have a room in this hotel, number 609, but right now they're enjoying a beer with me here in 812 as we discuss tomorrow's plan of attack. Here he is." Sam passed the phone to Marcus.

"Hello, Princess. We're back from dinner, and I'd planned to report in as soon as this planning session was over."

"Glad you haven't forgot about me, Sailor." Kelly paused before continuing in a somewhat suspicious tone, "Sam sounds cute. Sorry, ignore that jealous comment. Any progress on the case?"

Marcus chuckled. "Responses in the same order. Never. Yes. Ignored. And not much. We did find out more about the first aid stations than I ever wanted to know. But since they're not stocked with meds until right before the games start, we didn't find any evidence. Looks like the IOC staff is clean, but we will need to do some background work on them. I'll get Sam to find a personnel list, and we can pass that on to NISHQ. We are visiting an IOC warehouse tomorrow—doubt we'll find anything incriminating—but hope it will lead to the suppliers."

"Logical next step, babe. Just make sure Bob is watching your back."

Marcus swallowed a final sip of beer. "Yea, for sure. Anything new on your end?"

"Nothing much here either. Alvarez is still waiting for the high-priced lawyer to arrive from Chicago. The teams pulled a decent amount of evidence from the farm, and Allen, Rick, and I are spending hours helping with the sorting and cataloging. Elle got off okay. GT is trying to find next of kin for the remaining bodies now that the Thompkins were buried today. And when I got here to the mansion, Wendy called. She sent Brad back to D.C. this afternoon and needs to chat with you. Neither serious nor time sensitive, she said. Give her a call early tomorrow; she sounded exhausted. Oh, yea, one more thing …" Kelly said, then paused.

"What?"

"I love you. Stay safe, shoot straight, I need you, Sailor."

"Right back at ya, Deputy Doc. Have a good night, love."

A soft "'night" was all Marcus heard before the dial tone erupted in his ear.

Sam had a quizzical look. "I can usually pick up a lot from a one-sided conversation, but the first part of that one left me totally lost. Were you speaking in code?"

"No code," Marcus said, "just four years of marriage allowing us to finish each other's thoughts and being able to say much with few words."

A bit of sadness covered Samantha's face as she softly said, "I am jealous in so many ways." She cleared emotions from her throat with a small cough and allowed her work voice to return. "And finishing my thought before the call, I'll tell Henri that I want to follow the supply chain for the article, so getting the supplier data should be easy. The IOC personnel list you mentioned to Kelly might be more difficult."

"If you can't get the list, I know some people who know people. But first see what you can do quickly." Standing, Marcus continued, "Thanks for the beer, Sam. We'll meet for breakfast downstairs at 0730 hours. Okay?"

"Be here at that 0730 time thing, which I presume is half past seven in the morning, and I'll order room service. That way, if needed, we can discuss the operation privately. Eggs, bacon, and pancakes, okay?"

95

Bob Ledder was in the shower when Marcus called Wendy James at the Navy Lodge for an update. He knew it was only 0530 at Great Lakes, but had suspected correctly that Wendy was ready to hit the deck. As Marcus sipped on an excellent cup of coffee and munched on a fresh-baked croissant slathered with butter, he listened to Wendy's thoughts. The server who rolled in the room service cart earlier had said it was courtesy of room 812, including the gratuity, as Marcus found when he offered cash.

"So far, Todd's interrogation of Chief Diaz has been way less than beneficial. The only thing he gave up was that hint about 'games,' but nothing else. First off, I was hoping you had a crumb to toss me that I can use against him," Wendy said.

"Nothing yet, but hold off on your interrogation until the mid-afternoon. I might have something by then." Marcus then detailed his plan for the day.

"I have something that might help your search." Wendy explained the smear that should show up on all the bogus meds. "We checked supplies from several sources we knew to be good, and that smear, or tiny heart as Todd called it, was not on the labels. Our confidence is high that we can now identify contaminated supplies by this mark."

"Great work, Wendy. What's the status of those Cardinals you have in custody? Are they lawyered up?"

"Sort of. It's kinda weird, as they have called their attorney—they all called the same company—and no one has showed up yet. Similar to Alvarez in Princeton, who's still waiting to hear something from that same firm."

"Yea, that is strange. Get Todd to do a quick look at that company. Perhaps there's a link there we can use. And interrogate the Cardinals, letting them know that Alvarez and Marks, a.k.a. Marcano, are under arrest. Maybe that will loosen their tongues."

"Can do, boss. If you think it might help, I can tell them how Jesus Cabilla was killed by his associates."

"Do it. Maybe it will convince them they're not safe in that gang. Hopefully, by the time you finish with those five, I'll have something to tell you to use with Diaz," Marcus said. "Anything else?"

"I was going to say I'll let ya know, but since you will be out searching warehouses, I'll have to wait for your call. Make sure Bob has your back, partner. All for now," Wendy said.

"We'll talk soon," Marcus said right before he hung up.

Breakfast was waiting for them in Sam's room, and they went over the plan for the day as they ate. At the scheduled time, they met Henri at the main gate to the Olympic Village, and Sam's Land Rover followed Henri's BMW across the river to Brossard. A couple of stoplights and turns brought them to a modern warehouse. Security cameras covered all areas, and armed guards were in place at the gate. The guards verified Henri's identification and passed them into the parking lot. Another set of guards checked IDs and granted them entry into the warehouse.

With arm movements mimicking a circus ringmaster, Henri spun around and said, "And welcome to my world. Ten thousand square meters of storage space with the primary task of securely storing medical supplies that we all pray will never be needed. The bulk of the non-perishable items are here, and most of the perishable meds will be arriving two weeks before the opening ceremonies. We do have a small amount of perishables to stock the stations open for the construction crews. Now, if you will follow me ..."

Twenty minutes later, the tour had shown them row upon row of tall shelving units, which were crammed with boxes of every imaginable medical item that might be needed. Sam asked all the right questions as Marcus dropped the shutter on stacks of supplies. Henri recited from memory the exact number of cases of bandages, aspirin, tongue depressors, etc. that each first aid station would receive before the start of the games. With the tour and Henri winding down, they ended up facing several near-empty coolers that were waiting for the delivery of medications needing refrigeration.

A glance inside the first cooler revealed the bulk of the boxes were labeled *Tetanus*. Since the only first aid stations open were for the construction crews, tetanus was a logical concern. All the boxes were sealed, so Marcus couldn't check the vial labels.

Marcus gave a quick nod to Sam, and she picked up on the signal. "Henri, to write the best article, I want to give the readers a detailed look at the entire supply chain. Can I get the suppliers' contact information?"

Shrugging, Henri replied, "I don't think there would be any issues with that. They probably would appreciate the promotion. Come with me to my office and I'll get you a copy."

Laying a hand on Henri's arm and hitting him with her warmest smile, Sam asked, "Can my photographer wander around and shoot more photos?"

"Of course. We'll only be a couple of minutes, so he better be fast," Henri said as he led Sam toward the office.

Marcus motioned Bob to join him and they turned down between a close row of shelves. Marcus glanced around, then subtly said, "I need to get into that cooler again. Stand guard and do whatever you need to give me five uninterrupted minutes."

"Can do, sir," Bob replied.

Inside the cooler with the tetanus treatment, Marcus quickly opened two of the boxes and extracted three vials from each. None of the vials had the heart-shaped smear, but he shot photos anyway. He reloaded the boxes and placed them under two unopened ones in hopes no one would see they'd been opened.

As he turned to leave, Marcus heard some loud voices from outside the cooler. Devising an emergency plan, he snapped off the cooler's light and pushed open the door. "Hey, Bob, I saved the film and ..."

Marcus found an armed guard pointing his weapon at Bob's chest.

The guard yelled, "What the hell are you doing here?"

Bob stammered, "Henri said we could take more photos."

Confused, the guard shifted his weapon from Bob to Marcus and yelled, "What are you doing in the cooler?"

Raising his hands, Marcus rapidly yet calmly said, "I had a camera malfunction and used the cooler as a dark room. What's the problem?"

The guard looked like he shaved every couple of weeks and that this might be his first day on this—or any—job after leaving high school. Marcus saw that the boy's lack of experience could escalate into an accidental shooting unless he acted quickly. He spied the guard's nametag and used the information.

"Officer Taggert, I'm Marcus and this is Bob. We're here with a reporter working on a story for an American newspaper. Your boss Henri has just given us a tour of the facility, and he's with my boss in his office right now. What say we head that way and get this straightened out?" Marcus said in a matter-of-fact voice.

Before they could move, Henri and Sam came into view from the other side of the coolers. A shocked Henri, seeing the unholstered revolver, yelled, "Taggert, what are you doing? Put your gun away this minute!"

"Sir, I found them acting strange around the cooler," Taggert said as he holstered his weapon. "They claim to be photographers."

Marcus lowered his arms and raised his camera that was hanging around his neck. "Henri, my film's socket tore, and I needed a dark room to open the camera and manually advance the film. Otherwise all the shots from today would be lost. The cooler was perfect."

Henri nodded. "Continue your rounds, Taggert. Glad you were on the ball, but these are good people. And we are leaving now."

Sam delivered their appreciation for Henri's tour, and after a round of handshakes, the Land Rover was on the street heading toward Montréal. At least until Marcus spotted an old drive-in burger joint.

"Sam, find a spot there away from the other cars, please," Marcus said as he pointed.

"Hungry already?"

Marcus grinned. "Hungry for information—and a glass of iced tea, or more, would be nice: it *is* already past normal lunch time."

"Works for me," Bob interjected.

The carhop was quick to arrive and get their order. The three decided to go with cheeseburgers and fries all around. The old days of carhops on roller skates were long gone, but the orders were delivered quickly nevertheless.

"Henri was most obliging with access to his records. I have all the information on the suppliers, but he didn't have access to personnel records," Sam said between nibbles of slightly salty fries.

Marcus nodded in understanding. "I was able to check the vials in the cooler before almost getting shot by the wannabe Mountie. They are all normal; my speculation is they don't want the bad stuff to get out until the opening day."

"Greater impact that way. So, what next, Marcus?"

"We're back to the trigger event. Based on what Wendy told me this morning about the labels, there are more than anthrax-labeled vials being filled with the bad stuff. Penicillin is one of the frequently used meds, and that is one of the bogus labels," Marcus said. "Along with the tetanus and many others."

An experienced juggler of multiple tasks, Sam scanned the list of suppliers as she gobbled more fries and listened. Chewing the remains of a couple of fries, she mumbled, "We're in luck, boys." She swallowed the potato debris and continued, "There is only one supplier of refrigerated meds: a Chicago-based company called Positive Quest Medicals."

Marcus asked, "Is there a local warehouse address?"

Flipping a few more sheets, Sam shook her head. "Well, sort of local: closer than Chicago by about a thousand kilometers. There's an address in Ottawa. Should I call the IOC Medical and Scientific Director and have her open some doors for us?"

"What's the distance to Ottawa?"

Sam shrugged. "Eh. About two hundred kilometers or two hours' drive time."

"Or about thirty-five minutes' airtime in the *Songbird*, boss," Bob offered.

Marcus slowly chewed another bite of burger as he considered the new information. "We need to know more about Positive Quest Medicals before we go charging in. If they are dirty, we'll be giving them a heads-up going through the IOC. Let's head to the Olympic grounds. I saw some phone booths there; I'll make a couple of calls and then I want to do a casual look-around. Maybe I'll get lucky and see something."

96

THE PHONE BOOTH, PART OF the recently constructed Olympic Park, had a unique style, and unlike many in D.C., it was nearly hospital-room clean. Marcus didn't mind that it took the Beckley FBI office receptionist about five minutes to find SSA Ken Santoro; it got him out of a cold wind. It took another five minutes for Marcus to relate the updates and ask for Ken's help. Ken promised to get Marcus info on the Positive Quest Medicals people ASAP.

Ken added, "My DEA contact didn't have much new data to offer. Quispe is still reported to be in the Chicago area, but no one knows for sure. He's obviously using a false ID, and with his funds and connections, might have had surgery to change his face. She's hoping you turn up something, because they want him bad."

"Understood. Thanks for trying, Ken. We've got five drug-related suspects in custody in Chicago, so maybe one of them will crack and give us a lead. I'll keep you in the loop."

"Where can I reach you?"

Marcus gave Ken the room numbers at the hotel. "Not sure how often I'll be hanging around there, so if I don't answer, call NISO Great Lakes and pass the message on to Wendy. I'll be checking in with her frequently."

"Can do, Marcus. And be careful—this Quispe is an evil bastard."

Marcus chuckled. "That seems to be a requirement for us to be involved, right? Not too many bad guys are nice. Thanks, Ken, I'll be in touch."

Another collect call, this one to NISO Great Lakes, connected him to Wendy James. She answered with, "Hey, partner, about time you called. What ya got for me?"

"Two things, Wendy. There is no evidence of any tainted meds in either the Olympic Park first aid stations or the IOC warehouse. Sorry, nothing to use against the chief yet, so let him stew. We have the address for a medical supplier that's a couple hours away in Ottawa. I just put in a call to Ken Santoro to have him check on the company. You might want to snoop around, cautiously of course, and see what you can quickly find out about Positive Quest Medicals. They're based out of Chicago. I don't want to visit there cold tomorrow."

"We'll get right on it. What else?"

"Ken will be calling you with whatever he discovers about that company. Figured you'd be the best option for a central dispatch person: gathering, sorting, and disseminating information and keeping everyone informed. If I'm not in the hotel room, I'll be calling you every couple of hours. Okay?"

"Works for me! Otherwise, I'm twiddling my thumbs instead of waiting to start gathering, sorting, and disseminating," Wendy said with a laugh.

"All tasks are important, as you well know, whiner. If you have a better suggestion, I'm open to it."

"I got nothing." Wendy snickered. "Maybe one day we'll have those wrist radios like Dick Tracy, and then we'll have comms in the field that will work better."

It was Marcus's turn to chuckle. "I'll be first in line to buy one for both of us. While waiting for that radio watch and your report on that med company, we'll be wearing out shoe leather for the next couple of hours strolling around an empty Olympic Park. Maybe we'll see something that kicks off a new speculation on what the trigger will be. All for now."

Bob and Sam rose from the bench beside the phone booth as Marcus pushed open the door. "What's the word from headquarters, Commander? Full-speed-ahead time?" Sam asked whimsically.

"The FBI and NIS are now doing quiet backgrounds on our med supplier, and while they do that, we're going to wander around the Park.

Assuming the bad guys want to infect the largest number of people, and knowing the opening ceremonies is a big crowd drawing event, I'm hoping we will see something, anything—here in the Park or at the stadium—that could help with their cause."

Being a common sight around the Park, Sam garnered more than a few waves and greetings from IOC staff and construction workers. Marcus had asked her to guide him and Bob from the main entrance to the stadium, figuring that would be the most-used path on opening day. The weather cooperated somewhat, with clear skies and temps in the low forties. The wind chill sat around thirty.

The trek wasn't the longest Bob had done, but he was breathing heavy—he spent too many hours on a bulldozer seat and was a little out of shape. With the cold getting to him, he mumbled, "Damn glad we're not doing this in July; today's temps at least prevent losing a gallon of sweat."

"July in Canada isn't too bad, Bob. The temperatures around here run into the seventies, and the humidity is tolerable," Sam explained.

Marcus snorted. "Add in the body temps of fifty thousand plus people, and that seventy will get kicked up some."

Sam shook her head and pointed to tall poles that ran down both sides of the walkway. They were about twenty feet apart and alternately spaced on each side. "In addition to holding various cloth banners when the time comes, those poles are actually water misting devices."

Bob's face contorted as he looked up. "So they give the people showers as they walk by?"

"Nothing that drastic, Bob," Sam said with a laugh before switching into lecture mode. "It is a fine mist like those in the grocery store produce department and usually doesn't reach the people. It is a process called *evaporative cooling*, where the tiny droplets evaporate by pulling heat from the air to convert them from water to vapor. This action cools the area. A good system can drop temperatures in the area by twenty degrees or more."

"So you're both a journalist and a science nerd? Impressive," Marcus said.

"Not really into science. Like you, as an investigator, I ask a lot of questions and learn a lot of new and different things."

The walk continued with Sam playing tour guide. They examined each of the ingress points, and when they arrived at the stadium, their passes granted them access. In the areas inside the outer walls, Marcus noticed misting sprinkler heads mounted overhead and in the tunnels leading to the seating area. They exited one of the tunnels into the huge open arena and looked around.

"Looks like there is still a lot of work to do here," Bob said from the viewpoint of a construction professional.

Sam nodded. "Yea, it has been a sore subject. Construction strikes and cost overruns have hampered the project. Doubtful the roof will be on in time for the games, but miracles do occur."

"What's the capacity?" Marcus asked.

"Officially, it's fifty-six thousand, but there are rumors floating that another fifteen to twenty thou' will be here. Not sure where they will put them."

Marcus was lost in thought for a moment as the trio evaluated the place. Finally, he asked, "I saw spots for food vendors in the area before we entered the tunnel, just like our football stadiums. Will there be any food vendors outside the stadium?"

"Sorry, not sure, but I'll check. Guess I can tell them I'm also writing an article about the food," Sam said with raised hands of uncertainty. "Why?"

Marcus looked around again as he gathered his thoughts. He finally said, "Those misting things would be a perfect delivery system for a biological attack. I'm not sure if the anthrax spores would survive after the evaporation, but what if one or two holes in each misting nozzle are larger than the rest, thereby allowing larger drops to escape. Drops that are too big for the usual evaporation process, and they probably wouldn't be noticed as they land on people and whatever food or drink they carry."

Sam asked, "Wouldn't they have some filtration system in place?"

"Probably. But most filters cannot stop things as small as bacteria and viruses. A good dose of chlorine will kill anthrax, but I'm not sure what constitutes the safe ratio." Marcus's brow knotted and he bit his lower lip.

"And what are you not saying, Marcus?" Sam asked.

"Guess you need to write an article on water safety under the five rings. That could get us a look at the filter systems and see if they're adding chlorine, and how much."

"I can, but what do any of us know about water filter systems?"

"Nothing, but we could gather data, make, model numbers, et cetera, and photos to pass on to an expert. And then we could ..." Marcus paused and shook his head. He walked in a tight circle and rubbed his hands across his face as if clearing his mind. "No. We don't want to go there. What if, and I know this is a big if, so think about this. What if the people installing the filter systems are part of the Vampire's team, and in place of chlorine or whatever good chemical, they install anthrax? So the systems will look great on inspection, but can turn deadly on opening day."

Bob and Sam spoke over each other, but Sam was louder. "That's one hell of a conspiracy theory!"

"But it would work," Bob interjected again.

Marcus nodded. "Yea, it would. Spectators walk through a mist of anthrax getting to the stadium. And they get another dose here as they head to their seats. Some is inhaled, some falls on food or drink and is swallowed. Normally, it takes a few days for symptoms to show, but the stuff made in West Virginia is much stronger. No telling how quickly it will act. But even if it takes a day or two, most of those same people in the stadium will still be around for the games, and will go to the first aid stations when they start feeling bad. There they could get larger direct doses of the tainted drugs thinking they're getting a remedy."

Sam said, "So my job is to find out what company installed the misting systems, and who is maintaining it without raising suspicions, right?"

"That would be nice."

Sam smiled her most sexy smile and flipped her hair again. "It so happens that the man in charge of overseeing the contracts for the construction companies has wanted to take me to dinner since I arrived. If you boys can survive without me tonight, we just might get lucky. At least with information gathering."

"That would work," Marcus agreed.

"Now it's my turn to find a phone booth."

97

SAM BIGALOW WAS OFF ON her research assignment, leaving Bob Ledder and Marcus Colt to find dinner on their own. They agreed on room service, to allow them to freely talk about the events of the day and plan for tomorrow. Bob was pleasantly surprised by the bottle of Maker's Mark bourbon on the dinner cart, which they opened after stacking the empty dinner dishes.

"Sam certainly is formidable. I almost feel sorry for the guy buying her dinner tonight." Bob chuckled as he dropped ice in two glasses and splashed bourbon on top. He passed one to Marcus and dropped into the other easy chair in front of the television. It was tuned to a sitcom, *Welcome Back, Kotter*, with the volume turned all the way down.

Marcus nodded. "That she is. It's good to have people like her, and you, on the team. The Lord knows I couldn't do it alone."

Bob shrugged. "Listening to Harry, you did a lot by yourself over there. I know it wasn't a fun place—I was there multiple times."

"Remember, Harry is a politician, so take everything he says with a least two grains of salt," Marcus said, then lowered his voice. "I had two great SEAL teams with me who carried the heavy load. And I carry the regrets of losing several of them."

Bob sipped his drink and quietly nodded. "Yea, that's the hard part. Putting your buddy's body, one piece at a time, in a body bag is something we can't talk about to people who weren't there." Bob's voice broke as he finished. He regrouped his thoughts and tried to lighten up. "Good news this case is an easier one."

Marcus sighed before he muttered, "Except for the gutting of the victims, parentless children, and me then having to shoot the Vampire."

Bob flinched. "Sorry, Marcus." He wasn't sure if he saw pain or anger on Marcus's face. Either case, he knew he'd overstepped.

The ring of the phone broke the awkward silence. Marcus snapped, "Colt!"

"Guess I'll call sometime when your attitude is a bit sweeter," the soft, Virginia-accented voice of Wendy said.

"Sorry, Wendy. Reliving a few negative memories with Bob put me in a bitchy mood. Hopefully you're about to make my day better, right?"

"Ken called a short bit ago, and I figured I'd call your room every thirty minutes until I got ya. I've added his info to my report. Sorry, it's not much, but it beats nothing. Positive Quest Medicals is a privately owned corporation that filed its startup papers right at a year ago. Not sure who the owner is or owners are, but Ken is still checking."

"How about the staff?"

"Patience, young grasshopper," Wendy laughed through a quote from a popular martial arts TV show. "The CEO is a second-generation German named Claus Hermann Beck. According to his bio in a promotional pamphlet on the company, his parents left Germany in early 1928. Mother was a Jew, six months pregnant with Claus at the time. Couldn't find any confirmation on the parents; the bio said both died from natural causes in the late fifties. Beck's married, no children, graduated with a business degree and then an MBA in 1955 from USC. Wife is a California girl he met in college—maiden name was Carol Eckler—Ken's doing a BI on her. They have a nice house in Lake View on the north side of Chicago, and they are members of the Glen View Club where he plays a round every weekend unless the course is covered with snow. No criminal record. Beck's a registered Democrat who's been seen dining out with the mayor. Nothing screams evil."

"You know it usually doesn't scream, but I concur, at first glance he looks clean," Marcus said. "Got anything on other members of management?"

"Nothing yet, but Ken said to tell you he's working on it. Todd and I focused on the physical facilities and did find that their Chicago office is a standard four-story structure. Todd pulled the building plans from the zoning department. First floor and basement are dedicated to manufacturing and storage with offices above. Health department inspections have all been positive. They opened that warehouse in Ottawa early this summer strictly for the Olympic use. It's leased through the end of 1976."

"Wonder why Ottawa instead of Montréal?" Marcus pondered aloud.

"As an accountant, I'd speculate cost or availability or both."

"Yea, probably both. I'm always looking for nefarious acts when common sense is the usual answer."

"That's all I have for now, but the worker bees are busy," Wendy said.

"Hold one minute," Marcus said before going quiet. Wendy was accustomed to Marcus's need for thinking time and waited for the revelation.

"What did the Becks do between 1955 and him becoming CEO of Positive Quest Medicals? Have Ken dig up their work history and financials for those nineteen years. Might link to something."

"I take it you have a hunch? Care to share?"

"Nothing firm, partner, just one of those gut feelings."

Wendy knew to trust his gut. "I'll call Ken, soon as we hang up. He mentioned he'd be in the office late."

"Okay. Tomorrow morning, I should have some information about another company we need to check on ASAP. Share the following with GT and Ken, please." He spent the next few minutes updating Wendy on the misting devices and his wild theory of using them for biological weapon distribution. "Hopefully, Sam will come through with names and addresses. We'll talk more early in the morning."

Rattling the ice in his empty glass, Marcus stared at the cubes as they ran around the bottom of the tumbler. Bob noticed and picked up the Maker's Mark bottle.

"Need another small splash, boss?"

"Please. Now I need to make yet another phone call," Marcus said as his fingers did their magic on the phone dial.

"Hello?"

"Hey, Aunt Maude. Is Kelly there or still at the office?"

"She's right here, hon. We're sharing a touch of sadness about you not being here with us. Coming home soon?"

"Not for another day or two. Don't you two go chasing too many wild guys while I'm gone, okay?"

Maude laughed. "That'll be the day! Here she is, hon."

"About time you called, Sailor. I miss you," Kelly purred.

"Ditto, darling. I have a task for you and Rick to handle in the morning. What's he doing tonight?"

"I'm at your service, master. Rick's accepted GT's offer for one of Sally's home-cooked meals followed by a round or two of poker with Simpson and GT. I think he wanted to pick their brains doing some background on your early years!"

Marcus chuckled. "That's okay. When y'all get to the office in the morning, have Rick call the CDC under the premise he is putting together some NIS training manuals on possible terrorist attacks. It's not a lie since that'll be one of his tasks when we get back to D.C. Anyway, without tipping his hand about what's happening here, find out several things. Can anthrax be distributed in a water mist? How small a drop can be deadly? And what happens if a drop evaporates before hitting someone. Can the spores still be dangerous?"

"Sounds like you have a specific delivery system in mind."

"Maybe. Sam explained about a mist-based area cooling system that's installed almost everywhere on the Olympic grounds. It might work for bioweapon distribution, but the CDC's answers will firm it up or shoot it down. I have Wendy looking into the Chicago-based companies involved with the installation and operation."

"Wow, that's nasty. I'll call you as soon as we get the data," Kelly said.

"No, pass it on to Wendy at Great Lakes. I set her up as the information dispatcher to keep everyone current. We don't have the time or energy for each of us to call all the participants."

"Where do you plan to go tomorrow?"

"We're flying to Ottawa to check out a drug warehouse rented by Positive Quest Medicals. Should take just over half of the day."

"You know the routine, Sailor. Be careful, okay?"

"Always for you, Princess."

98

OTTAWA INTERNATIONAL AIRPORT WAS ACTIVE that morning. Air traffic control had Bob Ledder fly a racetrack-shaped holding pattern for ten minutes before giving him clearance to land, due to the exorbitant amount of air traffic. Still, they were in Ottawa over an hour faster than driving.

While the flight time was short, it was long enough for Marcus to consider all the new information received that morning. Sam's dinner date had provided her with the name of the misting equipment supplier, and the company that would service the system during the games. Perhaps it was only a coincidence: both companies were located in Chicago. Marcus silently reminded himself that he didn't believe in coincidences. He had told Wendy to look into both during their early morning call.

Wendy related that the FBI hadn't yet provided the complete history of Claus Beck, so that concern was hanging loose. As was info on the people working under him.

On top of that, Marcus was still trying to figure out what he was doing in Ottawa. He would do a drive-by of the Positive Quest Medicals' warehouse, but a sure method of accessing the inventory still escaped him. Sam thought that research for the article would cover them, but Marcus wasn't convinced. He started to belittle himself for his haste in coming to Ottawa, but realized that seeing the building might open mental pathways to the answer. Grasping at straws was standard procedure.

As Sam ran off to secure a rental car, Marcus turned to Bob. "I don't know how long we'll be gone, but I need you to stay here and get the *Songbird*'s tanks topped off. Do whatever pilot magic you need to do to get her ready to get out of here. There is a small possibility we'll need to do more than head straight back to Montréal."

"Can do, sir. Afterwards, you can find me hanging around the FBO lounge." Bob pointed to a building about a hundred yards away. "By then, it will be my burger time."

"Thanks." Marcus reinforced his comment with a clap on Bob's shoulder.

A short time later, Marcus shared his concern about accessing Positive Quest Medicals' warehouse with Sam, as she navigated there. She said, "Trust me, we can turn the lie I told Henri into the truth and tell them we're doing a story on the full medication supply chain."

"I'm out of ideas, so I hope that will work. If they balk, tell them to call Henri," Marcus said. "But first, I want to do a couple of drive-bys to look the place over."

The warehouse was a single-story structure of fairly new construction in the rear of an industrial park. A tall chain-link fence topped with rings of barbed wire surrounded the building and parking lot, containing several box trucks with refrigeration units. No signs, save for the street address posted on the mailbox that was accessed from both sides of the fence. Marcus noted the trucks were similar to the one his team had followed from Chicago to Princeton: boring paint jobs and tiny lettering on the door. He also noted that security cameras were spaced along the fence and at various places on the building.

The manned guardhouse rested beside the only access gate, which was inset about thirty feet so the guards could talk to approaching drivers without leaving the guardhouse. As expected, the gate was tightly closed. The whole place gave off a prison vibe that shouted, "Stay away!"

A small office featuring the only four windows in the building was located on the northwest corner, pointing toward the gate. A loading dock spanned three roll-up doors on the southern side of the building. Large air conditioning units sprouted from the roof. A tiny sign was next to the office door, but it was unreadable from the highway. Two sedans and one pickup truck were parked outside the office.

"What ya think, Marcus?" Sam raised her right eyebrow.

"I look forward to shooting photos there while you interview the manager. Time to head to the gate and see what happens."

Sam nosed their car up to the gate, rolled down the driver window, and pressed the red button on the speaker box. A stern face appeared at the window of the guardhouse.

"Hi. I'm Sam Bigalow from Garrett Publishing, and I'm here about the article," Sam announced into the speaker box.

"I have no record of your appointment. Please leave," an unpleasant metallic voice blasted from the speaker.

"My contact at the IOC, Henri Nomanic, should have called yesterday and set up the appointment. May I speak to your supervisor?" Sam asked.

Again the metallic voice replied, "No one is here right now. Call the number posted below the red button and set up an appointment. Goodbye." The stern face moved away from the window.

Sam drove about a mile from the warehouse and pulled in at a small diner, one of those made popular in the 1930s. Shaped to represent a railroad passenger car, it was constructed of polished stainless steel and sported large windows. Pink and blue 1960s-style neon lights glowed from the edges of the windows, with a large sign reading "Babe's Diner" reaching skyward over the double doors in the front. The aroma of tasty food hit Marcus as he held one of the doors open for Sam. They settled into a booth in the corner, a distance from the small crowd at the counter.

"Well, that was interesting," Sam said as she flipped through plastic-covered pages of the menu.

Marcus nodded as he fiddled with his menu. "Security seems to be extensive for a simple medical warehouse. Did you notice all the cameras?"

Sam said, "Oh, yea."

"And I think the guard was being honest. No one was there except for at least three security guards. I suspect the one in the guardhouse is watching feeds from the multiple cameras, and there are at least two others on roving patrol."

"So, *boss*, what do we do now?"

"Order lunch. And hopefully as we fly back to Montréal I will have an epiphany."

99

SAM BIGALOW'S ROOM WAS THEIR designated meeting room when they finally got to Montréal, much later than planned, after a frustrating afternoon. Arriving at the Ottawa airport somewhat after 1400 hours, Bob had dropped the news that an airline pilot had a brake issue on his new Lockheed L-1011 TriStar. He had run off the end of the runway upon landing, sinking the wheels into the soft, wet grass. Emergency vehicles coaxing the L-1011 off the grass now blocked the general aviation runway that Bob would be using.

An hour passed before they could fly out. It was after 1730 hours by the time they got to the hotel.

Passing out a round of beer in her room, Sam announced, "I don't have the energy to put up with a restaurant and all its noise, so I'm ordering room service, gentlemen. Shrimp cocktail, filet mignon, baked potato, and veggie du jour okay with you?"

"That works, Sam. Thanks. And as soon as you get that done, I need to call Wendy," Marcus said. Bob gave Sam an agreeing nod.

A few minutes after the food order was placed, Marcus reached Wendy James at NISO Great Lakes. "I hope your day was more fruitful than mine, Wendy," Marcus said.

"I'll start with the positives, since you sound somewhat down. Kelly called, and the CDC said a misting system would be a good way to deliver anthrax and many other evil diseases. After evaporation, the spores could still be inhaled, or fall on any open foodstuffs, so droplet size is not an issue. Both methods are pretty nasty weapons, with inhalation anthrax having a ninety-percent-plus death rate, and gastrointestinal anthrax running around a fifty-percent death rate. Rick is doing an in-depth write-up as you requested, but that's the summary."

"And when victims start feeling sick, they go to the first aid stations for help, only to receive an injection of super anthrax in place of a healing med," Marcus added.

"And I found that the company that makes that water misting system has been around for five years. No known issues with the product or the personnel."

"One of my wild thoughts just got a bit less wild."

"And that ends the positives," Wendy continued with reluctance. "Ken is still digging for info about the Becks and their people. And the company that will service the misting system is shut down for another week. Sign on the door said there was a family emergency this past weekend and they will be back next week."

"That's interesting that the emergency happened right after we shut down the Vampire's lab. Coincidence? Probably not."

"My thoughts exactly. We'll be doing more digging," Wendy said.

Marcus next related the events of the day, specifically the intense security they met at the Ottawa warehouse.

When he finished, Wendy asked, "Where do we go from here?"

"I think the links are coming together in my mind, but I need a few more pieces of information. When we finish here, send a NIR to NISO San Diego. I want them to get to USC immediately and find out all they can about Beck's time there. I want to know his friends, classmates, clubs, fraternity brothers, et cetera, and get his yearbooks. And also search for the name of the man who took Quispe under his wing; perhaps Quispe used his mentor's name and went there for his degree."

"Can do. Can I ask where you're going with this?"

"Nothing to share yet, Wendy. Next, get with Todd and set up surveillance on Beck's house and office. Get photos of everyone coming and going, and make damn sure you're not seen. Keep someone on Beck 24/7 and be ready to pick him up on a moment's notice. He might close down like that servicing company and try to vanish. Okay?"

"Okay, boss, but it will take more people than we have here," Wendy said.

"Get with the Shore Patrol skipper and order up some help. Call around other NISOs and see if they have anyone to spare. Get it set up yesterday! If it looks like he's going to run, pull him in."

"Can do. And what are your plans?"

Marcus chuckled. "Short term, dinner. Tomorrow, I'm not sure. There are several more things I might need to do here in the frozen north, and as soon as I can figure out what they are and how to do them, we'll head south."

"Whatever you do, keep watching your back. Unless there's anything else, I need to send a NIR and make some calls. Goodnight, Marcus."

"Until tomorrow, partner," Marcus said before he put the receiver in the cradle.

A gentle knock at the door stopped Sam from asking the questions that had formed as she listened to one side of that phone call. Dinner had arrived. After the server left and the three were digging into the meal, Sam got her question out. "Care to share an update, Marcus? You seem to have a lot going on inside your head."

Marcus nodded as he finished chewing a bite of mushrooms sautéed in red wine and butter. "The misting system can deliver the anthrax, and when the droplets dry, the anthrax spores are still in play. The company that will service the misting systems shut down for a family emergency right after we raided the Vampire's West Virginia farm and the Chicago repackaging site. I asked Wendy to get our people shadowing Claus Beck, Positive Quest Medicals' CEO, because I have a feeling he might be either the Chicago-based ring leader getting ready to run, or a good friend of Rodrigo Quispe, who he might be hiding or helping."

Sam cocked her head to the right and bit her lip. "What makes you think that?"

"An extremely weak, yet maybe connecting, straw. Quispe is reported to have gotten an MBA in 1955 at an American school, although his name doesn't show up anywhere. Beck's bio says he got his MBA from USC in 1955. What if a well-established wine producer in Bolivia sends his protégé to a prestigious university in Southern California, with its larger Hispanic population, and maybe greases the skids getting the kid into the school—and a fraternity—by claiming he's family? While there, going by his mentor's name, he strikes up a friendship with Claus Hermann Beck, who probably has respect for the old Nazi regime since his middle name is that of the World War II head of the Nazi air force. And these two followers of the Nazi propaganda maintained their mutual love of Hitler and later start working together importing illegal drugs. Like I said, an extremely weak straw without more information, attached to a lot of what-ifs."

Nodding, Sam said, "It's so far out there that it might be true. But why kill people at the Olympics?"

Marcus lifted his hands in frustration. "Still waiting to hear some background on all the players from our embassy in Bolivia. Sadly, they seem to have succumbed to the normal government slowness. But here's what's churning in my mind. What if, and that's a big damn if, there was a link, a friendship maybe, back in Bolivia between Nazi Perez and drug lord Quispe. Here they are chatting one day over a couple of cold cervezas in the early sixties, and Perez says, 'Man, I'd love to follow in my biological father's footsteps and kill more Jews. Papa Mengele did a good job, but I want to do more.' And Quispe laughingly replies, 'Get more Jews hooked on my drugs and that will happen. It's working with other Americans as they kill themselves.' They both laughed and life went on. Perez decided to move to the USA in 1967 but still maintains contact with his old buddy. They both hate Americans, but don't mind making money off us before they kill us."

Marcus paused to take another bite of steak and let that scenario solidify in Bob's and Sam's brains. Washing it down with a sip of beer, he continued. "Fast forward to 1972, and the Arabs attacked the Israeli Olympic Team, killing eleven members. Perez is impressed, but thinks he can do better. Nazis can always do better, right? Remembering the old advertising line about 'better living through chemistry,' he dreams up a plan to use drugs to kill more people at the next Olympics. He contacts his old buddy in Bolivia and they hash out the details. Drugs are possible, and selling same can generate the needed funds for the attack, but they decided that a nasty disease is so much better and faster at killing. Being a doctor, Perez looks at all the evil options and decides on anthrax. He realizes the backwoods of West Virginia is a great place to do his evil lab work in seclusion, and makes plans to move there when the time comes. Now there's still one problem: delivery. How to spread the disease."

Bob raised his hand briefly and asked, "So this is where Beck fits into this?"

"Gold star time, Bob," Marcus said. "Quispe remembers Beck from USC and his often positive comments about Hitler and his Third Reich, so he tracks him down and recruits him into the scheme. Beck sets up the companies in Chicago that will help push the illegal drugs to the population, helping Quispe financially, and sets up the delivery systems for the homegrown anthrax Perez wants to send to the Olympics. Dollars to donuts, Beck is also involved with the companies that manufacture and maintain the misting systems. But like I said, this is just a wild theory, and I need more data to firm it up. I didn't mention it to Wendy James because she has a tendency to take my theories as fact, and I need her open mind to keep working on the problem. She might come up with a different theory—probably a correct theory." Marcus stabbed another piece of steak and moved it to his mouth.

Sam said, "It's wild all right, but it would make a damn good movie!"

100

THE THRASHING AND BASHING OF the theory had gone on for another couple of hours in Sam Bigalow's room Wednesday night. Sam was good at spotting holes, and Bob was spot-on asking the difficult questions, pushing Marcus into deeper analysis. When they realized the same issues had been thrashed more than once, it was time to call it a night. Marcus announced an 0730 Thursday start time, with Sam again ordering a hearty room service breakfast—"pancakes would be nice," suggested Bob. But Marcus admitted he had no idea what they were going to do after eating.

The morning came faster than Marcus desired, and he was happy to find breakfast had arrived right on time. With the food consumed, they moved to the easy chairs to finish yet another cup of coffee. Marcus dialed the NISO Great Lakes number, and Wendy answered as though she had the receiver in her hand.

"Good morning, Marcus. Hope you're ready for a couple of pieces of possibly good news."

"I could use some good news. By the way, you are on speakerphone with Bob and Sam. I decided to read them into the case, figuring Sam's investigative reporting talents might help. And Bob's a good sounding board for some of my strange ideas."

"Makes sense to me, boss. Okay, what we have so far is that the administrators at USC were surprisingly accommodating to our NIS agents and opened their offices late last night. The lead agent being an alumnus might have helped. And with a ton of help from the Shore Patrol, we are quietly sitting on Beck."

Exasperation filled Marcus's sigh. "And?"

"Cool your jets, Marcus, I'm getting there. We now have copies of Beck's college records and yearbooks. In addition, the San Diego office is already checking on his friends and contacts from the various clubs."

"What about Quispe?"

"We struck out there. Neither Quispe nor Mendoza, name of his mentor from Bolivia, attended USC in the early 1950s, but your instincts were good. Quispe's mentor, Raul Mendoza, got his degree there in 1924," Wendy said.

Marcus rubbed his forehead. "Well, I can't hang around here forever. I want to call the Royal Canadian Mounted Police about my concerns and get their input, but I'm not sure they would take me seriously. Wish we had more solid evidence to lay on the table."

A subtle knock on the door interrupted the conversation. Marcus said, "Hold one, Wendy. Room service is here to collect the breakfast cart."

Sam opened the door to two serious men in dark suits. The shorter and slightly older one, mid-forties maybe, held out an open black ID case showing a gold badge on the right and a photo ID on the left. His receding hairline, weathered skin, and slight paunch matched his birth date of forty-four years ago. Otherwise, his look was plain, and he would never stand out in any crowd.

"Miss Bigalow, I'm Inspector Barillari, RCMP, Drug Division. I understand I might find Commander Colt here. Might I have a word, please?"

Stepping back from the door, Sam replied, "Certainly."

Marcus stood as the two men approached. "Good morning, I'm Colt," Marcus said as he reached for his military ID.

Barillari smiled as he held up a hand to indicate seeing Colt's ID was not necessary. "Yes, sir. I recognize you from your dossier. Here is my ID." He passed the black case to Marcus, who glanced at it before returning it.

Noticing a slight Italian accent from the inspector, Marcus turned to the second man and asked, "And you are?"

"Sorry, sir." The second man produced his ID case as he said, "RCMP Staff Sergeant Andrew Fortier." He reminded Marcus of Brad Neil: his dress was impeccable, his age was late twenties, and he spent time in the gym; he gave off a slight French accent.

"Commander," Barillari said, "we might have a small problem."

"And what might that be, Inspector?" Marcus said with his best Navy investigator voice of a senior officer irritated with a junior officer. He placed his hands on his hips and allowed his eyes to burrow into Barillari.

Realizing he was getting off on the wrong foot, Barillari quickly tried to correct the deteriorating situation. "Sir, please do not be offended. May we sit?"

Marcus pointed to the dining table. Sam joined them there after pouring two more cups of coffee. Bob stayed where he was on the sofa.

"Please consider this a courtesy call between two intelligence professionals," Barillari said, raising his hands in a disarming welcoming gesture.

Marcus returned the gesture and nodded. He felt his voice might inflame the situation, so he kept quiet.

Barillari continued, "Here's the situation. My officers tell me since your arrival, you have done an excellent job of impersonating a photojournalist. You would fool most people. Naturally, when we saw you enter Canada on a diplomatic passport, which covers the weapon resting in your shoulder holster, it raised a red flag, causing my superiors to contact your state department to ask why a decorated senior intelligence officer was coming here under the protection of a diplomat to act like a photographer."

Marcus gave a come-on gesture.

"My commanding officer was told, by your Secretary of State himself no less, that he sent you here to do an undercover security analysis at the Olympic site. Considering the events in 1972, that's understandable."

Marcus nodded. "All true, Inspector."

"Still, I can't help but wonder why a naval intelligence officer is working for the Secretary of State?" Barillari asked with raised eyebrows.

"Some events of a case I was working in my country led me to believe there might be a problem here. The key word is *might*. But I didn't have enough hard evidence to consider it a problem, so taking a look around seemed to be the next logical step. I have a personal friendship with the Secretary and asked his help with the diplomatic cover. Otherwise, I would be wasting time jumping through hoops getting permission to visit armed, which I felt was required due to the evil these men represent.

I needed quick answers and some evidence. Without evidence, my concerns carry as much weight as a Wang Chin fortune cookie's fortune."

"Knowing your record as I do, I personally would have put a lot of faith in your suppositions had you called me."

Marcus chuckled. "Hard to call someone I don't know. The FBI, CIA, and ONI do dossiers. My focus with NIS is with U.S. naval personnel and facilities; not foreign law enforcement personnel."

"Yet here you are in my country," Barillari said quietly. "All that aside, officially the RCMP does not have any problems with you being here or checking out the Olympic grounds. I guarantee you the RCMP has been doing the same since the first day they broke ground. And I hope if you see an issue, you'll share it with us."

"Of course."

"But the RCMP does have one small problem that I hope we can solve quickly and quietly. My people observed you and Miss Bigalow trying to get access to a Positive Quest Medicals warehouse in Ottawa yesterday. Your presence there might have damaged an ongoing illegal drug-related investigation. We're about ready to raid that warehouse and are waiting to see if we can catch a few of the principles there in addition to the military-trained security guards. I hope your visit doesn't shake them up."

Marcus sipped his coffee before saying, "Probably not. Our cover with the IOC is pretty good because of Sam's presence. And when you arrived, I was talking with my partner, who's working the Chicago end of the case, about my next move. Wendy, introduce yourself and tell Inspector Barillari what my next step was going to be." Marcus pointed to the phone resting on the coffee table.

The two RCMP officers hid their surprise as they looked to the phone. Wendy had been doing a good job listening in stealth mode.

"Good morning, gentlemen. I'm U.S. Navy Lieutenant Wendy James assigned to the Naval Investigative Service Internal Affairs Division in D.C., where I work for Commander Colt. Before you barged in, he was telling me of his desire to contact you, but was concerned about whether you would take him seriously. Let it be known that my boss has a history of having wild ideas that become factual after a bit of investigation. Marcus, I think this is the perfect time to bring the RCMP into the tent. Nothing to lose, it seems."

"Agreed, Wendy," Marcus said. "Welcome to the Vampire case, gents."

It took about ten minutes for Marcus to deliver a concise status report of the entire case, starting with his reason to visit West Virginia. He concluded with the wild theory he'd formulated the previous evening. Marcus wrapped it up by saying, "And that is why I consider Claus Beck, the man whose company runs the Ottawa warehouse, a key player. We just need more evidence."

"I like that theory, Marcus. All the pieces we have so far fit, but we need a few more pieces to fill in some holes," Wendy said.

"It's a unique, but possible theory, Dom," Staff Sergeant Fortier said, looking to Barillari for support.

Barillari glanced at Fortier, who gave a slight shrug. "Commander, it seems … excuse me, since it looks like we'll be working together, may we get on a more casual stance and switch from titles to given names, Marcus? I go by 'Dom' and the staff sergeant prefers to be called 'Andy' by his friends."

Pointing to his team, Marcus smiled. "Sam, you know, and the fellow lounging on the sofa is Bob Ledder, a Navy Reserve lieutenant I shanghaied to be part of my team for this case. You were saying something about working together, Dom?"

Barillari smiled as he dropped his head in a sideways nod. "It would be best if we use the resources of my office to plan the joint raid. It's a short drive."

"We can leave as soon as you give Wendy a phone number where she can reach us. I hope we get more information soon. Right, Wendy?"

"Aye, aye, Commander. You will know moments after I do."

IOI

THE RCMP DIVIDES THE COUNTRY into fourteen letter-identified divisions. 'A Division' is the national headquarters, in the country's capital of Ottawa, with responsibility over all other divisions. It is a huge law enforcement jurisdiction, as the RCMP performs the same tasks as the FBI, Secret Service, Customs and Border Patrol, State Police, Highway Patrol, and Embassy Security combined. And even with that workload, they take on anything else that gets thrown their way.

In Montréal, 'D Division' is responsible for all of Quebec, a land mass twice the size of Texas. The multiple-story HQ building is located a kilometer west of downtown Montréal. Barillari parked in the basement garage after directing Sam to a visitor's spot, and led the group to a conference room on the fifth floor. He put Marcus in a better mood by showing them the coffeepots in the break room before they got down to business.

As a courtesy request that sounded more like an order, Dom insisted they visit the top floor, the location of the upper management offices. There they met a deputy commissioner, two assistant commissioners, four chief superintendents, and three other inspectors who had interest in the drug case. While the time with each was brief, this wiped out most of the morning. It was the price to pay when playing in someone else's sandbox.

With the introductions now behind them, Marcus Colt spent the rest of the day reading the senior RCMP staff into the case and helping Dom's team set up the resources needed for the raid. The decision was reached to conduct the raid in the morning.

The RCMP had reservations about the involvement of a civilian reporter, but Marcus insisted Sam be part of the team documenting the assault, with Bob helping with the photography. As he explained, he owed her, and another set of eyes making a report would help. They would come in with one of the RCMP cars after the guards were subdued. Dom finally acquiesced and agreed that the documentation was a nice touch.

It was late afternoon when Inspector Dominic Barillari stood by the board covered with photos and drawings, finishing what he hoped would be his last overview of the final raid plans. He turned to Marcus. "Any comments on what you have seen and heard?"

"I have only one suggestion, Dom. Move the start time from 0700 to 0400 hours. 0400 is the time of day when people are least alert and less likely to successfully defend themselves. And with the changing of the guard happening at 0600, I'd rather go against a tired team than a fresh one."

"Agreed. Any other comments?"

Marcus pointed to the phone on the conference table. "Time to call Wendy and see if anything new is happening down south." A few moments and a couple of buttons on the speakerphone made the connection.

Introductions with the new team members were brief, and Wendy got right to the point. "Nothing much new to give you, Marcus. We found that Beck's wife is a principal investor in Cool Environment, Inc. It is strange that a high-end lawyer would be involved in a misting maintenance company. Sorry there's no more at this time, but we are continuing to dig."

"Fine. Interesting that the wife is involved too. Time to shift priorities. We'll be raiding the warehouse here at 0400 hours tomorrow, so be ready to arrest the Becks before that happens. They are involved, but I don't know to what degree. Pick them up if they start to run."

Wendy replied, "Todd said we probably don't have enough for an arrest warrant, so that could be a problem."

Dom raised his voice and interjected, "Wendy, my people will telex you what we have on Beck's warehouse. That should help solidify the warrant. It was enough for a search warrant here."

"Much appreciated, Dom. Anything else, Marcus?"

"No, we're good, Wendy. Thanks." Marcus hung up and turned to Dom with a smile. "So, do we get to wear red jackets and Mountie hats for the raid?"

Dom could not suppress a grin. "I think we'll go in a bit more subdued."

Andy turned to Sam. "Did your dinner contact give you more than that maintenance company's name? Like maybe an address for a local office here?"

Sam shook her head. "No. He said that he expected them to set up in a nearby motel for the three weeks, and if their home office gets more customers from their exposure here, then they might set up an office. He doubts anyone from the company will be here until the week before the opening ceremonies. They do have several tests scheduled for early June, but nothing else."

"Oh, well," Andy said with a shrug.

"Anything else, people?" Dom asked. Since there were no further changes, he instructed Marcus to have his team at the Montréal airport at 0200 hours.

102

A SECLUDED CORNER OF THE Ottawa International Airport became the staging area for the raid on the warehouse, which had been assigned the code name *Roundup*. Two Hueys adorned with RCMP markings and eight sedans—four with Ottawa Police Service (OPS) insignias and lights—were parked nearby.

Eight members of the assault team, including Marcus, Sam, and Bob, had arrived in the Hueys. Waiting for them were eight local officers: four from the OPS and four from the RCMP office. As the 0400 hour approached, the assault team went over the parameters one last time.

Inspector Dominic Barillari introduced Constable Sean McIlwaine of the OPS. "Sam, you and Bob will ride with McIlwaine and stay with him at all times. Understood?"

They both nodded and followed McIlwaine to his sedan. Sam leaned over to Bob and whispered, "Do we think fourteen officers to handle three security guys is overkill?"

Bob shrugged. "I'm only a dozer driver, and this is my first police raid, but that old line about safety in numbers comes to mind."

Sam chuckled. "I think it was the Confederate General Nathan Bedford Forrest who claimed his missions were successful because he was the 'fustest with the mostest.' So I like the three-to-one odds in our favor."

As they settled in McIlwaine's car, Sam replayed the assault plans in her mind. At 0355 hours, the power company, Hydro Ottawa, would cut the power to a four-block area around the warehouse. Bell Canada was to do the same for the phone service, leaving the warehouse isolated communication-wise, as well as dark. Right at 0400 hours, the two Hueys would take up overwatch at fifteen hundred feet, ready to follow any vehicles leaving the scene. Also at 0400, two of the OPS cars, with lights flashing, would work their way down the street under the pretext of checking buildings for problems.

One cruiser planned to pull into the warehouse gate insert and get the attention of the sentry on duty there. As he kept the sentry busy, Dom and Marcus would lead the assault team through a hole cut in the fence on the opposite side of the warehouse gate. Splitting up to cover all the exits from the warehouse, two other members of the team would move quietly to the gate and secure the guard. Opening the gate, two of the OPS cars, one including Sam and Bob, would enter the parking lot while the other two blocked the gate.

Two assault team officers would carry a special tool—Sam forgot the name—that could be used to literally rip open locked doors. Whether the door was locked or not, the bulk of the team would enter the front door of the warehouse and subdue the two guards. Then Sam could enter to help document the contraband they expected to find.

All of that looked great on the boards back at RCMP HQ, and sounded perfect as the team rehashed it again at the airport, but real life is never perfect. Prussian military strategist Helmuth von Moltke's comment that "No plan survives the first contact with the enemy" was true.

Marcus counted six private vehicles in the parking lot, indicating they would possibly be facing a few more security guards. Or perhaps Dom's desire to grab some of the higher-ups had actualized. Whatever the case, there might be more to find and secure as quickly as possible. And the ratio of good guys to bad started to shift in favor of the bad guys.

Seeing the OPS car at the gate—lights flashing and patrolmen motioning the guard to come out of the guardhouse—Dom ordered the team to move inside the already-cut fence. Per the plan, two RCMP officers quickly advanced to the gate and subdued the guard. Opening the gate, the designated vehicles entered and took their positions. The roll-up door area was covered as the rest of the team moved to the main door.

As they approached that main door, it opened and two men stepped out. Dom motioned those following him to flatten against the wall. A small emergency light above the door illuminated that one of them was an armed guard.

The other man was dressed only in trousers and shoes. Rubbing his hands over his face, he questioned the guard, "What the hell is going on?"

"Power outage at first," the guard answered, "but now I'm not sure. Best to get back inside."

As they turned to go in, Dom and Marcus stepped away from the wall, weapons drawn, and Dom announced, "Police. On your knees; hands on your head!"

The guard reached toward his weapon but hesitated when he saw the large dark bore of the Colt 1911 pointed toward his head. Marcus moved around to face the guard and said, "Not a wise move, ace. Who else is in there?"

Lowering his knees to the ground, the guard hesitated, but then he glanced between the frustration that Marcus exhibited and the nearness of the weapon. "There are three men from Chicago and two more guards."

"Good man," Marcus said. "And where will I find the guards?"

"I don't know."

Marcus gave a menacing stare. "Yea, you do. Think harder."

The guard sighed and replied, "One's in the office, first door on the left. The second is somewhere in the warehouse. No idea where. Really, I swear."

Dom motioned to one of the OPS men, who had been securing the prisoners with handcuffs. "Put these two in separate cars." Looking at Marcus, he continued, "Two of my men will take the office. You and I will find the roving guard. Okay?"

Marcus nodded. Dom pointed to two men and motioned them inside. Their stealth and speed was impressive as they moved into the building.

"We'll give them a moment, then start our search." Dom checked his watch.

"This should be fun. Try not to shoot me."

It wasn't surprising that the warehouse interior had battery-powered emergency lighting. It was subdued, providing enough light to safely move around without standing out, and leaving darkened areas where the assault team could vanish into the shadows. Bad news was, the bad guys could also move easily and hide.

Hearing steps heading their way, Dom moved into the darkness of the shelving on the left side as Marcus did the same on the right. The guard's flashlight slashed the subdued light in the aisle before him as he softly said, "Nick, where are you, man?"

Dom waited until the guard passed by, then he motioned to Marcus and stepped out behind the guard. "Police. On your knees, hands on your head, now!"

Moving faster than expected, the surprised guard spun around, drew his weapon, and fired. The lack of light and his jerking on the trigger in panic worked against him; the shot was intended for center mass, but ended up too far to the guard's left and hit Dom's right bicep. Dom fell to the floor, losing his weapon as his arm stopped working.

Marcus had been watching their backs in case another guard was following. He felt the bullet zip by his body, spun around, dropped to one knee and fired twice. The guard was pushed back several feet by the impact of the two 230-grain, .45 caliber slugs in his chest.

Even in the dim light, Marcus could see the surprise—that look of not understanding what had happened—cross the guard's face as he lost control of his limbs, dropped his weapon and flashlight, and sank to his knees before falling on his face. Marcus quickly retrieved the guard's weapon and checked him for a pulse. There was none.

Dom moaned as he tried to sit up. "Damn, this was a somewhat new jacket."

"What's your status?" Marcus asked as he moved from the dead guard to Dom.

"I'm hit in the right arm," Dom said. "Hurts some, but I'll live, since you stopped him from getting off a second shot."

"When I saw you down, I thought it was much worse," Marcus replied with concern.

Two of Dom's men came running to the scene. "We hear shots!" Andy yelled.

Marcus responded curtly, "Dom's been hit: flesh wound. Guard's dead. I'll get Dom to the office and check him out. You two check the rest of this place for other guards. Careful, this guy shot Dom without warning; his friends might do the same."

The guard from the office and the trio from Chicago had been relocated to the back seat of several OPS vehicles, leaving the office empty. As Dom and Marcus entered, the power came on, filling the room with light. Marcus pushed Dom onto the end of what looked to be a conference table.

Helping Dom out of his jacket as he sat on the table edge, Marcus saw the blood was already soaking his shirtsleeve. It was a small through-and-through wound. A jacketed 9mm round doesn't expand much unless it hits a bone, but Dom's arm was dumping blood at a rapid rate. Pulling out his handkerchief, Marcus said, "Hold this tight against the wound while I check for a first aid kit."

Marcus wasted a few precious minutes searching the office before Andy rushed in and said, "Place is clear, but I have people doing a double check. I called for an ambulance and the coroner. Here's a first aid kit from a squad car."

Through clenched teeth, Dom said, "Guess the adrenaline is wearing off 'cause this arm is starting to throb more. And I must have hit my head, I'm starting to feel fuzzy."

"Your arm wound's leaking pretty bad, and I don't see any blood or feel any lumps on your head, so I suspect you're getting lightheaded from blood loss and after effects of that adrenaline rush. That can be a real downer," Marcus said as he checked him over. He then grabbed Dom's arm and ordered, "Hold still."

Flipping open the knife pulled from his belt pouch, Marcus cut off the shirtsleeve at the shoulder. He grabbed a couple of gauze pads and, after pouring antibiotic on the wound, slapped the gauze in place and started to wrap the arm tight with tape.

"Are you a trained medic as well as investigator?" Dom asked through clenched teeth.

"No formal training beyond an ROTC first aid class, but too much experience in the field." Marcus pulled a bottle of ibuprofen from the kit and handed a couple to Dom. "This will take the edge off the pain."

Dom tried to get off the table but lost balance. Marcus pushed him into a prone position. "Andy, lift his legs and slide him further up on the table." Marcus folded Dom's jacket into a small square and placed it under his feet. "Lay still, Dom. This will help prevent shock."

Dom nodded and with an unsteady voice said, "Andy, Commander Colt is now in charge. He speaks with my voice. Understand?"

"Yes, sir."

The arrival of the medics precluded any further discussion as they pushed Andy and Marcus aside to check Dom's vitals. Marcus filled them in on what had happened and what aid he had given. They started an IV, hustled Dom onto a stretcher and out the door; he was on the way to the hospital in less than five minutes.

Marcus saw Bob and Sam standing at the door and motioned them inside. "You up to speed on what happened?"

Sam said, "We are. Dom going to be okay?" Seeing Marcus nod, she asked, "Okay for us to wander around and start documenting?"

"Yea. You know what drugs to look for, and there is one body that needs your photos. Shoot the entire area, but do not touch the body. Bob, get one of the OPS men to tape off the shooting area, then find and mark the locations for the shell casings. There should be three: two .45 and one nine-mil. I'll be with you two shortly."

After they left, Marcus looked hard at Andy and asked a question that sounded accusatory. "That 'speaks with my voice' sounds like a Mafia line from an old movie."

Andy shrugged as a slight smile crossed his face. "Dominic Barillari's parents came here from Palermo, Sicily in 1932 when Dom was two. They were not impressed with Mussolini and felt it was time to get out. Officially, the RCMP has no knowledge of Dom's father's history beyond him owning a fishing boat fleet there in the old country, but occasionally, especially in times of stress, Dom or his father will let something slip that hints at that type of upbringing. I ask that you please forget what you heard."

With a softer tone, Marcus said, "You sound more like a friend than a subordinate."

Andy again shrugged. "Dom went to high school with my older brother, David. When Canada decided to be a neutral player in the Vietnam conflict, David headed south in 1965 and joined your Marine Corps. Subsequently he became one of the 134-plus Canadians who died in Vietnam wearing the US uniform. Dom has filled in as my older brother since, so yes, I consider him family."

"Thanks for letting me know," Marcus solemnly said. "You know that blood loss makes people say strange things. Most of which are pure fantasies. Time to get back to work."

Andy smiled as he said in a voice filled with emotion, "Thank you, sir."

103

SSA Todd Burke shook his head as he studied the Quebec case board. He wasn't sure if he was frustrated or impressed with the situation. There were three boards set up in the agents' area: one for West Virginia, one for Chicago, and the latest one that was filling up quickly was for Quebec. Marcus was doing a good job of discovering, and speculating, on new scenarios. Todd hated to admit it, but Marcus's speculations were better than good.

Wendy had tacked up the latest bit of information on the Chicago board. Her wink and smile caused Todd to leave his desk and take a look.

Initially, Todd thought it was a boring read. The info had come from a complete FBI background check that Ken Santoro had gotten done in record time. Carol Anita Eckler, wife of Klaus Hermann Beck, was born on October 27, 1930 in San Diego, California, to Kenneth and Anita Eckler. Kenneth Eckler was a successful jeweler; he died of natural causes in 1967. Anita Eckler died of natural causes in 1970. Carol had no siblings and inherited a decent sum from her parents.

Then Todd saw what made Wendy smile. The law firm that the Southside Cardinals were trying to contact had been owned and operated by Anita Eckler for the last few years. Carol Beck was using part of her maiden name, and while it was not illegal, it did give off an air of impropriety. And further digging by the FBI found that a "Carol Eckler" was listed as the owner and manager of the misting equipment servicing company, Safety Monitoring LLC. Alarm bells started going off in Todd's mind: Carol had been busy.

"Carol sure has her fingers in many pies. Makes ya wonder if Claus is using multiple names for other activities," Todd mused.

Wendy nodded. "It would make sense. Ken said he would be digging into that scenario. But it forces the question why he didn't try to hide his involvement in Cool Environment, Inc."

"According to the records, Beck is only an investor. Could be Carol, as manager of Safety Monitoring, saw it as a good investment and pushed Claus to go for it. Perhaps Claus is clean and Carol is working with Quispe."

"At least Marcus has us watching both of them," Wendy said. "Can't wait for his call so I can tell him we have a couple more pieces of the puzzle. Just wish these were key pieces."

"Hell, they might be. We don't have a clear picture yet."

The phone on Todd's desk interrupted their discussion. "SSA Burke." He listened for a moment, then waved Wendy over as he pushed the speakerphone button. "I've got Wendy here on speakerphone."

Kelly Colt's voice was loud and clear. "Good morning to you both. Have ya heard from our wayward sailor yet this morning?"

Wendy laughed. "Nothing. He's probably enjoying an omelet right about now and putting off writing his ROI on the predawn raid. What do you have for us?"

"With the raid scheduled for this morning, I had hoped to hear some positives from him. Oh, well, I do have a few things. Manny Alvarez has decided to work with us since his attorney has yet to call him; he realized the big boss has cut him loose. We have a full statement that his boss in Chicago is Quispe, and he gave us names of the people they killed, and dump locations—at least as best he could recall—for the other bodies."

Todd interjected, "His high-end attorney is a lady who just so happens to be married to Claus Beck. She runs the firm under her maiden name, and she also owns the misting servicing company under another alias. We can use Alvarez's turning with the Cardinals we have in custody. Maybe that will get them talking. We will get you the particulars about her shortly, and they might help get more out of him."

Wendy asked, "Does Alvarez know where Quispe is hiding here in Chicago?"

"He claims he doesn't, but we'll keep pushing him," Kelly said. "With both Becks involved, I'll get Allen Chambers to use their names and aliases on Alvarez. If he knows them, then they're deeper involved."

"I'll telex their photos. He might know them by different names, at least the wife, since she is using at least three, so far," Todd said. "Ken's still digging to find aliases the husband might be using. And push Alvarez to see if he knows of any aliases used by Quispe."

"Can do. Anything else?" Kelly asked.

"Nothing I can think of, but I'll call as soon as we hear from Marcus," Wendy said.

"Thanks, Wendy. All for now," Kelly said before she hung up.

104

THE SUN HAD BEEN UP for a couple of hours when Marcus walked out of the warehouse. He grabbed a cup of coffee from the mobile canteen, often called the "roach coach" by naval personnel, but named *cantines* in Quebec. The RCMP had ordered it to be in place and covered the costs. Large teams of agents and tech personnel were on site, and quick access to food and drink would keep them happy and working. Marcus didn't care what they called the vehicle as long as the coffee was decent. And after the long stressful night, even a cup of GT's coffee would be considered decent. He needed caffeine.

"So, what ya thinkin' standing here all alone in the cold?" Sam asked as she grabbed a bottle of apple juice. She shook slightly from the chill in the air. "You look lost in thought."

Marcus stared at her for a moment as emotions churned. He often had trouble opening up to people, especially new acquaintances. Then he realized Sam was an old friend. He looked past the long blonde hair and saw the Samantha he knew from the wedding weekend some years ago: glowing brown hair curled up at her shoulders, framing a tanned face, a woman fully enjoying and absorbing her best friend's wedding. She was a friend he had shared time with, and one he trusted.

A painful frown crossed his face as he said, "Regrets over shooting the guard. Those feelings will pass eventually, at least the bulk of them, but I always think I've lost a piece of my soul when I kill someone."

Sam gently laid a hand on his arm and whispered in his ear, "Marcus, it is because you think that way that your soul is intact. You did what you had to do to save both your and Dom's life, not because you like it."

"Perhaps. Let's get back inside before you freeze." Changing the subject, Marcus headed to the warehouse. "Y'all about done with the documentation?"

"Between me and Bob, all my film—plus a few rolls courtesy of the RCMP—has been shot. Andy offered to have their lab process it quickly. They'll provide us with three sets of eight-by-ten prints. Saving the life of his boss put you in his 'good guy' column, big time!"

"Good. I assume two sets for me and one set for you?"

Sam nodded. "Yes, and I know … no publication without your specific approval, sir!" She gave a quick salute.

That made Marcus smile for the first time that morning. "Your following orders means I won't have to use the assassination rule."

Sam laughed as she said, "I never know when you're kidding."

Marcus held the door for her. "That's the plan."

"I'll keep that assassination rule out of the article."

That got a small laugh from Marcus.

Andy looked up from his notepad when they entered the office. He gestured to the older gent sitting at the conference table and said, "Marcus, the coroner has finished his investigation and is ready to take the body to the morgue. Uh, if that's all right by you. And we have completed the list of meds: some good and a lot bad, with the fake label you warned about. And a ton of the illegal drugs we expected to find before you arrived."

Marcus looked at the coroner. "Fine with me. I assume you found nothing out of order. And I will need a copy of your report."

"Of course, sir. I'll make sure Inspector Barillari has it soon, and you are correct: all is in order, and I have declared the shooting justified," the coroner said. "Excuse me, if there is nothing else, I need to get going."

Marcus waved the coroner toward the door and said, "So Andy, what are the inventory findings?"

"The illegal drugs run the gamut from marijuana to heroin. And the quantities are much more than Dom expected. As for your main concern, the four men from Chicago arrived yesterday afternoon in four different vehicles. In total, they brought eight five-gallon cans of your super anthrax, labeled as disinfectant for the misting systems. They used faked authorization letters from the IOC and entered at different locations to reduce suspicions. We found the cans hidden in a dark corner of one of the eighteen coolers they have here. They had installed a fake wall that hid the cans."

"I'm going to need one of those cans to take to Chicago as evidence. What else?"

Consulting his notepad again, Andy said, "We found a decent amount of real drugs and many empty shelves marked with the names of others I suspect were ordered to arrive closer to the opening day. So these guys were legit and evil at the same time."

"It's easier to hide an illegal activity within a respected one," Marcus said. "So what's the plan for all these drugs?"

Andy paused to gather his thoughts. "I have decided we keep everything here and set up a lab to test each one. The good meds we can then transfer to the IOC warehouse. Hate to admit it, but secure storage at the RCMP office is limited, and there is already a vast amount of security here, so we change the locks and set up RCMP guards. Assuming you concur."

"Yea, that should work. Oh, in addition to that five-gallon can, I need one case each of the anthrax that's labeled as something else. The rest you can keep here as further evidence," Marcus said. He paused and looked at Bob. "We'd be okay on weight with that?"

"Yes, sir. With the three of us and luggage, there's still around one thousand pounds that the *Songbird* can handle safely."

Marcus did a bit of a double take. "Three of us?"

Sam crossed her arms across her chest in defiant anticipation of an argument and coarsely said, "You don't think I'm staying here? The story goes where you go, and I will follow it." She took a deep breath and continued, "I will follow it and you to Chicago, West Virginia, D.C., or Timbuktu—whatever is necessary."

"I was planning to ask: happy you volunteered, Sam." Turning to Andy, Marcus asked, "Have you got everything in place here? If so, I think we should check on Dom."

105

THE RCMP ATMOSPHERE WAS HAPPY, almost giddy, as Sam, Andy, Bob, and Marcus came into the squad room. They were met with smiles and applause for a successful raid. Granted, Dom's shooting was a negative, but considering his light wound it didn't dampen the mood.

"Attention," Andy said as he raised his hands, then whistled. When silence finally occurred, he continued. "Before leaving Ottawa, I called the emergency room and spoke with Dom's doctor. He complimented our new friend, Commander Colt, on his nearly professional medical skills, and said Dom needed a few sutures and a new dressing. They gave him the standard tetanus shot and some antibiotics, then the OPS drove him home with his arm in a sling to rest for a few days. We stopped by his house just now and discovered the doc also gave him some pills to help him relax. Inspector Barillari sent his regards and thanks for a job 'well done' right before the pills kicked in. He's sleeping now."

The applause resumed, including a few laughs at the irony of a drug investigator using happy pills … albeit prescribed happy pills. And again, Andy had to calm the room.

"Before the ambulance hustled him off to the hospital, Dom ordered that Commander Colt take charge of Operation Roundup. While it might be unusual, I completely agree with the inspector's decision." Turning to Marcus, Andy asked, "So, Boss, what's the next step?"

"Thank you, Andy. I suspect Inspector Barillari will return sooner than expected, so you won't have to tolerate me for long. It has been a long, tiring day and fatigue often leads to mistakes. Mistakes we can't afford. Ladies and gentlemen, wrap up what you're doing right now, and we'll reconvene to do all that nasty paperwork at 0800 tomorrow. Working the weekend is never fun, but considering the importance of this case, I know you will understand the need for speed … rested, accurate speed."

Marcus was glad to hear the chuckles overpowered the moans about the weekend work. "Try to avoid the bars on your way home and follow Dom's lead and get plenty of sleep." That garnered a room of laughter as the Mounties returned to their desks to wrap up for the night.

Andy leaned toward Marcus and said, just loudly enough, "Well done, Sir."

"Thanks, Andy. Now can you lead us to a conference room with a speakerphone? I need to make a call to Chicago."

A few minutes later, Wendy's voice filled the room. "It's about time you called, Marcus, we were starting to worry. What's the status?"

"Sorry, but while the plan was a good one, the bad guys didn't play by the rules and that made for a long day. There were more guards and four visitors from Chicago, and one of our team caught a bullet: Inspector Dominic Barillari was shot in the right arm. He's okay, but he put me in charge of this operation."

"And was the anthrax there?"

"Yes, indeed. The Chicago boys each brought two five-gallon cans labeled as misting system disinfectant, and the coolers contained many cases of the stuff packaged at the lab you found. That mark on the label made them easy to find," Marcus said. "We'll bring some of the evidence to Chicago soon."

"Good. By the way, Ken came through with some interesting facts about Mrs. Beck." Wendy then laid out the multiple aliases she'd used and her involvement in the maintenance company.

Marcus smiled. "Perfect. We can use that with our interrogations tomorrow. Have the Becks made any moves?"

"No. Claus did a normal workday and just got back home. Carol hasn't left the house for three days now."

"Sure she's still there?" Marcus asked.

"Absolutely. We have photos of her on the back deck with a drink in her hand a few hours ago."

"Did you get the arrest warrants for the two?"

"Thanks to Dom we did. And we also have search warrants for all of their businesses and their house. Should we execute?"

"Yes, pull them in. We have hard evidence on Carol, and I think we have enough on Claus to push the illegal drug charge. Before you do, call Ken and get his DEA contact involved in both Chicago and with the RCMP. Between the FBI and the DEA, they can provide the extra manpower needed for the searches."

"Yes, sir."

Marcus thought for a moment, making sure he hadn't overlooked something. Finally he asked, "Anything else?"

"There is one thing. I know you designated me the central data retriever and disseminator, but I think you should call Kelly next with this update. I'll brief GT after I call Ken, so let her know she doesn't need to do that."

"As always, good thinking, Lieutenant. Thank you. Good night, Wendy."

With the call over, Marcus looked at Andy and asked, "Whom do you recommend to handle the interrogations?"

Andy bit his lower lip and said, "Dom is the best, but I'll have several selected by the morning."

"Fine. Do you think all the paperwork will be finished tomorrow?"

"Reports on the raid and the inventory will be done for sure. But unless the bad guys break on our first try, we might not have their full and final statements done until middle of next week. Or we might get lucky and they all turn tomorrow. Why?"

Marcus shrugged. "My two-day trip to Canada has grown to six days. I need to get back and start wrapping up things down south. I would like for us to leave on Sunday and head to Chicago with copies of all the reports."

Andy nodded. "Didn't think I'd ever say this about an American investigator, but I hate to see you go. If you ever decide to move north, I'm sure Dom has a Mountie hat just your size."

"I'll keep that option in my files, Andy. Thanks."

106

BOB FOLLOWED SAM TO HER room for a pre-dinner beer, leaving Marcus some privacy in their room. He asked them to hold off ordering dinner until he finished his call. As the tension of the raid faded, fatigue was taking over, so Marcus knew it would be a short night.

Marcus tried the sheriff's office first, and his instincts were accurate. Deputy Doc was still working the case. "Nice to hear your voice again, Sailor. I had hoped this call would've come sooner," Kelly said with a touch of sadness rather than anger.

"Sorry, Princess. Inspector Barillari caught a bullet in the raid, and he put me in charge of the operation as he left for the hospital. I've spent the day running the show, all while learning both the RCMP players and their procedures."

"You're okay, right? How bad's his wound?"

"I'm fine. Dom's wound is a through-and-through of his right bicep, with a jacketed nine-mil. He's home for a few days but will be as good as new soon," Marcus went on to give her all the details of the day's operation, and his plans for the next couple of days. After telling her that Wendy was updating GT, Marcus asked what the status was there.

Kelly replied, "Interesting things. Wendy sent photos of the Becks, and our lead suspect, Manny Alvarez, has identified Claus Hermann Beck as the man he called 'boss'—but he never knew his name. He was instructed to call him 'boss' or 'sir' and nothing else the couple of times he met him in Chicago before he sent him to West Virginia. He didn't remember ever seeing Carol Beck."

"That will help when Beck comes to trial. GT is still securing the Vampire's farm, right?"

"Yes, he is. Why?"

"Two thoughts on that place. First, Sam will be coming with us. She'll need to see the place for an article she's writing, one that I control editorially—I also control when it gets published. Second, it hit me that the Nazi hunter, Simon Wiesenthal, might find a few clues there. I'll run that by SecState to make sure it would be appropriate to invite him to visit," Marcus said. After a short pause, another thought hit. "And I bet the Smithsonian would love to get their hands on that collection."

"All good ideas, Marcus. With Elle and Sidney gone, there will be room for Sam at the mansion. And I'll run the Wiesenthal idea by Ken for the FBI's take; they might want first access. And I'm looking forward to meeting another of your old flames."

"GT technically has control of the farm, so the FBI cannot go running off with the collection, but they can shoot a lot of photos. Ditto for Wiesenthal," Marcus said.

"No comment on the old flame remark, Sailor?"

"Nothing to comment about, Princess. Besides, we both had lives before we met, but that's history, and the important part is now we are all each other needs."

"You do have a way with calming words. I agree. Hurry home because my back needs a good washing in a long hot shower."

They spent the next few minutes sharing normal husband-and-wife talk before the call ended and Marcus headed to meet his team for dinner.

Sam met Marcus at the door with a cold beer. "Thanks, Sam. That's a perfect way to start a relaxing evening. Ready to order dinner?"

After Sam placed the room service dinner order, the three settled down to discuss the day's events. And set up a plan for the morning.

"Andy should have all the photos ready by the morning, so I guess he and I will be spending the morning writing labels for them all," Sam said, nodding toward Bob. "I took a lot of notes as Bob shot the photos, so they'll be well documented."

Marcus nodded. "Good plan. I have my personal after-action report on the raid to write, then since Dom is out of service, I'll get with Andy and create the total operation analysis. Assuming that's the RCMP way."

Bob asked as he glanced at Sam, "Anything else for us to do?"

"Actually, yea there is. I want you both to write up what you saw during the raid. Sam, I know you've been documenting everything we've done this week, and will continue as we move back to Chicago, then Princeton, but I want this more of a technical piece rather than a novel, okay?"

Sam's face twisted in concern. "Eh, not my forte, but for you I'll give it a shot. My question is—why us, when so many professional crime fighters were there?"

Marcus chuckled. "A different perspective is always a good thing. Professionals often see what they expect to see or are so focused on one thing that small details are missed. And no matter how hard you focus on what you do see, small nuances can slip by. And include anything you didn't understand why it was being done, and if you saw something that might be done better."

"It sounds like fun, but my writing skills are on the *Dick and Jane* book level," Bob said. "Hope you grade on a curve."

"Sorry, no grades will be given. It is an experiment I've wanted to do at NIS. Always looking for ways to improve."

A gentle knock on the door announced the arrival of dinner. The dinner conversation and the short wind-down after centered on everything but the case. Sam enjoyed sharing her brother's passion for the Olympics, and Bob impressed everyone with his knowledge of Olympic boxing. He remembered it was a U.S. Navy man who fought for the USA in Munich but lost to a Cuban boxer. The conversation was a great escape from the stresses of the day.

107

MARCUS WAS SURPRISED TO SEE the squad room full at 0730 hours. He had set the start time for 0800, but was happy to see the team hard at work. Andy rushed to meet him at the door.

"Hope you don't mind, but everyone decided on their own to get an early start." A guilty look crossed Andy's face.

"I'm never one to squash enthusiasm," Marcus said as he gave Andy a pat on the back. "Sam and Bob need space to label the prints, right?"

"Yes, sir. I have all the photos on the conference table so they can get started."

"And I need a typewriter to do my after-action report. Point me to a spare one, please."

"You can use Dom's office, since he's resting at home. Follow me."

"Andy, does the RCMP have a specific standard for these reports?"

Andy laughed. "Every department is different. Rather than worrying about our standards, use your normal NIS format and that will be fine. I'll combine all the reports and do the final summary, which will need your approval as operation commander."

The morning was a blur of activity that morphed into the early afternoon too soon. To keep the team working at their desks, busy and happy, Andy ordered in trays of sandwiches. Marcus carried one and a cup of coffee to the conference room to check on the photos. He was happy to see that task was done. Five stacks of photos, two for RCMP, two for NIS, and one for Samantha Bigalow, rested at the end of the table while Sam and Bob devoured sandwiches at the other end.

"Welcome, Marcus. Pull up a chair," Sam said as she swallowed a bite. "Photos are done. Soon as we finish lunch, we'll get our sets packed and start our write-ups."

Marcus flipped through Sam's stack of photos as he finished his sandwich. Under Sam's guidance, Bob had done a good job with the camera. The labels on the back were professionally done. Marcus was impressed by his amateur team members and said so.

"Andy said he'd provide a cooler and dry ice for the evidence. I gave him the specs on the cargo space, so we should be good to go," Bob said. "And as soon as I finish my wimpy write-up, I'll get one of Andy's guys to run me out to the airport. Our late return from Ottawa did not give me time to top off the fluids and wind up the rubber bands. I'll make sure we're ready for a Sunday flight to Chicago."

Marcus gave him a thumbs-up. "Have you checked the weather?"

"I did, and there's good and bad news. A nasty thunderstorm is expected to arrive in Chicago late Sunday evening. High winds, dropping temps, and probably snow by Tuesday. If we get out of here no later than 1000 hours, we should have good weather from here to there and be in Chicago by 1400. Way ahead of the storm."

Marcus was lost in thought for a moment. "And how's the weather from Chicago to Princeton? Or from here to Princeton?"

Bob took a minute to frame his response. "The storm is coming from the Northwest, so from Chicago to Princeton we would be racing ahead of the storm … assuming it continues on a southeasterly flow. Here to Princeton would be a nice flight. What ya thinking?"

"Safety of the *Songbird* and logistics, actually. She would not be in a hangar when the storm hits Chicago. Then we might get snowed in, keeping us there longer than we need. Would you be safe to drop Sam, the evidence, and me off in Chicago, refuel, and fly home to Princeton? My gut is telling me that's the best option."

Bob let his disappointment show, but he said, "While I'd like to hang with you, this has been the best adventure I've had in a long time, I am at your orders, sir." There was no resentment in his voice as he continued, "I can safely make the trip to Princeton; it is about two hours' flight time.

And I can carry a copy of the report and photos with me so the sheriff can have them sooner."

"Okay, we'll do that. Sorry, Bob, but it's for the best. We need to be in the air at 0900 hours to give you more time in Chicago for the refueling and whatever pilot magic you do. I guess I'll need a day or two at NISO Great Lakes, so Sam and I will be there when the snow hits. As for us getting to Princeton, if flights are canceled due to the snow, we could rent a car. Or if the roads are a mess, take the train to Charleston and have one of GT's men pick us up. And as an added bonus, you'll be there with GT and Kelly to answer any questions about the photos or the report."

"You're putting a lot of trust in me, Marcus. But I'll do my best."

"I'm not worried, Lieutenant, I've seen you in action. Okay, y'all finish your lunch and write your reports. I'll be in Dom's office making a few phone calls. SecState has been more than patient, but I need to let him know the threat was real, and it has been eliminated. And letting Kelly and Wendy know our travel plans will help get us ground transportation. By the way, thanks for the great work on those photos."

108

"**ANDY, WE APPRECIATE THE RIDE,** but I could've left my Range Rover in long-term parking," Sam said as she gave Andy a quick hug.

"No need for you to waste money, Sam. The RCMP owes you all, and a ride is a small repayment. Let me know when you will be returning, and one of our men will pick you up," Andy said.

Marcus finished helping Bob stow their luggage and joined Andy and Sam. "Staff Sergeant Fortier, it has been a true pleasure working with you. If ever NIS can be of service to the RCMP, give me a call."

Before Andy could respond, a squad car with lights flashing approached. They were surprised to see Dom struggle to get out of the front passenger seat; his right arm was tight in a sling. He tried to hide the pain, but failed.

He stopped in front of Marcus and said, "I couldn't let you leave without giving you the highest regards of the RCMP and the IOC, and my personal thanks for saving my life. I am in your debt, Commander. Andy has kept me informed of your plans, and while I understand the need to get back to the states, I'm sorry to see you go. Take care, my friend Marcus."

"Glad I could help, Dom," Marcus said with respect. "I pray your wound heals quickly."

Dom continued, "Samantha. Bob. You also provided a great service to the RCMP and the IOC. We're grateful for your assistance."

"I have to admit it was different from what I expected. Especially the part where you got shot," Sam said. "Hope your healing goes quickly."

"Fortunately, it doesn't happen every day. Now I'll return home to continue my recuperation, and you good people need to get on your way. Although I do hate to see you go. *Bon voyage, mes amis.*" Unexpectedly, Dom pulled Marcus into a one-arm hug and nodded his head to the side. Then he briskly walked to his car.

Marcus yelled after him, "I'll keep in touch, my friend!"

Andy shook hands as he said his goodbyes. When he got to Marcus, he said, "Dom is not usually that emotional—he must really like you. Again, thank you."

"Until the next time, Andy." Marcus threw him a salute before climbing on the *Songbird*'s wing.

Although the airport looked calm, they had a ten-minute wait in line before they could take off. Once airborne, their flight was smooth in the clear blue November sky. Marcus took off his headset and leaned back to think. He looked as though he was getting some rest. Sam had requested the front seat, and she carried on a constant conversation with Bob about the airplane and flying in general.

Marcus ran the case through his mind as he had done many times in the past. The pieces he had fit nicely together, but there were still a number of holes. Important holes like … where the hell was Quispe hiding? What had Claus Beck been doing since 1955? And Mrs. Beck was another complicated can of worms. But Chicago was the key place, the Mount Olympus of the evil empire where the ultimate control existed. Ottawa and Princeton were minor players when compared to Chicago.

The Becks had to be high in the chain of command. As Marcus plotted a hierarchy chart in his mind, he placed Quispe at the top. On the next level down, he added Bruno Perez and Beck. He wasn't sure if that Beck should be Claus or Carol, but he penciled in Claus due to the matching MBA timing with Quispe. Then the more he considered the issues, he added Carol Beck to the same level as her husband. She was a busy lady, keeping up with all those aliases.

The Southside Cardinals were another question mark. Like most street gangs, they believed they were in charge of themselves, but in reality there was always a "Mr. Big" who controlled the gang. Could their "Mr. Big" be Quispe? Or did Claus dirty his hands dealing with a gang?

Marcus redrew the chart in his mind. This time, he placed Quispe and Perez on the same level at the top. It made more sense to consider them fifty/fifty partners. Below them, he added Claus Beck with Positive Quest Medicals and Cool Environment, Inc. under his control. Next to him, Marcus placed Carol Beck as controlling Safety Monitoring LLC.

And again, the Southside Cardinals didn't have a logical spot. Neither of the Becks would be issuing orders directly to individual members of the gang. They were too high on the social ladder to deal with gangs. The "Mr. Big" for the gang needed to be on the same authority level as the Becks, or did he? What if "Mr. Big" reported to both Becks, providing manpower where needed? He would be someone who could associate with the society types like the Becks, yet get down and dirty with the gangs. Marcus then remembered they had the perfect suspect already in custody; Chief Hospital Corpsman Hugo Diaz.

As a Navy chief petty officer, he carried the respect of his rate and time in service. Because of that, he could socialize with the society types and even be invited to play golf with the likes of the Becks. And as many senior Navy men do, he might be involved with the various youth programs in hopes of keeping good boys from going bad. So he was the logical interface between the two levels. If Claus needed men to work the drug warehouse, he called Diaz, who pulled in a few Cardinals. That puzzle piece fit.

Happy with his suppositions, Marcus erased the mental chart and replaced it with images of Kelly snuggled next to him on a sofa in the sanctuary. He drifted off into a restful sleep.

109

LT WENDY JAMES LEANED AGAINST her gray Navy-issue Plymouth Fury with her arms crossed across her chest. Her face lit up seeing Marcus wave from the back seat of the Cessna. While she enjoyed running her own cases at NIS, she missed working closely with Marcus, as she had done during and right after her training. Now, with a few years of experience, she was a lead agent and responsible for training new people as he had trained her.

Sam was the first out of the aircraft, and she waved at Wendy. Marcus followed and met Wendy as she approached the plane. "Welcome to Chi-town, Commander. I hope you've brought gifts from Canada in the form of a solved case."

"Will you settle for a few more puzzle pieces?" Marcus asked.

"Absolutely!" Wendy turned to Sam. "Wendy James, Miss Bigalow. Thanks for keeping an eye on Marcus for me."

Sam laughed. "He does need a keeper at times, right? Call me Sam and help me get the baggage unloaded so Bob can get out of here before the storm arrives."

"I checked the weather before I drove out here, and the storm is still about five hours out. No panic."

With a quizzical look, Sam asked, "If you don't mind my asking, how did you get permission to drive out here? I thought ramp access was tightly restricted due to all the hijackings."

It was Wendy's turn to laugh. "My NIS credentials and a mention of bio-hazard materials being transported made their decision easy. They would rather I load the stuff into the trunk here than tote it through the crowded building." That garnered laughs from both Sam and Marcus.

The baggage and evidence was quickly transferred to the Fury. Leaving Bob to top off the *Songbird*'s tanks and wing his way home to West Virginia, Wendy drove them to the NISO Great Lakes office.

As she pulled out of the airport property, Wendy asked, "Marcus, the drug warehouse is nearby. Would you like to do a walk-through since we're in the area? And we can leave the drug evidence there since it is under tight control of the Shore Patrol, and NIS has the only keys to the coolers."

"Might as well. Doubt that you or Todd missed anything, but it is always nice to actually see a crime scene," Marcus said.

"Can I shoot a few photos there?" Sam asked.

Marcus chuckled. "As long as you remember the rule."

"Oh, no," Wendy said. "He's threatening the assassination rule again? Well, since you're a reporter, Sam, it's appropriate and might be needed."

Sam shook her head. "You sailors and your weird sense of humor."

"Uh, Sam … it's not a joke," Wendy said.

The detour to the warehouse was silent as Sam wondered if it was a serious option. *Sailors have a wicked sense of humor, but still.*

Marcus saw that Todd and Wendy had set up the proper security over the site. Security cameras were in place inside and out, and roving patrols covered all access points. From the looks of the workbench components stacked against an empty wall, they anticipated setting up more work areas soon. That tied in with the increase of dead bodies in West Virginia, needed to brew more anthrax.

In addition to general area photos and shots of the packing equipment, Sam shot close-ups of the label machine that had been the indicator for contaminated drugs. She remembered reading an article about how it's often the little things that trip up the bad guys. *"Stopped by a Smudge" would be a good lead for the article*, she thought.

Their warehouse visit lasted about an hour, then Wendy drove on toward NISO Great Lakes office.

"Marcus, I reserved two rooms at the Navy Lodge for four nights. We can always extend that time, if needed. Todd promised to have another vehicle at the office for you to use," Wendy said as she weaved through the traffic heading north.

Sam asked, "The Navy has lodges?"

"Nothing like the splendor you have in Canada. Think of it as a basic Holiday Inn motel built on a Navy base. It's used for visiting low-level dignitaries, sailors' families, and transient folks like us who need a place to crash short term," Marcus explained. "It's more convenient than getting us into the transient BOQ."

Sam looked confused. "BOQ?"

"Bachelor Officers Quarters. Think of that as barracks for officers who need temporary quarters," Wendy said. "And Todd has issued you a set of temporary NIS credentials to eliminate any access issues, Sam."

"Wendy, has Chief Diaz had anything else to say?" Marcus asked.

"Nothing yet, and his JAG counsel has advised him to remain quiet. The Cardinals we picked up at the warehouse are getting antsy, so we might get a break there."

"Do you remember where the chief grew up?" Marcus asked.

"South side of Chicago. His family came here from Argentina after Juan Peron became president. They didn't like his wife Eva for some reason and got the 'hell out of Dodge.' All are naturalized citizens, and except for the chief, none have been on the wrong side of the law. Why?"

"I'll have to show you as soon as you get me to a clean white board. Is Todd working today?"

"No. Sorry, Marcus. He spent the entire day interrogating the Becks and felt he needed some free time to clear his mind. I agreed. I can call him in if you like," Wendy suggested.

Marcus considered that. "Let him have the day off; the next few are going to be hectic. Did he get anything from them?"

Wendy shook her head. "About as much silence as Diaz puts out. The DEA and FBI both want a crack at them, but gave us a few days to hit them first, since we broke the case."

The wind was picking up as they entered the NISO office right before 1600 hours. Marcus had Wendy take them to the Navy Lodge first to unload the luggage. With the storm approaching, he didn't want to unload in the rain. Another small delay resulted from stopping at the officers' club to pick up carryout burgers; breakfast in Canada had been many hours ago.

The three corkboards, filled with cards and photos, were set up in the conference room. Marcus did a slow walk-around, checking each board as he munched on a cheeseburger. Wendy secured a clean whiteboard from an office down the hall and handed Marcus several markers. "Okay, boss. I'm ready to be impressed."

That got a chuckle from Sam, who was surprised by the amount of information the boards held.

"Oh, ye of little faith. Hold your questions, please, while the artist works," Marcus quipped, and started to draw the hierarchy chart. As more boxes were added, and names and titles dropped in, Wendy moved closer to the board, mumbling incoherent comments as her accounting logic followed the management flow. Marcus intentionally left one box without a person's name.

"I can see it. Using your supposition from the other day, Quispe and Perez are equal partners using the same methods and supply chain to satisfy their individual goals: Quispe sells more drugs and Perez kills more Jews and Americans. Under them, Claus Beck runs Positive Quest Medicals, running drugs in America and Canada for Quispe, and he also controls Cool Environment, Inc., helping Perez deliver death in Canada. His wife, Carol Beck, operates Safety Monitoring LLC, assisting with the delivery of death at the Olympics, and she manages her law firm on that same level."

Marcus smiled and nodded.

Wendy continued, "Also on this second level is the head of the Southside Cardinals. When Claus or Carol need more workers, they call that person, who provides trusted people from the gang. The gang members know they either do the job right or die. And when any of the gang gets in trouble, the gang boss calls on Carol's legal team for help. And I'll wager that gang boss is our Chief Diaz. Did I miss anything?"

Marcus started drawing dotted lines to show the connections Wendy had vocalized. "Nope, I think you broke the code. Now we've got to get one of these bastards to talk."

"That's not looking good without a lucky break."

A strange look covered Marcus's face as he stared at the board for a minute or two. Then he walked to the other side of the room to contemplate the chart from afar. Biting his lower lip, he took a deep breath and let it go slowly. "In my mind's eye, this hierarchy chart looked realistic, but seeing it in ink, something looks off."

"Which part?" Wendy asked.

Marcus moved to the board, where he tapped on a box several times. "Beck. Beck is the problem. Claus Beck is a ghost from 1955 until a year or so ago, when he is suddenly CEO of this new startup company, Positive Quest Medicals."

"Ken's still working on that missing time. Maybe he'll call tomorrow."

"I can't help but wonder if Beck was in Bolivia with Quispe during that gap."

110

"I DIDN'T EXPECT TO SEE you in here so early, Kelly. Anything wrong?" GT asked when he saw Kelly Colt and Rick Gardener studying the boards in the conference room. He had decided to arrive at 0630 for an earlier start, expecting to be alone save for the duty deputy. Bob Ledder had delivered the packages of reports and photos late the previous afternoon after securing the *Songbird* in her airport hangar. GT made the hard decision to let the data sit until the morning. Fresh data deserved fresh eyes.

Kelly's smile kicked up to the left. "Nothing but the excitement of getting the case wrapped up. I have patients back in D.C., and I'm hoping this is the key to getting out of here." She laid her hands on the packages. "Sorry, I love you guys, but life in D.C. is calling.

"Hate to see y'all leave, but I get it. I didn't realize how much I missed Marcus," GT said as he changed the subject. "I asked Bob to join us at 0900 hours. He looked worn out, so a couple extra hours of sleep are deserved. That'll give us a chance to read everything before he gets here. Let's get started."

A steady flow of coffee and donuts sustained the three as they read the reports and studied the photos.

Bob Ledder arrived precisely at 0900 hours looking more rested. He sipped coffee while waiting for them to finish.

GT was impressed by the thoroughness of the RCMP reports. He was further impressed by the action Marcus had taken the day of the raid, and said so.

Kelly shook her head. "Try not to praise Marcus on taking out that guard. He knows he had to do it, but it weighs on his mind. He won't tell you—he rarely talks to me about it—but this one makes eleven kills since I met him in 1971. I don't know the number from the first three years he was with NIS. Nor the number wounded. No notches are carved on his Colt 1911 grips."

GT's face couldn't hide his shock, which morphed into sadness. "I didn't know, Kelly. All those medals don't come cheap, do they?"

Bob said, "Marcus was sleeping during the flight, and Sam told me he mentioned he felt he lost a piece of his soul every time he shot someone. She told him it was because of his concerns that his soul was intact. It might have helped."

Kelly smiled. "I'm not surprised he confided in her—after all, they are old friends. I'm glad he did. Makes me like her more and more. That's the same thing I tell him when he starts to get melancholy about it all."

"No jealousy?" GT asked.

Kelly gave him a look.

"Okay. Enough said about the forbidden subject. Back to work, Kelly."

When GT finished looking at the photos, he said, "Nice work, Bob. I didn't know you were a photographer."

"I wasn't until Sam gave me a crash course. Since the raid on the warehouse is well documented by the RCMP officers, Marcus asked that I give you a brief overview of what all we—Marcus, Sam, and me—discovered prior to the raid. I know Marcus included reports on all of that, but he wanted me to tell you anyway," Bob said.

Kelly nodded. "Marcus believes getting observations from everyone is important. And often, verbal reports include things not included in the written version, as memories are stimulated by conversation. So tell us what mischief my guy got you into up there."

Bob delivered a fairly accurate report off the cuff; it was nearly identical to the written version Marcus had included in the data package. He wrapped it up by saying, "And it was wild watching Marcus in action. He tied together things that Sam and I didn't even see. Most impressive. Makes me want to stay on active duty and transfer to NIS."

Rick smiled as he said, "He impressed me the same way a couple of years ago in Italy when I was a simple Marine corporal. That's why I'm in NIS today. He has that effect on people."

"Thanks, Bob. Good review. Okay, we have more information, so time to update the boards," GT said. "And get more coffee."

Norma knocked on the door casing to get attention. "Sheriff, this telex addressed to our missing Deputy Colt arrived." She entered and passed the papers to GT.

"Thanks, Norma." GT read the two sheets of paper in record time, then muttered, "Son of a bitch."

"What?" Kelly asked.

"The military attaché at our embassy in La Paz has finally responded to Marcus's request for background on Perez and associates. One of his pals happened to be Rodrigo Quispe."

"So Marcus's speculation was right on," Kelly said.

"Indeed. And here's the kicker: local law enforcement had been deceived. The photo of Quispe they passed to the DEA was actually one of his winery workers, who had been killed in an accident years ago. They said they didn't have any more photos that might be Quispe. To the attaché, that smelled of a payoff or two. He called in a favor from a friend in the Bolivian Army, and we now have a photo of the real Quispe. Granted, it's only one, and at least ten years old, but better than nothing."

GT slid the photo across the conference table. The face of the man in his early to middle twenties looked more European than Hispanic, but that's common, as many Europeans moved to South America when Hitler took over Germany. He looked familiar and had that every-fellow look about him. He could face a crowd standing on a soapbox waving a dead chicken and never be remembered by anyone.

Rick asked, "Did he find any other associates or relatives of Perez?"

"Relatives, no. Perez was the last of a long line of evil. Thank God for that! But our boy, Manny Alvarez, is the son of one of Perez's nurses from his days in Bolivia. That's how he got to the USA working for Perez. Another solid link," GT said.

"We need to get this to Marcus ASAP," Kelly said as she handed the telex to Rick. "This is the break we needed!"

"Norma can telex it to Wendy while we grab some lunch," GT announced as he motioned them out the door for a quick walk down the street.

Pansy was at her standard position behind the counter, supervising her bustling domain, when they entered the café. "Hello, GT. Usual table, hun?"

GT nodded and headed to the kitchen door. Pansy hustled to catch up and give Kelly a quick hug. "When's Marcus coming home?"

It warmed Kelly's heart to hear that. Thinking of Princeton as *home* was a different, but especially nice feeling. Being a Navy brat, home was always her dad's current duty station, and she was never there long enough to feel settled or build lasting friendships. "In a day or so, I think. He's in Chicago now."

Pansy looked concerned. "Have you been watching the news?"

"No, why?"

"Hun, a major storm hit Chicago last night. Lots of rain with winds over seventy miles an hour. There were some tornadoes in the area too."

Bob said, "Marcus knew about the storm. That's why he sent me home yesterday—so the *Songbird* would be safe."

"Don't worry, Pansy. He's actually a bit north of Chicago at a Navy base called Great Lakes. He should be all right. I'll call him after lunch and give you an update."

Pansy sighed. "I'll be saying a few prayers."

III

NISO GREAT LAKES, GREAT LAKES, ILLINOIS
LATE MONDAY MORNING
10 NOVEMBER 1975

SSA Todd Burke rushed into the conference room where Wendy and Marcus were checking cards on the boards. Sam was watching and listening intently as they tossed theories back and forth on the best way to break the Becks. The SSA's arrival stopped their discussion.

Todd tried to hide his guilty look as he said, "Sorry I'm late. They say bad things come in threes. After spilling coffee on my dress shirt as I was heading out the door, I lost time changing, and then I found a flat tire. When I finally got that changed, I required yet another clean shirt. Can't wait to see what number three in bad things will be. All that aside, it is good to see you, Marcus."

"You haven't met Sam Bigalow from Garrett Publishing, Todd. She's here gathering data for an article about tardy government employees and their wimpy excuses," Marcus said with a straight face.

Wendy couldn't contain a laugh at Todd's expression.

"Good to see you again, Todd. It's been too long," Marcus said as he shook hands. "I appreciate all your help on this case."

Todd nodded. "It's been an interesting one, that's for sure. What news do we have?"

"Marcus outlined the organization based on what we've discovered, but he thinks something is still amiss. What's your take on the chart?" Wendy asked.

Todd approached the board and folded his arms across his chest in silence. "I think you're right on with Diaz being the Cardinals' contact. Makes sense. I don't see any problems."

Marcus approached and again tapped the Mr. Beck box. "There is something nagging at me. Sorry, nothing firm or logical to base it on, but one of those gut feelings. He is more than we know or expect."

Todd shrugged. "Okay, we go with that. What's the next step? You want a shot at him?"

"Not yet. Let them both stew a bit more while I think about this freaking chart," Marcus said, frustration showing.

"Is a mere civilian allowed to offer a suggestion?" Sam asked.

"Samantha, you are far from a mere civilian. What's on your mind?" Marcus said with a slight smile.

Sam noticed Marcus used her full name, which made her wonder if there was a double meaning to that "far from" comment. She shook it off and approached the board, pointing to the top line. "What happens when you put Mr. Beck up here with Perez and Quispe? He might be an equal partner in this evil scheme. Ditto for the wife, since the female is usually the deadlier of the species."

Marcus stared for what seemed a long time, but it was only a few seconds. "That would help explain why he has been missing during that 1955 to 1974 time period. He was living in Bolivia with Quispe and working on the evil plan with Perez. Perhaps? Wendy, what ya think?"

Wendy shrugged. "Maybe. Possible. Probable. Hard to say without more information, but I agree with your theory that it would explain his dark period. We need more info, damn it!"

Marcus backed away from the white board and paced the opposite side of the room. Wendy, who'd seen this before, motioned for the others to keep quiet and try to ignore him. She went for fresh coffee while he paced. Sam joined her.

"Does he do that a lot?" Sam asked as she stirred the sugar and cream into her coffee.

Wendy chuckled. "Only when he believes the fate of the world is resting on his shoulders. Marcus thinks in a different dimension than the rest of us mortals. Best to leave him be for a bit."

"You care for him, don't you?" Sam asked. "I saw your smile at the airport … and it carried emotions."

Wendy bit her lip and paused before saying, with more than a touch of threat in her voice, "Honestly, I love him. I have since our first case together, where he saved my life. But never physically and nothing spoken, and I will eliminate anyone who tries to get between him and Kelly. Do. You. Understand. Me?"

Sam couldn't hold back a smile. "Wendy, I had my chance with Marcus nearly ten years ago and I blew it. I hadn't seen him since, but after the last week, I realize I also love him, and will be happy to help you eliminate anyone who tries to mess with his marriage. I look forward to meeting Kelly soon."

"Glad we are on the same page, Sam," Wendy said. "Less bloodshed that way."

"Well, pour him a fresh cup and let's see what he has figured out, eh?"

Wendy passed the fresh cup of coffee to Marcus. He nodded his thanks and continued the pacing.

SA Rodney Carth came into the conference room waving a few sheets of paper. "Sorry for the interruption, but we got this from Princeton." He handed the papers to Todd and left.

SSA Todd Burke spent less than a minute reading over the new data before a smile crossed his face. "Based on this, Marcus, you can stop your pacing." He handed the papers over.

It took only a few moments for Marcus to read the telex and study the photo. He snorted and said under his breath, "That son of a bitch."

Rushing to the white board, Marcus grabbed a marker and nearly yelled as he wrote, "We have Rodrigo Quispe in custody!"

"What the hell?" Wendy gasped.

After skimming the rest of the report from GT's office, Marcus gave more detail. "My contact in our embassy in Bolivia did some digging, and discovered the photo DEA provided of Quispe was not him, but a dead winery worker. Here is an old photo of Quispe. Does he look familiar?"

"Well, I'll be," Wendy said. "That's Beck. A few years younger, but still Beck."

Marcus laughed. "And now we know where Beck has been hiding. Hiding in plain sight as Quispe."

112

AFTER REALIZING BECK WAS ACTUALLY the drug kingpin Quispe, Marcus asked to be left alone for a bit. His expression was stoic as he watched them leave for lunch. When Wendy promised to bring him a burger, Marcus gave a short nod, lost in thought.

When they returned over an hour later, they saw a different expression. Marcus sat at the head of the table with his coffee and smiled as he typed madly on an IBM Selectric he confiscated from the front office. A small stack of paper was face down beside the typewriter as yet another sheet zipped through the machine. He filled several more before acknowledging their arrival.

"Welcome back. Todd, burn three copies of this report, then I want you, Sam, and Wendy to proof it. Thanks for the burger." Marcus grabbed the burger bag and left for the breakroom.

"Okay," Todd said with apprehension to the closing conference room door.

Wendy grinned. "He's on the cusp of making a big decision. I've seen this a couple of times before. Well, get the copies done, Todd. We have our orders!"

Sam finished reading the report and made a couple of grammar corrections. They might not have been needed, since she was not familiar with military phraseology, but from an investigative reporter's viewpoint, they were. She was amazed that so much had happened, and that while Marcus had shared some of the pre-Canada happenings, he'd barely scratched the surface. This case was exciting and scary at the same time.

"He didn't miss anything, as far as I can tell," Todd said as he laid the report on the table. Ever thorough, Marcus had given all the players and agencies the credit they deserved for the parts they played.

"In true Colt tradition, it's complete and concise," Wendy added.

Sam asked, "So what now?"

Before anyone could answer, Marcus entered the conference room and, walking around the conference table, asked, "So, what did I overlook?"

The three doing the proofing gave negative responses.

"Okay. Todd, can you get someone to get on the Teletype and convert this to an ROI?"

"Certainly," Todd said as he carried his copy out of the room.

"May I ask a question?" Sam asked.

"Of course."

"What now?"

Before Marcus could answer, Todd returned and took a seat. He nodded to Marcus that the task was underway.

"Todd, when this meeting is over, I need you to call the DEA and the FBI. Ask them to get here as soon as possible for an important case update. Just tell them we have figured it all out."

Again, Todd nodded.

Marcus glanced at the overhead for focus, then said, "For Sam's sake, I need to say a few things." He sat on the edge of the table and looked down at Sam. "The Department of Defense has a fairly strict set of written rules. And the Navy Department has a set that applies to the Navy, and NIS has a set that applies to us agents. We have to obey all three levels at all times. And as the director of NIS Internal Affairs, I also have a set that my people and I work under. I won't bore you with all of them, but two that are applicable here are—first, get the best people to do the job, and second, know your limitations. In most cases, those two rules work together because when you know your limitations, you know when to call in people who have more knowledge and/or resources. With me, so far?"

Sam nodded.

Marcus continued. "As you read in that Report of Investigation, I was tasked with helping the Mercer County Sheriff find a killer. He was found, and in doing so, we uncovered hints to this terrorist threat; I pursued that hint, discovering it was a fact and tied to international drug running."

Marcus noted Wendy's enlightened nod; she had figured out where he was going.

"So, it is time for NIS and the Mercer County Sheriff's office to pass what we have discovered to the DEA and the FBI. They have the resources and a lot more personnel trained to handle what we've uncovered. Questions?"

"What about Diaz and the other enlisted men we have picked up?" Todd asked.

"Work with our sister agencies for jurisdiction. I suspect they'll pass them to JAG for prosecution after they bleed them dry of information," Marcus said.

"Hate to admit it—and while your logic is perfect—I feel a bit let down," Todd said.

Marcus laughed. "Melancholy comes with the job, Supervising Special Agent Burke. It's there when we fail and sometimes even when we succeed."

"And I hate to tell you, but by passing the case to them, the FBI and DEA will hog all the credit," Sam said.

Again, Marcus laughed. "Samantha, Samantha, Samantha. You're not here just because of your beautiful face. On the table before you is a complete report to date on this case that any journalist would kill for. Such classified documents are numbered and tightly controlled, but since this is just a draft, and SSA Burke has not had time to properly set up the control log, no one will know if a copy is missing. And as we discussed about you writing my life's story, I always have editorial and release date control on this, right?"

"Of course, Commander," Sam purred as her copy slid off the table onto her lap.

"Wendy, are all your reports up to date?" Marcus asked.

"Yes, sir."

"Anything else pending?"

Wendy shook her head.

"I suspect our meeting shortly with the alphabet agencies will eat up the rest of the day. Plan on staying here through tomorrow in case they need more from NISHQ, then head back to D.C.," Marcus ordered. "All right with you, Todd?"

"Yes, sir."

"Todd, have your secretary get tickets for Sam and me for tomorrow morning from here to Kanawha Airport in Charleston, or Raleigh County Airport at Beaver; preferably the latter. Have her also set up a rental car in Sam's name for a week."

"What am I going to be doing in West Virginia for a week?" Sam asked.

"Investigating a story you will not believe," Marcus said as the grin covered his face.

Sam smirked. "Hell, after this one, my level of doubt about everything has greatly been reduced."

Answering her with a wink, Marcus said, "Todd, please call our friends in for the meeting, and then send that ROI to NISHQ, NISRA Charleston, and the Mercer County Sheriff's Office. Include SecDef and SecState in the distribution. Guess we'll need a few more copies of the report made for our guests. And set up the document control log, please, before something goes missing." Marcus augmented the last part with a grin and bouncing eyebrows.

113

GETTING OUT OF CHICAGO WAS bumpy due to the lingering nasty weather. News reports on the airport television focused on a missing ore freighter. The SS Edmund Fitzgerald, at over seven hundred feet long, was one of the largest ships on Lake Superior. She had radioed problems during the near hurricane-force winds and thirty-five-foot waves, and was now presumed lost with all hands. Little other news was covered.

Sam and Marcus caught a United flight that morning out of Midway to Pittsburgh. From there, they flew an Allegheny Airlines puddle jumper down to the airport a few miles outside of Beckley. The skies over West Virginia were clear and blue, resulting in a nice flight. A 1975 Ford LTD sedan in Ivy Green, with only five thousand or so miles on the odometer, was waiting at the rental car stand. "Damn, this thing is a tank compared to my little Range Rover," Sam commented as she drove south to Princeton. "It's a lot smoother ride—I must admit it is sweet."

Kelly was constantly looking out the war room window at the parking lot; Marcus was due any time now, and she felt the butterflies of anticipation. It had been a long eight days and lonely nights. GT had kidded about putting a chair outside the parking lot door for her convenience. She ignored him.

A green LTD pulled into the lot just as GT stepped out for some fresh air, and Marcus climbed out of the passenger seat. Kelly saw GT hurry up to him, slapping him on the back. She also watched Sam shake hands with GT as the trio headed toward the door. A small twinge of jealousy briefly came over her, seeing Sam smile as she punched Marcus in the shoulder about something he'd said. But it passed quickly when she remembered their old friendship.

Seeing Kelly at the war room door, Marcus rushed to her side, pulling her into the room and closing the door. In the quiet of the room, their embrace lasted an untold amount of time. Kelly and Marcus were left alone as GT introduced Sam to the rest of his people.

A gentle kiss calmed her butterflies but kindled a burning desire for more. "Sailor, I think you need a shower," Kelly whispered.

"You, too, but it has to wait until tonight," Marcus said as he kissed her forehead and stroked her back. "Think you can control yourself until then?"

"I'll try, but no guarantees. Now introduce me to your newest harem member."

They both laughed at the inside joke. Right after Kelly and Marcus met, Doc had commented on all the women that seemed to hang around Marcus. Doc asked if he was starting a harem, and that became a continuing joke with Kelly, Doc, and Marcus.

The war room table was filled with the principal investigators, most of them GT's people. The others joining the case review were FBI Supervisory Special Agent Ken Santoro, who'd driven down from Beckley at GT's request, Wallace Simpson, who was still in Princeton documenting his finds, and *Princeton Bugle* editor-in-chief Jerry Masterman, who Marcus had invited.

The afternoon passed quickly as everyone hashed out the new findings in the case. They all saw the logic of turning it over to the alphabet agencies, and Sam added that she was sure the Mercer County and NIS folks would get their due credit. "Right, Jerry?" she asked. He eagerly nodded.

Marcus added, "GT, as soon as we hear from NISO Great Lakes that all is well with the case transfer, probably tomorrow, you can call the governor and let him know the West Virginia side of the case is closed. Mention that Samantha Bigalow—a Pulitzer Prize-winning investigative reporter—is here from Garrett Publishing, and I suspect he will make time for a visit to thank you personally and hopefully release me from this TAD assignment. Get with Todd Burke about how much of the Chicago/

Canada issues the alphabet agencies want released. Nothing else I can do around here after I spend a day or so wrapping up all the reports."

"Sounds like a plan," GT said.

"I take it this is my chance to bid you all adieu and head back to my life in Beckley chasing bears," Simpson Wallace said as he started to stand.

Marcus held up a hand to stop Simpson. "Not so fast, bear guy. You have one more assignment before you vanish into the night."

"And what might that be?"

Marcus locked his fingers together on the table as he addressed everyone. "You all probably noticed that several unconfirmed—uh, I suppose *things* is the right word—were left out of the report you, the FBI, and DEA received yesterday. Sam will be here for about a week, and I want Simpson to show her all the samples he collected, and give her a tour of the various locations where we determined the things had been seen. I think Aunt Maude, Sally, and others will be happy to share their knowledge with her, and her investigative abilities might uncover some confirmation for us. And it might lead to another Pulitzer for her."

Sam looked confused. "What the hell are you talking about, Marcus?"

Tossing a quick smile to Kelly, Marcus said, "Oh, guess I failed to mention that a lot of the deaths around here were alongside some strange sightings: sightings strange enough to challenge everyone's doubts, and even caused Kelly to rethink her steadfast disbeliefs. She'll fill you in on what opened her mind to the unknown. Consider this your last order, Sam. Your mission is to investigate the recent sightings of Bigfoot and the Mothman. Who knows, you might even find more bodies of the Vampire's victims. Welcome to West Virginia, Samantha Bigalow."

114

STEPPING OFF THE NIS ELEVATOR for the first time that month, Marcus felt a little guilty. He'd spent the last couple of days at the Greenbrier, a luxury resort near White Sulphur Springs, West Virginia. But he had still been under the governor's orders until midnight the previous night.

The governor had shown up in Princeton last Wednesday, the day after the case review. Marcus gave him a complete review of the case, including the terrorism and drug trafficking, and the governor had understood the wisdom of not mentioning those aspects in his public statement of praise for the Mercer County Sheriff's Office and the Naval Investigative Service.

The governor's final order before releasing Marcus included a personal thank-you, in the form of an all-expense-paid Greenbrier R&R for him, GT, and their wives starting the following day. Marcus and GT then shared a golf game with the governor on Saturday while Kelly, Sally, and the governor's wife enjoyed the Greenbrier's Afternoon Tea in the upper lobby. Losing the golf game to the state's executive was easy, since Marcus always considered his golf scores would look better on a bowling alley score sheet.

Since that additional duty had been harrowing, resulting in more than a few hectic days dumped on top of his parents' memorial service, both he and Kelly had needed a few days to clear their minds. They both knew there were images of evil from that assignment that would never go away.

Now rested and back in D.C., Marcus opted to report to the admiral first rather than face the stacks of reports piled on his desk. He could catch up with Doc and the mountain of paper later. The admiral was happy to see him and to hear the synopsis of the Crazed Bear case.

With a shrug, Marcus wrapped up his verbal report: "And that about sums it up, Admiral. It was an interesting time, and NIS was able to stop an attack on our military and the Olympics, shut down a drug supplier, and close the books on an old Nazi plan. Sorry it took longer than either of us wanted."

Admiral Chance smiled. It was a look Marcus had seen too often, and it usually meant something was up. "Miss Bigalow's 'Crazed Bear' article ran yesterday in all of Garrett Publishing's papers and painted NIS in a good light. I won't ask how she got all that detailed information or what it cost you for her to leave your name out completely. Perhaps we should start calling you a 'highly placed unnamed Navy source.' Furthermore, I'm impressed that you somehow managed to stay out of the hospital this time."

Marcus chuckled. "Yes, sir, miracles do happen. If there's nothing else, sir, guess I now need to get up to speed with Doc on the Iceland issue and try to clear my desk."

Chance lost his smile and slightly grimaced. "Commander Colt, I've got some good news and regretfully much bad news to pass on to you. I'll start with the good. This is the last morning I can call you 'Commander.' You have been selected below the zone for captain, by direction of the president. As soon as we finish here, we head to the CNO's office for the swearing in. Kelly will be there, of course, as will many others. I took the liberty of getting you a new four-striped jacket: a small gift of gratitude for your years of service to me. Of course, the CNO and a representative from the RCMP will pin on your medals."

The shock caused Marcus to sit quietly for a moment. *Below the zone* meant he had been promoted above others with more time in rank; in short, he was being kicked to the head of the line.

"Well, this is a most unusual morning," the admiral said. "Rare to see you without a quick comeback, Marcus."

"Sir, I had heard I was on the promotion list, which I considered unusual due to my age, so never expected anything to happen for several years. May I ask what caused it? How did the president get involved? And what medals, sir?"

Chance could not hold a laugh at seeing Marcus so bewildered. "We now have a governor, two senators, several congressional representatives, and multiple cabinet members who love NIS and firmly believe you are a miracle worker who is a combination of John Wayne and James Bond. And they were a little disappointed that you would only be receiving a Legion of Merit medal for your actions in Canada and West Virginia. And when they heard the Canadian Government has decided you deserve the Royal Victorian Order for your—and I quote—'exemplary personal service to the RCMP,' the politicians' demands got even louder."

Chance paused for a sip of coffee and to let that info sink in. "As for the promotion, the politicians ganged up on the president, who dumped the problem on the Secretary of Defense. SecDef called in the Secretary of State, Admiral Gallagher, and me. SecDef considers us members of the Marcus Colt Career-Counseling fan club. We four discussed the situation and your future, and came up with the only viable solution to keep all parties happy."

With a deep sigh, Marcus said, "Wow. I'm a bit shocked since most O-6s are in their forties, nearing twenty years of service when the promotion comes through."

"Marcus, there is a precedent with the number of young O-6s we had in WWII, many younger than you, and frankly, you having completed your doctorate was a major factor. You will probably receive some resentment from older officers not yet promoted, but since you've handled the negativity that comes from being in NIS and especially Internal Affairs, as well as being the son-in-law of the CNO, we figure you can handle whatever they throw at you. Anyway, when we took our suggestions and justification back to the president, he immediately agreed. So, anyone seeing your service record will see POTUS signing off on your promotion. That carries a lot of respect; the rest you will have to earn."

"Admiral, I deserve neither the medal nor promotion. It was part of the job, sir."

"Your humility is commendable, but your opinion doesn't matter since, starting with me, everyone in the chain of command above thinks you do. Your date of rank was last Friday. I hope that piece of good news is enough to balance the bad. How well do you know Vice Admiral August Zimmers at ONI?"

"Not well. We met and chatted at a joint intelligence meeting last year, and we've had one or two phone conversations about cases. I had a great rapport with Vice Admiral Clarence Beckett, who retired last year, and still do with his staff. The Office of Naval Intelligence was always helpful to me while he was there. I haven't needed much contact with them since, but what I have has all been good."

A warm smile came to Chance as he said, "Auggie and I served together several times. I like to think he and I are cut from the same cloth. And he is looking forward to having Captain Colt join his ONI staff as soon as possible. Your transfer is effective today."

Marcus felt as if the weight of the world suddenly was suddenly sitting on his chest pushing all the air out. He couldn't hide the look of disappointment or keep his voice from starting to break as he muttered, "So I'm out of NIS. I knew it had to happen eventually."

"Marcus, going to ONI is another feather in your cap. You should think of it as an additional reward for a Bravo Zulu job leading the IA division. Admiral Gallagher and I have spent many hours trying to figure out how to keep your career on track. Having spent seven years in the same shore billet means the good people over at BUPERS have been pushing for over half that long to get you out to sea. And frankly, you need that experience, but you're a much better intelligence officer than you would be skipper of a destroyer. So, the CNO and I pushed back and kept you here."

Nodding, Marcus said, "I have often wondered what skill sets I've generated that would be useful as a line officer onboard a destroyer. In reality: not many. I have considered resigning if I received those orders, to spend the rest of my life as a civilian NIS special agent."

"That won't be necessary. Auggie assured me that in addition to vital staff work here in D.C., he can assign you to sea duty. You will probably go afloat as a senior intelligence officer on a carrier going on a Med Cruise next spring, which would keep BUPERS happy as they check off that sea duty box."

"Aside from missing this place and people, I guess the transfer is not that bad a piece of news, Admiral. I do appreciate you and the CNO watching out for my career."

Chance locked his hands together on the desk and let out a sigh of his own. "While we are all going to miss you, Marcus, that was not the bad news."

"Sir?"

"SA Stevens flew to Iceland last Tuesday to meet with a local contact reported to have information vital to the assignment from the CNO. When your West Virginia assignment took longer than anticipated, I asked Doc to start the prelim."

"Yes, sir, I know. I spoke with Doc about it a little over a week or so ago. Seemed he was making progress on the research needed before heading to Iceland."

"Well, he's there now, and the bad news is that as of Thursday night, we have not heard from him, nor can we contact him. I sent SA Neil to check, and so far, he has not found a trace of Doc. Hotel room is empty. He does not show on any flight manifests out of Iceland. Local law enforcement has nothing. Hospitals and morgues are negative."

"Any reason you didn't send Lieutenant James, Sir? She has more experience."

"When he returns, Doc will take over your old job as head of Internal Affairs. Until then, James is trying to control the ton of paperwork on your old desk and cannot be spared. Neil is waiting for you in Reykjavik."

"Not like Doc to go dark, sir," Marcus absentmindedly said, and then he comprehended the admiral's last words. "Waiting for me, sir?"

"Yes. Admiral Zimmers feels the Iceland issue is something for the ONI to pursue. He got the CNO to concur and approve it as a joint task force with ONI and NIS. Admiral Zimmers will also be at the CNO's office, to issue your first orders as lead member of the joint team. The orders are simple: find SA Stevens and handle the Iceland issue. Unless there is anything else, *Captain*, there are a large number of VIPs waiting for you at the Pentagon."

"Aye, aye, Sir. 'Boots and Saddles' time."

Chance laughed. "When you get to the fleet, you might want to drop that Army phrase and stick with 'Anchors Aweigh' as a get-moving cry."

GLOSSARY

IA—Internal Affairs.

BI—Background Information check. Used to determine eligibility for security clearances. Includes talking with friends, previous employers, and educators, looking into social memberships, and analyzing financials.

Bingo Fuel—The minimum amount of fuel required to safely reach a destination.

Bravo Zulu—International naval signal code for "well done."

Butter Bar—Slang for the single gold colored bar which is the rank insignia worn by a 2nd Lieutenant in the Army and Mariene Corps. As the lowest rank, there is an implied statement that this person has much to learn about being a "real" Officer.

CNO—Chief of Naval Operations. The military head of the U.S. Navy. Advisor and deputy of the Secretary of the Navy.

CO—Commanding Officer of a military unit.

Cover—Headgear. Hat.

CPO—Chief Petty Officer.

FUBAR—Navy version of SNAFU. Fouled Up Beyond All Recognition.

GS—General Schedule. GS followed by a number indicates the pay scale in the U.S. Civil Service.

Indian Country—Enemy Territory. A historical reference to the old West and the cavalry venturing into untamed areas.

JAG—Judge Advocate General. The legal arm of the U.S. Navy.

M.E.—Medical Examiner.

Klick—Military slang for a kilometer.

NIS—Naval Investigative Service.

NISHQ—Naval Investigative Service Headquarters, located in Washington, D.C.

NISO—Naval Investigative Service Office. Designation for the headquarters over a specific geographical area that contains multiple NISRAs. Staffed by both military and civilian personnel.

NISRA—Naval Investigative Service Resident Agency. Office that houses agents and staff that are responsible for a smaller portion of a NISO.

NTC—Naval Training Center.

Petty Officer—A noncommissioned officer that has shown skills and leadership, allowing them to advance over other enlisted personnel.

POTUS—Acronym that stands for "President Of The United States."

Rack—Military slang for a bunk or bed.

Rate—Navy's term for enlisted personnel's rank.

Rating—Occupational specialization within the enlisted Navy.

RTB—A military acronym that stands for "return to base".

SA—Special Agent.

SEALs—Special Warfare Operators. Acronym for Sea, Air, Land.

Shavetail—A newly commissioned officer at the lowest level.

SP—Shore Patrol. The police force of the Navy.

SSA—Supervisory Special Agent.

Swab Jockey—Slang for a sailor.

TAD—Temporary Additional Duty.

UA—Unauthorized Absence, same as Army's AWOL (Absent WithOut Leave).

UCMJ—Uniform Code of Military Justice. The foundation of military law in the United States.

UH-1— The Bell Iroquois is a utility military helicopter designed and produced by the Bell Helicopter. It is nicknamed "Huey" due to the phonetic sound of its military designation, HU-1. It was the work horse of the Army during the Vietnam War.

MARINE OFFICER RANKS

2ndLt—Abbreviation for the Marine rank of Second Lieutenant. Lowest level commissioned officer in the Marine Corps. Pay grade of O-1. Insignia is a collar device of a single gold bar, often called a "butter bar" due to the yellow color, on each shirt collar. The bar is also displayed on the shoulder boards and the right side of the garrison cover.

1stLt—Abbreviation for the Marine rank of First Lieutenant. Second lowest level commissioned officer in the Marine Corps. Pay grade of O-2. Insignia is a collar device of a single silver bar on each shirt collar. The bar is also displayed on the shoulder boards and the right side of the garrison cover.

Capt—Abbreviation for the Marine rank of Captain. Third lowest level commissioned officer in the Marine Corps. Pay grade of O-3. Insignia is a collar device of double silver bars, often called "railroad tracks" on each shirt collar. The bar is also displayed on the shoulder boards and the right side of the garrison cover.

ENS—Abbreviation for the Navy rank of Ensign. Lowest level commissioned officer in the Navy. Pay grade of O-1. Insignia is a single gold stripe around the jacket sleeve and on the shoulder board or a collar device of a single gold bar. This device is often referred to as a *butter bar.*

LTJG—Abbreviation for the Navy rank of Lieutenant Junior Grade. Second lowest level commissioned officer in the Navy. Pay grade of O-2. Insignia is a wide gold stripe and a narrow gold stripe around the jacket sleeve and on the shoulder board, or a collar device of a single silver bar.

LT—Abbreviation for the Navy rank of Lieutenant. Third lowest commissioned officer in the Navy. Pay grade of O-3. Insignia is a pair of wide gold stripes around the jacket sleeve and on the shoulder board, or a collar device of a pair of gold bars. This device is often referred to as *railroad tracks.*

LCDR—Abbreviation for the Navy rank of Lieutenant Commander. Fourth level commissioned officer in the Navy. Pay grade of O-4. Insignia is a single narrow gold stripe with a wide gold stripe above and below, around the jacket sleeve, and on the shoulder board, or a collar device of a gold leaf.

CDR—Abbreviation for the Navy rank of Commander. Fifth level commissioned officer in the Navy. Pay grade of O-5. Insignia is three wide gold stripes around the jacket sleeve and on the shoulder board, or a collar device of a silver leaf.

Capt—Abbreviation for the Navy rank of Captain. Sixth level commissioned officer in the Navy. Pay grade of O-6. Insignia is four wide gold stripes around the jacket sleeve and on the shoulder board, or a collar device of a silver eagle.

RDML—Abbreviation for the Navy rank of Rear Admiral (lower half). Seventh level commissioned officer in the Navy. Pay grade of O-7. Insignia is a single, very wide gold stripe around the jacket sleeve. Shoulder board and collar device is a single silver star.

RDM—Abbreviation for the Navy rank of Rear Admiral. Eighth level commissioned officer in the Navy. Pay grade of O-8. Insignia is a single very wide gold stripe, below a narrower single gold stripe around the jacket sleeve. Shoulder board and collar device is a pair of silver stars.

VADM—Abbreviation for the Navy rank of Vice Admiral. Ninth level commissioned officer in the Navy. Pay grade of O-9. Insignia is a single very wide gold stripe, below a pair of narrower single gold stripes, around the jacket sleeve. Shoulder board and collar device is a trio of silver stars.

ADM—Abbreviation for the Navy rank of Admiral. Tenth level commissioned officer in the Navy. Pay grade of O-10. Insignia is a single very wide gold stripe, below a trio of narrower single gold stripes, around the jacket sleeve. Shoulder board and collar device is a set of four silver stars.

AUTHOR'S NOTES

When it comes to cryptids and the supernatural, I suspect some of you harbor the same doubts Kelly Colt put forth through most of this story. That's understandable. When the conversation turns to the Mothman, Bigfoot, or a local ghost, people usually fall into three realms: true believers, somewhat believers, and total non-believers who are adamant that the other two groups are nut cases.

I fall somewhere between the first two realms, leaning more toward true believer. I've seen that, throughout history, many things once considered impossible were eventually proven true. A few of them are mentioned in the story.

In addition, I remember my father's stories of the haunting he experienced in an early family home on Walnut Avenue in Roanoke, Virginia. Stories he told with absolute belief in their truth. As an accountant, Dad lived in a world of facts, and wild stories were not in his nature.

I've had my own experiences. The events outlined in chapter 23 were true, except for the character names, of course. Seaman Wade experienced the haunting of that Yeoman "A" School building in early 1971. Other sailors confirmed hearing those haunting noises.

In the mid-1990s, I was on a train trip from D.C. to Tampa. Lunch in the dining car saw me sitting with a middle-aged lady and her mother, who looked to be in her eighties. Shortly after the introductions, the mother gave a knowing grin and said, "You're a writer." I responded in the negative and explained I was a mainframe computer systems analyst. She shook her head and said, "I can see auras, and your aura is telling me you are a writer. Or you will be." Nearly thirty years later, I remembered that lady's comment as I held my first novel in my hands. My aura knew what I needed to do.

And one other thing: the term *cryptid* first came into use sometime in 1983, a few years after the date of this story. I spend a lot of time and energy making sure all the bits in a story fit the timeline, but in fiction, the rules of time and space can be bent to fit the story. Especially if it is more fun that way! So, I used the term in the story. I hope you agree.

B. R. WADE, JR. BIO

B. R. WADE, JR., THOUGH relatively new to fiction writing, has been all too happy to add it to his list of life accomplishments. Born in Roanoke, Virginia, he spent his teen years and much of his adult life in the Tampa Bay area of Florida.

While in Tampa, Bill worked in retail management before switching to a career as a computer systems analyst for the local school system. He changed careers again, after nearly twenty years of working with mainframe computers, and started a manufacturing company. Shortly after the turn of the century, he made his self-proclaimed escape to the mountains of West Virginia, where he still owns and operates a hobby kit manufacturing business.

After enlisting in the U.S. Navy Reserve in 1969, he was called to active duty, and graduated top of his class from both basic training at Naval Training Center (NTC) Orlando, Florida, and Yeoman "A" School at NTC Bainbridge, Maryland. Soon after, he was assigned to the Naval Investigative Service Office in Norfolk, Virginia for nearly two years.

Bill left active service as a Petty Officer Third Class, then spent three more years as a weekend reservist at his local Navy Reserve Center, assisting with the clerical demands of the center and a Seabee unit. And despite his busy work schedule, Bill obtained degrees in Business Management and Computer Science. He also took his business training a step further and studied marketing at the University of South Florida.

Happily, all of Bill's business, educational, and military pursuits have provided him with plenty of inspiration and writing material. He has started the next adventure for his *Fair Winds* NIS novel protagonist, Marcus Colt. Bill attributes his new love of fiction writing to surviving brain surgery a few years ago. As he phrases it, some connections in his brain have found "new and definitely different pathways."